Pictorial map of London (ca. 1910).

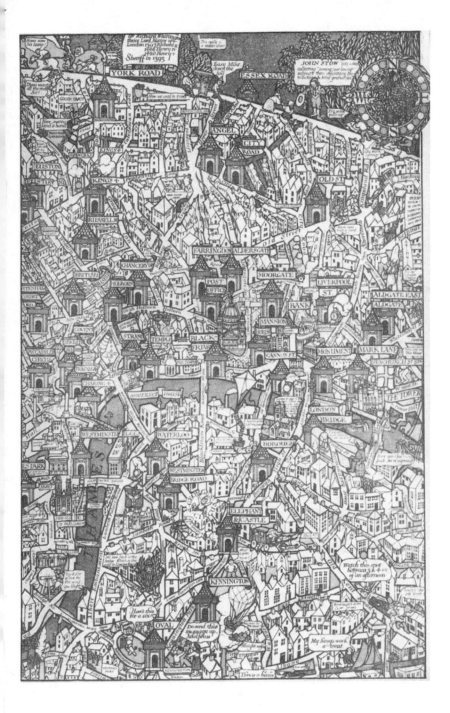

The Years

The Years

VIRGINIA
WOOLF

Annotated and with an introduction
by Eleanor McNees

Mark Hussey, General Editor

A Harvest Book • Harcourt, Inc.
Orlando Austin New York San Diego London

Copyright 1939 by Harcourt, Inc., and renewed 1965 by Leonard Woolf
Annotated Edition copyright © 2008 by Houghton Mifflin Harcourt Publishing Company
Preface copyright © 2005 by Mark Hussey
Introduction copyright © 2008 by Eleanor McNees

All rights reserved. No part of this publication may be reproduced
or transmitted in any form or by any means, electronic or mechanical,
including photocopy, recording, or any information storage and retrieval
system, without permission in writing from the publisher.

Requests for permission to make copies of any part of the work should be
submitted online at www.harcourt.com/contact or mailed to the following address:
Permissions Department, Houghton Mifflin Harcourt Publishing Company,
6277 Sea Harbor Drive, Orlando, Florida 32887-6777.

www.HarcourtBooks.com

Illustration credits appear on page 469, which constitutes
a continuation of the copyright page.

Library of Congress Cataloging-in-Publication Data
Woolf, Virginia, 1882–1941.
The years/Virginia Woolf; annotated and with an introduction
by Eleanor McNees; Mark Hussey, general editor.—Annotated ed., 1st ed.
p.   cm.
"A Harvest Book."
Includes bibliographical references.
1. Family—England—Fiction.   2. England—Social life and customs—Fiction.
3. Domestic fiction.   I. McNees, Eleanor Jane.   II. Hussey, Mark, 1956–   III. Title.
PR6045.O72Y4   2008
823'.912—dc22   2008002969
ISBN 978-0-15-603485-2

Text set in Garamond MT
Designed by Cathy Riggs

Printed in the United States of America

First annotated edition
A C E G I K J H F D B

CONTENTS

Illustrations

The Years

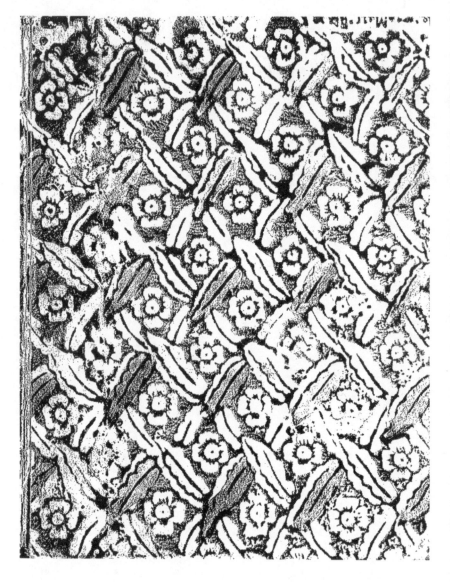

Front cover of Volume One Manuscript Notebook of *The Years*.

Virginia Woolf

Virginia Woolf was born into what she once described as "a very communicative, literate, letter writing, visiting, articulate, late nineteenth century world." Her parents, Leslie and Julia Stephen, both previously widowed, began their marriage in 1878 with four young children: Laura (1870–1945), the daughter of Leslie Stephen and his first wife, Harriet Thackeray (1840–1875); and George (1868–1934), Gerald (1870–1937), and Stella Duckworth (1869–1897), the children of Julia Prinsep (1846–1895) and Herbert Duckworth (1833–1870). In the first five years of their marriage, the Stephens had four more children. Their third child, Virginia, was born in 1882, the year her father began work on the monumental *Dictionary of National Biography* that would earn him a knighthood in 1902. Virginia, her sister, Vanessa (1879–1961), and brothers, Thoby (1880–1906) and Adrian (1883–1948), all were born in the tall house at 22 Hyde Park Gate in London where the eight children lived with numerous servants, their eminent and irascible father, and their beautiful mother, who, in Woolf's words, was "in the very centre of that great Cathedral space that was childhood."

Woolf's parents knew many of the intellectual luminaries of the late Victorian era well, counting among their close friends novelists such as George Meredith, Thomas Hardy, and Henry James. Woolf's great-aunt Julia Margaret Cameron was a pioneering photographer who made portraits of the poets Alfred

Tennyson and Robert Browning, of the naturalist Charles Darwin, and of the philosopher and historian Thomas Carlyle, among many others. Beginning in the year Woolf was born, the entire Stephen family moved to Talland House in St. Ives, Cornwall, for the summer. There the younger children would spend their days playing cricket in the garden, frolicking on the beach, or taking walks along the coast, from where they could look out across the bay to the Godrevy lighthouse.

The early years of Woolf's life were marred by traumatic events. When she was thirteen, her mother, exhausted by a punishing schedule of charitable visits among the sick and poor, died from a bout of influenza. Woolf's half sister Stella took over the household responsibilities and bore the brunt of their self-pitying father's sorrow until she escaped into marriage in 1897 with Jack Hills, a young man who had been a favorite of Julia's. Within three months, Stella (who was pregnant) was dead, most likely from peritonitis. In this year, which she called "the first really *lived* year of my life," Woolf began a diary. Over the next twelve years, she would record in its pages her voracious reading, her impressions of people and places, feelings about her siblings, and events in the daily life of the large household.[1]

In addition to the premature deaths of her mother and half sister, there were other miseries in Woolf's childhood. In autobiographical writings and letters, Woolf referred to the sexual abuse she suffered at the hands of her two older half brothers, George and Gerald Duckworth. George, in one instance, explained his behavior to a family doctor as his effort to comfort his half sister for the fatal illness of their father. Sir Leslie died

---

[1]Woolf's early diary is published as *A Passionate Apprentice: The Early Journals, 1897–1909,* edited by Mitchell A. Leaska. A 1909 notebook discovered in 2002 has been published as *Carlyle's House and Other Sketches,* edited by David Bradshaw (London: Hesperus, 2003).

from cancer in 1904, and shortly thereafter the four Stephen children—Vanessa, Virginia, Thoby, and Adrian—moved together to the then-unfashionable London neighborhood of Bloomsbury. When Thoby Stephen began to bring his Cambridge University friends to the house on Thursday evenings, what would later become famous as the "Bloomsbury Group" began to form.

In an article marking the centenary of her father's birth, Woolf recalled his "allowing a girl of fifteen the free run of a large and quite unexpurgated library"—an unusual opportunity for a Victorian young woman, and evidence of the high regard Sir Leslie had for his daughter's intellectual talents. In her diary, she recorded the many different kinds of books her father recommended to her—biographies and memoirs, philosophy, history, and poetry. Although he believed that women should be "as well educated as men," Woolf's mother held that "to serve is the fulfilment of women's highest nature." The young Stephen children were first taught at home by their mother and father, with little success. Woolf herself received no formal education beyond some classes in Greek and Latin in the Ladies' Department of King's College in London, beginning in the fall of 1897. In 1899 she began lessons in Greek with Clara Pater, sister of the renowned Victorian critic Walter Pater, and in 1902 she was tutored in the classics by Janet Case (who also later involved her in work for women's suffrage). Such homeschooling was a source of some bitterness later in her life, as she recognized the advantages that derived from the expensive educations her brothers and half brothers received at private schools and university. Yet she also realized that her father's encouragement of her obviously keen intellect had given her an eclectic foundation. In the early years of Bloomsbury, she reveled in the opportunity to discuss ideas with her brother Thoby and his friends, among whom were Lytton Strachey, Clive Bell, and

E. M. Forster. From them, she heard, too, about an intense young man named Leonard Woolf, whom she had met briefly when visiting Thoby at Cambridge, and also in 1904 when he came to dinner at Gordon Square just before leaving for Ceylon (now called Sri Lanka), where he was to administer a far-flung outpost of the British Empire.

Virginia Woolf's first publications were unsigned reviews and essays in an Anglo-Catholic newspaper called the *Guardian,* beginning in December 1904. In the fall of 1906, she and Vanessa went with a family friend, Violet Dickinson, to meet their brothers in Greece. The trip was spoiled by Vanessa's falling ill, and when she returned to London, Virginia found both her brother Thoby—who had returned earlier—and her sister seriously ill. After a misdiagnosis by his doctors, Thoby died from typhoid fever on November 20, leaving Virginia to maintain a cheerful front while her sister and Violet Dickinson recovered from their own illnesses. Two days after Thoby's death, Vanessa agreed to marry his close friend Clive Bell.

While living in Bloomsbury, Woolf had begun to write a novel that would go through many drafts before it was published in 1915 as *The Voyage Out.* In these early years of independence, her social circle widened. She became close to the art critic Roger Fry, organizer of the First Post-Impressionist Exhibition in London in 1910, and also entered the orbit of the famed literary hostess Lady Ottoline Morrell (cruelly caricatured as Hermione Roddice in D. H. Lawrence's 1920 novel *Women in Love*). Her political consciousness also began to emerge. In 1910 she volunteered for the movement for women's suffrage. She also participated that February in a daring hoax that embarrassed the British Navy and led to questions being asked in the House of Commons: She and her brother Adrian, together with some other Cambridge friends, gained access to a secret warship by dressing up and posing as the Emperor of Abyssinia and his retinue. The "Dreadnought Hoax" was front-page news, complete with photographs of the phony Ethiopians with flowing robes, blackened faces, and false beards.

To the British establishment, one of the most embarrassing aspects of the Dreadnought affair was that a woman had taken part in the hoax. Vanessa Bell was concerned at what might have happened to her sister had she been discovered on the ship. She was also increasingly worried about Virginia's erratic health, and by the early summer 1910 had discussed with Dr. George Savage, one of the family's doctors, the debilitating headaches her sister suffered; Dr. Savage prescribed several weeks in a nursing home. Another element in Vanessa's concern was that Virginia was twenty-eight and still unmarried. Clive Bell and Virginia had, in fact, engaged in a hurtful flirtation soon after the birth of Vanessa's first child in 1908. Although she had been proposed to twice in 1909 and once in 1911, Virginia had not taken these offers very seriously.

Dropping by Vanessa's house on a July evening in 1911, Virginia met Leonard Woolf, recently back on leave from Ceylon. Soon after this, Leonard became a lodger at the house Virginia shared with Adrian, the economist John Maynard Keynes, and the painter Duncan Grant. Leonard decided to resign from the Colonial Service, hoping that Virginia would agree to marry him. After some considerable hesitation, she did, and they married in August 1912.

By the end of that year, Woolf was again suffering from the tremendous headaches that afflicted her throughout her life, and in 1913 she was again sent to a nursing home for what was then called a "rest cure." In September of that year, she took an overdose of a sleeping drug and was under care until the following spring. In early 1915 she suffered a severe breakdown and was ill throughout most of the year in which her first novel was published.

Despite this difficult beginning, Virginia and Leonard Woolf's marriage eventually settled into a pattern of immense productivity and mutual support. Leonard worked for a time for the Women's Cooperative Guild, and became increasingly involved with advising the Labour Party and writing on international politics, as well as editing several periodicals. Virginia began to establish herself as an important novelist and influential critic. In 1917 the Woolfs set up their own publishing house, the Hogarth Press, in their home in Richmond. Their first publication was *Two Stories*—Leonard's "Three Jews" and Virginia's experimental "The Mark on the Wall." They had decided to make their livings by writing, and in 1919, a few months before Woolf's second novel, *Night and Day,* was published, they bought a cottage in the village of Rodmell in Sussex. After moving back into London from Richmond in 1923, Woolf would spend summers at Monk's House, returning to the social whirl of the city in the fall.

"The Mark on the Wall" was one of a number of what Woolf called "sketches" that she began to write around the time she and Leonard bought their printing press. *Night and Day* was the last of her books to be published in England by another press. In 1919 Hogarth published her short story *Kew Gardens,* with two woodcuts by Vanessa Bell, and two years later came *Monday or Tuesday,* the only collection of her short fiction published in Woolf's lifetime. Her next novel was *Jacob's Room* (1922), a slim elegy to the generation of 1914, and to her beloved brother Thoby, whose life of great promise had also been cut short so suddenly. Woolf had written to her friend Margaret Llewelyn Davies in 1916 that the Great War, as it was then called, was a "preposterous masculine fiction" that made her "steadily more feminist," and in her fiction and nonfiction she began to articulate and illuminate the connections between the patriarchal status quo, the relatively subordinate position of women, and war making. Thinking about a novel she was calling "The Hours," Woolf wrote in her diary in 1923 that she wanted to criticize "the social system." Her inclusion in the novel of a shell-shocked war veteran named Septimus Warren Smith would confuse many of the early reviewers of her fourth novel, *Mrs. Dalloway* (1925), but others recognized that Woolf was breaking new ground in the way she rendered consciousness and her understanding of human subjectivity.

By the time she wrote *Mrs. Dalloway,* Woolf was also a sought-after essayist and reviewer who, like many of her celebrated contemporaries, was staking out her own particular piece of modernist territory. The Hogarth Press published radical young writers like Katherine Mansfield, T. S. Eliot, and Gertrude Stein. Approached by Harriet Shaw Weaver with part of the manuscript of James Joyce's *Ulysses* in 1918, the Woolfs turned it down. Their own small press could not cope with the long and complex manuscript, nor could Leonard Woolf find a commercial printer willing to risk prosecution for obscenity by producing it. In 1924 the Hogarth Press became the official English publisher of the works of Sigmund Freud, translated by Lytton Strachey's brother James. Woolf's own literary criticism was collected in a volume published in 1925, *The Common Reader*—a title signaling her distrust of academics and love of broad, eclectic reading.

The staggering range of Woolf's reading is reflected in the more than five hundred essays and reviews she published during her lifetime. Her critical writing is concerned not only with the canonical works of English literature from Chaucer to her contemporaries, but also ranges widely through lives of the obscure, memoirs, diaries, letters, and biographies. Models of the form, her essays comprise a body of work that has only recently begun to attract the kind of recognition her fiction has received.

In 1922 Woolf met "the lovely and gifted aristocrat" Vita Sackville-West, already a well-known poet and novelist. Their close friendship slowly turned into a love affair, glowing most intensely from about 1925 to 1928, before modulating into friendship once more in the 1930s. The period of their intimacy was extremely creative for both writers, Woolf publishing essays such as "Mr. Bennett and Mrs. Brown" and "Letter to a Young Poet," as well as three very different novels: *To the Lighthouse* (1927), which evoked her own childhood and had at its center the figure of a modernist woman artist, Lily Briscoe; *Orlando* (1928), a fantastic biography inspired by Vita's own remarkable family history; and *The Waves* (1931), a mystical and profoundly meditative work that pushed Woolf's concept of novel form to its limit. Woolf also published a second *Common Reader* in 1932, and the "biography" of *Flush,* Elizabeth Barrett Browning's dog (1933). She went with Sackville-West to Cambridge in the fall of 1928 to deliver the second of the two lectures on which her great feminist essay *A Room of One's Own* (1929) is based.

As the political situation in Europe in the 1930s moved inexorably to its crisis in 1939, Woolf began to collect newspaper clippings about the relations between the sexes in England, France, Germany, and Italy. The scrapbooks she made became the matrix from which developed the perspectives of her penultimate novel, *The Years* (1937), and the arguments of her pacifist-feminist polemic *Three Guineas* (1938). In 1937 Vanessa's eldest son, Julian Bell, was killed serving as an ambulance driver in the Spanish Civil War. Woolf later wrote to Vanessa that she had written *Three Guineas* partly as an argument with Julian. Her work on *The Years* was grindingly slow and difficult. Ironically, given Woolf's reputation as a highbrow, it became a bestseller in the United States, even being published in an Armed Services edition. While she labored over the novel in 1934, the news came of the death of Roger Fry, one of her oldest and closest friends and the former lover of her sister, Vanessa. Reluctantly, given her distaste for the conventions of biography, Woolf agreed to write his life, which was published in 1940.

In 1939, to relieve the strain of writing Fry's biography, Woolf began to write a memoir, "A Sketch of the Past," which remained unpublished until 1976, when the manuscripts were edited by Jeanne Schulkind for a collection of Woolf's autobiographical writings, *Moments of Being*. Withdrawing with Leonard to Monk's House in Sussex, where they could see the German airplanes flying low overhead on their way to bomb London, Woolf continued to write for peace and correspond with antiwar activists in Europe and the United States. She began to write her last novel, *Between the Acts,* in the spring of 1938, but by early 1941 was dissatisfied with it. Before completing her final revisions, Woolf ended her own life, walking into the River Ouse on the morning of March 28, 1941. To her sister, Vanessa, she wrote, "I can hardly think clearly any more. If I could I would tell you what you and the children have meant to me. I think you know." In her last note to Leonard, she told him he had given her "complete happiness," and asked him to destroy all her papers.

BY THE END of the twentieth century, Virginia Woolf had become an iconic figure, a touchstone for the feminism that revived in the 1960s as well as for the conservative backlash of the 1980s. Hailed by many as a radical writer of genius, she has also been dismissed as a narrowly focused snob. Her image adorns T-shirts, postcards, and even a beer advertisement, while phrases from her writings occur in all kinds of contexts, from peace-march slogans to highbrow book reviews. That Woolf is one of those figures on whom the myriad competing narratives of twentieth- and twenty-first-century Western culture inscribe themselves is testified to by the enormous number of biographical works about her published in the decades since her nephew Quentin Bell broke the ground in 1972 with his two-volume biography of his aunt.

Argument continues about the work and life of Virginia Woolf: about her experience of incest, her madness, her class attitudes, her sexuality, the difficulty of her prose, her politics, her feminism, and her legacy. Perhaps, though, these words from her essay "How Should One Read a Book?" are our best guide: "The only advice, indeed, that one person can give another about reading is to take no advice, to follow your own instincts, to use your own reason, to come to your own conclusions."

—MARK HUSSEY, GENERAL EDITOR

CHRONOLOGY

Information is arranged in this order: 1. Virginia Woolf's family and her works; 2. Cultural and political events; 3. Significant publications and works of art.

1878 Marriage of Woolf's parents, Leslie Stephen (1832–1904) and Julia Prinsep Duckworth (née Jackson) (1846–1895). Leslie Stephen publishes *Samuel Johnson,* first volume in the English Men of Letters series. England at war in Afghanistan.

1879 Vanessa Stephen (Bell) born (d. 1961). Edward Burne-Jones paints Julia Stephen as the Virgin Mary in *The Annunciation.* Leslie Stephen, *Hours in a Library,* 3rd series.
Somerville and Lady Margaret Hall Colleges for women founded at Oxford University.
Anglo-Zulu war in South Africa.

1880 Thoby Stephen born (d. 1906).
William Gladstone becomes prime minister for second time. First Boer War begins (1880–81). Deaths of Gustave Flaubert (b. 1821) and George Eliot (b. 1819). Lytton Strachey born (d. 1932).
Fyodor Dostoyevsky, *The Brothers Karamazov.*

1881   Leslie Stephen buys lease of Talland House, St. Ives, Cornwall.

Cambridge University Tripos exams opened to women. Henrik Ibsen, *Ghosts;* Henry James, *The Portrait of a Lady, Washington Square;* Christina Rossetti, *A Pageant and Other Poems;* D. G. Rossetti, *Ballads and Sonnets;* Oscar Wilde, *Poems.*

1882   Adeline Virginia Stephen (Virginia Woolf) born January 25. Leslie Stephen begins work as editor of the *Dictionary of National Biography (DNB)*; publishes *The Science of Ethics.* The Stephen family spends its first summer at Talland House.

Married Women's Property Act enables women to buy, sell, and own property and keep their own earnings. Triple Alliance between Germany, Italy, and Austria. Phoenix Park murders of British officials in Dublin, Ireland. James Joyce born (d. 1941). Death of Charles Darwin (b. 1809).

1883   Adrian Leslie Stephen born (d. 1948). Julia Stephen's *Notes from Sick Rooms* published.

Olive Schreiner, *The Story of an African Farm;* Robert Louis Stevenson, *Treasure Island.*

1884   Leslie Stephen delivers the Clark Lectures at Cambridge University.

Third Reform Act extends the franchise in England. Friedrich Engels, *The Origin of the Family, Private Property and the State;* John Ruskin, *The Storm-Cloud of the Nineteenth Century;* Mark Twain, *The Adventures of Huckleberry Finn.*

1885   First volume of Leslie Stephen's *Dictionary of National Biography* published.

Redistribution Act further extends the franchise in England. Ezra Pound born (d. 1972); D. H. Lawrence born (d. 1930).

George Meredith, *Diana of the Crossways;* Émile Zola, *Germinal.*

1887   Queen Victoria's Golden Jubilee.

Arthur Conan Doyle, *A Study in Scarlet;* H. Rider Haggard, *She;* Thomas Hardy, *The Woodlanders.*

1891   Leslie Stephen gives up the *DNB* editorship. Laura Stephen (1870–1945) is placed in an asylum.

William Gladstone elected prime minister of England a fourth time.

Thomas Hardy, *Tess of the D'Urbervilles;* Oscar Wilde, *The Picture of Dorian Gray.*

1895   Death of Julia Stephen.

Armenian Massacres in Turkey. Discovery of X-rays by William Röntgen; Guglielmo Marconi discovers radio; invention of the cinematograph. Trials of Oscar Wilde.

Thomas Hardy, *Jude the Obscure;* H. G. Wells, *The Time Machine;* Oscar Wilde, *The Importance of Being Earnest.*

1896   Vanessa Stephen begins drawing classes three afternoons a week.

Death of William Morris (b. 1834); F. Scott Fitzgerald born (d. 1940).

Anton Chekhov, *The Seagull.*

1897   Woolf attends Greek and history classes at King's College, London, and begins to keep a regular diary. Vanessa, Virginia, and Thoby watch Queen Victoria's Diamond Jubilee procession. Stella Duckworth (b. 1869) marries Jack Hills in April, but dies in July. Gerald Duckworth (1870–1937) establishes a publishing house.
Paul Gauguin, *Where Do We Come From? What Are We? Where Are We Going?;* Bram Stoker, *Dracula.*

1898   Spanish-American War (1898–99). Marie Curie discovers radium. Death of Stéphane Mallarmé (b. 1842). H. G. Wells, *The War of the Worlds;* Oscar Wilde, *The Ballad of Reading Gaol.*

1899   Woolf begins Latin and Greek lessons with Clara Pater. Thoby Stephen goes up to Trinity College, Cambridge University, entering with Lytton Strachey, Leonard Woolf (1880–1969), and Clive Bell (1881–1964). The Second Boer War begins (1899–1902) in South Africa. Ernest Hemingway born (d. 1961).

1900   Woolf and Vanessa attend the Trinity College Ball at Cambridge University.
Deaths of Friedrich Nietzsche (b. 1844), John Ruskin (b. 1819), and Oscar Wilde (b. 1854).
Sigmund Freud, *The Interpretation of Dreams.*

1901   Vanessa enters Royal Academy Schools.
Queen Victoria dies January 22. Edward VII becomes king. Marconi sends messages by wireless telegraphy from Cornwall to Newfoundland.

1902   Woolf begins classics lessons with Janet Case. Adrian
Stephen enters Trinity College, Cambridge University.
Leslie Stephen is knighted.

Joseph Conrad, *Heart of Darkness;* Henry James, *The
Wings of the Dove;* William James, *The Varieties of Religious
Experience.*

1903   The Wright Brothers fly a biplane 852 feet. Women's
Social and Political Union founded in England by Emmeline Pankhurst.

1904   Sir Leslie Stephen dies. George Duckworth (1868–
1934) marries Lady Margaret Herbert. The Stephen
children—Vanessa, Virginia, Thoby, and Adrian—move
to 46 Gordon Square, in the Bloomsbury district of
London. Woolf contributes to F. W. Maitland's biography of her father. Leonard Woolf comes to dine before
sailing for Ceylon. Woolf travels in Italy and France.
Her first publication is an unsigned review in the
Guardian, a church weekly.

"Empire Day" inaugurated in London and in Britain's
colonies.

Anton Chekhov, *The Cherry Orchard;* Henry James, *The
Golden Bowl.*

1905   Woolf begins teaching weekly adult education classes at
Morley College. Thoby invites Cambridge friends to
their home for "Thursday Evenings"—the beginnings
of the Bloomsbury Group. Woolf travels with Adrian to
Portugal and Spain. The Stephens visit Cornwall for the
first time since their mother's death.

Revolution in Russia.

Albert Einstein, *Special Theory of Relativity;* E. M. Forster, *Where Angels Fear to Tread;* Sigmund Freud, *Essays in the Theory of Sexuality;* Edith Wharton, *The House of Mirth;* Oscar Wilde, *De Profundis.*

1906   The Stephens travel to Greece. Vanessa and Thoby fall ill. Thoby dies November 20; on November 22, Vanessa agrees to marry Clive Bell.
Deaths of Paul Cézanne (b. 1839) and Henrik Ibsen (b. 1828). Samuel Beckett born (d. 1989).

1907   Woolf moves with her brother Adrian to Fitzroy Square. Vanessa marries Clive Bell.
First Cubist exhibition in Paris. W. H. Auden born (d. 1973).
Joseph Conrad, *The Secret Agent;* E. M. Forster, *The Longest Journey;* Edmund Gosse, *Father and Son;* Pablo Picasso, *Demoiselles d'Avignon.*

1908   Birth of Vanessa Bell's first child, Julian. Woolf travels to Italy with Vanessa and Clive Bell.
Herbert Asquith becomes prime minister.
E. M. Forster, *A Room with a View;* Gertrude Stein, *Three Lives.*

1909   Woolf receives a legacy of £2,500 on the death of her Quaker aunt, Caroline Emelia Stephen. Lytton Strachey proposes marriage to Woolf, but they both quickly realize this would be a mistake. Woolf meets Lady Ottoline Morrell for the first time. She travels to the Wagner festival in Bayreuth.
Chancellor of the Exchequer David Lloyd George (1863–1945) introduces a "People's Budget," taxing

wealth to pay for social reforms. A constitutional crisis ensues when the House of Lords rejects it. Death of George Meredith (b. 1828).

Filippo Marinetti, "The Founding and Manifesto of Futurism"; Henri Matisse, *Dance.*

1910   Woolf participates in the Dreadnought Hoax. She volunteers for the cause of women's suffrage. Birth of Vanessa Bell's second child, Quentin (d. 1996).

First Post-Impressionist Exhibition ("Manet and the Post-Impressionists") organized by Roger Fry (1866–1934) at the Grafton Galleries in London. Edward VII dies May 6. George V becomes king. Death of Leo Tolstoy (b. 1828).

E. M. Forster, *Howards End;* Igor Stravinsky, *The Firebird.*

1911   Woolf rents Little Talland House in Sussex. Leonard Woolf returns from Ceylon; in November, he, Adrian Stephen, John Maynard Keynes (1883–1946), Woolf, and Duncan Grant (1885–1978) share a house together at Brunswick Square in London.

Ernest Rutherford makes first model of atomic structure. Rupert Brooke, *Poems;* Joseph Conrad, *Under Western Eyes;* D. H. Lawrence, *The White Peacock;* Katherine Mansfield, *In a German Pension;* Ezra Pound, *Canzoni;* Edith Wharton, *Ethan Frome.*

1912   Woolf leases Asheham House in Sussex. Marries Leonard on August 10; they move to Clifford's Inn, London.

Captain Robert Scott's expedition reaches the South Pole, but he and his companions die on the return

journey. The *Titanic* sinks. Second Post-Impression-
ist Exhibition, for which Leonard Woolf serves as
secretary.
Marcel Duchamp, *Nude Descending a Staircase;* Wassily
Kandinsky, *Concerning the Spiritual in Art;* Thomas
Mann, *Death in Venice;* George Bernard Shaw, *Pygmalion.*

1913 *The Voyage Out* manuscript delivered to Gerald Duckworth. Woolf enters a nursing home in July; in September, she attempts suicide.
Roger Fry founds the Omega Workshops.
Sigmund Freud, *Totem and Taboo;* D. H. Lawrence, *Sons
and Lovers;* Marcel Proust, *Du côté de chez Swann;* Igor
Stravinsky, *Le Sacre du printemps.*

1914 Leonard Woolf, *The Wise Virgins;* he reviews Freud's
The Psychopathology of Everyday Life.
World War I ("The Great War") begins in August.
Home Rule Bill for Ireland passed.
Clive Bell, *Art;* James Joyce, *Dubliners;* Wyndham Lewis
et al., "Vorticist Manifesto" (in *BLAST*); Gertrude
Stein, *Tender Buttons.*

1915 *The Voyage Out,* Woolf's first novel, published by Duck-
worth. In April the Woolfs move to Hogarth House in
Richmond. Woolf begins again to keep a regular diary.
First Zeppelin attack on London. Death of Rupert
Brooke (b. 1887).
Joseph Conrad, *Victory;* Ford Madox Ford, *The Good Sol-
dier;* D. H. Lawrence, *The Rainbow;* Dorothy Richardson,
Pointed Roofs.

1916   Woolf discovers Charleston, where her sister, Vanessa (no longer living with her husband, Clive), moves in October with her sons, Julian and Quentin, and Duncan Grant (with whom she is in love) and David Garnett (with whom Duncan is in love).

Easter Rising in Dublin. Death of Henry James (b. 1843).

Albert Einstein, *General Theory of Relativity;* James Joyce, *A Portrait of the Artist as a Young Man;* Dorothy Richardson, *Backwater.*

1917   The Hogarth Press established by Leonard and Virginia Woolf in Richmond. Their first publication is their own *Two Stories,* with woodcuts by Dora Carrington (1893–1932).

Russian Bolshevik Revolution destroys the rule of the czar. The United States enters the European war.

T. S. Eliot, *Prufrock and Other Observations;* Sigmund Freud, *Introduction to Psychoanalysis;* Carl Jung, *The Unconscious;* Dorothy Richardson, *Honeycomb;* W. B. Yeats, *The Wild Swans at Coole.*

1918   Woolf meets T. S. Eliot (1888–1965). Harriet Shaw Weaver comes to tea with the manuscript of James Joyce's *Ulysses.* Vanessa Bell and Duncan Grant's daughter, Angelica Garnett, born; her paternity is kept secret from all but a very few intimates.

Armistice signed November 11; Parliamentary Reform Act gives votes in Britain to women of thirty and older and to all men.

G. M. Hopkins, *Poems;* James Joyce, *Exiles;* Katherine Mansfield, *Prelude* (Hogarth Press); Marcel Proust, *À l'ombre des jeunes filles en fleurs;* Lytton Strachey, *Eminent Victorians;* Rebecca West, *The Return of the Soldier.*

1919   The Woolfs buy Monk's House in Sussex. Woolf's second novel, *Night and Day,* is published by Duckworth. Her essay "Modern Novels" (republished in 1925 as "Modern Fiction") appears in the *Times Literary Supplement; Kew Gardens* published by Hogarth Press.

Bauhaus founded by Walter Gropius in Weimar. Sex Disqualification (Removal) Act opens many professions and public offices to women. Election of first woman member of Parliament, Nancy Astor. Treaty of Versailles imposes harsh conditions on postwar Germany, opposed by John Maynard Keynes, who writes *The Economic Consequences of the Peace.* League of Nations created. T. S. Eliot, "Tradition and the Individual Talent," *Poems;* Dorothy Richardson, *The Tunnel, Interim;* Robert Wiene, *The Cabinet of Dr. Caligari* (film).

1920   The Memoir Club, comprising thirteen original members of the Bloomsbury Group, meets for the first time. *The Voyage Out* and *Night and Day* are published in the United States by George H. Doran.

Mohandas Gandhi initiates mass passive resistance against British rule in India.

T. S. Eliot, *The Sacred Wood;* Sigmund Freud, *Beyond the Pleasure Principle;* Roger Fry, *Vision and Design;* D. H. Lawrence, *Women in Love;* Katherine Mansfield, *Bliss and Other Stories;* Ezra Pound, *Hugh Selwyn Mauberley;* Marcel Proust, *Le Côté de Guermantes I;* Edith Wharton, *The Age of Innocence.*

1921   Woolf's short story collection *Monday or Tuesday* published by Hogarth Press, which will from this time publish all her books in England. The book is also published in the United States by Harcourt Brace, which from now on is her American publisher.

Aldous Huxley, *Crome Yellow;* Pablo Picasso, *Three Musicians;* Luigi Pirandello, *Six Characters in Search of an Author;* Marcel Proust, *Le Côté de Guermantes II, Sodome et Gomorrhe I;* Dorothy Richardson, *Deadlock;* Lytton Strachey, *Queen Victoria.*

1922   *Jacob's Room* published. Woolf meets Vita Sackville-West (1892–1962) for the first time.

Bonar Law elected prime minister. Mussolini comes to power in Italy. Irish Free State established. British Broadcasting Company (BBC) formed. Discovery of Tutankhamen's tomb in Egypt. Death of Marcel Proust (b. 1871).

T. S. Eliot, *The Waste Land;* James Joyce, *Ulysses;* Katherine Mansfield, *The Garden Party;* Marcel Proust, *Sodome et Gomorrhe II;* Ludwig Wittgenstein, *Tractatus Logico-Philosophicus.*

1923   The Woolfs travel to Spain, stopping in Paris on the way home. Hogarth Press publishes *The Waste Land.*

Stanley Baldwin succeeds Bonar Law as prime minister. Death of Katherine Mansfield (b. 1888).

Mina Loy, *Lunar Baedeker;* Marcel Proust, *La Prisonnière;* Dorothy Richardson, *Revolving Lights;* Rainer Maria Rilke, *Duino Elegies.*

1924   The Woolfs move to Tavistock Square. Woolf lectures on "Character in Fiction" to the Heretics Society at Cambridge University.

The Labour Party takes office for the first time under

the leadership of Ramsay MacDonald but is voted out within the year. Death of Joseph Conrad (b. 1857).
E. M. Forster, *A Passage to India;* Thomas Mann, *The Magic Mountain.*

1925   *Mrs. Dalloway* and *The Common Reader* published. Woolf stays with Vita Sackville-West at her house, Long Barn, for the first time.
Nancy Cunard, *Parallax;* F. Scott Fitzgerald, *The Great Gatsby;* Ernest Hemingway, *In Our Time;* Adolf Hitler, *Mein Kampf;* Franz Kafka, *The Trial;* Alain Locke, ed., *The New Negro;* Marcel Proust, *Albertine disparue;* Dorothy Richardson, *The Trap;* Gertrude Stein, *The Making of Americans.*

1926   Woolf lectures on "How Should One Read a Book?" at Hayes Court School. "Cinema" published in *Arts* (New York), "Impassioned Prose" in *Times Literary Supplement,* and "On Being Ill" in *New Criterion.* Meets Gertrude Stein (1874–1946).
The General Strike in support of mine workers in England lasts nearly two weeks.
Ernest Hemingway, *The Sun Also Rises;* Langston Hughes, *The Weary Blues;* Franz Kafka, *The Castle;* A. A. Milne, *Winnie-the-Pooh.*

1927   *To the Lighthouse,* "The Art of Fiction," "Poetry, Fiction and the Future," and "Street Haunting" published. The Woolfs travel with Vita Sackville-West and her husband, Harold Nicolson, to Yorkshire to see the total eclipse of the sun. They buy their first car.
Charles Lindbergh flies the Atlantic solo.
E. M. Forster, *Aspects of the Novel;* Ernest Hemingway, *Men without Women;* Franz Kafka, *Amerika;* Marcel

Proust, *Le Temps retrouvé;* Gertrude Stein, *Four Saints in Three Acts.*

1928   *Orlando: A Biography* published. In October, Woolf delivers two lectures at Cambridge on which she will base *A Room of One's Own.* Femina-Vie Heureuse prize awarded to *To the Lighthouse.*
The Equal Franchise Act gives the vote to all women over twenty-one. Sound films introduced. Death of Thomas Hardy (b. 1840).
Djuna Barnes, *Ladies Almanack;* Radclyffe Hall, *The Well of Loneliness;* D. H. Lawrence, *Lady Chatterley's Lover;* Evelyn Waugh, *Decline and Fall;* W. B. Yeats, *The Tower.*

1929   *A Room of One's Own* published. "Women and Fiction" in *The Forum* (New York).
Labour Party returned to power under Prime Minister MacDonald. Discovery of penicillin. Museum of Modern Art opens in New York. Wall Street crash.
William Faulkner, *The Sound and the Fury;* Ernest Hemingway, *A Farewell to Arms;* Nella Larsen, *Passing.*

1930   Woolf meets the pioneering composer, writer, and suffragette Ethel Smyth (1858–1944), with whom she forms a close friendship.
Death of D. H. Lawrence (b. 1885).
W. H. Auden, *Poems;* T. S. Eliot, *Ash Wednesday;* William Faulkner, *As I Lay Dying;* Sigmund Freud, *Civilisation and Its Discontents.*

1931   *The Waves* is published. First of six articles by Woolf about London published in *Good Housekeeping;* "Introductory Letter" to *Life As We Have Known It.* Lectures to London branch of National Society for Women's Service on "Professions for Women." Meets John Lehmann (1907–1987), who will become a partner in the Hogarth Press.

Growing financial crisis throughout Europe and beginning of the Great Depression.

1932 *The Common Reader, Second Series* and "Letter to a Young Poet" published. Woolf invited to give the 1933 Clark Lectures at Cambridge, which she declines.

Death of Lytton Strachey (b. 1880).

Aldous Huxley, *Brave New World*.

1933 *Flush: A Biography,* published. The Woolfs travel by car to Italy.

Adolf Hitler becomes chancellor of Germany, establishing the totalitarian dictatorship of his National Socialist (Nazi) Party.

T. S. Eliot, *The Use of Poetry and the Use of Criticism;* George Orwell, *Down and Out in Paris and London;* Gertrude Stein, *The Autobiography of Alice B. Toklas;* Nathanael West, *Miss Lonelyhearts;* W. B. Yeats, *The Collected Poems*.

1934 Woolf meets W. B. Yeats at Ottoline Morrell's house. Writes "Walter Sickert: A Conversation."

George Duckworth dies. Roger Fry dies.

Samuel Beckett, *More Pricks Than Kicks;* Nancy Cunard, ed., *Negro: An Anthology;* F. Scott Fitzgerald, *Tender Is the Night;* Wyndham Lewis, *Men Without Art;* Henry Miller, *Tropic of Cancer;* Ezra Pound, *ABC of Reading;* Evelyn Waugh, *A Handful of Dust*.

1935   The Woolfs travel to Germany, where they accidentally get caught up in a parade for Göring. They return to England via Italy and France.

1936   Woolf reads "Am I a Snob?" to the Memoir Club, and publishes "Why Art Today Follows Politics" in the *Daily Worker*.

Death of George V, who is succeeded by Edward VIII, who then abdicates to marry Wallis Simpson. George VI becomes king. Spanish Civil War (1936–38) begins when General Franco, assisted by Germany and Italy, attacks the Republican government. BBC television begins.

Djuna Barnes, *Nightwood;* Charlie Chaplin, *Modern Times* (film); Aldous Huxley, *Eyeless in Gaza;* J. M. Keynes, *The General Theory of Employment, Interest and Money;* Rose Macaulay, *Personal Pleasures;* Margaret Mitchell, *Gone with the Wind.*

1937   *The Years* published. Woolf's nephew Julian Bell killed in the Spanish Civil War.

Neville Chamberlain becomes prime minister.

Zora Neale Hurston, *Their Eyes Were Watching God;* David Jones, *In Parenthesis;* Pablo Picasso, *Guernica;* John Steinbeck, *Of Mice and Men;* J. R. R. Tolkien, *The Hobbit.*

1938   *Three Guineas* published.

Germany annexes Austria. Chamberlain negotiates the Munich Agreement ("Peace in our time"), ceding Czech territory to Hitler.

Samuel Beckett, *Murphy;* Elizabeth Bowen, *The Death of the Heart;* Jean-Paul Sartre, *La Nausée.*

1939   The Woolfs visit Sigmund Freud, living in exile in London having fled the Nazis. They move to Mecklenburgh Square.

Germany occupies Czechoslovakia; Italy occupies Albania; Russia makes a nonaggression pact with Germany. Germany invades Poland and war is declared by Britain and France on Germany, September 3. Deaths of W. B. Yeats (b. 1865), Sigmund Freud (b. 1856), and Ford Madox Ford (b. 1873).

James Joyce, *Finnegans Wake;* John Steinbeck, *The Grapes of Wrath;* Nathanael West, *The Day of the Locust.*

1940   *Roger Fry: A Biography* published. "Thoughts on Peace in an Air Raid" in the *New Republic.* Woolf lectures on "The Leaning Tower" to the Workers Educational Association in Brighton.

The Battle of Britain leads to German night bombings of English cities. The Woolfs' house at Mecklenburgh Square is severely damaged, as is their former house at Tavistock Square. Hogarth Press is moved out of London.

Ernest Hemingway, *For Whom the Bell Tolls;* Christina Stead, *The Man Who Loved Children.*

1941   Woolf drowns herself, March 28, in the River Ouse in Sussex. *Between the Acts* published in July.

Death of James Joyce (b. 1882).

Rebecca West, *Black Lamb and Grey Falcon.*

INTRODUCTION
BY ELEANOR MCNEES

It remains for me to explain. . . . The Pargiters are intended to
tell . . . I need not say to represent. . . . The family of Pargiter is
meant. . . . my intention in this book to give. . . . (Virginia Woolf,
[*The Years*] "The Pargiters," vol. 1).

THE FIVE-YEAR composition process of *The Years,* initially ex-
hilarating, gradually became torturous when Virginia Woolf realized that the new form—a "novel-essay"—she had invented for
The Pargiters (the manuscript title of *The Years*) represented an ir-
reconcilable collision of genres. Ultimately, she would need to
extricate the didactic and interpretive essays she had alternated
with chapters of fiction from the novel. Much of the material
from the essays would appear several years later in her polemical
nonfiction tract, *Three Guineas* (1938). What Woolf learned from
this process of excision was something she had suspected all
along—the critical and creative faculties were, for her, opposing
forces. They manifested themselves in the two paths of her vocation—those of the literary critic and the novelist. Her one attempt to fuse the two in *The Years* was destined to fail.

The seeds of *The Years,* first tentatively called "The Open
Door" (January 1931, *Diary* 4: 6) or "A Knock on the Door"
(May 1931, *Diary* 4: 28) and planned as a sequel to *A Room of
One's Own* (1929), were sown on January 20, 1931, while Virginia
Woolf was taking a bath (*Diary* 4: 6) and pondering a talk to be
delivered to the London National Society for Women's Service.[1]

Volume Four Manuscript Notebook, inside front cover, of *The Years*.

Volume Eight Manuscript Notebook, inside front cover, of *The Years*.

The image of a door—closed to women but about to open—
would become significant as Woolf labored to depict the social
and political shift from Victorian to post–World War I England.
By February 1933 Woolf finally abandoned her original intention of interspersing novel chapters with essayistic commentary
and deleted the six essays, leaving only the fictional first section
(later labeled "1880") of the novel. In the rest of the nearly eight

manuscript notebooks that constitute the holograph of the novel, she withdrew her authorial voice, parceling it out instead among the characters and especially embedding her views within the two Pargiter cousins, Eleanor and Sara. She likewise buried political and historical facts within conversational allusions or couched them in the lyrical prefaces to the eleven chronological sections of the novel. In effacing a specific authorial presence and allowing factual details to appear almost as asides, Woolf created a new novelistic genre, one that Mitchell Leaska in his introduction to the "1880" section of the manuscript termed "documented vision in union with poeticized truth" (Woolf, *Pargiters* xviii). Trying to achieve such an oxymoronic union would harass her over the next five years, through revisions of the galleys and page proofs and even beyond the novel's publication in March 1937.

Origins of the Novel

WOOLF'S SPEECH to the London National Society for Women's Service (LNSWS) on January 21, 1931, later severely truncated and published posthumously in *The Death of the Moth and Other Essays* (1942) as "Professions for Women," was addressed to a group of about two hundred professional women who, although they had finally received the vote, still fell far below their male counterparts in economic and educational opportunities.[2] In the surviving twenty-five-page typescript of the talk, Woolf demonstrates for her audience the female novelist's battle between reason and imagination, opposites that recall terms from an earlier essay, "granite" and "rainbow."[3] In her speech to the professional women, Woolf figures the novelist (a thinly disguised version of herself) as a fisherwoman whose fishing line represents reason dropped into the deep waters of imagination.

Volume One Manuscript Notebook, page 48, of *The Years*.

Reason—masculine, faithful to the factual, conventional world—acts as the disciplinarian, the censor who insists that women cannot yet write about their deepest instincts, about sex and the body. Grudgingly, the feminine imagination agrees to wait another fifty years until men can be "educated to stand free speech in women" (*Pargiters* xl). In a rather awkward transition from her own profession as a writer to the working women she is addressing, Woolf acknowledges that their tasks are materially different from and more difficult than hers, since in post–World War I England these women are actively competing with men for jobs and salaries. She concedes that, for the present, being self-supporting is an adequate achievement for women. Her conclusion, however, offers the metaphor of a door about to open, at which point "there will take place between you [her audience of working women] and some one else the most interesting, exciting, and important conversation that has ever been heard" (*Pargiters* xliv).

Adopting the image of a door in her tentative titles for *The Years* in her diary, she would at first try to chronicle the steps various members of one extended family, the Pargiters, would take toward that door from the late Victorian period of 1880 to the Present Day of the mid-1930s. But instead of reporting the exciting conversation about to occur, both the lecture (ending with the teasing statement "I am not going to talk about that now. My time is up" [*Pargiters* xliv]) and the novel (concluding with Eleanor Pargiter and her siblings deciding to open the door and walk home in the early summer morning) invite the reader to imagine those conversations. To provide them for the reader would be too didactic, would close instead of open that door to new possibilities. Consequently, although *The Years* is more filled with conversation than any of Woolf's earlier novels, those conversations are invariably fragmented, interrupted, and almost always unfinished. Neither an author nor any specific narrative

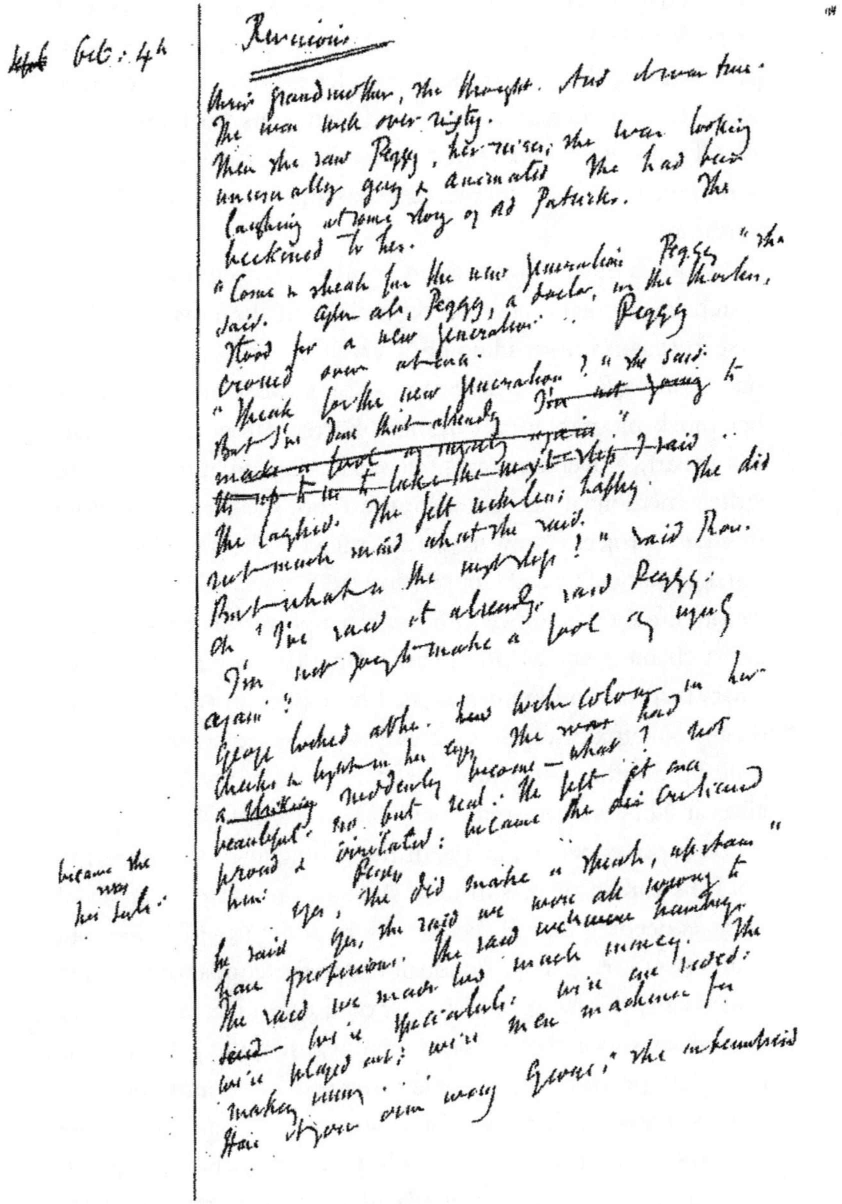

~~Wed~~ Feb: 4th

Revisions

Her grandmother, she thought. And it was true. She was well over sixty. Then she saw Peggy, her niece; she was looking unusually gay & animated. She had been laughing at some story of Sir Patrick's. She beckoned to her.

"Come & speak for the new generation Peggy" she said. After all, Peggy, a doctor, in the kitchen, stood for a new generation.. Peggy crossed over at once.

"Speak for the new generation?" she said. But I've done that already. ~~I'm not going to make a fool of myself again."~~ ~~She stopped to take the next step~~ I said.. She laughed. She felt extraordinarily happy. She did not much mind what she said.

"But what is the next step?" said Rose.

Oh I've said it already, said Peggy. I'm not going to make a fool of myself again!"

George looked at her. How the colour in her cheeks & light in her eyes. She ~~was~~ had suddenly become—what? Not a ~~striking~~ beautiful; no, but real. He felt it at once proud & irritated: because she did embarrass him: Peggy

because the way her sister.

Yes, she did make a speech, upstairs" he said. Yes, she said we were all trying to have professions. She said we made too much money. She said we were speculators; we're mere machines for ~~doing~~ making money; we're played out; ... Have it your own way George;" she interrupted

Volume Eight Manuscript Notebook, page 14, of *The Years.*

perspective, Woolf seems to suggest, can present a unified story of discrete lives. Unlike the Victorian family chronicles of its predecessors, *The Years* refuses to offer a summary or even to suggest any particular destiny for its characters. Such an ending, Woolf implies, would contradict reality, if indeed reality lies within the characters' consciousnesses and not in an omniscient narrator.

Woolf's burst of inspiration in 1931 took well over a year to materialize into the tangible beginnings of the novel. She had first to finish proofreading both *The Waves* (1931) and her second *Common Reader* (1932). She was also at work on *Flush* (1933), her mock biography of Elizabeth Barrett Browning's spaniel. But in early November 1932, fresh from digging into her past to write a memoir of her father for the *Times,* she is exultant about this new project. Now it will be called "The Pargiters," she states in her diary, and "its [*sic*] to take in everything, sex, education, life &c; & come, with the most powerful & agile leaps, like a chamois across precipices from 1880 to here & now— Thats [*sic*] the notion anyhow, & I have been in such a haze & dream & intoxication, declaiming phrases, seeing scenes, as I walk up Southampton Row that I can hardly say I have been alive at all, since the 10th Oct" (*Diary* 4: 129). At this point, Woolf reprises her old image of the fishing line; determined to hold the thread of reason taut, she vows to write a "novel of fact," conceding that "I feel now & then the tug to vision, but resist it" (*Diary* 4: 129). Gradually, over the course of the next three years, this "tug to vision" would cause her considerable anguish. In successive revisions from typescript to galleys to the final page proofs, Woolf would struggle to find an impossible balance between fact and vision, granite and rainbow. In her 1927 review of Harold Nicolson's *Some People,* she first articulates the challenge that faces the modern biographer (and the modern novelist as well) in a world devoid of fixed standards: "Truth of fact and truth of fiction," she argues, "are incompatible; yet he [the biographer] is now more than ever urged to combine them" ("The New Biography" 155). In *The Years* Woolf steeled herself to meet the biographer's challenge, one she would encounter again in her biography of her friend the painter Roger Fry, written immediately after publication of *The Years*. Always anxious to avoid duplicating herself, Woolf was determined in *The Years* not to stick to one method or genre.

In her most complete overview of the art of fiction, "Phases of Fiction," published in 1929 in *The Bookman,* she coins a series of labels to designate the various types of novels and novelists. Among the most disparate are the "Truth-Tellers" and the "Psychologists." The former, exemplified by such seemingly diverse writers as Daniel Defoe and Guy de Maupassant, make us believe completely in the solidity of their world. Woolf notes of their works that "we seem wedged among solid objects in a solid universe" ("Phases" 95). Conversely, the psychologists—Henry James and Marcel Proust—have virtually abandoned this solid world: "The usual supports, the props and struts of the conventions, expressed or observed by the writer, are removed" ("Phases" 121). Their emphasis instead falls on the tangible world only insofar as that world impresses itself upon the characters and elicits sensations. In her most famous essay on character, "Mr. Bennett and Mrs. Brown," written in response to a truth-telling novelist, Arnold Bennett, Woolf coins new terms to illustrate this difference between truth-tellers and psychologists: *materialists* vs. *spiritualists.* The materialists, epitomized by Arnold Bennett, John Galsworthy, and other Edwardian novelists, emphasize the factual details of their characters; while the spiritualists, the new Georgian novelists like James Joyce and Woolf herself, stress the internal consciousness of their characters.[4] The true challenge in *The Years* would be to synthesize these two methods, to blend material and spiritual, truth-teller and psychologist.

In her diaries and letters Woolf complains of the cleft between the critical and creative minds, a division closely related to her opposition between fact and fiction, reason and imagination, truth-teller and psychologist. Throughout her literary career she divided her time between critical essays and reviews for newspapers and journals and short stories and novels. Writing furiously throughout the late fall of 1932, she interspersed the fictional chapters of her novel-essay, "The Pargiters," with critical interpretations of the issues — social, political, and economic — that her characters faced. She finished the first section by Christmas, and on December 31 records her yearning to begin the next section, in which she will extend the Pargiter family to include the two female cousins, Elvira (later Sara) and Maggie. In a final image of 1932, Woolf's fisherwoman, dipping the line of reason into the waters of imagination, has been transformed into a sailboat that "long[s] to feel my sails blow out, & to be careering with Elvira, Maggie & the rest over the whole of human life" (*Diary* 4: 134).

By February 1933 Woolf had revised the first chapter — the "1880" section — and had made her most significant generic change. She extracted the explanatory interchapters, instead "compacting them in the text" (*Diary* 4: 146), and envisioned an appendix with dates. She would not adopt the nonfictional interchapter commentary in any of the later sections, fearing the danger of appearing too didactic. The loss of these critical passages in a sense broke the structural backbone of the novel but accorded with Woolf's distrust of an overbearing narrative voice. The tug toward vision over fact would grow stronger in the next ("1891") section with the creation of Elvira (Sara in the final version), the most poetic and visionary of all the Pargiter

characters and the one with whom Woolf most closely identi-
fied.[5] Still, Woolf believed that *The Years* could achieve a delicate
balance between her early novel of fact, *Night and Day* (1919),
and her novel of vision, *The Waves*. While in writing *Mrs. Dalloway* (1925) she had discovered a new method of giving depth
to character—her "tunneling process" (*Diary* 2: 272)—in *The
Years* she grappled with both breadth and depth, trying to find
a form that would be expansive enough to deliver both. What
Henry James had once termed the generic dilemma of the
novel—the "baggy monster"—at first challenged and later
dismayed Woolf.[6] To achieve the "immense breadth" and the
"immense intensity" she wanted, she hoped to combine extra-
novelistic genres—"satire, comedy, poetry ... [and perhaps] a
play, letters, poems ..." (*Diary* 4: 152). She aspired to cram the
book full of everything she knew, to sum up but not to preach.
Yet as late as November 1935 she still found herself battling
with this mixed genre. In a diary entry she complains, "Now
again I pay the penalty of mixing fact & fiction: cant [*sic*] concentrate on The Years. I have a sense that one cannot control
this terrible fluctuation between the 2 worlds" (*Diary* 4: 350).

Revisions

CRITICS WHO first traced Woolf's revisions and relentless re-
ductions from manuscript to final published novel (Hoffmann,
Radin, and Leaska) generally conclude that the compacting of
the factual portion harms the novel's unity. Harshest in this
judgment is Charles G. Hoffmann, one of the first critics to eval-
uate the holograph against the final version. Hoffmann finds the
novel too "diffuse at its center" (88) and blames this on Woolf's
failure to punctuate each chronological section with moments
of vision. He suggests that the balance between external and

internal, fact and vision, might have worked better had Woolf continued to write interchapters for each section and then, as in the "1880" section, compacted them into the text of the novel.

In 1977 Mitchell Leaska transcribed and published the holograph version of the "1880" section with the six interchapters so that readers can now track Woolf's changes and thus literally see a writer at work in the process of revising. The publication of the complete *Diary,* especially volumes 4 and 5 in 1982 and 1984, further enables readers to trace Woolf's thoughts and anxieties as she writes and rewrites the novel. As Leonard Woolf, who first published some of his wife's entries in *A Writer's Diary* in 1953, claimed, she had a particularly thorough and reflective tendency to record her writing process in her diaries:

> She uses these pages as Beethoven used his Notebooks to jot down an idea or partially work out a theme to be used months or years later in a novel or a symphony. While writing a book, in the diary she communes with herself about it and its meaning and object, its scenes and characters. She reveals, more nakedly perhaps than any other writer has done, the exquisite pleasure and pains, the splendours and miseries, of artistic creation, the relation of the creator both to his creation and his creatures and also to his critics and public. (Leonard Woolf 48)

Though he refrains from much critical commentary in his effort simply to put before the reader Woolf's original manuscript, Leaska offers an insight into her method of composition in his definition of the word *parget* from Joseph Wright's *English Dialect Dictionary.* The two entries that shed light on the working title of the novel, *The Pargiters,* give the meaning of *parget* as "to plaster with cement or mortar" and "to whitewash" (Leaska 173).[7] Leaska suggests that in her revisions, Woolf metaphorically acted to "parget"—both to cement the novel's segments and to whitewash or gloss over the deeper social and political issues. In addition, he argues that the Victorian Pargiter families of 1880 and 1891 left to their children the dubious legacy of pargeting ideas and social issues too dangerous to voice clearly (introduction, Woolf, *The Pargiters* xix).

Building on her original reprisal of the two large portions of the manuscript that Woolf omitted shortly before publication of *The Years,* Grace Radin offers the most thorough discussion of Woolf's progression from manuscript to published novel in her study *Virginia Woolf's 'The Years': The Evolution of a Novel.* Radin chronicles the final date of the seven and one-quarter holograph notebooks (November 15, 1934), the receipt of the first set of galley proofs (March 1936), and the page proofs (December 1936), and analyzes the omission of what she terms the "two enormous chunks" (Radin, "'Two enormous chunks'") as late as the galley stage of March 1936. She views the omission of a large portion of the wartime "1917" section and of an entire "1921" section as a softening of Woolf's antiwar commentary and a consequent loosening of any explicit connection between *The Years* and the extended polemical essay *Three Guineas (Evolution of a Novel* 121). At the galley stage also Radin notes the addition of the servants' (especially Crosby's) points of view to provide a broader perspective on class consciousness in late Victorian and early twentieth-century England. In response to criticism that the published novel lacks unity, Radin argues that Woolf's successive revisions, especially those between March and December 1936, lent the book a "reverberative structure" whereby various characters echo thoughts and phrases and recall actions from earlier episodes.

A final significant revision, reminiscent of Woolf's "Time Passes" middle section of *To the Lighthouse* (1927) and the seasonal preludes in *The Waves,* was the insertion of the lyrical descriptions of the seasons and the dates that open each section of the novel. Here, Woolf blends poetic description with specific material fact to draw the reader forward chronologically and at the same time to fuse the linear progression of the years with spatial depictions of weather and seasons. The descriptions of the weather in four spring sections ("1880," "1908," "1910," "1914"), three summer ones ("1907," "1911," "Present Day"), two autumn ones ("1891," "1918"), and two winter ones ("1913," "1917") furthermore allow Woolf to insert, subtly and anonymously, factual references to nationally significant events—deaths of monarchs and political figures, war at home and abroad, the armistice, suffragette meetings and actions. Yet in spite of Woolf's revisions and the insertion of reverberative echoes to meld past and present within both the characters' consciousnesses and that of the reader, Radin, like earlier critics, ultimately concludes that the novel lacks unity. For Radin, this is not so much a problem of technique as a failure of "some perspective that transcends daily life" (*Evolution of a Novel* 154). Both Eleanor and Sara, the two characters whose perspectives dominate the novel, in the end deliberately fail to offer any steady or consistent point of view.

A New Genre?

IF *THE YEARS* lacks a unified vision, it may be because Woolf refused to repeat herself generically. All nine of her novels, from her first, *The Voyage Out* (1915), a sort of truncated bildungsroman, to her novel of fact, *Night and Day,* to her most poetic and experimental novel, *The Waves,* composed entirely of interior monologues, seek to push against the novel genre while still retaining some of its traditional conventions. In *The Years* Woolf was surely conscious of the legacy of the family chronicle per-

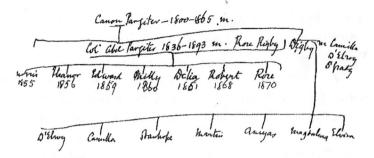

Genealogical tree, inside front cover of Volume One Manuscript Notebook of *The Years*.

fected in England by the major Victorian novelists Thackeray, Eliot, Trollope, and Dickens and, in her own time, by John Galsworthy, author of *The Forsyte Saga,* a multivolume work that Woolf derided in her essay "Mr. Bennett and Mrs. Brown." Galsworthy died while she was in the initial stages of writing *The Years.* In her diary she curtly remarks, "That stark man lies dead" (*Diary* 4: 147). Woolf was also clearly aware of her own attempt to recapitulate and reform her own family past as she had more obviously done in her admittedly autobiographical novel *To the Lighthouse.* The two branches of the Pargiter family spawned by the two brothers, Abel and Digby Pargiter, closely correspond in numbers and ages to the families of James Fitzjames and Leslie Stephen, Woolf's uncle and father, respectively. While it would be presumptuous and reductive to argue for close correspondences between the siblings of both families and their fictional counterparts, it may not be far-fetched to note certain parallels between Eleanor Pargiter and Woolf's oldest cousin, Katherine Stephen (secretary and later principal of Newnham College, Cambridge), and Delia Pargiter and Dorothea Stephen (Katherine's sister, who spent her adulthood in Ireland), Edward Pargiter and Jem (J. K.) Stephen (Cambridge scholar and poet). Closer to home, the intimacy between Maggie and Sara (with Maggie's new kind of marriage and Sara's iconoclastic behavior) is reminiscent of that between Virginia and her sister, Vanessa Bell.

During the early stages of writing *The Years,* Woolf constantly alludes in her diary to the problem of form and revision as reshaping. Finishing her rewriting of the first section as she was reading the Russian author Ivan Turgenev's works, she contrasts Turgenev with Fyodor Dostoyevsky in an attempt to elucidate her own form. As she pares and cuts her manuscript she seems to ally herself more with Turgenev, asking, "How do we know if the D. [Dostoyevsky] form is better or worse than the T. [Turgenev]. It seems less permanent. T.'s idea that you the writer states [*sic*] the essential & lets the reader do the rest. D. to supply the reader with every possible help & suggestion. T. reduces the possibilities" (*Diary* 4: 172–73). Following Turgenev instead of Dostoyevsky, *The Years* calls for more work on the reader's part. Like the unreported conversation about to occur, the novel offers fragmentary thought and speech as the essential entrance to each character's mind.

Resisting generic labels used to designate many of her nineteenth-century predecessors (social problem novel, novel of manners, bildungsroman, romance), and even ones used to categorize her and other twentieth-century experimental novelists (stream of consciousness, psychological novel), Woolf forges new territory with her generic blending in *The Years.* Both Jane Marcus and Pamela Caughie in different ways have tried to stake this new ground, with Marcus calling the novel's structure operatic and Caughie seeing it as postmodern in its emphasis on relations instead of representation.[8] Rather, it seems from evidence of Woolf's own frequent comments on the process of writing and revision that she sought and was frustrated by a new method that would present actions, thoughts, and events simultaneously as if, she notes in an August 1933 entry, "I could see the same thing from two different views" (*Diary* 4: 173). In the final section, "Present Day," she comes closest to success with the juxtaposed scenes and conversations between the elderly Eleanor and her niece Peggy, and between Sara and her cousin North. Could she have achieved true simultaneity, however, these scenes would have had to be staged with the audience hearing both conversations at the same time.[9] This is precisely what the final party in Delia's rented rooms tries to do. Here in the last pages of the novel no conversation is complete, because no central character dominates the scene, and no narrator offers a commanding perspective. Instead, the reader becomes a privileged eavesdropper on the characters' external conversations and internal thoughts. The burden of interpretation, as Woolf had noted with Turgenev, thus rests quite explicitly on the reader, especially when the caretakers' children sing their unintelligible song (407). Each character (as well as a number of critics of the novel) who responds to the song tries feebly to interpret it, but no one can reach consensus. After *The Years* was published in March 1937, Woolf wrote to the poet Stephen Spender about her intention:

> But what I meant I think was to give a picture of society as a whole; give characters from every side; turn them towards society, not private life; exhibit the effect of ceremonies; keep one toe on the ground by means of dates, facts: envelop the whole in a changing temporal atmosphere; compose into one vast many-sided group at the end; and then shift the stress from present into the future — suggesting that there is no break, but a continuous development, possibly a recurrence of some pattern; of which of course we actors are ignorant. And the future was gradually to dawn. (*Letters* 6: 116)

Throughout her writing, both in her essays and novels and in her late memoir "A Sketch of the Past," Woolf speaks of her search for a pattern. In an early essay, "Modern Novels," written in 1919 for the *Times Literary Supplement* and later revised as "Modern Fiction" for *The Common Reader* (1925), she most articulately calls for a redefinition of the genre of the modern novel. Offering James Joyce as an example of this new genre, she states, "Let us record the atoms as they fall upon the mind in the order in which they fall, let us trace the pattern, however disconnected and incoherent in appearance, which each sight or incident scores upon the consciousness" (*Essays* 3: 33–34). In *The Years* the two principal voices of the novel, Eleanor and her cousin Sara, each demonstrate Woolf's maxim in different ways. Eleanor, originally the surrogate mother to her siblings after their mother's death and subsequently her father's caretaker, gradually learns how to open herself to the seemingly random play of atoms. Searching for a pattern, Eleanor never truly finds one, though she, like Woolf's modern novelist, comes to believe that no method is wrong. Sara, an outsider, a writer and reader, and an observer from the beginning, chants fragments of songs, bursts out with disconnected phrases, and adamantly refuses others' attempts to tame or place her. She is, in a very real sense, an example of Woolf's character "Mrs. Brown," from "Mr. Bennett and Mrs. Brown." In a version of that essay published in the *Criterion* in 1924 under the title "Character in Fiction," Woolf warns readers that their duty is to demand a true and original as opposed to ready-made character in fiction: "You should insist that she is an old lady of unlimited capacity and infinite variety; capable of appearing in any place; wearing any dress; saying anything and doing heaven knows what" (*Essays* 3: 436). In this context, Sara serves as an adviser to the reader; by making us slightly uncomfortable and frequently frustrated, she gestures toward a new openness to experience, just as Eleanor's final words to her brother Morris, "And now?," advise us to approach the text as open-ended, a door opening instead of closing.[10]

Cultural and Historical Context

PRECISELY BECAUSE Woolf expunged so many of the factual details from the final version of *The Years,* it is instructive to survey the principal political and cultural events to which discrete phrases and images obliquely refer. While reading *Three Guineas* as a sort of documentary companion to *The Years* is illuminating, the far more polemical tone and issue-laden content of *Three Guineas* presents a more propagandistic view than Woolf desired in *The Years.* She railed against novels with a set purpose, and thus the allusions to external events serve more to undergird the novel and to illuminate particular associations than to argue for a particular agenda. The period covered by the novel— 1880 to Present Day (the mid-1930s)—witnessed an enormous shift from Victorian to modern, post–World War I England. Woolf marks this shift on a number of levels: historically, with references to specific British monarchs, statues, and memorials; politically, with allusions to British imperialism in Africa, India, Egypt, and Ireland, to national elections, female suffrage, and war; socially and culturally, with the mention of new words such as "poppycock," "wireless," and "tosh," and with allusions to the large new London department stores of the 1870s and 1880s and the enormous change from horse-drawn to motorized transport; geographically, as the characters move from more to less established London residences; and literarily, with paraphrases and quotations from a wide range of authors, from Sophocles and Dante to Maupassant and T. S. Eliot. In each dated section Woolf weaves a thicket of asides and allusions that define the characters' class and perspective. The novel is divided into eleven sections of varying length with the longest two, the first ("1880") and the last ("Present Day"), enclosing the others— the first two decades of the twentieth century—like bookends.

The two Victorian sections, "1880" and "1891," place both Pargiter families as relatively well-to-do middle-class residents of late Victorian London. The daughters of Colonel Abel Pargiter shop at the large new department store, Whiteley's, instead of the poorer Army and Navy Stores. Abel's family, like Leslie Stephen's family, live in a respectable middle-class area, while Abel's mistress, Mira, lives in a less reputable section near Westminster Abbey where representatives of the next generation, Maggie and Renny, will live during the war. Colonel Pargiter frequents a club in Piccadilly where he meets other retired military friends who discuss past imperialistic campaigns in the British colonies in India, Africa, and Egypt. Colonel Pargiter has lost two fingers in the Indian Mutiny of 1857, an allusion that had been more explicit in Woolf's first version, "The Pargiters." In both the "1880" and "1891" sections, Irish Home Rule and the life of Charles Stewart Parnell, leader of the Irish Home Rule Party, define various characters' views and affiliations. Delia dreams of aiding Parnell in 1880 in the cause of "Justice" and "Liberty" (22), and when Eleanor reads that he has died in 1891, she rushes to find Delia to comfort her. When we meet Delia again in the 1930s she has married a conservative Anglo-Irishman, Patrick, who regrets the partition of Ireland and the formation of the Republic. The "1880" section mentions two sites closely connected with Britain's military victories earlier in the century—Marble Arch, commemorating Admiral Nelson's naval victories, and Apsley House, residence of the Duke of Wellington after the British victory at the Battle of Waterloo. It is here in the London spring—the beginning of the city's social season—that one sees Princess Alexandra, mentioned again in the "1891" and then in the "1910" section that closes with King Edward's death. The "1880" section also alludes to the general election of 1880, in which the Liberal Party under William Gladstone defeated Benjamin Disraeli's Tory Party. Woolf subtly grounds the long "1880" section in these factual details while introducing other themes and images that will accrue associations as the chronological sections progress.

In addition to the allusive political details of 1880, Woolf hints at the severe social restrictions on young women's behavior in late Victorian Britain. Their sheltered and chaperoned lives do not permit them to wander freely amid the London streets. The excised explanation of "Street Love," for example, in the original draft of "The Pargiters" is largely submerged in the experience of the youngest child, Rose Pargiter, of the man who exposes himself one evening as Rose sneaks out of the house to buy a box of toy ducks at the local corner store, Lamley's. Aware that she has already broken an implicit rule never to go out alone, Rose sees a man standing by a pillar-box, "unbuttoning his clothes" (28), and that image will haunt her for the rest of the novel, though she will never quite bring herself to discuss it. Rose's experience and her ensuing reticence illustrate Woolf's skill in connecting psychic trauma with concrete character traits. Though Woolf excised specific reference to Rose's lesbianism in the published version of the novel, by the "1907" section Rose will be a militant suffragette and later militantly in favor of World War I. As a counterpoint to Rose's response to trauma, Sara Pargiter's physical deformity will, in part, explain her later status as an odd and ill-dressed outsider and a pacifist, whose primary companion is the homosexual foreigner Nicholas. While Sara and Eleanor remain the two main centers of consciousness through which we read the novel, Sara and Rose emerge as the two most vocal and opinionated characters. Spokeswomen for conflicting attitudes toward suffrage and war, pacifism and militarism, the cousins allow Woolf to indicate the divisions within the women's movement in the early twentieth century and to confine specific commentary—"Force is always wrong"—to Kitty Lasswade, who has married an aristocrat and who presumably opposes the more militant Women's Social and Political Union founded in 1903 by Emmeline and Christabel Pankhurst.[11]

The "1880" section initiates the thread of literary allusions that will wind throughout the novel. The Oxford scene, the longest section with a setting outside of London, introduces both Kitty Malone (later Lasswade) and her cousin Edward Pargiter, second of the three Pargiter sons. Destined to be an Oxford don, Edward chooses a career representing the third profession open to middle-class Victorian men after the law, which his older brother, Morris, chooses, and the military, adopted and later dropped by his younger brother, Martin. In 1880 Edward is studying for his final examinations in classics and hoping to obtain a fellowship that will allow him to remain at Oxford as a tutor. He is reading Sophocles' *Antigone* in preparation for the examination, a play he will later translate and one that will echo throughout later sections of the novel as Sara reads his translation in 1907 and imagines herself Antigone, buried alive. In the final section of the novel, Edward quotes a line in Greek from the play but refuses to translate it when North asks him (393). In fact, Woolf purposely refuses to translate Edward's character for the reader. In the final proof stages she excised the only scene that would have fleshed out his thwarted relationship with his cousin Kitty Lasswade. There, in 1921, they walk together in Richmond Park, and again after Edward leaves, Kitty is frustrated by his refusal to indicate the source of a quotation or to finish a sentence.

The two Victorian sections of "1880" and "1891" introduce a material chronology of London transport between 1880 and 1935. In "1880" Woolf mentions the various forms of horse-drawn transportation, from the aristocratic landaus and victorias

Hansom cab, London (ca. 1880).

London omnibus (ca. 1880).

London omnibus
(ca. 1920).

of wealthy Londoners to the more middle-class omnibuses and hansom cabs and the working-class vans. In 1891 Eleanor takes a yellow omnibus (omnibuses were color-coded to mark their routes) and later, when she is in a hurry to reach the Law Courts, a hansom cab. The General London Omnibus Company had operated in London since 1856, and by the 1890s it was the largest omnibus company in the world.[12] It was a largely middle-class conveyance, and the Pargiter women—especially Eleanor, who has an active life of meetings and visits to her housing projects—take it frequently. In 1917 Eleanor travels on a motorized omnibus to and from Maggie and Renny's house in Westminster. The omnibus's lights are "shrouded with blue paint" because of the city blackout during the war (284). The old Pargiter servant Crosby will be afraid to take the London Underground (the Tube) in 1908; though the Underground had first operated as early as 1869, not until 1906 were most of the main Tube lines opened. Only Kitty has her own motorcar in 1910, though she is embarrassed by the status it represents and tells Martin that it belongs to her husband. By 1914, Martin thinks about how easily the city has made the transition to "cars without horses" (222). London cabs crisscross the novel, with the Pargiter girls in 1880 watching a hansom cab stop at a house two doors down the street to drop off a man; in the 1930s, Eleanor reprises that scene as she watches a taxi deposit a couple at a flat two doors down. The final scene recalls Woolf's taxicab image from *A Room of One's Own* that initiates the narrator's peroration on androgyny (103). Here, in *The Years,* the use of the hansom cab and later the taxi indicates a movement from a male-centered environment where women are not supposed to stare out the window to a more modern, egalitarian society where a couple enter a building together and Eleanor comments simply, "There! . . . There!" (372). At the end of the Pargiter party in the "Present Day" section, the Tube and omnibuses have ceased running for the night, and the characters decide to walk home in the early summer morning.

A London Novel

ABOVE ALL, however, as several critics have remarked, *The Years* is a London novel.[13] More than either the early *Night and Day* or *Mrs. Dalloway,* which covers a single day in 1920s postwar London, *The Years* captures the vibrancy of the city in and out of "the season." It records the changes in transportation, commerce, and street life as city noises shift from the jingling

Traffic scene in Queen Victoria Street showing a number of hansom cabs (1880).

of hansom cabs and horses' hooves to the honking of motorcar horns and buses. Throughout all the sections Woolf tethers the middle-class Pargiters to the lower classes through such street sounds as hawkers of wares, barrel organ players, and newsboys carrying placards. As she draws the reader chronologically through the London of Victorian times to the London of the 1930s, Woolf maintains the unchanging background noises of nature as a sort of refrain. Pigeons coo in both the "1880" and "Present Day" sections; wind rages over the city in autumn and winter, scattering leaves and garbage. The only sustained forays out of the city are the sections on Oxford in "1880," where Kitty Malone and Edward Pargiter live, and Dorsetshire of "1911," where Eleanor goes to visit Morris's family at the home of his mother-in-law. Yet by her allusions to caretakers and house agents and especially to the old Pargiter servant Crosby, Woolf reaches toward the outskirts of London and its burgeoning suburbs, the less fashionable areas where the lower classes and lower middle classes live: Bermondsey, Hoxton, Pimlico, Wandsworth. After she is forced to leave Abercorn Terrace, Crosby moves to a lodging house in Richmond, and Sara and Maggie Pargiter move to a lower-class area south of the Thames after their parents die in 1908. Eleanor Pargiter visits her housing projects in Grove Street in Marylebone. The final party that brings all the Pargiter siblings, their cousins, and their children together at the end is somewhere off Holborn—possibly, as Dorothy Brewster comments, Red Lion Square, where Delia rents rooms in an office building and where some of the group had assembled for a suffrage meeting in the "1910" section (Brewster 93–94). Though Brewster suggests that Abercorn Terrace is in St. John's Wood, its description closely resembles the Stephen house where Woolf grew up in Hyde Park Gate, minutes from Kensington Gardens, the Round Pond, and the Serpentine, which all figure frequently in the novel.

In the longest and most detailed journey through London in the novel, Martin and his cousin Sara meet on the steps of St. Paul's Cathedral in the City, eat lunch in a city chophouse, and walk down Fleet Street and along the Strand to Charing Cross, where they board a bus to Hyde Park Corner and then walk to Kensington Gardens to meet Maggie and her baby. Their journey is significant, as it allows for a final pre–World War I summary both of the characters' movements within London from 1880 to 1914 and the various religious, commercial, monarchical, legal, and civilian aspects of a city on the brink of a war that would alter if not the landscape (as would World War II), then the consciousness of the people. Cassandra-like, Sara quotes former prime minister William Pitt's response to an early nineteenth-century battle between France and Russia: " 'Roll up the map of Europe,' said the man to the flunkey" (220). The map of Europe will be changed by the impending war, and Sara

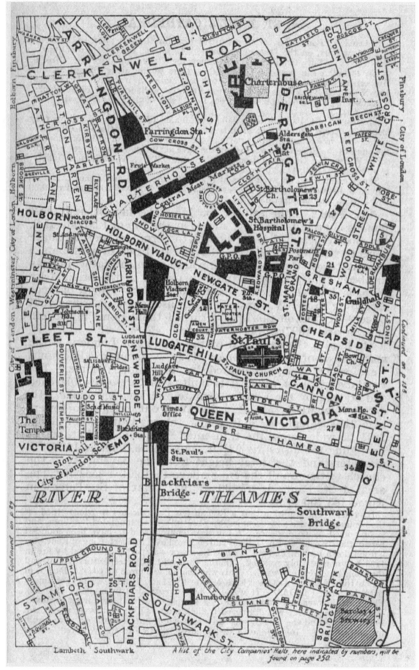

Street map of London (1933) (a).

will remain a staunch opponent of all wars. In her mind Sara appears to connect Rose Pargiter's militant suffragette stance to war as well. Rose, we find, is in prison, having thrown a brick during one of the suffragette demonstrations. Ironically, the "Present Day" section will allude to the decoration she would receive for her patriotic war work.

As Martin and Sara approach Temple Bar separating the City of London from Westminster, Martin laughs at the grotesque statues of Queen Victoria and King Edward that represent the years of their childhood and young adulthood. They pass the Law Courts, where Eleanor had heard Morris argue a case in 1891, and later see from the bus's window Colonel Pargiter's old club on Piccadilly. Walking in the wrong direction, away from Kensington Gardens, they pause at Speakers' Corner, where they listen to fragments of speeches by three anonymous citizens and where both Martin and Sara mock the lower-class speech. The cockney-edged words "Joostice and liberty" (227), repeated by Martin, parody Parnell's words in the "1880" section where Delia imagines herself at Parnell's side. At the gate to Kensington Gardens they suddenly enter fashionable and peaceful Kensington, where "[a] primal innocence seemed to brood over the scene" (229) and where they are for the last time back in the Victorian world of their childhood with the white marble statue of Queen Victoria before them. The "1914" section ends with a party hosted by Kitty Lasswade in her aristocratic Grosvenor Square home. Fragments of desultory conversations about the arts—from Canaletto's landscape paintings to the Russian ballet—dominate the party and bore Martin, the only representative of the Pargiter family to attend. The section ends with Kitty leaving London by train and returning to her home in the north, where, perfectly happy and peaceful, she feels time has stopped. The entire "1914" section comprises Woolf's farewell to pre–World War I London. Spatially the section connects the City of

Street map of London (1933) (b).

London with Westminster, legal London with royal Kensington, a city chophouse with a fancy dinner party. Statues of Queen Victoria bracket Martin and Sara's journey and mark a stable order about to be permanently disrupted.

From prewar 1914 the reader is plunged into the midst of a winter's night in the shrouded wartime London of 1917 on which Eleanor, Sara, Maggie, her husband Renny, and Sara's new friend Nicholas converge in the basement of Maggie's house during an air raid. Suddenly the Pargiter circle has expanded to include foreigners, the French Renny and the Russian or Polish Nicholas. England's imperialist days have ended, as have those of Napoléon, around whom the conversation briefly revolves. The "1917" section is followed by a brief "1918" section, the only one to focus entirely on Crosby's point of view. It is November 11, Armistice Day, and Crosby hears the guns booming, announcing the end of the war. Woolf has succeeded in these two wartime sections in reducing the war to its immediate impact on the family dining in the basement during an air raid, and then on an old servant who remains virtually untouched by historical and political events. Here, as opposed to the more overt intrusion of World War I into the lives of the characters in *Jacob's Room* (1922), *Mrs. Dalloway*, or *To the Lighthouse*, Woolf has chosen to confine the war's significance to the impressions of a few loud sounds on the characters' physical senses—the booming of bombs during an air raid and the booming of guns announcing the end of the war. One section, deleted in the final proof stage, would have given brief glimpses of soldiers on leave, the repeated headlines THREE BRITISH CRUISERS SUNK, and Eleanor's guilty musings about wounded soldiers on battlefields as she walks to meet a friend at a theater near Trafalgar Square.

Skipping entirely over the decade of the 1920s, the "Present Day" section at first appears to offer a final composed portrait of two generations of the Pargiters. As in *Mrs. Dalloway,* the novel culminates in a dinner-party reunion in which all the characters are confined to a specific space. Here, Woolf can allow both covert and overt commentary as characters collide and separate, speak and reflect. The characters can also sum each other up without the aid of an external narrator, so common in the nineteenth-century family chronicle, where the narrator/author neatly glosses each character's future. By contrast, the summing-up at the end of *The Years* remains partial, biased, and incomplete, and thwarts any urge for closure. Where *Mrs. Dalloway* had placed the final focus on the central character, Clarissa, with Peter Walsh's closing comment, "There she was," and where *The Waves* had handed the summary to the most verbal of the six characters, Bernard, *The Years* extends and disperses the focus on the two generations of the Pargiter family. This method allows Woolf to contrast the younger generation with the older in light of such material inventions as lipstick (which Peggy wears but Eleanor doesn't), electricity, and running taps for the bath. Through the conversations of two elderly people, neither of them members of the Pargiter families, we overhear negative views about the newly won freedom of women—the suffrages of 1918 and 1928, and the professions recently opened to women like Peggy, who is a doctor but who remains critical of her profession and dissatisfied. In the novel's ambivalent view of political and professional advances for women, Woolf avoids the didacticism of a specific agenda. Instead she chooses to chart innovations—material, political, professional—by her characters' responses. *The Years* have rung changes, but the characters constantly wonder whether they are indeed better off than before. Only Eleanor, now over seventy, seems to be optimistic, because she has learned to avoid judgment. This abeyance of judgment requires a relinquishment of personality, a move toward anonymity that Woolf would pursue in her last writings, and paradoxically positions Eleanor to have the last words in the novel.

Critical Reception

WOOLF'S FIRST and (for the future of the novel) most important critic was her husband. Leonard Woolf read the manuscript of *The Years* late — in November 1936, when it was already in galley proofs. In his autobiography he admits to softening, indeed to eliminating, any criticism save for that of its length, because of Virginia's precarious mental state and her fear that the novel was a failure:

> The verdict on *The Years* which I now gave her was not absolutely and completely what I thought about it. As I read it I was greatly relieved. It was obviously not in any way as bad as she thought it to be; it was in many ways a remarkable book and many authors and most publishers would have been glad to publish it as it stood. I thought it a good deal too long, particularly in the middle, and not really as good as *The Waves, To the Lighthouse,* and *Mrs. Dalloway.* (Leonard Woolf 155)

Leonard notes somewhat ironically that *The Years* sold better than any of her previous novels. His chart of figures indicates how relatively rich the novel made them in the years immediately following its publication. To him, this was an ironic instance of the public's lack of taste and of its inability to appreciate the true art of Virginia's better novels. Nevertheless, his praise, prevaricating as it might have been, was an immense relief to Virginia, who commented in her diary, "The miracle is accomplished. L. put down the last sheet about 12 last night; &

could not speak. He was in tears. He says it is 'a most remarkable book—he *likes* it better than The Waves'" (*Diary* 5: 30). Leonard's praise was timely; it allowed Virginia to persevere through the final page proofs and to see the novel published the following spring.

Lacking access to Virginia Woolf's previous drafts of the novel, early reviewers saw *The Years* as a further instance either of her poetic prowess, of her ability to capture the "quality of infinity in all experience" (Basil de Selincourt in Majumdar and McLaurin 374), or of her failure to depict convincing characters. Both British and American reviewers read the novel in comparison to its predecessor, *The Waves,* and they consequently mined *The Years* for the same lyrical prose and the same theme— the passage of time. Woolf was, as usual, buffeted by the criticism, alternately feeling the novel an achievement or a complete failure. Buoyed by de Selincourt's long and eulogistic review in the *Observer,* where he saw the novel as an advance on her ability in *The Waves* to render "tiny cubes of live experience" in a "kaleidoscopic" manner, she finds herself so excited that she can hardly continue writing *Three Guineas* (*Diary* 5: 67–68). And Desmond MacCarthy's opinion later that spring followed the same line. Dismissing the complaint of the "Communist historian of literature" (and the persistent view of the *Scrutiny* critics) that the novel lacked adequate contact with the tangible world, MacCarthy praised Woolf's ability to capture moments that suggested a mystical depth beneath the surface (Majumdar and McLaurin 114). She was pleased to read Howard Spring's review in the *Evening Standard,* in which he perceived her intention to submerge historical fact yet still convey "the blood and marrow of history" (Majumdar and McLaurin 377). Though she appeared satisfied with her friend David Garnett's assessment in the *New Statesman and Nation,* in which he praised her ability to convey the immediacy of "sense impression" far better than her contemporary Galsworthy, Garnett's review was to signal an ongoing debate about lack of unity in the novel. Garnett likened the book to a quilt made up of "scraps of a hundred old frocks" (Majumdar and McLaurin 384), but concluded that the pieces were discontinuous, never woven together. The negative reviews complained of Woolf's inability to depict character and of the artificiality of her technique. She was depressed by Edwin Muir's assessment in the *Listener,* in which he compared *The Years* to Tolstoy's *War and Peace* and found Woolf's novel to lack both story and continuity. He thought her characters insignificant (Majumdar and McLaurin 387), as did W. H. Mellers in the most scathing of the reviews, published in *Scrutiny* in June. Complaining that Woolf's sensuous impressions, her poetic method, were not matched by intellectual capacity, Mellers faulted her for cheating with technique and witheringly called the novel "a document of purposelessness" (Majumdar and McLaurin 397).

With the publication of *A Writer's Diary* in 1953, critics were able to see Woolf's original intention of the book as a novel-essay and to witness her struggle between internal vision and external fact. Criticism of the later 1950s and 1960s, especially that of James Hafley and Herbert Marder, lauded her ability to link external objects and settings as objective correlatives for characters' psyches. Marder labeled her technique in *The Years* "narrative pointillism," in which the characters manage both to blend with their settings and to retain their distinctness (McNees 4: 124). For both Marder and Hafley, Woolf's experiment with fact and vision succeeds and silences earlier criticism about the novel's lack of unity. The influential French critic Jean Guiguet, however, saw the novel as a failure of the "synthesis of the two orders of reality, that of facts and that of vision" (312).

The most important event in critical evaluations of *The Years* was the publication of Mitchell Leaska's transcription of the holograph of the first one and three-quarters of Woolf's manuscript notebooks, titled *The Pargiters* (1977), followed by an entire issue of the *Bulletin of the New York Public Library* (Winter 1977). In the latter, Grace Radin published her transcription of the "two enormous chunks" from "1917" and an excised "1921" section, which further enabled readers to compare the final version with earlier ones and, in particular, to see how Woolf had buried her factual materials, transforming historical, social, and political events into allusions, symbols, and fragments of conversation. From Woolf's complete diaries, especially volumes 4 (1982) and 5 (1984), as well as her *Letters,* especially volume 5 (1979), we have more evidence of the writing process and the mental and physical toll it took on Woolf than we have for any of the other novels. The exposition of her revisionary process has spawned a number of useful, if at times recapitulative, studies of the genre of *The Years.*[14]

Two other significant critical strains that run throughout the late twentieth and early twenty-first centuries are feminist and cultural studies approaches to *The Years.* Although the novel was a bestseller in America in 1937, netting Woolf enough money to buy a new car for Leonard and affording her the possibility of no longer having to write for a living, many critics have followed Leonard Woolf's view in designating *The Years* a second-rate novel within her corpus. Thus it has often been dropped from book-length studies of her more "canonical" novels like *Mrs. Dalloway, To the Lighthouse,* and *The Waves.* A number of critics have explored the connections between feminism and politics in the novel, and others have discussed Woolf's anti-Fascist stance in the aftermath of World War I and the buildup to World War II.[15] The trend of recent essays on *The Years* has tended to view the novel in light of specific historical and cultural events in late Victorian and early twentieth-century Britain. In an essay that evaluates *A Room of One's Own* and *Three Guineas* as well as *The Years,* Sowon Park offers a perceptive critique of

Woolf's feminism based on Woolf's ambivalent attitude toward suffragettes. In "Sounds of the City: Virginia Woolf and Modern Noise," Kate Flint addresses the evolution of sounds in London between 1880 and the 1930s, and suggests that Woolf's sensitivity to sound was a not uncommon phenomenon among city dwellers of her generation, who lived through the transition from horse-drawn vehicles and street musicians to motor vehicles. Though she concludes that *The Years* is ultimately a "crippled text," because Woolf could not overtly attack the issues of war, patriarchal privilege, and women's suppression (665), Hermione Lee states in her biography that "[i]n a way *The Years* rewrote [Woolf's] earlier books" (627). This seems a fitting way to open a door to *The Years* for the reader who, perhaps having missed the earlier novels, will read backward from this novel to earlier ones to discover Woolf's constant experiments with genre, character, vision, and fact. Alternatively, for a reader who comes later to *The Years,* especially after *Mrs. Dalloway, To the Lighthouse,* and *The Waves,* the novel offers a more comprehensive, if more diffuse, world than one finds in the earlier works. This world, melding fact and vision and moving rapidly in and out of multiple points of view, feels at times as though the earlier three works had been turned inside out, their centripetal movement having become in *The Years* centrifugal — characters, years, and events spinning outward and only superficially drawn together at the final "Present Day" party. Yet it may be that in the final novel published during her lifetime, Woolf came closer than ever before to presenting her own mimetic view of reality as a continuous succession of unfinished and often unrealized possibilities. If this is so, Eleanor's final question to Morris, one that echoes Sara's question at the subterranean dinner during the war in 1917, "And now?," (274) is a fitting conclusion to a work that refuses plot and closure in its insistence on dramatizing the moment. In a diary entry from December 1932 in the midst of her first frenetic writing of the manuscript, Woolf advises herself to wallow in the moment instead of trying to define it:

> . . . to use ones hands & eyes; to talk to people; to be a straw on the river, now & then—passive, not striving to say this is this. If one does not lie back & sum up & say to the moment, this very moment, stay you are so fair, what will be one's gain, dying? No: stay, this moment. No one ever says that enough. (*Diary* 4: 135)

To read *The Years* as a series of moments in time, each personally significant yet none more significant than another, to see these moments accumulate in memory as the characters age, is one way of appreciating the pattern of the novel and a means, too, of countering the complaint that Woolf failed to create living characters.

NOTES

[1]Over the course of writing the first draft, Woolf repeatedly suggested other titles for *The Years*. In the holograph notebook dated June 19, 1933, she jots in addition to "The Pargiters," "Time Passes" (recalling the middle section of *To the Lighthouse*), "Here & Now," and "In the Flesh." In the eighth and final notebook, dated September 27, 1934, she lists, in addition to "The Pargiters" and "Here and Now," "Brothers and Sisters," "Dawn," "Uncles & Aunts," "Ordinary People," and "Sons and Daughters." "A Knock on the Door" would eventually become, after several revisions, *Three Guineas*.

[2]See Hermione Lee's account of the meeting in her biography, *Virginia Woolf*, 590–91.

[3]"The New Biography," 1927; reprinted in *Granite and Rainbow: Essays*, 149 (New York: Harcourt Brace Jovanovich, 1958).

[4]Woolf referred to the previous generation of writers as "Edwardian" because their heyday was during the reign of King Edward VII (1901–1910); her own generation flourished during the reign of George V (1910–1936).

[5]In March 1933, Woolf is so immersed in writing Elvira's character that she notes in her diary, "I hardly know which I am, or where: Virginia or Elvira; in the Pargiters or outside" (*Diary* 4: 148); and several weeks later, just before a trip to Italy that would force a hiatus in the writing, she worries that Elvira "may become too dominant" (*Diary* 4: 152).

[6]Speaking in his preface to *The Tragic Muse* (1908) of the lack of artistry of big novels that capture life but fail to adhere to any form, James asks, ". . . but what do such large, loose, baggy monsters, with their queer elements of the accidental and the arbitrary artistically mean?" (*French Writers, Other European Writers, The Prefaces to the New York Edition,* ed. Leon Edel, 1107 [New York: Library of America, 1984]). Like Woolf, James preferred the taut novels of Turgenev.

[7]In "Virginia Woolf, The Pargeter," Leaska credits Jane Marcus with initially suggesting further exploration of this word (173).

[8]In "*The Years* as Greek Drama, Domestic Novel, and Götterdämmerung," Jane Marcus acknowledges Woolf's move away from conventionally identifiable novelistic forms: "Woolf wanted a form for the novel which would dispense with the conventional plot. . . . She longed to *compose* her novel, to score arias, duets, trios, quartets, as for voices and orchestra; above all to bring forward the chorus" (296). Writing over a decade later, Caughie extends this performative model to argue that *The Years* resists any attempt at defining and therefore fixing the form: "Woolf does not tell us what a novel is or should be; instead she shows us how it functions in the world" (107). Caughie's view seems to recall Woolf's discussion of Turgenev, save for one major point: Reading Turgenev, Woolf still believes in the division between essential and nonessential. Jeri Johnson's introduction to the Penguin edition of the novel is especially perceptive on genre. Johnson states that Woolf has replaced "narrative history" with " 'historical narrative' " (xiii), and later stresses both the dramatic and uncertain qualities of the novel: ". . . meaning must be performed in action in the full face of uncertainty, from within a narrative of doubt" (xxvi).

[9]In her posthumous novel, *Between the Acts,* Woolf literally and metaphorically played with dramatic forms, staging an outdoor pageant at a country estate. The pageant, however, like so many scenes in *The Years,* is constantly interrupted by external events and other characters' thoughts.

[10]Margaret Comstock's "The Loudspeaker and the Human Voice: Politics and the Form of *The Years*" speaks of the novel as anti-Fascist in form, with no central dictatorial character, and though she does not allude to Woolf's

critical essays, she reads the novel as a cooperation between the reader and the author in which both collaborate to achieve a nonhierarchical vision. Such a partnership would allow for a more fluid interpretation of the genre.

[11]Members and sympathizers of the Women's Social and Political Union were called suffragettes, as opposed to the suffragists, who had been working more quietly for the vote. By contrast, the National Union of Women's Suffrage Societies, led by Millicent Fawcett, were grouped in the latter (suffragist) category.

[12]According to Frank E. Huggett's *Carriages at Eight,* the omnibuses of the late nineteenth century had licenses to carry ten to twelve (usually female) passengers inside and ten to fourteen outside. They were slow, traveling at about five miles per hour; thus Eleanor's decision to take a hansom cab when she is in a hurry to get to the Law Courts to hear Morris argue his case (100).

[13]The first study of Woolf's London was Dorothy Brewster's *Virginia Woolf's London.* Brewster's work is particularly helpful in identifying specific streets and locations of the Pargiter families. Susan Squier's *Virginia Woolf and London: The Sexual Politics of the City* moves beyond Brewster's study to read the novel as a feminist plea for women's equality, noting that "women's war for sexual and professional equality is waged on the battlefield of London, where men and women struggle with each other for control of the streets" (140).

[14]See especially Jane Marcus's and Victoria Middleton's essays in the special issue of the *Bulletin of the New York Public Library* 80 (Winter 1977), and Anna Snaith's chapter on *The Pargiters* in *Virginia Woolf: Public and Private Negotiations,* 88–112.

[15]See Susan Squier's "'A Track of Our Own': The Typescript Draft of *The Years*"; Sallie Sears, "Notes on Sexuality: *The Years* and *Three Guineas*"; Patricia Cramer, "'Loving in the War Years'"; and Madeline Moore, *The Short Season Between Two Silences.* On Woolf's anti-Fascism and *The Years,* see Margaret Comstock, "The Loudspeaker and the Human Voice"; and Karen Levenback, "Virginia Woolf's 'War in the Village' and 'The War from the Street.'"

WORKS CITED

Brewster, Dorothy. *Virginia Woolf's London.* New York: New York University Press, 1960.

Caughie, Pamela L. *Virginia Woolf and Postmodernism.* Urbana: University of Illinois Press, 1991.

Comstock, Margaret. "The Loudspeaker and the Human Voice: Politics and the Form of *The Years.*" *Bulletin of the New York Public Library* 80 (1977): 252–75.

Cramer, Patricia. "'Loving in the War Years': The War of Images in *The Years.*" In *Virginia Woolf and War: Fiction, Reality, and Myth.* Edited by Mark Hussey, 203–24. Syracuse, NY: Syracuse University Press, 1991.

Flint, Kate. "Sounds of the City: Virginia Woolf and Modern Noise." In *Literature, Science, Psychoanalysis, 1830–1970: Essays in Honor of Gillian Beer.* Edited by Helen Small and Trudi Tate, 181–94. Oxford: Oxford University Press, 2003.

Guiguet, Jean. *Virginia Woolf and Her Works.* Translated by Jean Stewart. New York: Harcourt, Brace & World, 1965.

Hafley, James. *The Glass Roof: Virginia Woolf as Novelist.* Berkeley: University of California Press, 1954.

Hoffmann, Charles G. "Virginia Woolf's Manuscript Revisions of *The Years.*" *PMLA* 84 (January 1969): 79–89.

Huggett, Frank E. *Carriages at Eight: Horse-drawn Society in Victorian and Edwardian Times.* Fakenham, Norfolk, England: Lutterworth Press, 1979.

James, Henry. *French Writers, Other European Writers, The Prefaces to the New York Edition.* Vol. 2. Edited by Leon Edel. New York: Library of America, 1984.

Johnson, Jeri. Introduction. In *The Years* by Virginia Woolf, ix–xxxviii. London: Penguin, 1998.

Leaska, Mitchell A. "Virginia Woolf, The Pargeter: A Reading of *The Years.*" *Bulletin of the New York Public Library* 80 (1977): 172–210.

Lee, Hermione. *Virginia Woolf.* New York: Vintage Books, 1996.

Levenback, Karen. "Virginia Woolf's 'War in the Village' and 'The War from the Street': An Illusion of Immunity." In *Virginia Woolf and War: Fiction, Reality and Myth.* Edited by Mark Hussey, 40–57. Syracuse, NY: Syracuse University Press, 1991.

Majumdar, Robin, and Allen McLaurin, eds. *Virginia Woolf: The Critical Heritage.* New York: Routledge, 1975.

Marcus, Jane. "*The Years* as Greek Drama, Domestic Novel, and Götterdämmerung." *Bulletin of the New York Public Library* 80 (1977): 276–301.

Marder, Herbert. *Feminism and Art: A Study of Virginia Woolf.* Chicago: University of Chicago Press, 1968.

McNees, Eleanor, ed. *Virginia Woolf: Critical Assessments.* Vol. 4. East Sussex, England: Helm Information Ltd., 1994.

Middleton, Victoria. "*The Years:* 'A Deliberate Failure.'" *Bulletin of the New York Public Library* 80 (1977): 158–71.

Moore, Madeline. *The Short Season Between Two Silences: The Mystical and Political in the Novels of Virginia Woolf.* Boston: Allen and Unwin, 1984.

Park, Sowon S. "Suffrage and Virginia Woolf: 'The Mass Behind the Single Voice.'" *The Review of English Studies* 56 (2005): 119–34.

Radin, Grace. "'Two enormous chunks': Episodes Excluded during the Final Revisions of *The Years.*" *Bulletin of the New York Public Library* 80 (1977): 221–51.

———. *Virginia Woolf's 'The Years': The Evolution of a Novel.* Knoxville: Tennessee University Press, 1982.

Sears, Sallie. "Notes on Sexuality: *The Years* and *Three Guineas.*" *Bulletin of the New York Public Library* 80 (1977): 211–20.

Snaith, Anna. *Virginia Woolf: Public and Private Negotiations.* London: Macmillan Publishing, 2000.

Squier, Susan. "'A Track of Our Own': The Typescript Draft of *The Years.*" *Modernist Studies* 4 (1982): 218–31.

———. *Virginia Woolf and London: The Sexual Politics of the City.* Chapel Hill: University of North Carolina Press, 1985.

Woolf, Leonard. *Downhill All the Way: An Autobiography of the Years 1919 to 1939.* San Diego: Harcourt Brace Jovanovich, 1967.

Woolf, Virginia. "Character in Fiction." In *The Essays of Virginia Woolf.* Vol. 3 (1919–24). Edited by Andrew McNeillie, 420–36. San Diego: Harcourt Brace Jovanovich, 1988.

———. *The Diary of Virginia Woolf.* Edited by Anne Olivier Bell, assisted by Andrew McNeillie. Vol. 2 (1920–24). New York: Harcourt Brace Jovanovich, 1979.

———. *The Diary of Virginia Woolf.* Edited by Anne Olivier Bell, assisted by Andrew McNeillie. Vol. 4 (1931–35). New York: Harcourt Brace Jovanovich, 1982.

———. *The Diary of Virginia Woolf.* Edited by Anne Olivier Bell, assisted by Andrew McNeillie. Vol. 5 (1936–41). New York: Harcourt Brace Jovanovich, 1984.

———. *The Essays of Virginia Woolf.* Vol. 3 (1919–24). Edited by Andrew McNeillie. San Diego: Harcourt Brace Jovanovich, 1988.

———. *The Letters of Virginia Woolf.* Vol. 6 (1936–41). Edited by Nigel Nicolson and Joanne Trautmann. New York: Harcourt Brace Jovanovich, 1980.

———. "Modern Novels." In *The Essays of Virginia Woolf.* Vol. 3 (1919–24). Edited by Andrew McNeillie, 30–37. San Diego: Harcourt Brace Jovanovich, 1988.

———. "The New Biography." In *Granite and Rainbow,* 149–55. 1958. Reprint, New York: Harcourt Brace Jovanovich, 1975.

————. "Phases of Fiction." In *Granite and Rainbow,* 93–145. 1958. Reprint, New York: Harcourt Brace Jovanovich, 1975.

————. [*The Years*] The Pargiters; a novel-essay based upon a paper read to the London National Society for Women's Service. Holograph, unsigned, dated Oct. 11, 1932–Nov. 15, 1934. 8 volumes. Berg Collection of English and American Literature, New York Public Library. *Major Authors on CD-ROM: Virginia Woolf.* Edited by Mark Hussey. Woodbridge, CT: Research Publications, 1997.

————. *The Pargiters by Virginia Woolf. The Novel-Essay Portion of* The Years. Edited with an introduction by Mitchell A. Leaska. New York: New York Public Library, 1977.

————. *A Room of One's Own.* Annotated and with an introduction by Susan Gubar. Orlando: Harcourt, 2005.

The Years

1 8 8 0

It was an uncertain spring. The weather, perpetually changing,
sent clouds of blue and of purple flying over the land. In the
country farmers, looking at the fields, were apprehensive; in
London umbrellas were opened and then shut by people looking up at the sky. But in April such weather was to be expected.
Thousands of shop assistants made that remark, as they handed
neat parcels to ladies in flounced dresses standing on the other
side of the counter at Whiteley's and the Army and Navy Stores.
Interminable processions of shoppers in the West end, of business men in the East, paraded the pavements, like caravans perpetually marching,—so it seemed to those who had any reason
to pause, say, to post a letter, or at a club window in Piccadilly.
The stream of landaus, victorias and hansom cabs was incessant; for the season was beginning. In the quieter streets musicians doled out their frail and for the most part melancholy pipe
of sound, which was echoed, or parodied, here in the trees of
Hyde Park, here in St. James's by the twitter of sparrows and the
sudden outbursts of the amorous but intermittent thrush. The
pigeons in the squares shuffled in the tree tops, letting fall a twig
or two, and crooned over and over again the lullaby that was always interrupted. The gates at the Marble Arch and Apsley
House were blocked in the afternoon by ladies in many-
coloured dresses wearing bustles, and by gentlemen in frock

coats carrying canes, wearing carnations. Here came the Princess, and as she passed hats were lifted. In the basements of the long avenues of the residential quarters servant girls in cap and apron prepared tea. Deviously ascending from the basement the silver teapot was placed on the table, and virgins and spinsters with hands that had staunched the sores of Bermondsey and Hoxton carefully measured out one, two, three, four spoonfuls of tea. When the sun went down a million little gaslights, shaped like the eyes in peacocks' feathers, opened in their glass cages, but nevertheless broad stretches of darkness were left on the pavement. The mixed light of the lamps and the setting sun was reflected equally in the placid waters of the Round Pond and the Serpentine. Diners-out, trotting over the Bridge in hansom cabs, looked for a moment at the charming vista. At length the moon rose and its polished coin, though obscured now and then by wisps of cloud, shone out with serenity, with severity, or perhaps with complete indifference. Slowly wheeling, like the rays of a searchlight, the days, the weeks, the years passed one after another across the sky.

COLONEL ABEL PARGITER was sitting after luncheon in his club talking. Since his companions in the leather armchairs were men of his own type, men who had been soldiers, civil servants, men who had now retired, they were reviving with old jokes and stories now their past in India, Africa, Egypt, and then, by a natural transition, they turned to the present. It was a question of some appointment, of some possible appointment.

Suddenly the youngest and the sprucest of the three leant forward. Yesterday he had lunched with . . . Here the voice of the speaker fell. The others bent towards him; with a brief wave of his hand Colonel Abel dismissed the servant who was removing the coffee cups. The three baldish and greyish heads remained close together for a few minutes. Then Colonel Abel threw himself back in his chair. The curious gleam which had come into all their eyes when Major Elkin began his story had faded completely from Colonel Pargiter's face. He sat staring ahead of him with bright blue eyes that seemed a little screwed up, as if the glare of the East were still in them; and puckered at the corners as if the dust were still in them. Some thought had struck him that made what the others were saying of no interest to him; indeed, it was disagreeable to him. He rose and looked out of the window down into Piccadilly. Holding his cigar suspended he looked down on the tops of omnibuses, hansom cabs, victorias, vans and landaus. He was out of it all, his attitude seemed to say; he had no longer any finger in that pie. Gloom settled on his red handsome face as he stood gazing. Suddenly a thought struck him. He had a question to ask; he turned to ask it; but his friends were gone. The little group had broken up. Elkins was already hurrying through the door; Brand had moved off to talk to another man. Colonel Pargiter shut his mouth on the thing he might have said, and turned back again to the window overlooking Piccadilly. Everybody in the crowded street, it seemed, had some end in view. Everybody was hurrying along to keep some appointment. Even the ladies in their victorias and broughams were trotting down Piccadilly on some errand or other. People were coming back to London; they were settling in for the season. But for him there would be no season; for him there was nothing to do. His wife was dying; but she did not die. She was better today; would be worse tomorrow; a new nurse was coming; and so it went on. He picked up a paper and turned over the pages. He looked at a picture of the west front of Cologne Cathedral. He tossed the paper back into its place among the other papers. One of these days—that was his euphemism for the time when his wife was dead—he would give up London, he thought, and live in the country. But then there was the house; then there were the children; and there was also . . . his face changed; it became less discontented; but also a little furtive and uneasy.

He had somewhere to go, after all. While they were gossiping he had kept that thought at the back of his mind. When he turned round and found them gone, that was the balm he clapped on his wound. He would go and see Mira; Mira at least would be glad to see him. Thus when he left the club he turned not East, where the busy men were going; nor West where his own house in Abercorn Terrace was; but took his way along the hard paths through the Green Park towards Westminster. The grass was very green; the leaves were beginning to shoot; little green claws, like birds' claws, were pushing out from the branches; there was a sparkle, an animation everywhere; the air smelt clean and brisk. But Colonel Pargiter saw neither the grass nor the trees. He marched through the Park, in his closely buttoned coat, looking straight ahead of him. But when he came to Westminster he stopped. He did not like this part of the business at all. Every time he approached the little street that lay under the huge bulk of the Abbey, the street of dingy little houses, with yellow curtains and cards in the window, the street where the muffin man seemed always to be ringing his bell, where children screamed and hopped in and out of white chalk-marks on the pavement, he paused, looked to the right, looked to the left; and then walked very sharply to Number Thirty and rang the bell. He gazed straight at the door as he waited with his head rather sunk. He did not wish to be seen standing on that door-step. He did not like waiting to be let in. He did not like it when Mrs. Sims let him in. There was always a smell in the house; there were always dirty clothes hanging on a line in the back garden. He went up the stairs, sulkily and heavily, and entered the sitting-room.

Nobody was there; he was too early. He looked round the room with distaste. There were too many little objects about.

He felt out of place, and altogether too large as he stood upright before the draped fireplace in front of a screen upon which was painted a kingfisher in the act of alighting on some bulrushes. Footsteps scurried about hither and thither on the floor above. Was there somebody with her? he asked himself, listening. Children screamed in the street outside. It was sordid; it was mean; it was furtive. One of these days, he said to himself . . . but the door opened and his mistress, Mira, came in.

"Oh, Bogy, dear!" she exclaimed. Her hair was very untidy; she was a little fluffy-looking; but she was very much younger than he was and really glad to see him, he thought. The little dog bounced up at her.

"Lulu, Lulu," she cried, catching the little dog in one hand while she put the other to her hair, "come and let Uncle Bogy look at you."

The Colonel settled himself in the creaking basket-chair. She put the dog on his knee. There was a red patch—possibly eczema—behind one of its ears. The Colonel put on his glasses and bent down to look at the dog's ear. Mira kissed him where his collar met his neck. Then his glasses fell off. She snatched them and put them on the dog. The old boy was out of spirits today, she felt. In that mysterious world of clubs and family life of which he never spoke to her something was wrong. He had come before she had done her hair, which was a nuisance. But her duty was to distract him. So she flitted—her figure, enlarging as it was, still allowed her to glide between table and chair— hither and thither; removed the firescreen and set a light, before he could stop her, to the grudging lodging-house fire. Then she perched on the arm of his chair.

"Oh, Mira!" she said, glancing at herself in the looking-glass and shifting her hair-pins, "what a dreadfully untidy girl you are!" She loosed a long coil and let it fall over her shoulders. It was beautiful gold-glancing hair still, though she was nearing

forty and had, if the truth were known, a daughter of eight
boarded out with friends at Bedford. The hair began to fall of
its own accord, of its own weight, and Bogy seeing it fall
stooped and kissed her hair. A barrel-organ had begun to play
down the street and the children all rushed in that direction,
leaving a sudden silence. The Colonel began to stroke her neck.
He began fumbling, with the hand that had lost two fingers,
rather lower down, where the neck joins the shoulders. Mira
slipped onto the floor and leant her back against his knee.

Then there was a creaking on the stairs; someone tapped as
if to warn them of her presence. Mira at once pinned her hair
together, got up and shut the door.

The Colonel began in his methodical way to examine the
dog's ears again. Was it eczema? or was it not eczema? He
looked at the red patch, then set the dog on its legs in the basket and waited. He did not like the prolonged whispering on the
landing outside. At length Mira came back; she looked worried;
and when she looked worried she looked old. She began hunting about under cushions and covers. She wanted her bag, she
said; where had she put her bag? In that litter of things, the
Colonel thought, it might be anywhere. It was a lean, poverty-
stricken-looking bag when she found it under the cushions in
the corner of the sofa. She turned it upside down. Pocket handkerchiefs, screwed up bits of paper, silver and coppers fell out
as she shook it. But there should have been a sovereign, she
said. "I'm sure I had one yesterday," she murmured.

"How much?" said the Colonel.

It came to one pound—no, it came to one pound eight and
sixpence, she said, muttering something about the washing. The
Colonel slipped two sovereigns out of his little gold case and
gave them to her. She took them and there was more whispering on the landing.

"Washing . . . ?" thought the Colonel, looking round the room. It was a dingy little hole; but being so much older than she was it did not do to ask questions about the washing. Here she was again. She flitted across the room and sat on the floor and put her head against his knee. The grudging fire which had been flickering feebly had died down now. "Let it be," he said impatiently, as she took up the poker. "Let it go out." She resigned the poker. The dog snored; the barrel-organ played. His hand began its voyage up and down her neck, in and out of the long thick hair. In this small room, so close to the other houses, dusk came quickly; and the curtains were half drawn. He drew her to him; he kissed her on the nape of the neck; and then the hand that had lost two fingers began to fumble rather lower down where the neck joins the shoulders.

A SUDDEN SQUALL of rain struck the pavement, and the children, who had been skipping in and out of their chalk cages, scudded away home. The elderly street singer, who had been swaying along the kerb, with a fisherman's cap stuck jauntily on the back of his head, lustily chanting: "Count your blessings, Count your blessings—" turned up his coat collar and took refuge under the portico of a public house where he finished his injunction: "Count your blessings. Every One." Then the sun shone again; and dried the pavement.

"IT'S NOT BOILING," said Milly Pargiter, looking at the tea-kettle. She was sitting at the round table in the front drawing-room of the house in Abercorn Terrace. "Not nearly boiling," she repeated. The kettle was an old-fashioned brass kettle, chased with a design of roses that was almost obliterated. A feeble little flame flickered up and down beneath the brass bowl. Her sister Delia, lying back in a chair beside her, watched it too.

"Must a kettle boil?" she asked idly after a moment, as if she expected no answer, and Milly did not answer. They sat in silence watching the little flame on a tuft of yellow wick. There were many plates and cups as if other people were coming; but at the moment they were alone. The room was full of furniture. Opposite them stood a Dutch cabinet with blue china on the shelves; the sun of the April evening made a bright stain here and there on the glass. Over the fireplace the portrait of a red-haired young woman in white muslin holding a basket of flowers on her lap smiled down on them.

Milly took a hairpin from her head and began to fray the wick into separate strands so as to increase the size of the flame.

"But that doesn't do any good," Delia said irritably as she watched her. She fidgeted. Everything seemed to take such an intolerable time. Then Crosby came in and said, should she boil the kettle in the kitchen? and Milly said No. How can I put a stop to this fiddling and trifling, she said to herself, tapping a knife on the table and looking at the feeble flame that her sister was teasing with a hairpin. A gnat's voice began to wail under the kettle; but here the door burst open again and a little girl in a stiff pink frock came in.

"I think Nurse might have put you on a clean pinafore," said Milly severely, imitating the manner of a grown-up person. There was a green smudge on her pinafore as if she had been climbing trees.

"It hadn't come back from the wash," said Rose, the little girl, grumpily. She looked at the table, but there was no question of tea yet.

Milly applied her hairpin to the wick again. Delia leant back and glanced over her shoulder out of the window. From where she sat she could see the front door steps.

"Now, there's Martin," she said gloomily. The door slammed; books were slapped down on the hall table, and Martin, a boy of twelve, came in. He had the red hair of the woman in the picture, but it was rumpled.

"Go and make yourself tidy," said Delia severely. "You've plenty of time," she added. "The kettle isn't boiling yet."

They all looked at the kettle. It still kept up its faint melancholy singing as the little flame flickered under the swinging bowl of brass.

"Blast that kettle," said Martin, turning sharply away.

"Mama wouldn't like you to use language like that," Milly reproved him as if in imitation of an older person; for their mother had been ill so long that both sisters had taken to imitating her manner with the children. The door opened again.

"The tray, Miss . . ." said Crosby, keeping the door open with her foot. She had an invalid's tray in her hands.

"The tray," said Milly. "Now who's going to take up the tray?" Again she imitated the manner of an older person who wishes to be tactful with children.

"Not you, Rose. It's too heavy. Let Martin carry it; and you can go with him. But don't stay. Just tell Mama what you've been doing; and then the kettle . . . the kettle . . ."

Here she applied her hairpin to the wick again. A thin puff of steam issued from the serpent-shaped spout. At first intermittent, it gradually became more and more powerful, until, just as they heard steps on the stairs, one jet of powerful steam issued from the spout.

"It's boiling!" Milly exclaimed. "It's boiling!"

THEY ATE in silence. The sun, judging from the changing lights on the glass of the Dutch cabinet, seemed to be going in and out. Sometimes a bowl shone deep blue; then became livid. Lights rested furtively upon the furniture in the other room. Here was a pattern; here was a bald patch. Somewhere there's beauty, Delia thought, somewhere there's freedom, and somewhere, she thought, *he* is—wearing his white flower. . . . But a stick grated in the hall.

"It's Papa!" Milly exclaimed warningly.

Instantly Martin wriggled out of his father's armchair; Delia sat upright. Milly at once moved forward a very large rose-sprinkled cup that did not match the rest. The Colonel stood at the door and surveyed the group rather fiercely. His small blue eyes looked round them as if to find fault; at the moment there was no particular fault to find; but he was out of temper; they knew at once before he spoke that he was out of temper.

"Grubby little ruffian," he said, pinching Rose by the ear as he passed her. She put her hand at once over the stain on her pinafore.

"Mama all right?" he said, letting himself down in one solid mass into the big armchair. He detested tea; but he always sipped a little from the huge old cup that had been his father's. He raised it and sipped perfunctorily.

"And what have you all been up to?" he asked.

He looked round him with the smoky but shrewd gaze that could be genial, but was surly now.

"Delia had her music lesson, and I went to Whiteley's—" Milly began, rather as if she were a child reciting a lesson.

"Spending money, eh?" said her father sharply, but not unkindly.

"No, Papa; I told you. They sent the wrong sheets—"

"And you, Martin?" Colonel Pargiter asked, cutting short his daughter's statement. "Bottom of the class as usual?"

"Top!" shouted Martin, bolting the word out as if he had restrained it with difficulty until this moment.

"Hm—you don't say so," said his father. His gloom relaxed a little. He put his hand into his trouser pocket and brought out a handful of silver. His children watched him as he tried to single out one sixpence from all the florins. He had lost two fin-

gers of the right hand in the Mutiny, and the muscles had
shrunk so that the right hand resembled the claw of some aged
bird. He shuffled and fumbled; but as he always ignored the in-
jury, his children dared not help him. The shiny knobs of the
mutilated fingers fascinated Rose.

"Here you are, Martin," he said at length, handing the sixpence to his son. Then he sipped his tea again and wiped his
moustaches.

"Where's Eleanor?" he said at last, as if to break the silence.

"It's her Grove day," Milly reminded him.

"Oh, her Grove day," muttered the Colonel. He stirred the
sugar round and round in the cup as if to demolish it.

"The dear old Levys," said Delia tentatively. She was his
favourite daughter; but she felt uncertain in his present mood
how much she could venture.

He said nothing.

"Bertie Levy's got six toes on one foot," Rose piped up suddenly. The others laughed. But the Colonel cut them short.

"You hurry up and get off to your prep., my boy," he said,
glancing at Martin, who was still eating.

"Let him finish his tea, Papa," said Milly, again imitating the
manner of an older person.

"And the new nurse?" the Colonel asked, drumming on the
edge of the table. "Has she come?"

"Yes . . ." Milly began. But there was a rustling in the hall
and in came Eleanor. It was much to their relief; especially to
Milly's. Thank goodness, there's Eleanor she thought, looking
up—the soother, the maker-up of quarrels, the buffer between
her and the intensities and strifes of family life. She adored her
sister. She would have called her goddess and endowed her with
a beauty that was not hers, with clothes that were not hers, had
she not been carrying a pile of little mottled books and two
black gloves. Protect me, she thought, handing her a teacup,

who am such a mousy, downtrodden, inefficient little chit, compared with Delia, who always gets her way, while I'm always snubbed by Papa, who was grumpy for some reason. The Colonel smiled at Eleanor. And the red dog on the hearthrug looked up too and wagged his tail, as if he recognised her for one of those satisfactory women who give you a bone, but wash their hands afterwards. She was the eldest of the daughters, about twenty-two, no beauty, but healthy, and though tired at the moment, naturally cheerful.

"I'm sorry I'm late," she said. "I got kept. And I didn't expect—" She looked at her father.

"I got off earlier than I thought," he said hastily. "The meeting—" he stopped short. There had been another row with Mira.

"And how's your Grove, eh?" he added.

"Oh, my Grove—" she repeated; but Milly handed her the covered dish.

"I got kept," Eleanor said again, helping herself. She began to eat; the atmosphere lightened.

"Now tell us, Papa," said Delia boldly—she was his favourite daughter—"what you've been doing with yourself. Had any adventures?"

The remark was unfortunate.

"There aren't any adventures for an old fogy like me," said the Colonel surlily. He ground the grains of sugar against the walls of his cup. Then he seemed to repent of his gruffness; he pondered for a moment.

"I met old Burke at the Club; asked me to bring one of you to dinner; Robin's back, on leave," he said.

He drank up his tea. Some drops fell on his little pointed beard. He took out his large silk handkerchief and wiped his chin impatiently. Eleanor, sitting on her low chair, saw a curious look first on Milly's face, then on Delia's. She had an impression of hostility between them. But they said nothing. They went on eating and drinking until the Colonel took up his cup, saw there was nothing in it, and put it down firmly with a little chink. The ceremony of tea-drinking was over.

"Now, my boy, take yourself off and get on with your prep.," he said to Martin.

Martin withdrew the hand that was stretched towards a plate.

"Cut along," said the Colonel imperiously. Martin got up and went, drawing his hand reluctantly along the chairs and tables as if to delay his passage. He slammed the door rather sharply behind him. The Colonel rose and stood upright among them in his tightly-buttoned frock coat.

"And I must be off too," he said. But he paused a moment, as if there was nothing particular for him to be off to. He stood there very erect among them, as if he wished to give some order, but could not at the moment think of any order to give. Then he recollected.

"I wish one of you would remember," he said, addressing his daughters impartially, "to write to Edward. . . . Tell him to write to Mama."

"Yes," said Eleanor.

He moved towards the door. But he stopped.

"And let me know when Mama wants to see me," he remarked. Then he paused and pinched his youngest daughter by the ear.

"Grubby little ruffian," he said, pointing to the green stain on her pinafore. She covered it with her hand. At the door he paused again.

"Don't forget," he said, fumbling with the handle, "don't forget to write to Edward." At last he had turned the handle and was gone.

———

THEY WERE SILENT. There was something strained in the atmosphere, Eleanor felt. She took one of the little books that she had dropped on the table and laid it open on her knee. But she did not look at it. Her glance fixed itself rather absent-mindedly upon the farther room. The trees were coming out in the back garden; there were little leaves—little ear-shaped leaves on the bushes. The sun was shining, fitfully; it was going in and it was going out, lighting up now this, now—

"Eleanor," Rose interrupted. She held herself in a way that was oddly like her father's.

"Eleanor," she repeated in a low voice, for her sister was not attending.

"Well?" said Eleanor, looking at her.

"I want to go to Lamley's," said Rose.

She looked the image of her father, standing there with her hands behind her back.

"It's too late for Lamley's," said Eleanor.

"They don't shut till seven," said Rose.

"Then ask Martin to go with you," said Eleanor.

The little girl moved off slowly towards the door. Eleanor took up her account-books again.

"But you're not to go alone, Rose; you're not to go alone," she said, looking up over them as Rose reached the door. Nodding her head in silence, Rose disappeared.

SHE WENT UPSTAIRS. She paused outside her mother's bedroom and snuffed the sour-sweet smell that seemed to hang about the jugs, the tumblers, the covered bowls on the table outside the door. Up she went again, and stopped outside the schoolroom door. She did not want to go in, for she had quarrelled with Martin. They had quarrelled first about Erridge and the microscope and then about shooting Miss Pym's cats next door. But Eleanor had told her to ask him. She opened the door.

"Hullo, Martin—" she began.

He was sitting at a table with a book propped in front of him, muttering to himself—perhaps it was Greek, perhaps it was Latin.

"Eleanor told me—" she began, noting how flushed he looked, and how his hand closed on a bit of paper as if he were going to screw it into a ball. "To ask you . . ." she began, and braced herself and stood with her back against the door.

ELEANOR LEANT BACK in her chair. The sun now was on the trees in the back garden. The buds were beginning to swell. The spring light of course showed up the shabbiness of the chair-covers. The large armchair had a dark stain on it where her father had rested his head, she noticed. But what a number of chairs there were—how roomy, how airy it was after that bedroom where old Mrs. Levy— But Milly and Delia were both silent. It was the question of the dinner-party, she remembered. Which of them was to go? They both wanted to go. She wished people would not say, "Bring one of your daughters." She wished they would say, "Bring Eleanor," or "Bring Milly," or "Bring Delia," instead of lumping them all together. Then there could be no question.

"Well," said Delia abruptly, "I shall . . ."

She got up as if she were going somewhere. But she stopped. Then she strolled over to the window that looked out onto the street. The houses opposite all had the same little front gardens; the same steps; the same pillars; the same bow windows. But now dusk was falling and they looked spectral and insubstantial in the dim light. Lamps were being lit; a light glowed in the drawing-room opposite; then the curtains were drawn, and the room was blotted out. Delia stood looking down at the street. A woman of the lower classes was wheeling a perambulator; an old man tottered along with his hands behind his back. Then the street was empty; there was a pause. Here came a hansom jingling down the road. Delia was momentarily interested. Was it going to stop at their door or not? She gazed more intently. But then, to her regret, the cabman jerked his reins, the horse stumbled on; the cab stopped two doors lower down.

"Someone's calling on the Stapletons," she called back, holding apart the muslin blind. Milly came and stood beside her sister, and together, through the slit, they watched a young man in a top-hat get out of the cab. He stretched his hand up to pay the driver.

"Don't be caught looking," said Eleanor warningly. The young man ran up the steps into the house; the door shut upon him and the cab drove away.

But for the moment the two girls stood at the window looking into the street. The crocuses were yellow and purple in the front gardens. The almond trees and privets were tipped with green. A sudden gust of wind tore down the street, blowing a piece of paper along the pavement; and a little swirl of dry dust followed after. Above the roofs was one of those red and fitful London sunsets that make window after window burn gold. There was a wildness in the spring evening; even here, in Abercorn Terrace the light was changing from gold to black, from black to gold. Dropping the blind, Delia turned, and coming back into the drawing-room, said suddenly:

"Oh, my God!"

Eleanor, who had taken her books again, looked up disturbed.

"Eight times eight . . ." she said aloud. "What's eight times eight?"

Putting her finger on the page to mark the place, she looked
at her sister. As she stood there with her head thrown back and
her hair red in the sunset glow, she looked for a moment defiant, even beautiful. Beside her Milly was mouse-coloured and
nondescript.

"Look here, Delia," said Eleanor, shutting her book,
"you've only got to wait . . ." She meant but she could not say
it, "until Mama dies."

"No, no, no," said Delia, stretching her arms out. "It's hope-
less . . ." she began. But she broke off, for Crosby had come in.
She was carrying a tray. One by one with an exasperating little
chink she put the cups, the plates, the knives, the jam-pots, the
dishes of cake and the dishes of bread and butter, on the tray.
Then, balancing it carefully in front of her, she went out. There
was a pause. In she came again and folded the table-cloth and
moved the tables. Again there was a pause. A moment or two
later back she came carrying two silk-shaded lamps. She set one
in the front room, one in the back room. Then she went, creaking in her cheap shoes, to the window and drew the curtains.
They slid with a familiar click along the brass rod, and soon the
windows were obscured by thick sculptured folds of claret-
coloured plush. When she had drawn the curtains in both rooms,
a profound silence seemed to fall upon the drawing-room. The
world outside seemed thickly and entirely cut off. Far away down
the next street they heard the voice of a street hawker droning;
the heavy hooves of van horses clopped slowly down the road.
For a moment wheels ground on the road; then they died out
and the silence was complete.

Two yellow circles of light fell under the lamps. Eleanor
drew her chair up under one of them, bent her head and went
on with the part of her work that she always left to the last because she disliked it so much—adding up figures. Her lips

moved and her pencil made little dots on the paper as she added eights to sixes, fives to fours.

"There!" she said at last. "That's done. Now I'll go and sit with Mama."

She stooped to pick up her gloves.

"No," said Milly, throwing aside a magazine she had opened, "I'll go . . ."

Delia suddenly emerged from the back room in which she had been prowling.

"I've nothing whatever to do," she said briefly. "I'll go."

SHE WENT UPSTAIRS, step by step, very slowly. When she came to the bedroom door with the jugs and glasses on the table outside, she paused. The sour-sweet smell of illness slightly sickened her. She could not force herself to go in. Through the little window at the end of the passage she could see flamingo-coloured curls of cloud lying on a pale-blue sky. After the dusk of the drawing-room, her eyes dazzled. She seemed fixed there for a moment by the light. Then on the floor above she heard children's voices—Martin and Rose quarrelling.

"Don't then!" she heard Rose say. A door slammed. She paused. Then she drew in a deep breath of air, looked once more at the fiery sky, and tapped on the bedroom door.

The nurse rose quietly; put her finger to her lips, and left the room. Mrs. Pargiter was asleep. Lying in a cleft of the pillows with one hand under her cheek, Mrs. Pargiter moaned slightly as if she wandered in a world where even in sleep little obstacles lay across her path. Her face was pouched and heavy; the skin was stained with brown patches; the hair which had been red was now white, save that there were queer yellow patches in it, as if some locks had been dipped in the yolk of an egg. Bare of all rings save her wedding ring, her fingers alone seemed to indicate that she had entered the private world of illness. But she did not look as if she were dying; she looked as if she might go on existing in this borderland between life and death for ever. Delia could see no change in her. As she sat down, everything seemed to be at full tide in her. A long narrow glass by the bedside reflected a section of the sky; it was dazzled at the moment with red light. The dressing-table was illuminated. The light struck on silver bottles and on glass bottles, all set out in the perfect order of things that are not used. At this hour of the evening the sick-room had an unreal cleanliness, quiet and order. There by the bedside was a little table set with spectacles, prayer-book and a vase of lilies of the valley. The flowers, too, looked unreal. There was nothing to do but to look.

She stared at the yellow drawing of her grandfather with the high light on his nose; at the photograph of her Uncle Horace in his uniform; at the lean and twisted figure on the crucifix to the right.

"But you don't believe in it!" she said savagely, looking at her mother sunk in sleep. "You don't want to die."

She longed for her to die. There she was—soft, decayed but everlasting, lying in the cleft of the pillows, an obstacle, a prevention, an impediment to all life. She tried to whip up some feeling of affection, of pity. For instance, that summer, she told herself, at Sidmouth, when she called me up the garden steps. . . . But the scene melted as she tried to look at it. There was the other scene of course—the man in the frock coat with the flower in his button-hole. But she had sworn not to think of that till bedtime. What then should she think of? Grandpapa with the white light on his nose? The prayer-book? The lilies of the valley? Or the looking-glass? The sun had gone in; the glass was dim and reflected now only a dun-coloured patch of sky. She could resist no longer.

"Wearing a white flower in his button-hole," she began. It required a few minutes' preparation. There must be a hall; banks of palms; a floor beneath them crowded with people's heads. The charm was beginning to work. She became permeated with delicious starts of flattering and exciting emotion. She was on the platform; there was a huge audience; everybody was shouting, waving handkerchiefs, hissing and whistling. Then she stood up. She rose all in white in the middle of the platform; Mr. Parnell was by her side.

"I am speaking in the cause of Liberty," she began, throwing out her hands, "in the cause of Justice. . . ." They were standing side by side. He was very pale but his dark eyes glowed. He turned to her and whispered. . . .

There was a sudden interruption. Mrs. Pargiter had raised herself on her pillows.

"Where am I?" she cried. She was frightened and bewildered, as she often was on waking. She raised her hand; she seemed to appeal for help. "Where am I?" she repeated. For a moment Delia was bewildered too. Where was she?

"Here, Mama! Here!" she said wildly. "Here, in your own room."

She laid her hand on the counterpane. Mrs. Pargiter clutched it nervously. She looked round the room as if she were seeking someone. She did not seem to recognise her daughter.

"What's happening?" she said. "Where am I?" Then she looked at Delia and remembered.

"Oh, Delia—I was dreaming," she murmured half apologetically. She lay for a moment looking out of the window. The lamps were being lit, and a sudden soft spurt of light came in the street outside.

"It's been a fine day . . ." she hesitated, "for . . ." It seemed as if she could not remember what for.

"A lovely day, yes, Mama," Delia repeated with mechanical cheerfulness.

". . . for . . ." her mother tried again.

What day was it? Delia could not remember.

". . . for your Uncle Digby's birthday," Mrs. Pargiter at last brought out.

"Tell him from me — tell him how very glad I am."

"I'll tell him," said Delia. She had forgotten her uncle's birthday; but her mother was punctilious about such things.

"Aunt Eugénie —" she began.

But her mother was staring at the dressing-table. Some gleam from the lamp outside made the white cloth look extremely white.

"Another clean table-cloth!" Mrs. Pargiter murmured peevishly. "The expense, Delia, the expense — that's what worries me —"

"That's all right, Mama," said Delia dully. Her eyes were fixed upon her grandfather's portrait; why, she wondered, had the artist put a dab of white chalk on the tip of his nose?

"Aunt Eugénie brought you some flowers," she said.

For some reason Mrs. Pargiter seemed pleased. Her eyes rested contemplatively on the clean table-cloth that had suggested the washing bill a moment before.

"Aunt Eugénie . . ." she said. "How well I remember," her voice seemed to get fuller and rounder, "the day the engagement was announced. We were all of us in the garden; there came a letter." She paused. "There came a letter," she repeated. Then she said no more for a time. She seemed to be going over some memory.

"The dear little boy died, but save for that . . ." She stopped again. She seemed weaker tonight, Delia thought; and a start of joy ran through her. Her sentences were more broken than usual. What little boy had died? She began counting the twists on the counterpane as she waited for her mother to speak.

"You know all the cousins used to come together in the summer," her mother suddenly resumed. "There was your Uncle Horace. . . ."

"The one with the glass eye," said Delia.

"Yes. He hurt his eye on the rocking-horse. The aunts thought so much of Horace. They would say . . ." Here there was a long pause. She seemed to be fumbling to find the exact words.

"When Horace comes . . . remember to ask him about the dining-room door."

A curious amusement seemed to fill Mrs. Pargiter. She actually laughed. She must be thinking of some long-past family joke, Delia supposed, as she watched the smile flicker and fade away. There was complete silence. Her mother lay with her eyes shut; the hand with the single ring, the white and wasted hand, lay on the counterpane. In the silence they could hear a coal click in the grate and a street hawker droning down the road. Mrs. Pargiter said no more. She lay perfectly still. Then she sighed profoundly.

The door opened, and the nurse came in. Delia rose and went out. Where am I? she asked herself, staring at a white jug stained pink by the setting sun. For a moment she seemed to be in some borderland between life and death. Where am I? she repeated, looking at the pink jug, for it all looked strange. Then she heard water rushing and feet thudding on the floor above.

"HERE YOU ARE, Rosie," said Nurse, looking up from the wheel of the sewing-machine as Rose came in.

The nursery was brightly lit; there was an unshaded lamp on the table. Mrs. C., who came every week with the washing, was sitting in the armchair with a cup in her hand. "Go and get your sewing, there's a good girl," said Nurse as Rose shook hands with Mrs. C., "or you'll never be done in time for Papa's birthday," she added, clearing a space on the nursery table.

Rose opened the table drawer and took out the boot-bag that she was embroidering with a design of blue and red flowers for her father's birthday. There were still several clusters of little pencilled roses to be worked. She spread it on the table and examined it as Nurse resumed what she was saying to Mrs. C. about Mrs. Kirby's daughter. But Rose did not listen.

Then I shall go by myself, she decided, straightening out the boot-bag. If Martin won't come with me, then I shall go by myself.

"I left my work-box in the drawing-room," she said aloud.

"Well, then, go and fetch it," said Nurse, but she was not attending; she wanted to go on with what she was saying to Mrs. C. about the grocer's daughter.

NOW THE ADVENTURE has begun, Rose said to herself as she stole on tiptoe to the night nursery. Now she must provide herself with ammunition and provisions; she must steal Nurse's latchkey; but where was it? Every night it was hidden in a new place for fear of burglars. It would be either under the handkerchief-case or in the little box where she kept her mother's gold watchchain. There it was. Now she had her pistol and her shot, she thought, taking her own purse from her own drawer, and enough provisions, she thought, as she hung her hat and coat over her arm, to last a fortnight.

She stole past the nursery, down the stairs. She listened intently as she passed the schoolroom door. She must be careful not to tread on a dry branch, or to let any twig crack under her, she told herself, as she went on tiptoe. Again she stopped and listened as she passed her mother's bedroom door. All was silent. Then she stood for a moment on the landing, looking down into the hall. The dog was asleep on the mat; the coast was clear; the hall was empty. She heard voices murmuring in the drawing-room.

She turned the latch of the front door with extreme gentleness, and closed it with scarcely a click behind her. Until she was round the corner she crouched close to the wall so that nobody could see her. When she reached the corner under the laburnum tree she stood erect.

"I am Pargiter of Pargiter's Horse," she said, flourishing her hand, "riding to the rescue!"

She was riding by night on a desperate mission to a besieged garrison, she told herself. She had a secret message — she clenched her fist on her purse — to deliver to the General in person. All their lives depended upon it. The British flag was still flying on the central tower—Lamley's shop was the central tower; the General was standing on the roof of Lamley's shop with his telescope to his eye. All their lives depended upon her riding to them through the enemy's country. Here she was galloping across the desert. She began to trot. It was growing dark. The street lamps were being lit. The lamplighter was poking his stick up into the little trap-door; the trees in the front gardens made a wavering network of shadow on the pavement; the pavement stretched before her broad and dark. Then there was the crossing; and then there was Lamley's shop on the little island of shops opposite. She had only to cross the desert, to ford the river, and she was safe. Flourishing the arm that held the pistol, she clapped spurs to her horse and galloped down Melrose Avenue. As she ran past the pillar-box the figure of a man suddenly emerged under the gas lamp.

"The enemy!" Rose cried to herself. "The enemy! Bang!" she cried, pulling the trigger of her pistol and looking him full in the face as she passed him. It was a horrid face; white, peeled, pock-marked; he leered at her. He put out his arm as if to stop her. He almost caught her. She dashed past him. The game was over.

She was herself again, a little girl who had disobeyed her sister, in her house shoes, flying for safety to Lamley's shop.

FRESH-FACED Mrs. Lamley was standing behind the counter folding up the newspapers. She was pondering among her two-penny watches, cards of tools, toy boats and boxes of cheap stationery something pleasant, it seemed; for she was smiling. Then Rose burst in. She looked up enquiringly.

"Hullo, Rosie!" she exclaimed. "What d'you want, my dear?"

She kept her hand on the pile of newspapers. Rose stood there panting. She had forgotten what she had come for.

"I want the box of ducks in the window," Rose at last remembered.

Mrs. Lamley waddled round to fetch it.

"Isn't it rather late for a little girl like you to be out alone?" she asked, looking at her as if she knew she had come out in her house shoes, disobeying her sister.

"Goodnight, my dear, and run along home," she said, giving her the parcel. The child seemed to hesitate on the door-step: she stood there staring at the toys under the hanging oil lamp; then out she went reluctantly.

I GAVE MY message to the General in person, she said to herself as she stood outside on the pavement again. And this is the trophy, she said, grasping the box under her arm. I am returning in triumph with the head of the chief rebel, she told herself, as she surveyed the stretch of Melrose Avenue before her. I must set spurs to my horse and gallop. But the story no longer worked. Melrose Avenue remained Melrose Avenue. She looked down it. There was the long stretch of bare street in front of her. The trees were trembling their shadows over the pavement. The lamps stood at great distances apart, and there were pools of darkness between. She began to trot. Suddenly, as she passed the lamp-post, she saw the man again. He was leaning with his back against the lamp-post, and the light from the gas lamp flickered over his face. As she passed he sucked his lips in and out. He made a mewing noise. But he did not stretch his hands out at her; they were unbuttoning his clothes.

She fled past him. She thought that she heard him coming after her. She heard his feet padding on the pavement. Everything shook as she ran; pink and black spots danced before her eyes as she ran up the door-step, fitted her key in the latch and opened the hall door. She did not care whether she made a noise or not. She hoped somebody would come out and speak to her. But nobody heard her. The hall was empty. The dog was asleep on the mat. Voices still murmured in the drawing-room.

"AND WHEN IT does catch," Eleanor was saying, "it'll be much too hot."

Crosby had piled the coals into a great black promontory. A plume of yellow smoke was sullenly twining round it; it was beginning to burn, and when it did burn it would be much too hot.

"She can see Nurse stealing the sugar, she says. She can see her shadow on the wall," Milly was saying. They were talking about their mother.

"And then Edward," she added, "forgetting to write."

"That reminds me," said Eleanor. She must remember to write to Edward. But there would be time after dinner. She did not want to write; she did not want to talk; always when she came back from the Grove she felt as if several things were going on at the same time. Words went on repeating themselves in her mind—words and sights. She was thinking of old Mrs. Levy, sitting propped up in bed with her white hair in a thick flop like a wig and her face cracked like an old glazed pot.

"Them that's been good to me, them I remember . . . them

that's ridden in their coaches when I was a poor widder woman scrubbing and mangling—" here she stretched out her arm, which was wrung and white like the root of a tree. "Them that's been good to me, them I remember . . ." Eleanor repeated as she looked at the fire. Then the daughter came in who was working for a tailor. She wore pearls as big as hen's eggs; she had taken to painting her face; she was wonderfully handsome. But Milly made a little movement.

"I was thinking," said Eleanor on the spur of the moment, "the poor enjoy themselves more than we do."

"The Levys?" said Milly absent-mindedly. Then she brightened.

"Do tell me about the Levys," she added. Eleanor's relations with "the poor"—the Levys, the Grubbs, the Paravicinis, the Zwinglers and the Cobbs—always amused her. But Eleanor did not like talking about "the poor" as if they were people in a book. She had a great admiration for Mrs. Levy, who was dying of cancer.

"Oh, they're much as usual," she said sharply. Milly looked at her. Eleanor's "broody" she thought. The family joke was, "Look out. Eleanor's broody. It's her Grove day." Eleanor was ashamed, but she always was irritable for some reason when she came back from the Grove—so many different things were going on in her head at the same time: Canning Place; Abercorn Terrace; this room; that room. There was the old Jewess sitting up in bed in her hot little room; then one came back here, and there was Mama ill; Papa grumpy; and Delia and Milly quarrelling about a party. . . . But she checked herself. She ought to try to say something to amuse her sister.

"Mrs. Levy had her rent ready, for a wonder," she said. "Lily helps her. Lily's got a job at a tailor's in Shoreditch. She came in all covered with pearls and things. They do love finery—Jews," she added.

"Jews?" said Milly. She seemed to consider the taste of the Jews; and then to dismiss it.

"Yes," she said. "Shiny."

"She's extraordinarily handsome," said Eleanor, thinking of the red cheeks and the white pearls.

Milly smiled; Eleanor always would stick up for the poor. She thought Eleanor the best, the wisest, the most remarkable person she knew.

"I believe you like going there more than anything," she said. "I believe you'd like to go and live there if you had your way," she added, with a little sigh.

Eleanor shifted in her chair. She had her dreams, her plans, of course; but she did not want to discuss them.

"Perhaps you will, when you're married?" said Milly. There was something peevish yet plaintive in her voice. The dinner-party; the Burkes' dinner-party, Eleanor thought. She wished Milly did not always bring the conversation back to marriage. And what do they know about marriage? she asked herself. They stay at home too much, she thought; they never see any-one outside their own set. Here they are cooped up, day after day. . . . That was why she had said, "The poor enjoy themselves more than we do." It had struck her coming back into that drawing-room, with all the furniture and the flowers and the hospital nurses. . . . Again she stopped herself. She must wait till she was alone — till she was brushing her teeth at night. When she was with the others she must stop herself from thinking of two things at the same time. She took the poker and struck the coal.

"Look! What a beauty!" she exclaimed. A flame danced on top of the coal, a nimble and irrelevant flame. It was the sort of flame they used to make when they were children, by throwing salt on the fire. She struck again, and a shower of gold-eyed sparks went volleying up the chimney. "D'you remember," she said, "how we used to play at firemen, and Morris and I set the chimney on fire?"

"And Pippy went and fetched Papa," said Milly. She paused. There was a sound in the hall. A stick grated; someone was hanging up a coat. Eleanor's eyes brightened. That was Morris—yes; she knew the sound he made. Now he was coming in. She looked round with a smile as the door opened. Milly jumped up.

Morris tried to stop her.

"Don't go—" he began.

"Yes!" she exclaimed. "I shall go. I shall go and have a bath," she added on the spur of the moment. She left them.

MORRIS SAT DOWN in the chair she had left empty. He was glad to find Eleanor alone. Neither of them spoke for a moment. They watched the yellow plume of smoke, and the little flame dancing nimbly, irrelevantly, here and there on the black promontory of coals. Then he asked the usual question:

"How's Mama?"

She told him; there was no change: "except that she sleeps more," she said. He wrinkled his forehead. He was losing his boyish look, Eleanor thought. That was the worst of the Bar, everyone said; one had to wait. He was devilling for Sanders Curry; and it was dreary work, hanging about the Courts all day, waiting.

"How's old Curry?" she asked—old Curry had a temper.

"A bit liverish," said Morris grimly.

"And what have you been doing all day?" she asked.

"Nothing in particular," he replied.

"Still Evans *v.* Carter?"

"Yes," he said briefly.

"And who's going to win?" she asked.

"Carter, of course," he replied.

Why "of course" she wanted to ask? But she had said something silly the other day—something that showed that she had not been attending. She muddled things up; for example, what was the difference between Common Law and the other kind of law? She said nothing. They sat in silence, and watched the flame playing on the coals. It was a green flame, nimble, irrelevant.

"D'you think I've been an awful fool," he asked suddenly. "With all this illness, and Edward and Martin to be paid for—Papa must find it a bit of a strain." He wrinkled his brow up in the way that made her say to herself that he was losing his boyish look.

"Of course not," she said emphatically. Of course it would have been absurd for him to go into business; his passion was for the Law.

"You'll be Lord Chancellor one of these days," she said. "I'm sure of it." He shook his head, smiling.

"Quite sure," she said, looking at him as she used to look at him when he came back from school and Edward had all the prizes and Morris sat silent—she could see him now—bolting his food with nobody making a fuss of him. But even while she looked, a doubt came over her. Lord Chancellor, she had said. Ought she not to have said Lord Chief Justice? She never could remember which was which: and that was why he would not discuss Evans *v.* Carter with her.

She never told him about the Levys either, except by way of a joke. That was the worst of growing up, she thought; they couldn't share things as they used to share them. When they met they never had time to talk as they used to talk—about things in general—they always talked about facts—little facts. She poked the fire. Suddenly a blare of sound rang through the room. It was Crosby applying herself to the gong in the hall. She was like a savage wreaking vengeance upon some brazen victim. Ripples of rough sound rang through the room. "Lord, that's the dressing-bell!" said Morris. He got up and stretched himself. He raised his arms and held them for a moment suspended above his head. That's what he'll look like when he's the father of a family, Eleanor thought. He let his arms fall and left the room. She sat brooding for a moment; then she roused herself. What must I remember? she asked herself. To write to Edward, she mused, crossing over to her mother's writing-table. It'll be my table now, she thought, looking at the silver candlestick, the miniature of her grandfather, the tradesmen's books—one had a gilt cow stamped on it—and the spotted walrus with a brush in its back that Martin had given his mother on her last birthday.

CROSBY HELD OPEN the door of the dining-room as she waited for them to come down. The silver paid for polishing, she thought. Knives and forks rayed out round the table. The whole room, with its carved chairs, oil paintings, the two daggers on the mantelpiece, and the handsome sideboard—all the solid objects that Crosby dusted and polished every day—looked at its best in the evening. Meat-smelling and serge-curtained by day, it looked lit up, semi-transparent in the evening. And they were a handsome family, she thought as they filed in—the young ladies in their pretty dresses of blue and white sprigged muslin; the gentlemen so spruce in their dinner jackets. She pulled the Colonel's chair out for him. He was always at his best in the evening; he enjoyed his dinner; and for some reason his gloom had vanished. He was in his jovial mood. His children's spirits rose as they noted it.

"That's a pretty frock you're wearing," he said to Delia as he sat down.

"This old one?" she said, patting the blue muslin.

There was an opulence, an ease and a charm about him

when he was in a good temper that she liked particularly. People always said she was like him; sometimes she was glad of it— tonight for instance. He looked so pink and clean and genial in his dinner-jacket. They became children again when he was in this mood, and were spurred on to make family jokes at which they all laughed for no particular reason.

"Eleanor's broody," said her father, winking at them. "It's her Grove day."

Everybody laughed; Eleanor had thought he was talking about Rover, the dog, when in fact he was talking about Mrs. Egerton, the lady. Crosby, who was handing the soup, crinkled up her face because she wanted to laugh too. Sometimes the Colonel made Crosby laugh so much that she had to turn away and pretend to be doing something at the sideboard.

"Oh, Mrs. Egerton—" said Eleanor, beginning her soup.

"Yes, Mrs. Egerton," said her father, and went on telling his story about Mrs. Egerton, "whose golden hair was said by the voice of slander not to be entirely her own."

Delia liked listening to her father's stories about India. They were crisp, and at the same time romantic. They conveyed an atmosphere of officers dining together in mess jackets on a very hot night with a huge silver trophy in the middle of the table.

He used always to be like this when we were small, she thought. He used to jump over the bonfire on her birthday, she remembered. She watched him flicking cutlets dexterously on to plates with his left hand. She admired his decision, his common sense. Flicking the cutlets on to plates, he went on—

"Talking of the lovely Mrs. Egerton reminds me—did I ever tell you the story of old Badger Parkes and—"

"Miss—" said Crosby in a whisper, opening the door behind Eleanor's back. She whispered a few words to Eleanor privately.

"I'll come," said Eleanor, getting up.

"What's that—what's that?" said the Colonel, stopping in the middle of his sentence. Eleanor left the room.

"Some message from Nurse," said Milly.

The Colonel, who had just helped himself to cutlets, held his knife and fork in his hand. They all held their knives suspended. Nobody liked to go on eating.

"Well, let's get on with our dinner," said the Colonel, abruptly attacking his cutlet. He had lost his geniality. Morris helped himself tentatively to potatoes. Then Crosby reappeared. She stood at the door, with her pale-blue eyes looking very prominent.

"What is it, Crosby? What is it?" said the Colonel.

"The Mistress, sir, taken worse, I think, sir," she said with a curious whimper in her voice. Everybody got up.

"You wait. I'll go and see," said Morris. They all followed him out into the hall. The Colonel was still holding his dinner napkin. Morris ran upstairs; in a moment he came down again.

"Mama's had a fainting-fit," he said to the Colonel. "I'm going to fetch Prentice." He snatched his hat and coat and ran down the front steps. They heard him whistling for a cab as they stood uncertainly in the hall.

"Finish your dinner, girls," said the Colonel peremptorily. But he paced up and down the drawing-room, holding his dinner napkin in his hand.

"IT HAS COME," Delia said to herself; "it has come!" An extraordinary feeling of relief and excitement possessed her. Her father was pacing from one drawing-room to the other; she followed him in; but she avoided him. They were too much alike; each knew what the other was feeling. She stood at the window looking up the street. There had been a shower of rain. The street was wet; the roofs were shining. Dark clouds were moving across the sky; the branches were tossing up and down in the light of the street lamps. Something in her was tossing up and down too. Something unknown seemed to be approaching. Then a gulping sound behind her made her turn. It was Milly. She was standing by the mantelpiece under the picture of the white-robed girl with the flower-basket, and the tears slid slowly down her cheeks. Delia moved towards her; she ought to go up to her and put her arms round her shoulders; but she could not do it. Real tears were sliding down Milly's cheeks. But her own eyes were dry. She turned to the window again. The street was empty—only the branches were tossing up and down in the lamplight. The Colonel paced up and down; once he knocked against a table and said "Damn!" They heard steps moving about in the room upstairs. They heard voices murmuring. Delia turned to the window.

A hansom came trotting down the street. Morris jumped out directly the cab stopped. Dr. Prentice followed him. He went straight upstairs and Morris joined them in the drawing-room.

"Why not finish your dinner?" the Colonel said gruffly, coming to a halt and standing upright before them.

"Oh, after he's gone," said Morris irritably.

The Colonel resumed his pacing.

Then he stopped his pacing, and stood with his hands behind him in front of the fire. He had a braced look as if he were holding himself ready for an emergency.

We're both acting, Delia thought to herself, stealing a glance at him, but he's doing it better than I am.

She looked out of the window again. The rain was falling. When it crossed the lamplight it glanced in long strips of silver light.

"It's raining," she said in a low voice, but nobody answered her.

At last they heard footsteps on the stairs and Dr. Prentice came in. He shut the door quietly but said nothing.

"Well?" said the Colonel, facing up to him.

There was a prolonged pause.

"How d'you find her?" said the Colonel.

Dr. Prentice moved his shoulders slightly.

"She's rallied," he said. "For the moment," he added.

Delia felt as if his words struck her violently a blow on the head. She sank down on the arm of a chair.

So you're not going to die, she said, looking at the girl balanced on the trunk of a tree; she seemed to simper down at her daughter with smiling malice. You're not going to die — never, never! she cried clenching her hands together beneath her mother's picture.

"Now, shall we get on with our dinner?" said the Colonel, taking up the napkin which he had dropped on the drawing-room table.

IT WAS A PITY — the dinner was spoilt, Crosby thought, bringing up the cutlets from the kitchen again. The meat was dried up, and the potatoes had a brown crust on top of them. One of the candles was scorching its shade too, she observed as she put the dish down in front of the Colonel. Then she shut the door on them, and they began to eat their dinner.

ALL WAS QUIET in the house. The dog slept on its mat at the foot of the stairs. All was quiet outside the sickroom door. A faint sound of snoring came from the bedroom where Martin lay asleep. In the day nursery Mrs. C. and the nurse had resumed their supper, which they had interrupted when they heard sounds in the hall below. Rose lay asleep in the night nursery. For some time she slept profoundly, curled round with the blankets tight twisted over her head. Then she stirred and stretched her arms out. Something had swum up on top of the blackness. An oval white shape hung in front of her dangling, as if it hung from a string. She half opened her eyes and looked at it. It bubbled with grey spots that went in and out. She woke completely. A face was hanging close to her as if it dangled on a bit of string. She shut her eyes; but the face was still there, bubbling in and out, grey, white, purplish and pock-marked. She put out her hand to touch the big bed next hers. But it was empty. She listened. She heard the clatter of knives and the chatter of voices in the day nursery across the passage. But she could not sleep.

She made herself think of a flock of sheep penned up in a hurdle in a field. She made one of the sheep jump the hurdle; then another. She counted them as they jumped. One, two, three, four—they jumped over the hurdle. But the fifth sheep would not jump. It turned round and looked at her. Its long narrow face was grey; its lips moved; it was the face of the man at the pillar-box, and she was alone with it. If she shut her eyes there it was; if she opened them, there it was still.

She sat up in bed and cried out, "Nurse! Nurse!"

There was dead silence everywhere. The clatter of knives and forks in the next room had ceased. She was alone with something horrible. Then she heard a shuffling in the passage. It came closer and closer. It was the man himself. His hand was on the door. The door opened. An angle of light fell across the washstand. The jug and basin were lit up. The man was actually in the room with her . . . but it was Eleanor.

"WHY AREN'T you asleep?" said Eleanor. She put down her candle and began to straighten the bedclothes. They were all crumpled up. She looked at Rose. Her eyes were very bright and her cheeks were flushed. What was the matter? Had they woken her, moving about downstairs in Mama's room?

"What's been keeping you awake?" she asked. Rose yawned again; but it was a sigh rather than a yawn. She could not tell Eleanor what she had seen. She had a profound feeling of guilt; for some reason she must lie about the face she had seen.

"I had a bad dream," she said. "I was frightened." A queer nervous jerk ran through her body as she sat up in bed. What was the matter? Eleanor wondered again. Had she been fighting with Martin? Had she been chasing cats in Miss Pym's garden again?

"Have you been chasing cats again?" she asked. "Poor cats," she added; "they mind it just as much as you would," she said. But she knew that Rose's fright had nothing to do with the cats. She was grasping her finger tightly; she was staring ahead of her with a queer look in her eyes.

"What was your dream about?" she asked, sitting down on the edge of the bed. Rose stared at her; she could not tell her; but at all costs Eleanor must be made to stay with her.

"I thought I heard a man in the room," she brought out at last. "A robber," she added.

"A robber? Here?" said Eleanor. "But, Rose, how could a robber get into your nursery? There's Papa, there's Morris—they would never let a robber come into your room."

"No," said Rose. "Papa would kill him," she added. There was something queer about the way she twitched.

"But what are you all doing?" she said restlessly. "Haven't you gone to bed yet? Isn't it very late?"

"What are we all doing?" said Eleanor. "We're sitting in the drawing-room. It's not very late." As she spoke a faint sound boomed through the room. When the wind was in the right direction they could hear St. Paul's. The soft circles spread out in the air: one, two, three, four—Eleanor counted eight, nine, ten. She was surprised that the strokes stopped so soon.

"There, it's only ten o'clock, you see," she said. It had

seemed to her much later. But the last stroke dissolved in the air. "So now you'll go to sleep," she said. Rose clutched her hand.

"Don't go, Eleanor; not yet," she implored her.

"But tell me, what's frightened you?" Eleanor began. Something was being hidden from her, she was sure.

"I saw . . ." Rose began. She made a great effort to tell her the truth; to tell her about the man at the pillar-box. "I saw . . ." she repeated. But here the door opened and Nurse came in.

"I don't know what's come over Rosie tonight," she said, bustling in. She felt a little guilty; she had stayed downstairs with the other servants gossiping about the mistress.

"She sleeps so sound generally," she said, coming over to the bed.

"Now here's Nurse," said Eleanor. "She's coming to bed. So you won't be frightened any more, will you?" She smoothed down the bed-clothes and kissed her. She got up and took her candle.

"Good-night, Nurse," she said, turning to leave the room.

"Good-night, Miss Eleanor," said Nurse, putting some sympathy into her voice; for they were saying downstairs that the mistress couldn't last much longer.

"Turn over and go to sleep, dearie," she said, kissing Rose on the forehead. For she was sorry for the little girl who would so soon be motherless. Then she slipped the silver links out of her cuffs and began to take the hairpins out of her hair, standing in her petticoats in front of the yellow chest of drawers.

"I SAW," Eleanor repeated, as she shut the nursery door. "I saw . . ." What had she seen? Something horrible, something hidden. But what? There it was, hidden behind her strained eyes. She held the candle slightly slanting in her hand. Three drops of grease fell on the polished skirting before she noticed them. She straightened the candle and walked down the stairs. She listened

as she went. There was silence. Martin was asleep. Her mother
was asleep. As she passed the doors and went downstairs a
weight seemed to descend on her. She paused, looking down
into the hall. A blankness came over her. Where am I? she asked
herself, staring at a heavy frame. What is that? She seemed to be
alone in the midst of nothingness; yet must descend, must carry
her burden—she raised her arms slightly, as if she were carrying a pitcher, an earthenware pitcher on her head. Again she
stopped. The rim of a bowl outlined itself upon her eyeballs;
there was water in it; and something yellow. It was the dog's
bowl, she realised; that was the sulphur in the dog's bowl; the
dog was lying curled up at the bottom of the stairs. She stepped
carefully over the body of the sleeping dog and went into the
drawing-room.

THEY ALL looked up as she came in; Morris had a book in his
hand but he was not reading; Milly had some stuff in her hand
but she was not sewing; Delia was lying back in her chair, doing
nothing whatever. She stood there hesitating for a moment.
Then she turned to the writing-table. "I'll write to Edward," she
murmured. She took up the pen, but she hesitated. She found
it difficult to write to Edward, seeing him before her, when she
took up the pen, when she smoothed the notepaper on the
writing-table. His eyes were too close together; he brushed up
his crest before the looking-glass in the lobby in a way that irritated her. 'Nigs' was her nickname for him. "My dear Edward,"
she began to write, choosing 'Edward' not 'Nigs' on this oc-
casion.

Morris looked up from the book he was trying to read. The
scratching of Eleanor's pen irritated him. She stopped; then she
wrote; then she put her hand to her head. All the worries were
put on her of course. Still she irritated him. She always asked
questions; she never listened to the answers. He glanced at his

book again. But what was the use of trying to read? The atmosphere of suppressed emotion was distasteful to him. There was
nothing that anybody could do, but there they all sat in attitudes
of suppressed emotion. Milly's stitching irritated him, and Delia
lying back in her chair doing nothing as usual. There he was
cooped up with all these women in an atmosphere of unreal
emotion. And Eleanor went on writing, writing, writing. There
was nothing to write about—but here she licked the envelope
and dabbed down the stamp.

"SHALL I TAKE IT?" he said, dropping his book.

He got up as if he were glad to have something to do.
Eleanor went to the front door with him and stood holding it
open while he went to the pillar-box. It was raining gently, and
as she stood at the door, breathing in the mild damp air, she
watched the curious shadows that trembled on the pavement
under the trees. Morris disappeared under the shadows round
the corner. She remembered how she used to stand at the door
when he was a small boy and went to a day school with a satchel
in his hand. She used to wave to him; and when he got to the
corner he always turned and waved back. It was a curious little
ceremony, dropped now that they were both grown up. The
shadows shook as she stood waiting; in a moment he emerged
from the shadows. He came along the street and up the steps.

"He'll get that tomorrow," he said—"anyhow by the second post."

He shut the door and stooped to fasten the chain. It seemed
to her, as the chain rattled, that they both accepted the fact that
nothing more was going to happen tonight. They avoided each
other's eyes; neither of them wanted any more emotion tonight.
They went back into the drawing-room.

"Well," said Eleanor, looking round her, "I think I shall go
to bed. Nurse will ring," she said, "if she wants anything."

"We may as well all go," said Morris. Milly began to roll up her embroidery. Morris began to rake out the fire.

"What an absurd fire—" he exclaimed irritably. The coals were all stuck together. They were blazing fiercely.

Suddenly a bell rang.

"Nurse!" Eleanor exclaimed. She looked at Morris. She left the room hurriedly. Morris followed her.

But what's the good? Delia thought to herself. It's only another false alarm. She got up. "It's only Nurse," she said to Milly, who was standing up with a look of alarm on her face. She can't be going to cry again, she thought, and strolled off into the front room. Candles were burning on the mantelpiece; they lit up the picture of her mother. She glanced at the portrait of her mother. The girl in white seemed to be presiding over the protracted affair of her own death-bed with a smiling indifference that outraged her daughter.

"You're not going to die—you're not going to die!" said Delia bitterly, looking up at her. Her father, alarmed by the bell, had come into the room. He was wearing a red smoking-cap with an absurd tassel.

But it's all for nothing, Delia said silently, looking at her father. She felt that they must both check their rising excitement. "Nothing's going to happen—nothing whatever," she said, looking at him. But at that moment Eleanor came into the room. She was very white.

"Where's Papa?" she said, looking round. She saw him. "Come, Papa, come," she said, stretching out her hand. "Mama's dying. . . . And the children," she said to Milly over her shoulder.

Two little white patches appeared above her father's ears, Delia noticed. His eyes fixed themselves. He braced himself. He strode past them up the stairs. They all followed in a little procession behind. The dog, Delia noticed, tried to come upstairs with them; but Morris cuffed him back. The Colonel went first into the bedroom; then Eleanor; then Morris; then Martin came down, pulling on a dressing-gown; then Milly brought Rose wrapped in a shawl. But Delia hung back behind the others. There were so many of them in the room that she could get no further than the doorway. She could see two nurses standing with their backs to the wall opposite. One of them was crying—the one, she observed, who had only come that afternoon. She could not see the bed from where she stood. But she could see that Morris had fallen on his knees. Ought I to kneel too, she wondered? Not in the passage, she decided. She looked away; she saw the little window at the end of the passage. Rain was falling; there was a light somewhere that made the raindrops shine. One drop after another slid down the pane; they slid and they paused; one drop joined another drop and then they slid again. There was complete silence in the bedroom.

Is this death? Delia asked herself. For a moment there seemed to be something there. A wall of water seemed to gape apart; the two walls held themselves apart. She listened. There was complete silence. Then there was a stir, a shuffle of feet in the bedroom and out came her father, stumbling.

"Rose!" he cried. "Rose! Rose!" He held his arms with the fists clenched out in front of him.

You did that very well, Delia told him as he passed her. It was like a scene in a play. She observed quite dispassionately that the raindrops were still falling. One sliding met another and together in one drop they rolled to the bottom of the window-pane.

IT WAS RAINING. A fine rain, a gentle shower, was peppering the pavements and making them greasy. Was it worth while opening an umbrella, was it necessary to hail a hansom, people coming out from the theatres asked themselves, looking up at

the mild, milky sky in which the stars were blunted. Where it fell
on earth, on fields and gardens, it drew up the smell of earth.
Here a drop poised on a grass-blade; there filled the cup of a
wild flower, till the breeze stirred and the rain was spilt. Was it
worth while to shelter under the hawthorn, under the hedge, the
sheep seemed to question; and the cows, already turned out in
the grey fields, under the dim hedges, munched on, sleepily
chewing with raindrops on their hides. Down on the roofs it
fell—here in Westminster, there in the Ladbroke Grove; on the
wide sea a million points pricked the blue monster like an innumerable shower bath. Over the vast domes, the soaring spires
of slumbering University cities, over the leaded libraries, and the
museums, now shrouded in brown holland, the gentle rain slid
down, till, reaching the mouths of those fantastic laughers, the
many-clawed gargoyles, it splayed out in a thousand odd inden-
tations. A drunken man slipping in a narrow passage outside the
public house, cursed it. Women in childbirth heard the doctor
say to the midwife, "It's raining." And the walloping Oxford
bells, turning over and over like slow porpoises in a sea of oil,
contemplatively intoned their musical incantations. The fine
rain, the gentle rain, poured equally over the mitred and the
bareheaded with an impartiality which suggested that the god
of rain, if there were a god, was thinking Let it not be restricted
to the very wise, the very great, but let all breathing kind, the
munchers and chewers, the ignorant, the unhappy, those who
toil in the furnace making innumerable copies of the same pot,
those who bore red hot minds through contorted letters, and
also Mrs. Jones in the alley, share my bounty.

IT WAS RAINING in Oxford. The rain fell gently, persistently,
making a little chuckling and burbling noise in the gutters. Edward, leaning out of the window, could still see the trees in the
college garden, whitened by the falling rain. Save for the rustle

of the trees and the rain falling, it was perfectly quiet. A damp, earthy smell came up from the wet ground. Lamps were being lit here and there in the dark mass of the college; and there was a pale-yellowish mound in one corner where lamplight fell upon a flowering tree. The grass was becoming invisible, fluid, grey, like water.

He drew in a long breath of satisfaction. Of all the moments in the day he liked this best, when he stood and looked out into the garden. He breathed in again the cool damp air, and then straightened himself and turned back into the room. He was working very hard. His day was parcelled out on the advice of his tutor into hours and half-hours; but he still had five minutes before he need begin. He turned up the reading-lamp. It was partly the green light that made him look a little pale and thin, but he was very handsome. With his clear-cut features and the fair hair that he brushed up with a flick of his fingers into a crest, he looked like a Greek boy on a frieze. He smiled. He was thinking as he watched the rain how, after the interview between his father and his tutor—when old Harbottle had said, "Your son has a chance"—the old boy had insisted upon looking up the rooms that his own father had had when his father was at college. They had burst in and found a chap called Thompson on his knees blowing up the fire with a bellows.

"My father had these rooms, sir," the Colonel had said, by way of apology. The young man had got very red and said, "Don't mention it." Edward smiled. "Don't mention it," he repeated. It was time to begin. He turned the lamp a little higher. When the lamp was turned higher he saw his work cut out in a sharp circle of bright light from the surrounding dimness. He looked at the textbooks, at the dictionaries lying before him. He always had some doubts before he began. His father would be frightfully cut-up if he failed. His heart was set on it. He had

sent him a dozen of fine old port "by way of a stirrup-cup," so
he said. But after all Marsham was in for it; then there was the
clever little Jew-boy from Birmingham—but it was time to
begin. One after another the bells of Oxford began pushing
their slow chimes through the air. They tolled ponderously, un-
equally, as if they had to roll the air out of their way and the air
was heavy. He loved the sound of the bells. He listened till the
last stroke had struck; then pulled his chair to the table; time was
up; he must work now.

A little dint sharpened between his brows. He frowned as
he read. He read; and made a note; then he read again. All
sounds were blotted out. He saw nothing but the Greek in front
of him. But as he read, his brain gradually warmed; he was conscious of something quickening and tightening in his forehead.
He caught phrase after phrase exactly, firmly, more exactly, he
noted, making a brief note in the margin, than the night before.
Little negligible words now revealed shades of meaning, which
altered the meaning. He made another note; *that* was the meaning. His own dexterity in catching the phrase plumb in the
middle gave him a thrill of excitement. There it was, clean and
entire. But he must be precise; exact; even his little scribbled
notes must be clear as print. He turned to this book; then that
book. Then he leant back to see, with his eyes shut. He must
let nothing dwindle off into vagueness. The clocks began striking. He listened. The clocks went on striking. The lines that
had graved themselves on his face slackened; he leant back; his
muscles relaxed; he looked up from his books into the dimness.
He felt as if he had thrown himself down on the turf after running a race. But for a moment it seemed to him that he was still
running; his mind went on without the book. It travelled by itself without impediments through a world of pure meaning; but
gradually it lost its meaning. The books stood out on the wall:

he saw the cream-coloured panels; a bunch of poppies in a blue vase. The last of the strokes had sounded. He gave a sigh and rose from the table.

He stood by the window again. It was raining, but the whiteness had gone. Save for a wet leaf shining here and there, the garden was all dark now—the yellow mound of the flowering tree had vanished. The college buildings lay round the garden in a low couched mass, here red-stained, here yellow-stained, where lights burnt behind curtains; and there lay the chapel, huddling its bulk against the sky which, because of the rain, seemed to tremble slightly. But it was no longer silent. He listened; there was no sound in particular; but, as he stood looking out, the building hummed with life. There was a sudden roar of laughter; then the tinkle of a piano; then a nondescript clatter and chatter—of china partly; then again the sound of rain falling, and the gutters chuckling and burbling as they sucked up the water. He turned back into the room.

It had grown chilly; the fire was almost out; only a little red glowed under the grey ash. Opportunely he remembered his father's gift—the wine that had come that morning. He went to the side table and poured himself out a glass of port. As he raised it against the light he smiled. He saw again his father's hand with two smooth knobs instead of fingers holding the glass, as he always held the glass, to the light before he drank.

"You can't drive a bayonet through a chap's body in cold blood," he remembered him saying.

"And you can't go in for an exam. without drinking," said Edward. He hesitated; he held the glass to the light in imitation of his father. Then he sipped. He set the glass on the table in front of him. He turned again to the *Antigone*. He read; then he sipped, then he read; then he sipped again. A soft glow spread over his spine at the nape of his neck. The wine seemed to press open little dividing doors in his brain. And whether it was the wine or the words or both, a luminous shell formed, a purple fume, from which out stepped a Greek girl; yet she was English. There she stood among the marble and the asphodel, yet there she was among the Morris wall-papers and the cabinets—his cousin Kitty, as he had seen her last time he dined at the Lodge. She was both of them—Antigone and Kitty; here in the book; there in the room; lit up, risen, like a purple flower. No, he exclaimed, not in the least like a flower! For if ever a girl held herself upright, lived, laughed and breathed, it was Kitty, in the white and blue dress that she had worn last time he dined at the Lodge. He crossed to the window. Red squares showed through the trees. There was a party at the Lodge. Who was she talking to? What was she saying? He went back to the table.

"Oh, damn!" he exclaimed, prodding the paper with his pencil. The point broke. Then there was a tap at the door, a sliding tap, not a commanding tap, the tap of one who passes, not of one who comes in. He went and opened the door. There on the stair above loomed the figure of a huge young man who was leaning over the bannisters. "Come in," said Edward.

The huge young man came slowly down the stairs. He was very large. His eyes, which were prominent, became apprehensive at the sight of the books on the table. He looked at the books on the table. They were Greek. But there was wine after all.

Edward poured out wine. Beside Gibbs he looked what Eleanor called 'finicky.' He felt the contrast himself. The hand with which he lifted his glass was like a girl's beside Gibbs's great red paw. Gibbs's hand was burnt bright scarlet; it was like a piece of raw meat.

Hunting was the subject they had in common. They talked about hunting. Edward leant back and let Gibbs do the talking. It was all very pleasant, listening to Gibbs, riding through these English lanes. He was talking about cubbing in September; and a raw but handy hack. He was saying, "You remember that farm

on the right as you go up to Stapleys? and the pretty girl?"—he
winked—"worse luck, she's married to a keeper." He was saying—Edward watched him gulping down his port—how he
wished this damned summer were over. Then, again, he was
telling the old story about the spaniel bitch. "You'll come and
stop with us in September," he was saying when the door
opened so silently that Gibbs did not hear it, and in glided another man—quite another man.

It was Ashley who came in. He was the very opposite of
Gibbs. He was neither tall nor short, neither dark nor fair. But
he was not negligible—far from it. It was partly the way he
moved, as if chair and table rayed out some influence which he
could feel by means of some invisible antennae, or whiskers, like
a cat. Now he sank down, cautiously, gingerly, and looked at the
table and half read a line in a book. Gibbs stopped in the middle
of his sentence.

"Hullo, Ashley," he said rather curtly. He stretched out and
poured himself another glass of the Colonel's port. Now the de-
canter was empty.

"Sorry," he said, glancing at Ashley.

"Don't open another bottle for me," said Ashley quickly.
His voice sounded a little squeaky, as if he were ill at ease.

"Oh, but we shall want some more too," said Edward casually. He went into the dining-room to fetch it.

"Damned awkward," he reflected as he stooped among the
bottles. It meant, he reflected grimly as he chose his bottle, another row with Ashley, and he had had two rows with Ashley
about Gibbs already this term.

He went back with the bottle and sat down on a low stool
between them. He uncorked the wine and poured it out. They
both looked at him, as he sat between them, admiringly. The
vanity, which Eleanor always laughed at in her brother, was flattered. He liked to feel their eyes on him. And yet he was at his

ease with both of them, he thought; the thought pleased him; he could talk hunting with Gibbs and books with Ashley. But Ashley could only talk about books, and Gibbs — he smiled — could only talk about girls. Girls and horses. He poured out three glasses of wine.

Ashley sipped gingerly, and Gibbs, with his great red hands on the glass, gulped rather. They talked about races; then they talked about examinations. Then Ashley, glancing at the books on the table, said:

"And what about you?"

"I've not the ghost of a chance," said Edward. His indifference was affected. He pretended to despise examinations; but it was pretence. Gibbs was taken in by him; but Ashley saw through him. He often caught Edward out in small vanities like this; but they only served to endear him the more. How beautiful he looks, he was thinking: there he sat between them with the light falling on the top of his fair hair; like a Greek boy; strong; yet in some way, weak, needing his protection.

He ought to be rescued from brutes like Gibbs, he thought savagely. For how Edward could tolerate that clumsy brute, he thought, looking at him, who always seemed to smell of beer and horses (he was listening to him), Ashley could not conceive. As he came in he had caught the tail of an infuriating sentence — of a sentence that seemed to show that they had made some plan together.

"Well, then, I'll see Storey about that hack," Gibbs was saying now, as if he were finishing some private talk that they had been having before he came in. A spasm of jealousy ran through Ashley. To hide it, he stretched out his hand and took up a book that lay open on the table. He pretended to read it.

He did it to insult him, Gibbs felt. Ashley, he knew, thought him a great hulking brute; the dirty little swine came in, spoilt the talk, and then began to give himself airs at Gibbs's expense.

Very well; he had been going to go; now he would stay; he
would twist his tail for him—he knew how. He turned to Edward and went on talking.

"You won't mind pigging it," he said. "My people will be up
in Scotland."

Ashley turned a page viciously. They would be alone then.
Edward began to relish the situation; he played up to it
maliciously.

"All right," he said. "But you'll have to see I don't make a
fool of myself," he added.

"Oh, it'll only be cubbing," said Gibbs. Ashley turned another page. Edward glanced at the book. It was being held upside down. But as he glanced at Ashley he caught his head
against the panels and the poppies. How civilised he looked, he
thought, compared with Gibbs; and how ironical. He respected
him immensely. Gibbs had lost his glamour. There he was,
telling the same old story of the spaniel bitch all over again.
There would be a devil's own row tomorrow, he thought, and
glanced surreptitiously at his watch. It was past eleven; and he
must do an hour's work before breakfast. He swallowed down
the last drops of his wine, stretched himself, yawned ostenta-
tiously and rose.

"I'm off to bed," he said. Ashley looked at him appealingly.
Edward could torture him horribly. Edward began unbuttoning
his waistcoat; he had a perfect figure, Ashley thought, looking
at him, standing between them.

"But don't you hurry," said Edward, yawning again. "Finish
your drinks." He smiled at the thought of Ashley and Gibbs finishing their drinks together.

"There's plenty more in there if you want it." He indicated
the next room and left them.

"Let 'em fight it out together," he thought as he shut the
bedroom door. His own fight would come soon enough; he

knew that from the look on Ashley's face. He was infernally jealous. He began to undress. He put his money methodically in
two heaps on either side of the looking-glass; for he was a little
near about money; folded his waistcoat carefully on a chair; then
glanced at himself in the looking-glass, and brushed his crest up
with the half-conscious gesture that irritated his sister. Then he
listened.

A door slammed outside. One of them had gone — either
Gibbs or Ashley. But one, he rather thought, was still there. He
listened intently. He heard someone moving about in the sitting-
room. Very quickly, very firmly, he turned the key in the door.
A moment later the handle moved.

"Edward!" said Ashley. His voice was low and controlled.
Edward made no answer.

"Edward!" said Ashley, rattling the handle.

The voice was sharp and appealing.

"Good-night," said Edward sharply. He listened. There was
a pause. Then he heard the door shut. Ashley was gone.

"Lord! What a row there'll be tomorrow," said Edward,
going to the window and looking out at the rain that was still
falling.

THE PARTY at the Lodge was over. The ladies stood in the
doorway in their flowing gowns, and looked up at the sky from
which a gentle rain was falling.

"Is that a nightingale?" said Mrs. Larpent, hearing a bird twitter in the bushes. Then old Chuffy—the great Dr. Andrews—
standing slightly behind her with his domed head exposed to
the drizzle and his hirsute, powerful but not prepossessing
countenance turned upward, gave a roar of laughter. It was a
thrush, he said. The laughter was echoed back like a hyena
laughing from the stone walls. Then, with a wave of the hand
dictated by centuries of tradition, Mrs. Larpent drew back her

foot, as if she had encroached upon one of the chalk marks which decorate academic lintels and, signifying that Mrs. Lathom, wife of the Divinity professor, should precede her, they passed out into the rain.

IN THE LONG drawing-room at the Lodge they were all standing up.

"I'm so glad Chuffy—Dr. Andrews—came up to your expectations," Mrs. Malone was saying in her courteous manner. As residents they called the great Doctor "Chuffy"; he was Dr. Andrews to American visitors.

The other guests had gone. But the Howard Fripps, the Americans, were staying in the house. Mrs. Howard Fripp was saying that Dr. Andrews had been perfectly charming to her. And her husband, the Professor, was saying something equally polite to the Master. Kitty, the daughter, standing a little in the background, wished that they would get it over and come to bed. But she had to stand there until her mother gave the signal for them to move.

"Yes, I never knew Chuffy in better form," her father continued, implying a compliment to the little American lady who had made such a conquest. She was small and vivacious, and Chuffy liked ladies to be small and vivacious.

"I adore his books," she said in her queer nasal voice. "But I never expected to have the pleasure of sitting next him at dinner."

Did you really like the way he spits when he talks? Kitty wondered, looking at her. She was extraordinarily pretty and gay. All the other women had looked dowdy and dumpy beside her, except her mother. For Mrs. Malone, standing by the fireplace with her foot on the fender, with her crisp white hair curled stiffly, never looked in the fashion or out of it. Mrs. Fripp, on the contrary, looked in the fashion.

And yet they laughed at her, Kitty thought. She had caught the Oxford ladies lifting their eyebrows at some of Mrs. Fripp's American phrases. But Kitty liked her American phrases; they were so different from what she was used to. She was American, a real American; but nobody would have taken her husband for an American, Kitty thought, looking at him. He might have been any professor, from any University, she thought, with his distinguished wrinkled face, his goatee beard and the black ribbon of his eyeglass crossing his shirt-front as if it were some foreign order. He spoke without any accent—at least without any American accent. Yet he too was different somehow. She had dropped her handkerchief. He stooped at once and gave it her with a bow that was almost too courteous—it made her shy. She bent her head and smiled at the Professor, rather shyly, as she took the handkerchief.

"Thank you so much," she said. He made her feel awkward. Beside Mrs. Fripp she felt even larger than usual. Her hair, of the true Rigby red, never lay smooth as it should have done; Mrs. Fripp's hair looked beautiful, glossy and tidy.

But now Mrs. Malone, glancing at Mrs. Fripp, said, "Well, ladies—?" and waved her hand.

There was something authoritative about her action—as if she had done it again and again; and been obeyed again and again. They moved towards the door. Tonight there was a little ceremony at the door; Professor Fripp bent very low over Mrs. Malone's hand, not quite so low over Kitty's hand, and held the door wide open for them.

"He rather overdoes it," Kitty thought to herself as they passed out.

The ladies took their candles and went in single file up the wide low stairs. Portraits of former masters of Katharine's looked down on them as they mounted. The light of the candles flickered over the dark gold-framed faces as they went up stair after stair.

Now she'll stop, thought Kitty, following behind, and ask who *that* is.

But Mrs. Fripp did not stop. Kitty gave her good marks for that. She compared favourably with most of their visitors, Kitty thought. She had never done the Bodleian quite so quick as she had done it that morning. Indeed, she had felt rather guilty. There were a great many more sights to be seen, had they wished it. But in less than an hour of it Mrs. Fripp had turned to Kitty and had said in her fascinating, if nasal, voice:

"Well, my dear, I guess you're a bit fed-up with sights— what d'you say to an ice in that dear old bun-shop with the bow windows?"

And they had eaten ices when they ought to have been going round the Bodleian.

The procession had now reached the first landing, and Mrs. Malone stopped at the door of the famous room where distinguished guests always slept when they stayed at the Lodge. She gave one look round as she held the door open.

"The bed where Queen Elizabeth did *not* sleep," she said, making the usual little joke as they looked at the great four-poster. The fire was burning; the water-jug was swaddled up like an old woman with the toothache; and the candles were lit on the dressing-table. But there was something strange about the room tonight, Kitty thought, glancing over her mother's shoulder; a dressing-gown flashed green and silver upon the bed. And on the dressing-table there were a number of little pots and jars and a large powder-puff stained pink. Could it be, was it possible, that the reason why Mrs. Fripp looked so very bright and the Oxford ladies looked so very dingy was that Mrs. Fripp— But Mrs. Malone was saying, "You have everything you want?" with such extreme politeness that Kitty guessed

that Mrs. Malone too had seen the dressing-table. Kitty held
out her hand. To her surprise, instead of taking it, Mrs. Fripp
pulled her down and kissed her.

"Thanks a thousand times for showing me all those sights,"
she said. "And remember, you're coming to stay with us in
America," she added. For she had liked the big shy girl who had
so obviously preferred eating ices to showing her the Bodleian;
and she had felt sorry for her too for some reason.

"Good-night, Kitty," said her mother as she shut the door;
and they touched each other perfunctorily on the cheek.

KITTY WENT on upstairs to her own room. She still felt the
spot where Mrs. Fripp had kissed her; the kiss had left a little
glow on her cheek.

She shut the door. The room was very stuffy. It was a
warm night, but they always shut the windows and drew the
curtains. She opened the windows and drew the curtains. It
was raining as usual. Arrows of silver rain crossed the dark
trees in the garden. Then she kicked off her shoes. That was
the worst of being so large—shoes were always too tight;
white satin shoes in particular. Then she began to unhook her
dress. It was difficult; there were so many hooks and all at the
back; but at last the white satin dress was off and laid neatly
across the chair; and then she began to brush her hair. It had
been Thursday at its very worst, she reflected; sights in the
morning; people for lunch; undergraduates for tea; and a
dinner-party in the evening.

However, she concluded, tugging the comb through her
hair, it's over . . . it's over.

The candles flickered and then the muslin blind, blowing
out in a white balloon, almost touched the flame. She opened
her eyes with a start. She was standing at the open window with
a light beside her in her petticoat.

"Anybody might see in," her mother had said, scolding her only the other day.

Now, she said, moving the candles to a table at the right, nobody can see in.

She began to brush her hair again. But with the light at the side instead of in front she saw her face from a different angle.

Am I pretty? she asked herself, putting down her comb and looking in the glass. Her cheek-bones were too prominent; her eyes were set too far apart. She was not pretty; no, her size was against her. What did Mrs. Fripp think of me, she wondered?

She kissed me, she suddenly remembered with a start of pleasure, feeling again the glow on her cheek. She asked me to go with them in America. What fun that would be! she thought. What fun to leave Oxford and go to America! She tugged the comb through her hair, which was like a fuzz bush.

But the bells were making their usual commotion. She hated the sound of the bells; it always seemed to her a dismal sound; and then, just as one stopped, here was another beginning. They went walloping one over another, one after another, as if they would never be finished. She counted eleven, twelve, and then they went on thirteen, fourteen ... clock repeating clock through the damp, drizzling air. It was late. She began to brush her teeth. She glanced at the calendar above the washstand and tore off Thursday and screwed it into a ball, as if she were saying, "That's over! That's over!" Friday in large red letters confronted her. Friday was a good day; on Friday she had her lesson with Lucy; she was going to tea with the Robsons. "Blessed is he who has found his work," she read on the calendar. Calendars always seemed to be talking at you. She had not done her work. She glanced at a row of blue volumes, *The Constitutional History of England, by Dr. Andrews*. There was a paper slip in volume three. She should have finished her chapter for

Lucy; but not tonight. She was too tired tonight. She turned to
the window. A roar of laughter floated out from the undergraduates' quarters. What are they laughing at, she wondered as she
stood by the window. It sounded as if they were enjoying themselves. They never laugh like that when they come to tea at the
Lodge, she thought, as the laughter died away. The little man
from Balliol sat twisting his fingers, twisting his fingers. He
would not talk; but he would not go. Then she blew out the
candle and got into bed. I rather like him, she thought, stretching out in the cool sheets, though he twists his fingers. As for
Tony Ashton, she thought, turning on her pillow, I don't like
him. He always seemed to be cross-examining her about Edward, whom Eleanor, she thought, calls 'Nigs.' His eyes were
too close together. A bit of a barber's block, she thought. He
had followed her at the picnic the other day—the picnic when
the ant got into Mrs. Lathom's skirts. There he was always beside her. But she didn't want to marry him. She didn't want to
be a Don's wife and live in Oxford for ever. No, no, no! She
yawned, turned on her pillow, and listening to a belated bell that
went walloping like a slow porpoise through the thick drizzling
air, yawned once more and fell asleep.

THE RAIN FELL steadily all night long, making a faint mist over
the fields, chuckling and burbling in the gutters. In gardens it fell
over flowering bushes of lilac and laburnum. It slipped gently
over the leaden domes of libraries, and splayed out of the laughing mouths of gargoyles. It smeared the window where the Jew-
boy from Birmingham sat mugging up Greek with a wet towel
round his head; where Dr. Malone sat up late writing another
chapter in his monumental history of the college. And in the
garden of the Lodge outside Kitty's window it sluiced the ancient tree under which Kings and poets had sat drinking three

centuries ago, but now it was half fallen and had to be propped
up by a stake in the middle.

"UMBRELLA, MISS?" said Hiscock, offering Kitty an umbrella
as she left the house rather later than she should have left it the
following afternoon. There was a chilliness in the air which
made her glad, as she caught sight of a party with white and yellow frocks and cushions bound for the river, that she was not
going to sit in a boat today. No parties today, she thought, no
parties today. But she was late, the clock warned her.

She strode along until she came to the cheap red villas that
her father disliked so much that he would always make a round
to avoid them. But as it was in one of these cheap red villas that
Miss Craddock lived, Kitty saw them haloed with romance. Her
heart beat faster as she turned the corner by the new chapel and
saw steep steps of the house where Miss Craddock actually
lived. Lucy went up those steps and down them every day; that
was her window; this was her bell. The bell came out with a jerk
when she pulled it; but it did not go back again, for everything
was ramshackle in Lucy's house; but everything was romantic.
There was Lucy's umbrella in the stand; and it too was not like
other umbrellas; it had a parrot's head for a handle. But as she
went up the steep shiny stairs excitement became mixed with
fear: once more she had scamped her work; she had not "given
her mind to it" again this week.

"SHE'S COMING!" thought Miss Craddock, holding her pen
suspended. Her nose was red-tipped; there was something owl-
like about the eyes, round which there was a sallow, hollow depression. There was the bell. The pen had been dipped in red
ink; she had been correcting Kitty's essay. Now she heard her
step on the stairs. "She's coming!" she thought with a little catch
of her breath, laying down the pen.

"I'm awfully sorry, Miss Craddock," Kitty said, taking off her things and sitting down at the table. "But we had people staying in the house."

Miss Craddock brushed her hand over her mouth in a way she had when she was disappointed.

"I see," she said. "So you haven't done any work this week either."

Miss Craddock took up her pen and dipped it in the red ink. Then she turned to the essay.

"It wasn't worth correcting," she remarked, pausing with her pen in the air.

"A child of ten would have been ashamed of it." Kitty blushed bright red.

"And the odd thing is," said Miss Craddock, putting down her pen when the lesson was over, "that you've got quite an original mind."

Kitty flushed bright red with pleasure.

"But you don't use it," said Miss Craddock. "Why don't you use it?" she added, looking at her out of her fine grey eyes.

"You see, Miss Craddock," Kitty began eagerly, "my mother—"

"Hm . . . hm . . . hm . . ." Miss Craddock stopped her. Confidences were not what Dr. Malone paid her for. She got up.

"Look at my flowers," she said, feeling that she had snubbed her too severely. There was a bowl of flowers on the table; wild flowers, blue and white, stuck into a cushion of wet green moss.

"My sister sent them from the moors," she said.

"The moors?" said Kitty. "Which moors?" She stooped and touched the little flowers tenderly. How lovely she is, Miss Craddock thought; for she was sentimental about Kitty. But I will not be sentimental, she told herself.

"The Scarborough moors," she said aloud. "If you keep the

moss damp but not too damp, they'll last for weeks," she added, looking at the flowers.

"Damp, but not too damp," Kitty smiled. "That's easy in Oxford, I should think. It's always raining here." She looked at the window. Mild rain was falling.

"If I lived up there, Miss Craddock—" she began, taking her umbrella. But she stopped. The lesson was over.

"You'd find it very dull," said Miss Craddock, looking at her. She was putting on her cloak. Certainly she looked very lovely, putting on her cloak.

"When I was your age," Miss Craddock continued, remembering her rôle as teacher, "I would have given my eyes to have the opportunities you have, to meet the people you meet; to know the people you know."

"Old Chuffy?" said Kitty, remembering Miss Craddock's profound admiration for that light of learning.

"You irreverent girl!" Miss Craddock expostulated. "The greatest historian of his age!"

"Well, he doesn't talk history to me," said Kitty, remembering the damp feel of a heavy hand on her knee.

She hesitated; but the lesson was over; another pupil was coming. She glanced round the room. There was a plate of oranges on the top of a pile of shiny exercise-books: a box that looked as if it contained biscuits. Was this her only room, she wondered? Did she sleep on the lumpy-looking sofa with the shawl thrown over it? There was no looking-glass, and she stuck her hat on rather to one side, thinking as she did so that Miss Craddock despised clothes.

But Miss Craddock was thinking how wonderful it was to be young and lovely and to meet brilliant men.

"I'm going to tea with the Robsons," said Kitty, holding out her hand. The girl, Nelly Robson, was Miss Craddock's favourite pupil; the only girl, she used to say, who knew what work meant.

"Are you walking?" said Miss Craddock, looking at her clothes. "It's some way, you know. Down Ringmer Road, past the gasworks."

"Yes, I'm walking," said Kitty, shaking hands.

"And I will try to work hard this week," she said, looking down on her with eyes full of love and admiration. Then she descended the steep stairs whose oilcloth shone bright with romance; and glanced at the umbrella that had a parrot for handle.

THE SON of the Professor, who had done it all off his own bat, "a most creditable performance," to quote Dr. Malone, was mending the hen coops in the back garden at Prestwich Terrace—a scratched up little place. Hammer, hammer, hammer, he went, fixing a board to the rotten roof. His hands were white, unlike his father's, and long fingered too. He had no love of doing these jobs himself. But his father mended the boots on Sunday. Down came the hammer. He went at it, hammering the long shiny nails that sometimes split the wood, or drove outside. For it was rotten. He hated hens too, imbecile fowls, a huddle of feathers, watching him out of their red beady eyes. They scratched up the path; left little curls of feather here and there on the beds, which were more to his fancy. But nothing grew there. How grow flowers like other people if one kept hens? A bell rang.

"Curse it! There's some old woman come to tea," he said, holding his hammer suspended; and then brought it down on the nail.

AS SHE STOOD on the step, noting the cheap lace curtains and the blue and orange glass, Kitty tried to remember what it was that her father had said about Nelly's father. But a little maid let her in. I'm much too large, Kitty thought, as she stood for a moment in the room to which the maid had admitted her. It was a small room, crowded with objects. And I'm too well dressed, she thought, looking at herself in the glass over the fireplace. But here her friend Nelly came in. She was dumpy; over her large grey eyes she wore steel spectacles, and her brown holland overall seemed to increase her air of uncompromising veracity.

"We're having tea in the back room," she said, looking her up and down. What has she been doing? Why is she dressed in an overall? Kitty thought, following her into the room where tea had already begun.

"Pleased to see you," said Mrs. Robson formally, looking over her shoulder. But nobody seemed in the least pleased to see her. Two children were already eating. Slices of bread and butter were in their hands, but they stayed the bread and butter and stared at Kitty as she sat down.

She seemed to see the whole room at once. It was bare yet crowded. The table was too large; there were hard green-plush chairs; yet the table-cloth was coarse; darned in the middle; and the china was cheap with its florid red roses. The light was extraordinarily bright in her eyes. A sound of hammering came in from the garden outside. She looked at the garden; it was a scratched-up, earthy garden without flower-beds; and there was a shed at the end of the garden from which the sound of hammering came.

They're all so short too, Kitty thought, glancing at Mrs. Robson. Only her shoulders came above the tea things; but her shoulders were substantial. She was a little like Bigge, the cook at the Lodge, but more formidable. She gave one brief look at Mrs. Robson and then began to pull off her gloves secretly, swiftly, under the cover of the table-cloth. But why does nobody talk? she thought nervously. The children kept their eyes fixed upon her with a look of solemn amazement. Their owl-like stare went up and down over her uncompromisingly. Happily before they could express their disapproval, Mrs. Robson told them sharply to go on with their tea; and the bread and butter slowly rose to their mouths again.

Why don't they say something? Kitty thought again, glancing at Nelly. She was about to speak when an umbrella grated in the hall; and Mrs. Robson looked up and said to her daughter: "There's Dad!"

Next moment in trotted a little man, who was so short that he looked as if his jacket should have been an Eton jacket, and his collar a round collar. He wore, too, a very thick watch-chain, made of silver, like a schoolboy's. But his eyes were keen and fierce, his moustache bristly, and he spoke with a curious accent.

"Pleased to see you," he said, and gripped her hand hard in his. He sat down, tucked a napkin under his chin so that it obscured his heavy silver watch-chain under its stiff white shield. Hammer, hammer, hammer came from the shed in the garden.

"Tell Jo tea's on the table," said Mrs. Robson to Nelly, who had brought in a dish with a cover on it. The cover was removed. Actually they were going to eat fried fish and potatoes at tea-time, Kitty remarked.

But Mr. Robson had turned his rather alarming blue eyes upon her. She expected him to say, "How is your father, Miss Malone?"

But he said:

"You're reading history with Lucy Craddock?"

"Yes," she said. She liked the way he said Lucy Craddock, as if he respected her. So many of the Dons sneered at her. She liked feeling too, as he made her feel, that she was nobody's daughter in particular.

"You're interested in history?" he said, applying himself to his fish and potatoes.

"I love it," she said. His bright blue eyes, gazing straight at her rather fiercely, seemed to make her say quite shortly what she meant.

"But I'm frightfully lazy," she added. Here Mrs. Robson looked at her rather sternly, and handed her a thick slice of bread on the point of a knife.

Anyhow their taste is awful, she said by way of revenge for the snub that she felt was intended. She focussed her eyes on a picture opposite—an oily landscape in a heavy gilt frame. There was a blue and red Japanese plate on either side of it. Everything was ugly, especially the pictures.

"The moor at the back of our house," said Mr. Robson, seeing her look at a picture.

It struck Kitty that the accent with which he spoke was a Yorkshire accent. In looking at the picture he had increased his accent.

"In Yorkshire?" she said. "We come from there too. My mother's family I mean," she added.

"Your mother's family?" said Mr. Robson.

"Rigby," she said, and blushed slightly.

"Rigby?" said Mrs. Robson, looking up. "I wur-r-rked for a Miss Rigby before I married."

What sort of wur-r-rk had Mrs. Robson done? Kitty wondered. Sam explained.

"My wife was a cook, Miss Malone, before we married," he said. Again he increased his accent as if he were proud of it. I had a great-uncle who rode in a circus, she felt inclined to say: and an aunt who married . . . but here Mrs. Robson interrupted her.

"The Hollies," she said. "Two very old ladies; Miss Ann and Miss Matilda." She spoke more gently.

"But they must be dead long ago," she concluded. For the first time she leant back in her chair and stirred her tea, just as old Snap at the farm, Kitty thought, stirred her tea round and round and round.

"Tell Jo we're not sparing the cake," said Mr. Robson, cut-

ting himself a slice of that craggy-looking object; and Nell went
out of the room once more. The hammering stopped in the garden. The door opened. Kitty, who had altered the focus of her
eyes to suit the smallness of the Robson family, was taken by
surprise. The young man seemed immense in that little room.
He was a handsome young man. He brushed his hand through
his hair as he came in, for a wood shaving had stuck in it.

"Our Jo," said Mrs. Robson, introducing them. "Go and get
the kittle, Jo," she added; and he went at once as if he were used
to it. When he came back with the kettle, Sam began chaffing
him about a hencoop.

"It takes you a long time, my son, to mend a hencoop," he
said. There was some family joke which Kitty could not follow
about mending boots and hencoops. She watched him eating
steadily under his father's banter. He was not Eton or Harrow,
or Rugby or Winchester; or reading or rowing. He reminded her
of Alf, the farm hand up at Carter's, who had kissed her under
the shadow of the haystack when she was fifteen, and old Carter
loomed up leading a bull with a ring through its nose and said
"Stop that!" She looked down again. She would rather like Jo to
kiss her; better than Edward, she thought to herself suddenly.
She remembered her own appearance, which she had forgotten.
She liked him. Yes, she liked them all very much, she told herself; very much indeed. She felt as if she had given her nurse the
slip and run off on her own.

Then the children began scrambling down off their chairs;
the meal was over. She began to fish under the table for her
gloves.

"These them?" said Jo, picking them up off the floor. She
took them and crumpled them up in her hand.

He cast one quick sulky look at her as she stood in the doorway. She's a stunner, he said to himself, but my word, she gives
herself airs!

Mrs. Robson ushered her into the little room where, before tea, she had looked in the glass. It was crowded with objects. There were bamboo tables; velvet books with brass hinges; marble gladiators askew on the mantelpiece and innumerable pictures. . . . But Mrs. Robson, with a gesture that was exactly like Mrs. Malone's when she pointed to the Gainsborough that was not quite certainly a Gainsborough, was displaying a huge silver salver with an inscription.

"The salver my husband's pupils gave him," Mrs. Robson began, pointing to the inscription. Kitty began to spell out the inscription.

"And this . . ." said Mrs. Robson, when she had done, pointing to a document framed like a text on the wall.

But here Sam, who stood in the background fiddling with his watch-chain, stepped forward and indicated with his stubby forefinger the picture of an old woman looking rather over life size in the photographer's chair.

"My mother," he said and stopped. He gave a queer little chuckle.

"Your mother?" Kitty repeated, stooping to look. The unwieldy old lady, posed in all the stiffness of her best clothes, was plain in the extreme. And yet Kitty felt that admiration was expected.

"You're very like her, Mr. Robson," was all she could find to say. Indeed they had something of the same sturdy look; the same piercing eyes; and they were both very plain. He gave an odd little chuckle.

"Glad you think so," he said. "Brought us all up. Not one of them a patch on her though." He gave his odd little chuckle again.

Then he turned to his daughter, who had come in and was standing there in her overall.

"Not a patch on her," he repeated, pinching Nell on the

shoulder. As she stood there with her father's hand on her shoulder under the portrait of her grandmother, a sudden rush of self-pity came over Kitty. If she had been the daughter of people like the Robsons, she thought; if she had lived in the north—but it was clear they wanted her to go. Nobody ever sat down in this room. They were all standing up. Nobody pressed her to stay. When she said that she must go, they all came out into the little hall with her. They were all about to go on with what they were doing, she felt. Nell was about to go into the kitchen and wash up the tea things; Jo was about to return to his hencoops; the children were about to be put to bed by their mother; and Sam—what was he about to do? She looked at him standing there with his heavy watch-chain, like a schoolboy's. You are the nicest man I have ever met, she thought, holding out her hand.

"Pleased to have made your acquaintance," said Mrs. Robson in her stately way.

"Hope you'll come again soon," said Mr. Robson, grasping her hand very hard.

"Oh, I should love to!" she exclaimed, pressing their hands as hard as she could. Did they know how much she admired them? she wanted to say. Would they accept her in spite of her hat and her gloves? she wanted to ask. But they were all going off to their work. And I am going home to dress for dinner, she thought as she walked down the little front steps, pressing her pale kid gloves in her hands.

THE SUN was shining again; the damp pavements gleamed; a gust of wind tossed up the wet branches of the almond trees in the villa gardens; little twigs and tufts of blossom whirled onto the pavement and stuck there. As she stood still for a second at a crossing she too seemed to be tossed aloft out of her usual surroundings. She forgot where she was. The sky, blown into a blue open space, seemed to be looking down not here upon streets and houses, but upon open country, where the wind brushed the moors, and sheep, with grey fleeces ruffled, sheltered under stone walls. She could almost see the moors brighten and darken as the clouds passed over them.

But then in two strides the unfamiliar street became the street she had always known. Here she was again in the paved alley; there were the old curiosity shops with their blue china and their brass warming-pans; and next moment she was out in the famous crooked street with all the domes and steeples. The sun lay in broad stripes across it. There were the cabs and the awnings and the book-shops; the old men in black gowns billowing; the young women in pink and blue dresses flowing; and the young men in straw hats carrying cushions under their arms. But for a moment all seemed to her obsolete, frivolous, inane. The usual undergraduate in cap and gown with books under his arm looked silly. And the portentous old men, with their exaggerated features, looked like gargoyles, carved, mediaeval, unreal. They were all like people dressed up and acting parts, she thought. Now she stood at her own door and waited for Hiscock, the butler, to take his feet off the fender and waddle upstairs. Why can't you talk like a human being, she thought, as he took her umbrella and mumbled his usual remark about the weather.

SLOWLY, as if a weight had got into her feet too, she went upstairs, seeing through open windows and open doors the smooth lawn, the recumbent tree and the faded chintzes. Down she sank on the edge of her bed. It was very stuffy. A blue-bottle buzzed round and round; a lawn mower squeaked in the garden below. Far away pigeons were cooing — Take two coos, Taffy. Take two coos. Tak . . . Her eyes half shut. It seemed to her that she was sitting on the terrace of an Italian inn. There was her father pressing gentians on to a rough sheet of blotting paper. The lake below lapped and dazzled. She plucked up courage and said to her father: "Father . . ." He looked up very kindly over his spectacles. He held the little blue flower between his thumb and finger. "I want . . ." she began, slipping off the balustrade upon which she was sitting. But here a bell struck. She rose and crossed to the washing-table. What would Nell think of this, she thought, tilting up the beautifully polished brass jug and dipping her hands in the hot water. Another bell tolled. She crossed to the dressing-table. The air from the garden outside was full of murmurings and cooings. Wood shavings, she said as she took up her brush and comb—he had wood shavings in his hair. A servant passed with a pile of tin dishes on his head. The pigeons were cooing Take two coos, Taffy. Take two coos. . . . But there was the dinner bell. In a moment she had pinned her hair up, hooked her dress on, and ran down the slippery stairs, sliding her palm along the bannisters as she used to do when she was a child in a hurry. And there they all were.

HER PARENTS were standing in the hall. A tall man was with them. His gown was thrown back and one last ray of sunshine lit up his genial, authoritative face. Who was he? Kitty could not remember.

"My word!" he exclaimed, looking up at her with admiration.

"It *is* Kitty, isn't it?" he said. Then he took her hand and pressed it.

"How you've grown!" he exclaimed. He looked at her as if he were looking not at her but at his own past.

"You don't remember me?" he added.

"Chingachgook!" she exclaimed, recalling some childish memory.

"But he is now Sir Richard Norton," said her mother, giving him a proud little pat on the shoulder; and they turned away, for the gentlemen were dining in Hall.

IT WAS DULL FISH, Kitty thought; the plates were half cold. It was stale bread, she thought, cut in meagre little squares; the colour, the gaiety of Prestwich Terrace, was still in her eyes, in her ears. She granted, as she looked round, the superiority of the Lodge china and silver; and the Japanese plates and the picture had been hideous; but this dining-room with its hanging creepers and its vast cracked canvases was so dark. At Prestwich Terrace the room was full of light; the sound of hammer, hammer, hammer still rang in her ears. She looked out at the fading greens in the garden. For the thousandth time she echoed her childish wish that the tree would either lie down or stand up instead of doing neither. It was not actually raining, but gusts of whiteness seemed to blow about the garden as the wind stirred the thick leaves on the laurels.

"Didn't you notice it?" Mrs. Malone suddenly appealed to her.

"What, Mama?" Kitty asked. She had not been attending.

"The odd taste in the fish," said her mother.

"I don't think I did," she said; and Mrs. Malone went on talking to the butler. The plates were changed; another dish was brought in. But Kitty was not hungry. She bit one of the green sweets that were provided for her, and then the modest dinner, retrieved for the ladies from the relics of last night's party, was over and she followed her mother into the drawing-room.

It was too big when they were alone, but they always sat there. The pictures seemed to be looking down at the empty chairs, and the empty chairs seemed to be looking up at the pictures. The old gentleman who had ruled the college over a hundred years ago seemed to vanish in the daytime, but he came back when the lamps were lit. The face was placid, solid and smiling, and singularly like Dr. Malone, who, had a frame been set round him, might have hung over the fireplace too.

"It's nice to have a quiet evening once in a way," Mrs. Malone was saying, "though the Fripps . . ." Her voice tailed off as she put on her spectacles and took up *The Times*. This was her moment of relaxation and recuperation after the day's work. She suppressed a little yawn as she glanced up and down the columns of the newspaper.

"What a charming man he was," she observed casually, as she looked at the births and deaths. "One would hardly have taken him for an American."

Kitty recalled her thoughts. She was thinking of the Robsons. Her mother was talking about the Fripps.

"And I liked her too," she said rashly. "Wasn't she lovely?"

"Hum-m-m. A little overdressed for my taste," said Mrs. Malone dryly. "And that accent—" she went on, looking through the paper, "I sometimes hardly understood what she said."

Kitty was silent. Here they differed; as they did about so many things.

Suddenly Mrs. Malone looked up:

"Yes, just what I was saying to Bigge this morning," she said, laying down the paper.

"What, Mama?" said Kitty.

"This man—in the leading article," said Mrs. Malone. She touched it with her finger.

"'With the best flesh, fish and fowl in the world,'" she read, "'we shall not be able to turn them to account because we have none to cook them'—what I was saying to Bigge this morning." She gave her quick little sigh. Just when one wanted to impress people, like those Americans, something went wrong. It had been the fish this time. She foraged for her work things, and Kitty took up the paper.

"It's the leading article," said Mrs. Malone. That man almost always said the very thing that she was thinking, which comforted her, and gave her a sense of security in a world which seemed to her to be changing for the worse.

" 'Before the rigid and now universal enforcement of school attendance . . . ?' " Kitty read out.

"Yes. That's it," said Mrs. Malone, opening her work-box and looking for her scissors.

" '. . . the children saw a good deal of cooking which, poor as it was, yet gave them some taste and inkling of knowledge. They now see nothing and they do nothing but read, write, sum, sew or knit,' " Kitty read out.

"Yes, yes," said Mrs. Malone. She unrolled the long strip of embroidery upon which she was working a design of birds pecking at fruit copied from a tomb at Ravenna. It was for the spare bedroom.

The leading article bored Kitty with its pompous fluency. She searched the paper for some little piece of news that might interest her mother. Mrs. Malone liked someone to talk to her or read aloud to her as she worked. Night after night her embroidery served to weave the after-dinner talk into a pleasant harmony. One said something and stitched; looked at the design, chose another coloured silk, and stitched again. Sometimes Dr. Malone read poetry aloud—Pope, Tennyson. Tonight she would have liked Kitty to talk to her. But she was becoming increasingly conscious of difficulty with Kitty. Why? She glanced at her. What was wrong? she wondered. She gave her quick little sigh.

Kitty turned over the large pages. Sheep had the fluke; Turks wanted religious liberty; there was the General Election.

"Mr. Gladstone—" she began.

Mrs. Malone had lost her scissors. It annoyed her.

"Who can have taken them again?" she began. Kitty went down on the floor to look for them. Mrs. Malone ferreted in the work-box; then she plunged her hand into the fissure between the cushion and the chair frame and brought up not only the scissors but also a little mother-of-pearl paper-knife that had been missing for ever so long. The discovery annoyed her. It proved Ellen never shook up the cushions properly.

"Here they are, Kitty," she said. They were silent. There was always some constraint between them now.

"Did you enjoy your party at the Robsons', Kitty?" she asked, resuming her embroidery. Kitty did not answer. She turned the paper.

"There's been an experiment," she said. "An experiment with electric light. 'A brilliant light,'" she read, "'was seen to shoot forth suddenly shooting out a profound ray across the water to the Rock. Everything was lit up as if by daylight.'" She paused. She saw the bright light from the ships on the drawing-room chair. But here the door opened and Hiscock came in with a note on a salver.

Mrs. Malone took it and read it in silence.

"No answer," she said. From the tone of her mother's voice Kitty knew that something had happened. She sat holding the note in her hand. Hiscock shut the door.

"Rose is dead!" said Mrs. Malone. "Cousin Rose."

The note lay open on her knee.

"It's from Edward," she said.

"Cousin Rose is dead?" said Kitty. A moment before she had been thinking of a bright light on a red rock. Now everything looked dingy. There was a pause. There was silence. Tears stood in her mother's eyes.

"Just when the children most wanted her," she said, sticking the needle into her embroidery. She began to roll it up very slowly. Kitty folded *The Times* and laid it on a little table, slowly, so that it should not crackle. She had only seen Cousin Rose once or twice. She felt awkward.

"Fetch me my engagement book," said her mother at last. Kitty brought it.

"We must put off our dinner on Monday," said Mrs. Malone, looking through her engagements.

"And the Lathoms' party on Wednesday," Kitty murmured, looking over her mother's shoulder.

"We can't put off everything," said her mother sharply, and Kitty felt rebuked.

But there were notes to be written. She wrote them at her mother's dictation.

Why is she so ready to put off all our engagements? thought Mrs. Malone, watching her write. Why doesn't she enjoy going out with me any more? She glanced through the notes that her daughter brought her.

"Why don't you take more interest in things here, Kitty?" she said irritably, pushing the letters away.

"Mama, dear—" Kitty began, deprecating the usual argument.

"But what is it you want to do?" her mother persisted. She had put away her embroidery; she was sitting upright, she was looking rather formidable.

"Your father and I only want you to do what you want to do," she continued.

"Mama, dear—" Kitty repeated.

"You could help your father if it bores you helping me," said Mrs. Malone. "Papa told me the other day that you never come to him now." She referred, Kitty knew, to his history of the college. He had suggested that she should help him. Again she saw the ink flowing—she had made an awkward brush with her arm—over five generations of Oxford men, obliterating hours of her father's exquisite penmanship; and could hear him say with his usual courteous irony, "Nature did not intend you to be a scholar, my dear," as he applied the blotting-paper.

"I know," she said guiltily. "I haven't been to Papa lately. But then there's always something—" She hesitated.

"Naturally," said Mrs. Malone, "with a man in your father's position . . ." Kitty sat silent. They both sat silent. They both disliked this petty bickering; they both detested these recurring scenes; and yet they seemed inevitable. Kitty got up, took the letters she had written and put them in the hall.

What does she want? Mrs. Malone asked herself, looking up at the picture without seeing it. When I was her age . . . she thought, and smiled. How well she remembered sitting at home on a spring evening like this up in Yorkshire, miles from anywhere. You could hear the beat of a horse's hoof on the road miles away. She could remember flinging up her bedroom window and looking down on the dark shrubs in the garden and crying out, "Is this life?" And in the winter there was the snow. She could still hear the snow flopping off the trees in the garden. And here was Kitty, living in Oxford, in the midst of everything.

Kitty came back into the drawing-room and yawned very slightly. She raised her hand to her face with an unconscious gesture of fatigue that touched her mother.

"Tired, Kitty?" she said. "It's been a long day; you look pale."

"And you look tired too," said Kitty.

The bells came pushing forth one after another, one on top of another, through the damp, heavy air.

"Go to bed, Kitty," said Mrs. Malone. "There! It's striking ten."

"But aren't you coming too, Mama?" said Kitty, standing beside her chair.

"Your father won't be back just yet," said Mrs. Malone, putting on her spectacles again.

Kitty knew it was useless to try to persuade her. It was part of the mysterious ritual of her parents' lives. She bent down and

gave her mother the little perfunctory peck that was the only
sign they ever gave each other outwardly of their affection. Yet
they were very fond of each other; yet they always quarrelled.

"Good night, and sleep well," said Mrs. Malone.

"I don't like to see your roses fade," she added, putting her
arm round her for once in a way.

She sat still after Kitty had gone. Rose is dead, she
thought—Rose who was about her own age. She read the note
again. It was from Edward. And Edward, she mused, is in love
with Kitty, but I don't know that I want her to marry him, she
thought, taking up her needle. No, not Edward. . . . There was
young Lord Lasswade. . . . That would be a nice marriage, she
thought. Not that I want her to be rich, not that I care about
rank, she thought, threading her needle. No, but he could give
her what she wants. . . . What was it? . . . Scope, she decided, beginning to stitch. Then again her thoughts turned to Rose. Rose
was dead. Rose who was about her own age. That must have
been the first time he proposed to her, she thought, the day we
had the picnic on the moors. It was a spring day. They were sitting on the grass. She could see Rose wearing a black hat with a
cock's feather in it over her bright red hair. She could still see
her blush and look extremely pretty when Abel rode up, much
to their surprise—he was stationed at Scarborough—the day
they had the picnic on the moors.

The house at Abercorn Terrace was very dark. It smelt
strongly of spring flowers. For some days now wreaths had been
piled one on top of another on the hall table in Abercorn Terrace. In the dimness—all the blinds were drawn—the flowers
gleamed; and the hall smelt with the amorous intensity of a hot-
house. Wreath after wreath, they kept arriving. There were lilies

with broad bars of gold in them; others with spotted throats sticky with honey; white tulips, white lilac—flowers of all kinds, some with petals as thick as velvet, others transparent, paper-thin, but all white, and clubbed together, head to head, in circles, in ovals, in crosses so that they scarcely looked like flowers. Black-edged cards were attached to them, "With deep sympathy from Major and Mrs. Brand"; "With love and sympathy from General and Mrs. Elkin"; "For dearest Rose from Susan." Each card had a few words written on it.

Even now with the hearse at the door the bell rang; a messenger boy appeared bearing more lilies. He raised his cap, as he stood in the hall, for men were lurching down the stairs carrying the coffin. Rose, in deep black, prompted by her nurse, stepped forward and dropped her little bunch on the coffin. But it slipped off as it swayed down the brilliant sun-lit steps on the slanting shoulders of Whiteley's men. The family followed after.

IT WAS AN uncertain day, with passing shadows and darting rays of bright sunshine. The funeral started at a walking pace. Delia, getting into the second carriage with Milly and Edward, noticed that the houses opposite had their blinds drawn in sympathy, but a servant peeped. The others, she noticed, did not seem to see her; they were thinking of their mother. When they got into the main road the pace quickened, for the drive to the cemetery was a long one. Through the slit of the blind, Delia noticed dogs playing; a beggar singing; men raising their hats as the hearse passed them. But by the time their own carriage passed, the hats were on again. The men walked briskly and unconcernedly along the pavement. The shops were already gay with spring clothing; women paused and looked in at the windows. But they would have to wear nothing but black all the summer, Delia thought, looking at Edward's coal-black trousers.

They scarcely spoke, or only in little formal sentences, as if they were already taking part in the ceremony. Somehow their relations had changed. They were more considerate, and a little important too, as if their mother's death had laid new responsibilities on them. But the others knew how to behave; it was only she who had to make an effort. She remained outside, and so did her father, she thought. When Martin suddenly burst out laughing at tea, and then stopped and looked guilty, she felt—that is what Papa would do, that is what I should do if we were honest.

She glanced out of the window again. Another man raised his hat—a tall man, a man in a frock coat, but she would not allow herself to think of Mr. Parnell until the funeral was over.

At last they reached the cemetery. As she took her place in the little group behind the coffin and walked up the church, she was relieved to find that she was overcome by some generalised and solemn emotion. People stood up on both sides of the church and she felt their eyes on her. Then the service began. A clergyman, a cousin, read it. The first words struck out with a rush of extraordinary beauty. Delia, standing behind her father, noticed how he braced himself and squared his shoulders.

"I am the resurrection and the life."

Pent up as she had been all these days in the half-lit house which smelt of flowers, the outspoken words filled her with glory. This she could feel genuinely; this was something that she said herself. But then, as Cousin James went on reading, something slipped. The sense was blurred. She could not follow with her reason. Then in the midst of the argument came another burst of familiar beauty. "And fade away suddenly like the grass, in the morning it is green, and groweth up; but in the evening it is cut down, dried up, and withered." She could feel the beauty of that. Again it was like music; but then Cousin James seemed to hurry, as if he did not altogether believe what he was saying. He seemed to pass from the known to the unknown; from what he believed to what he did not believe; even his voice altered. He looked clean, he looked starched and ironed like his robes. But what did he mean by what he was saying? She gave it up. Either one understood or one did not understand, she thought. Her mind wandered.

But I will not think of him, she thought, seeing a tall man who stood beside her on a platform and raised his hat, until it's over. She fixed her eyes upon her father. She watched him dab a great white pocket-handkerchief to his eyes and put it in his pocket; then he pulled it out and dabbed his eyes with it again. Then the voice stopped; he put his handkerchief finally in his pocket; and again they all formed up, the little group of the family, behind the coffin and again the dark people on either side rose, and watched them and let them go first and followed after.

It was a relief to feel the soft damp air blowing its leafy smell in her face again. But again now that she was out of doors, she began to notice things. She noticed how the black funeral horses were pawing the ground; they were scraping little pits with their hooves in the yellow gravel. She remembered hearing that funeral horses came from Belgium and were very vicious. They looked vicious, she thought; their black necks were flecked with foam—but she recalled herself. They went straggling in ones and twos along a path until they reached a fresh mound of yellow earth heaped beside a pit; and there again she noticed how the grave-diggers stood at a little distance, rather behind, with their spades.

There was a pause; people kept on arriving and took up their positions, some a little higher, some a little lower. She observed a poor-looking shabby woman prowling on the outskirts, and tried to think whether she were some old servant, but she could not put a name to her. Her Uncle Digby, her father's brother, stood directly opposite her, with his top-hat held like some sacred vessel between his hands, the image of grave decorum.

Some of the women were crying; but not the men; the men had one pose; the women had another, she observed. Then it all began again. The splendid gust of music blew through them— "Man that is born of a woman": the ceremony had renewed itself; once more they were grouped, united. The family pressed a little closer to the graveside and looked fixedly at the coffin which lay with its polish and its brass handles there in the earth to be buried for ever. It looked too new to be buried for ever. She stared down into the grave. There lay her mother; in that coffin—the woman she had loved and hated so. Her eyes dazzled. She was afraid that she might faint; but she must look; she must feel; it was the last chance that was left her. Earth dropped on the coffin; three pebbles fell on the hard shiny surface; and as they dropped she was possessed by a sense of something everlasting; of life mixing with death, of death becoming life. For as she looked she heard the sparrows chirp quicker and quicker; she heard wheels in the distance sound louder and louder; life came closer and closer. . . .

"We give thee hearty thanks," said the voice, "for that it has pleased thee to deliver this our sister out of the miseries of this sinful world—"

What a lie! she cried to herself. What a damnable lie! He had robbed her of the one feeling that was genuine; he had spoilt her one moment of understanding.

She looked up. She saw Morris and Eleanor side by side; their faces were blurred; their noses were red; the tears were running down them. As for her father he was so stiff and so rigid that she had a convulsive desire to laugh aloud. Nobody can feel like that, she thought. He's overdoing it. None of us feel anything at all, she thought: we're all pretending.

Then there was a general movement; the attempt at concentration was over. People strolled off this way and that; there was no attempt now to form into a procession; little groups came together; people shook hands rather furtively, among the graves, and even smiled.

"How good of you to come!" said Edward, shaking hands with old Sir James Graham, who gave him a little pat on the shoulder. Ought she to go and thank him too? The graves made it difficult. It was becoming a shrouded and subdued morning party among the graves. She hesitated — she did not know what she ought to do next. Her father had walked on. She looked back. The grave-diggers had come forward; they were piling the wreaths one on top of another neatly; and the prowling woman had joined them and was stooping down to read the names on the cards. The ceremony was over; rain was falling.

THE AUTUMN wind blew over England. It twitched the leaves
off the trees, and down they fluttered, spotted red and yellow,
or sent them floating, flaunting in wide curves before they
settled. In towns coming in gusts round the corners, the wind
blew here a hat off; there lifted a veil high above a woman's
head. Money was in brisk circulation. The streets were crowded.
Upon the sloping desks of the offices near St. Paul's, clerks
paused with their pens on the ruled page. It was difficult to
work after the holidays. Margate, Eastbourne and Brighton had
bronzed them and tanned them. The sparrows and starlings,
making their discordant chatter round the eaves of St. Martin's,
whitened the heads of the sleek statues holding rods or rolls of
paper in Parliament Square. Blowing behind the boat train, the
wind ruffled the channel, tossed the grapes in Provence, and
made the lazy fisher boy, who was lying on his back in his boat
in the Mediterranean, roll over and snatch a rope.

But in England, in the North, it was cold. Kitty, Lady Lasswade, sitting on the terrace beside her husband and his spaniel,
drew the cloak round her shoulders. She was looking at the hill
top, where the snuffer-shaped monument raised by the old Earl
made a mark for ships at sea. There was mist on the woods. Near
at hand the stone ladies on the terrace had scarlet flowers in their
urns. Thin blue smoke drifted across the flaming dahlias in the

long beds that went down to the river. "Burning weeds," she said aloud. Then there was a tap on the window, and her little boy in a pink frock stumbled out, holding his spotted horse.

In Devonshire where the round red hills and the steep valleys hoarded the sea air leaves were still thick on the trees—too thick, Hugh Gibbs said at breakfast. Too thick for shooting, he said, and Milly, his wife, left him to go to his meeting. With her basket on her arm she walked down the well-kept crazy pavement with the swaying movement of a woman with child. There hung the yellow pears on the orchard wall, lifting the leaves over them, they were so swollen. But the wasps had got at them—the skin was broken. With her hand on the fruit she paused. Pop, pop, pop sounded in the distant woods. Someone was shooting.

The smoke hung in veils over the spires and domes of the University cities. Here it choked the mouth of a gargoyle; there it clung to the walls that were peeled yellow. Edward, who was taking his brisk constitutional, noted smell, sound and colour; which suggested how complex impressions are; few poets compress enough; but there must be some line in Greek or Latin, he was thinking, which sums up the contrast—when Mrs. Lathom passed him and he raised his cap.

In the Law Courts the leaves lay dry and angular on the flagstones. Morris, remembering his childhood, shuffled his feet through them on his way to his chambers, and they scattered edgeways along the gutters. Not yet trodden down they lay in Kensington Gardens, and children, crunching the shells as they ran, scooped up a handful and scudded on through the mist down the avenues, with their hoops.

Racing over the hills in the country the wind blew vast rings of shadow that dwindled again to green. But in London the streets narrowed the clouds; mist hung thick in the East End by the river; made the voices of men crying, "Any old iron to sell, any old iron," sound distant; and in the suburbs the organs were muted. The wind blew the smoke — for in every back garden in the angle of the ivy-grown wall that still sheltered a few last geraniums, leaves were heaped up; keen-fanged flames were eating them — out into the street, into windows that stood open in the drawing-room in the morning. For it was October, the birth of the year.

ELEANOR WAS sitting at her writing-table with her pen in her hand. It's awfully queer, she thought, touching the ink-corroded patch of bristle on the back of Martin's walrus with the point of her pen, that *that* should have gone on all these years. That solid object might survive them all. If she threw it away it would still exist somewhere or other. But she never had thrown it away because it was part of other things — her mother for example. . . . She drew on her blotting paper; a dot with strokes raying out round it. Then she looked up. They were burning weeds in the back garden; there was a drift of smoke; a sharp acrid smell; and leaves were falling. A barrel-organ was playing up the street. "Sur le pont d'Avignon" she hummed in time to it. How did it go? — the song Pippy used to sing as she wiped your ears with a piece of slimy flannel.

"Ron, ron, ron, et plon, plon plon," she hummed. Then the tune stopped. The organ had moved further away. She dipped her pen in the ink.

"Three times eight," she murmured, "is twenty-four," she said decidedly; wrote a figure at the bottom of the page, swept together the little red and blue books and took them to her father's study.

"HERE'S THE HOUSEKEEPER!" he said good-humouredly as she came in. He was sitting in his leather armchair reading a pinkish financial paper.

"Here's the housekeeper," he repeated, looking up over his glasses. He was getting slower and slower, she thought; and she was in a hurry. But they got on extremely well; they were almost like brother and sister. He put down his paper and went to the writing-table.

But I wish you would hurry, Papa, she thought as she watched the deliberate way in which he unlocked the drawer in which he kept his cheque-book, or I shall be late.

"Milk's very high," he said, tapping the book with the gilt cow. "Yes. It's eggs in October," she said.

As he made out the cheque with extreme deliberation she glanced round the room. It looked like an office, with its files of papers and its deed-boxes, except that horses' bits hung by the fireplace, and there was the silver cup he had won at polo. Would he sit there all the morning reading the financial papers and considering his investments, she wondered? He stopped writing.

"And where are you off to now?" he asked with his shrewd little smile.

"A Committee," she said.

"A Committee," he repeated, signing his firm heavy signature. "Well, stand up for yourself; don't be sat on, Nell." He entered a figure in the ledger.

"Are you coming with me this afternoon, Papa?" she said as he finished writing the figure. "It's Morris's case you know; at the Law Courts."

He shook his head.

"No; I've got to be in the City at three," he said.

"Then I shall see you at lunch," she said, making a movement to go. But he held up his hand. He had something to say, but he hesitated. He was getting rather heavier in the face, she noted; there were little veins in his nose; he was getting rather too red and heavy.

"I was thinking of looking in at the Digbys'," he said, at length. He got up and walked to the window. He looked out at the back garden. She fidgeted.

"How the leaves are falling!" he remarked.

"Yes," she said. "They're burning weeds."

He stood looking at the smoke for a moment.

"Burning weeds," he repeated, and stopped.

"It's Maggie's birthday," at last he came out with it. "I thought I'd take her some little present—" He paused. He meant that he wished her to buy it, she knew.

"What would you like to give her?" she asked.

"Well," he said vaguely, "something pretty you know— something she could wear."

Eleanor reflected—Maggie, her little cousin; was she seven or eight?

"A necklace? A brooch? Something like that?" she asked quickly.

"Yes, something like that," said her father, settling down in his chair again. "Something pretty, something she could wear, you know." He opened the paper and gave her a little nod. "Thank you, my dear," he said as she left the room.

ON THE HALL TABLE, between a silver salver laden with visiting-cards—some with their corners turned down, some large, some small—and a piece of purple plush with which the Colonel polished his top hat—lay a thin foreign envelope with "England" marked in large letters in the corner. Eleanor, running down the stairs in a hurry, swept it into her bag as she passed. Then she ran at a peculiar ambling trot down the Terrace. At the corner she stopped and looked anxiously down the road. Among the other traffic she singled out one bulky form; mercifully, it was yellow; mercifully she had caught her bus. She hailed it and climbed on top. She sighed with relief as she pulled

the leather apron over her knees. All responsibility now rested
with the driver. She relaxed; she breathed in the soft London air;
she heard the dull London roar with pleasure. She looked along
the street and relished the sight of cabs, vans and carriages all
trotting past with an end in view. She liked coming back in October to the full stir of life after the summer was over. She had
been staying in Devonshire with the Gibbses. That's turned out
very well, she thought, thinking of her sister's marriage to Hugh
Gibbs, seeing Milly with her babies. And Hugh—she smiled.
He rode about on a great white horse, breaking up litters. But
there are too many trees and cows and too many little hills instead of one big one, she thought. She did not like Devonshire.
She was glad to be back in London, on top of the yellow bus,
with her bag stuffed with papers, and everything beginning
again in October. They had left the residential quarter; the
houses were changing; they were turning into shops. This was
her world; here she was in her element. The streets were
crowded; women were swarming in and out of shops with their
shopping baskets. There was something customary, rhythmical
about it, she thought, like rooks swooping in a field, rising and
falling.

She, too, was going to her work—she turned her watch on
her wrist without looking at it. After the Committee, Duffus;
after Duffus, Dickson. Then lunch; and the Law Courts . . .
then lunch and the Law Courts at two-thirty, she repeated. The
bus trundled along the Bayswater Road. The streets were becoming poorer and poorer.

Perhaps I oughtn't to have given the job to Duffus, she said
to herself—she was thinking of Peter Street where she had built
houses; the roof was leaking again; there was a bad smell in the
sink. But here the omnibus stopped; people got in and out; the
omnibus went on again—but it's better to give the work to a
small man, she thought, looking at the huge plate-glass windows

of one of the large shops, instead of going to one of those big firms. There were always small shops side by side with big shops. It puzzled her. How did the small shops manage to make a living? she wondered. But if Duffus, she began—here the omnibus stopped; she looked up, she rose "—if Duffus thinks he can bully me," she said as she went down the steps, "he'll find he's mistaken."

She walked quickly up the cinder path to the galvanised iron shed in which the meeting took place. She was late; there they were already. It was her first meeting since the holidays, and they all smiled at her. Judd even took his toothpick out of his mouth—a sign of recognition that flattered her. Here we all are again, she thought, taking her place and laying her papers on the table.

But she meant "them," not herself. She did not exist; she was not anybody at all. But there they all were—Brocket, Cufnell, Miss Sims, Ramsden, Major Porter and Mrs. Lazenby. The Major preaching organisation; Miss Sims (ex-mill hand) scenting condescension; Mrs. Lazenby, offering to write to her cousin Sir John, upon which Judd, the retired shopkeeper, snubbed her. She smiled as she took her seat. Miriam Parrish was reading letters. But why starve yourself, Eleanor asked as she listened. She was thinner than ever.

She looked round the room as the letters were read. There had been a dance. Festoons of red and yellow paper were slung across the ceiling. The coloured picture of the Princess of Wales had loops of yellow roses at the corners; a sea-green ribbon across her breast, a round yellow dog on her lap, and pearls slung and knotted over her shoulders. She wore an air of serenity, of indifference; a queer comment upon their divisions, Eleanor thought; something that the Lazenbys worshipped; that Miss Sims derided; that Judd looked at cocking his eyebrows, picking his teeth. If he had had a son, he had told her, he would

have sent him to the Varsity. But she recalled herself. Major
Porter had turned to her.

"Now, Miss Pargiter," he said, drawing her in, because they
were both of the same social standing, "you haven't given us
your opinion."

She pulled herself together and gave him her opinion. She
had an opinion—a very definite opinion. She cleared her throat
and began.

THE SMOKE blowing through Peter Street had condensed, between the narrowness of the houses, into a fine grey veil. But
the houses on either side were clearly visible. Save for two in the
middle of the street, they were all precisely the same—yellow-
grey boxes with slate tents on top. Nothing whatever was happening; a few children were playing in the street, two cats turned
something over in the gutter with their paws. Yet a woman leaning out of the windows searched this way, that way, up and
down the street as if she were raking every cranny for something
to feed on. Her eyes, rapacious, greedy, like the eyes of a bird of
prey, were also sulky and sleepy, as if they had nothing to feed
their hunger upon. Nothing happened—nothing whatever. Still
she gazed up and down with her indolent dissatisfied stare.
Then a trap turned the corner. She watched it. It stopped in
front of the houses opposite which, since the sills were green,
and there was a plaque with a sunflower stamped on it over the
door, were different from the others. A little man in a tweed cap
got out and rapped at the door. It was opened by a woman who
was about to have a baby. She shook her head; looked up
and down the street; then shut the door. The man waited. The
horse stood patiently with the reins drooping and its head bent.
Another woman appeared at the window, with a white many-
chinned face, and an under lip that stood out like a ledge. Leaning out of the window side by side the two women watched the

man. He was bandy-legged; he was smoking. They passed some remark about him together. He walked up and down as if he were waiting for somebody. Now he threw away his cigarette. They watched him. What would he do next? Was he going to give his horse a feed? But here a tall woman wearing a coat and skirt of grey tweed came round the corner hastily; and the little man turned and touched his cap.

"SORRY I'M LATE," Eleanor called out, and Duffus touched his cap with the friendly smile that always pleased her.

"That's all right, Miss Pargiter," he said. She always hoped that he did not feel that she was the ordinary employer.

"Now we'll go over it," she said. She hated the job, but it had to be done.

The door was opened by Mrs. Toms, the downstairs lodger.

Oh, dear, thought Eleanor, observing the slant of her apron, another baby coming, after all I told her.

They went from room to room of the little house, Mrs. Toms and Mrs. Groves following after. There was a crack here; a stain there. Duffus had a foot-rule in his hand with which he tapped the plaster. The worst of it is, she thought, as she let Mrs. Toms do the talking, that I can't help liking him. It was his Welsh accent largely; he was a charming ruffian. He was as supple as an eel, she knew; but when he talked like that, in that sing-song, which reminded her of Welsh valleys . . . But he had cheated her at every point. There was a hole you could poke your finger through in the plaster.

"Look at that, Mr. Duffus, there —" she said, stooping and poking her finger. He was licking his pencil. She loved going to his yard with him and seeing him size up planks and bricks; she loved his technical words for things, his little hard words.

"Now we'll go upstairs," she said. He seemed to her like a fly struggling to haul itself up out of a saucer. It was touch and go with small employers like Duffus; they might haul themselves up and become the Judds of their day and send their sons to the Varsity; or on the other hand they might fall in and then— He had a wife and five children; she had seen them in the room behind the shop, playing with reels of cotton on the floor. And she always hoped that they would ask her in. . . . But here was the top floor where old Mrs. Potter lay bedridden. She knocked; she called out in a loud cheerful voice, "May we come in?"

There was no answer. The old woman was stone deaf; so in they went. There she was, as usual, doing nothing whatever, propped up in the corner of her bed.

"I've brought Mr. Duffus to look at your ceiling," Eleanor shouted.

The old woman looked up and began plucking with her hands like a large tousled ape. She looked at them wildly, suspiciously.

"The ceiling, Mr. Duffus," said Eleanor. She pointed to a yellow stain on the ceiling. The house had only been built five years; and yet everything wanted repairing. Duffus threw open the window and leant out. Mrs. Potter clutched hold of Eleanor's hand, as if she suspected that they were going to hurt her.

"We've come to look at your ceiling," Eleanor repeated very loudly. But the words conveyed nothing. The old woman went off into a whining plaint; the words ran themselves together into a chant that was half plaint, half curse. If only the Lord would take her. Every night, she said, she implored Him to let her go. All her children were dead.

"When I wake in the morning . . ." she began.

"Yes, yes, Mrs. Potter," Eleanor tried to soothe her; but her hands were firmly grasped.

"I pray Him to let me go," Mrs. Potter continued.

"It's the leaves in the gutter," said Duffus, popping his head in again.

"And the pain—" Mrs. Potter stretched out her hands; they were knotted and grooved like the gnarled roots of a tree.

"Yes, yes," said Eleanor. "But there's a leak; it's not only the dead leaves," she said to Duffus.

Duffus put his head out again.

"We're going to make you more comfortable," Eleanor shouted to the old woman. Now she was cringing and fawning; now she had pressed her hand to her lips.

Duffus drew his head in again.

"Have you found out what's wrong?" Eleanor said to him sharply. He was entering something in his pocket-book. She longed to go. Mrs. Potter was asking her to feel her shoulder. She felt her shoulder. Her hand was still grasped. There was medicine on the table; Miriam Parrish came every week. Why do we do it? she asked herself as Mrs. Potter went on talking. Why do we force her to live? she asked, looking at the medicine on the table. She could stand it no longer. She withdrew her hand.

"Good-bye, Mrs. Potter," she shouted. She was insincere; she was hearty. "We're going to mend your ceiling," she shouted. She shut the door. Mrs. Groves waddled in advance of her to show her the sink in the scullery. A wisp of yellow hair hung down behind her dirty ears. If I had to do this every day of my life, Eleanor thought, as she followed them down into the scullery, I should become a bag of bones like Miriam; with a string of beads. . . . And what's the use of that, she thought, stooping to smell the sink in the scullery.

"Well, Duffus," she said, facing him when the inspection was over, with the smell of drains still in her nose. "What d'you propose to do about it?"

Her anger was rising; it was his fault largely. He had swindled her. But as she stood facing him and observed his little under-fed body, and how his bow tie had worked up over his collar, she felt uncomfortable.

He shuffled and squirmed; she felt that she was going to lose her temper.

"If you can't make a good job of it," she said curtly, "I shall employ somebody else." She adopted the tone of the Colonel's daughter; the upper middle-class tone that she detested. She saw him turn sullen before her eyes. But she rubbed it in.

"You ought to be ashamed of it," she told him. He was impressed she could see. "Good morning," she said briefly.

The ingratiating smile was not produced for her benefit again, she observed. But you have to bully them or else they despise you, she thought as Mrs. Toms let her out, and once more she observed the slant in her apron. A crowd of children stood round staring at Duffus's pony. But none of them, she noticed, dared stroke the pony's nose.

SHE WAS LATE. She gave one look at the sunflower on the terra-cotta plaque. That symbol of her girlish sentiment amused her grimly. She had meant it to signify flowers, fields in the heart of London; but now it was cracked. She broke into her usual ambling trot. The movement seemed to break up the disagreeable crust; to jolt off the grasp of the old woman's hand that was still on her shoulder. She ran; she dodged. Shopping women got in her way. She dashed into the road waving her hand among the carts and horses. The conductor saw her, curved his arm round her and hauled her up. She had caught her bus.

She trod on the toe of a man in the corner, and pitched down between two elderly women. She was panting slightly; her hair was coming down; she was red with running. She cast a glance at her fellow-passengers. They all looked settled, elderly, as if their minds were made up. For some reason she always felt that she was the youngest person in an omnibus, but today, since she had won her scrap with Judd, she felt that she was grown up. The grey line of houses jolted up and down before her eyes as the omnibus trundled along the Bayswater Road. The shops were turning into houses; there were big houses and little houses; public houses and private houses. And here a church raised its filigree spire. Underneath were pipes, wires, drains. . . . Her lips began moving. She was talking to herself. There's always a public house, a library and a church, she was muttering.

THE MAN on whose toe she had trodden sized her up; a well-known type; with a bag; philanthropic; well nourished; a spinster; a virgin; like all the women of her class, cold; her passions had never been touched; yet not unattractive. She was laughing. . . . Here she looked up and caught his eye. She had been talking aloud to herself in an omnibus. She must cure herself of the habit. She must wait till she brushed her teeth. But luckily the bus was stopping. She jumped out. She began to walk quickly up Melrose Place. She felt vigorous and young. She noticed every-thing freshly after Devonshire. She looked down the long many-pillared vista of Abercorn Terrace. The houses, with their pillars and their front gardens, all looked highly respectable; in every front room she seemed to see a parlourmaid's arm sweep over the table, laying it for luncheon. In several rooms they were al-ready sitting down to luncheon; she could see them between the tent-shaped opening made by the curtains. She would be late for her own luncheon, she thought as she ran up the front steps and fitted her latch-key in the door. Then, as if someone were speak-ing, words formed in her mind. "Something pretty, something to wear." She stopped with her key in the lock. Maggie's birthday; her father's present; she had forgotten it. She paused. She turned, she ran down the steps again. She must go to Lamley's.

Mrs. Lamley, who had grown stout these last years, was masticating a mouthful of cold mutton in the back room when she saw Miss Eleanor through the glass door.

"Good morning, Miss Eleanor," she began, coming out.

"Something pretty, something to wear," Eleanor panted. She was looking very well—quite brown after her holiday, Mrs. Lamley noticed.

"For my niece—I mean cousin. Sir Digby's little girl," Eleanor brought out.

Mrs. Lamley deprecated the cheapness of her goods.

There were toy boats; dolls; twopenny gold watches—but nothing nice enough for Sir Digby's little girl. But Miss Eleanor was in a hurry.

"There," she said, pointing to a card of bead necklaces. "That'll do."

It looked a little cheap, Mrs. Lamley thought; reaching down a blue necklace with gold spots, but Miss Eleanor was in such a hurry that she wouldn't even have it wrapped in brown paper.

"I shall be late as it is, Mrs. Lamley," she said, with a genial wave of her hand; and off she ran.

Mrs. Lamley liked her. She always seemed so friendly. It was such a pity she didn't marry—such a mistake to let the younger sister marry before the elder. But then she had the Colonel to look after, and he was getting on now, Mrs. Lamley concluded, going back to her mutton in the back shop.

"MISS ELEANOR won't be a minute," said the Colonel as Crosby brought in the dishes. "Leave the covers on." He stood with his back to the fireplace waiting for her. Yes, he thought, I don't see why not. "I don't see why not," he repeated, looking at the dish-cover. Mira was on the scene again; the other fellow had turned out, as he knew he would, a bad egg. And what provision was he to make for Mira? What was he to do about it? It had struck him that he would like to put the whole thing before Eleanor. Why not after all? She's not a child any longer, he thought; and he didn't like this business of—of—shutting things up in drawers. But he felt some shyness at the thought of telling his own daughter.

"Here she is," he said abruptly to Crosby, who stood waiting mutely behind him.

No, no, he said to himself with sudden conviction, as Eleanor came in. I can't do it. For some reason when he saw her he realised that he could not tell her. And after all, he thought, seeing how bright-cheeked, how unconcerned she looked, she has her own life to live. A spasm of jealousy passed through him. She's got her own affairs to think about, he thought as they sat down.

She pushed a necklace across the table towards him.

"Hullo, what's that?" he said, looking at it blankly.

"Maggie's present, Papa," she said. "The best I could do. . . . I'm afraid it's rather cheap."

"Yes; that'll do very nicely," he said, glancing at it absent-mindedly. "Just what she'll like," he added, shoving it to one side. He began to carve the chicken.

She was very hungry; she was still rather breathless. She felt a little "spun round," as she put it to herself. What did you spin things round on? she wondered, helping herself to bread sauce — a pivot? The scene had changed so often that morning; and every scene required a different adjustment; bringing this to the front; sinking that to the depths. And now she felt nothing; hungry merely; merely a chicken-eater; blank. But as she ate, the sense of her father imposed itself. She liked his solidity, as he sat opposite her munching his chicken methodically. What had he been doing, she wondered. Taking shares out of one company and putting them in another? He roused himself.

"Well, how was the Committee?" he asked. She told him, exaggerating her triumph with Judd.

"That's right. Stand up to 'em, Nell. Don't let yourself be sat on," he said. He was proud of her in his own way; and she liked him to be proud of her. At the same time she did not mention Duffus and Rigby Cottages. He had no sympathy with people who were foolish about money, and she never got a penny interest: it all went on repairs. She turned the conversation to Morris and his case at the Law Courts. She looked at her watch again. Her sister-in-law Celia had told her to meet her at the Law Courts at two-thirty sharp.

"I shall have to hurry," she said.

"Ah, but these lawyer chaps always know how to spin things out," said the Colonel. "Who's the Judge?"

"Sanders Curry," said Eleanor.

"Then it'll last till Domesday," said the Colonel.

"Which Court's he sitting in?" he asked.

Eleanor did not know.

"Here, Crosby—" said the Colonel. He sent Crosby for *The Times*. He began opening and turning the great sheets with his clumsy fingers as Eleanor swallowed her tart. By the time she had poured out coffee he had found out in which court the case was being heard.

"And you're going to the City, Papa?" she said as she put down her cup.

"Yes. To a meeting," he said. He loved going to the City, whatever he did there.

"Odd it should be Curry who's trying the case," she said, rising. They had dined with him not long ago in a dreary great house somewhere off Queen's Gate.

"D'you remember that party?" she said, getting up. "The old oak?" Curry collected chests.

"All shams I suspect," said her father. "Don't hurry," he expostulated. "Take a cab, Nell—if you want any change—" he began, fumbling with his curtailed fingers for silver. As she watched him Eleanor felt the old childish feeling that his pockets were bottomless silver mines from which half-crowns could be dug eternally.

"Well then," she said, taking the coins, "we shall meet at tea."

"No," he reminded her, "I'm going round by the Digbys'."

He took the necklace in his large hairy hand. It looked a little cheap, Eleanor was afraid.

"And what about a box for this, eh?" he asked.

"Crosby, find a box for the necklace," said Eleanor. And Crosby, suddenly radiating importance, hurried off to the basement.

"It'll be dinner then," she said to her father. That'll mean, she thought with relief, that I needn't be back for tea.

"Yes, dinner," he said. He held a spill of paper in his hand which he was applying to the end of his cigar. He sucked. A little puff of smoke rose from the cigar. She liked the smell of cigars. She stood for a moment and drew it in.

"And give my love to Aunt Eugénie," she said. He nodded as he puffed at his cigar.

IT WAS A TREAT to take a hansom—it saved fifteen minutes. She leant back in the corner, with a little sigh of content, as the flaps clicked above her knees. For a minute her mind was completely vacant. She enjoyed the peace, the silence, the rest from exertion as she sat there in the corner of the cab. She felt detached, a spectator, as it trotted along. The morning had been a rush; one thing on top of another. Now, until she reached the Law Courts, she could sit and do nothing. It was a long way; and the horse was a plodding horse, a red-coated hairy horse. It kept up its steady jog-trot all down the Bayswater Road. There was very little traffic; people were still at luncheon. A soft grey mist filled up the distance; the bells jingled; the houses passed. She ceased to notice what houses they were passing. She half shut

her eyes, and then, involuntarily, she saw her own hand take a
letter from the hall table. When? That very morning. What had
she done with it? Put it in her bag? Yes. There it was, unopened;
a letter from Martin in India. She would read it as they drove
along. It was written on very thin paper in Martin's little hand.
It was longer than usual; it was about an adventure with somebody called Renton. Who was Renton? She could not remember. "We started at dawn," she read.

She looked out of the window. They were being held up by
traffic at the Marble Arch. Carriages were coming out of the
Park. A horse pranced; but the coachman had him well in hand.

She read again: "I found myself alone in the middle of the
jungle. . . ."

But what were you doing? she asked.

She saw her brother; his red hair; his round face; and the
rather pugnacious expression which always made her afraid that
he would get himself into trouble one of these days. And so he
had, apparently.

"I had lost my way; and the sun was sinking," she read.

"The sun was sinking . . ." Eleanor repeated, glancing ahead
of her down Oxford Street. The sun shone on dresses in a window. A jungle was a very thick wood, she supposed; made of
stunted little trees; dark green in colour. Martin was in the
jungle alone, and the sun was sinking. What happened next? "I
thought it better to stay where I was." So he stood in the midst
of little trees alone, in the jungle; and the sun was sinking. The
street before her lost its detail. It must have been cold, she
thought, when the sun sank. She read again. He had to make a
fire. "I looked in my pocket and found that I had only two
matches . . . The first match went out." She saw a heap of dry
sticks and Martin alone watching the match go out. "Then I lit
the other, and by sheer luck it did the trick." The paper began
to burn; the twigs caught; a fan of fire blazed up. She skipped

on in her anxiety to reach the end . . . "—once I thought I heard voices shouting, but they died away."

"They died away!" said Eleanor aloud.

They had stopped at Chancery Lane. An old woman was being helped across the road by a policeman; but the road was a jungle.

"They died away," she said. "And then?"

". . . I climbed a tree . . . I saw the track . . . the sun was rising. . . . They had given me up for dead."

The cab stopped. For a moment Eleanor sat still. She saw nothing but stunted little trees, and her brother looking at the sun rising over the jungle. The sun was rising. Flames for a moment danced over the vast funereal mass of the Law Courts. It was the second match that did the trick, she said to herself as she paid the driver and went in.

"OH, THERE YOU ARE!" cried a little woman in furs, who was standing by one of the doors.

"I had given you up. I was just going in." She was a small cat-faced woman, worried, but very proud of her husband.

They pushed through the swing doors into the Court where the case was being tried. It seemed dark and crowded at first. Men in wigs and gowns were getting up and sitting down and coming in and going out like a flock of birds settling here and there on a field. They all looked unfamiliar; she could not see Morris. She looked about her, trying to find him.

"There he is," Celia whispered.

One of the barristers in the front row turned his head. It was Morris; but how odd he looked in his yellow wig! His glance passed over them without any sign of recognition. Nor did she smile at him; the solemn sallow atmosphere forbade personalities; there was something ceremonial about it all. From where she sat she could see his face in profile; the wig squared his forehead, and gave him a framed look, like a picture. Never had she seen him to such advantage; with such a brow, with such a nose. She glanced round. They all looked like pictures; all the barristers looked emphatic, cut out, like eighteenth-century portraits hung upon a wall. They were still rising and settling, laughing, talking. . . . Suddenly a door was thrown open. The usher demanded silence for his lordship. There was silence; everybody stood up; and the Judge came in. He made one bow and took his seat under the Lion and the Unicorn. Eleanor felt a little thrill of awe run through her. That was old Curry. But how transformed! Last time she had seen him he was sitting at the head of a dinner-table; a long yellow strip of embroidery went rippling down the middle; and he had taken her, with a candle, round the drawing-room to look at his old oak. But now, there he was, awful, magisterial, in his robes.

A barrister had risen. She tried to follow what the man with a big nose was saying; but it was difficult to pick it up now. She listened, however. Then another barrister rose—a chicken-breasted little man, wearing gold pince-nez. He was reading some document; then he too began to argue. She could understand parts of what he was saying; though how it bore on the case she did not know. When was Morris going to speak, she wondered? Not yet apparently. As her father had said, these lawyer chaps knew how to spin things out. There had been no need to hurry over luncheon; an omnibus would have done just as well. She fixed her eyes on Morris. He was cracking some joke with the sandy man next to him. Those were his cronies, she thought; this was his life. She remembered his passion for the Bar as a boy. It was she who had talked Papa round; one morning she had taken her life in her hand and gone to his study . . . but now, to her excitement, Morris himself got up.

She felt her sister-in-law stiffen with nervousness and clasp her little bag tightly. Morris looked very tall, and very black and white as he began. One hand was on the edge of his gown. How well she knew that gesture of Morris's, she thought—grasping something, so that you saw the white scar where he had cut himself bathing. But she did not recognise the other gesture— the way he flung his arm out. That belonged to his public life, his life in the Courts. And his voice was unfamiliar. But every now and then as he warmed to his speech, there was a tone in his voice that made her smile; it was his private voice. She could not help half turning to her sister-in-law as if to say, How like Morris! But Celia was looking with absolute fixity ahead of her at her husband. Eleanor, too, tried to fix her mind upon the argument. He spoke with extraordinary clearness; he spaced his words beautifully. Suddenly the Judge interrupted:

"Do I understand you to hold, Mr. Pargiter . . . ?" he said in urbane yet awful tones; and Eleanor was thrilled to see how instantly Morris stopped short; how respectfully he bent his head as the Judge spoke.

But will he know the answer? she thought, as if he were a child, shifting in her seat with nervousness lest he might break down. But he had the answer at his finger-ends. Without hurry or flutter he opened a book; found his place; read out a passage, upon which old Curry nodded, and made a note in the great volume that lay open in front of him. She was immensely relieved.

"How well he did that!" she whispered. Her sister-in-law nodded; but she still grasped her bag tightly. Eleanor felt that she could relax. She glanced round her. It was an odd mixture of solemnity and licence. Barristers kept coming in and out. They stood leaning against the wall of the Court. In the pale top light all their faces looked parchment-coloured; all their features seemed cut out. They had lit the gas. She gazed at the Judge himself. He was now lying back in his great carved chair under the Lion and the Unicorn, listening. He looked infinitely sad and wise, as if words had been beating upon him for centuries. Now he opened his heavy eyes, wrinkled his forehead, and the little hand that emerged frailly from the enormous cuff wrote a few words in the great volume. Then again he lapsed with half-shut eyes into his eternal vigil over the strife of unhappy human beings. Her mind wandered. She leant back against the hard wooden seat and let the tide of oblivion flow over her. Scenes from her morning began to form themselves; to obtrude themselves. Judd at the Committee; her father reading the paper; the old woman plucking at her hand; the parlourmaid sweeping the silver over the table; and Martin lighting his second match in the jungle. . . .

She fidgeted. The air was fuggy; the light dim; and the Judge now that the first glamour had worn off, looked fretful; no longer immune from human weakness, and she remembered with a smile how very gullible he was, there in that hideous house in Queen's Gate, about old oak. "This I picked up at Whitby," he had said. And it was a sham. She wanted to laugh; she wanted to move. She rose and whispered:

"I'm going."

Her sister-in-law made a little murmur, perhaps of protest. But Eleanor made her way as silently as she could through the swing doors, out into the street.

THE UPROAR, the confusion, the space of the Strand came upon her with a shock of relief. She felt herself expand. It was still daylight here; a rush, a stir, a turmoil of variegated life came racing towards her. It was as if something had broken loose — in her, in the world. She seemed, after her concentration, to be dissipated, tossed about. She wandered along the Strand, looking with pleasure at the racing street; at the shops full of bright chains and leather cases; at the white-faced churches; at the irregular jagged roofs laced across and across with wires. Above

was the dazzle of a watery but gleaming sky. The wind blew in
her face. She breathed in a gulp of fresh wet air. And that man,
she thought, thinking of the dark little Court and its cut-out
faces, has to sit there all day, every day. She saw Sanders Curry
again, lying back in his great chair, with his face falling in folds
of iron. Every day, all day, she thought, arguing points of law.
How could Morris stand it? But he had always wanted to go to
the Bar.

Cabs, vans and omnibuses streamed past; they seemed to
rush the air into her face; they splashed the mud onto the pavement. People jostled and hustled and she quickened her pace in
time with theirs. She was stopped by a van turning down one of
the little steep streets that led to the river. She looked up and
saw the clouds moving between the roofs, dark clouds, rain-
swollen; wandering, indifferent clouds. She walked on.

Again she was stopped at the entrance to Charing Cross station. The sky was wide at that point. She saw a file of birds flying high, flying together; crossing the sky. She watched them.
Again she walked on. People on foot, people in cabs were being
sucked in like straws round the piers of a bridge; she had to wait.
Cabs piled with boxes went past her.

She envied them. She wished she were going abroad; to
Italy, to India. . . . Then she felt vaguely that something was happening. The paper boys at the gates were dealing out papers
with unusual rapidity. Men were snatching them and opening
them and reading them as they walked on. She looked at a placard that was crumpled across a boy's legs. "Death" was written
in very large black letters.

Then the placard blew straight, and she read another word:
"Parnell."

"Dead" . . . she repeated. "Parnell." She was dazed for a
moment. How could he be dead—Parnell? She bought a paper.
They said so. . . .

"Parnell is dead!" she said aloud. She looked up and saw the sky again; clouds were passing; she looked down into the street. A man pointed at the news with his forefinger. Parnell is dead, he was saying. He was gloating. But how could he be dead? It was like something fading in the sky.

She walked slowly along towards Trafalgar Square, holding the paper in her hand. Suddenly the whole scene froze into immobility. A man was joined to a pillar; a lion was joined to a man; they seemed stilled, connected, as if they would never move again.

She crossed into Trafalgar Square. Birds chattered shrilly somewhere. She stopped by the fountain and looked down into the large basin full of water. The water rippled black as the wind ruffled it. There were reflections in the water, branches and a pale strip of sky. What a dream, she murmured; what a dream . . . But someone jostled her. She turned. She must go to Delia. Delia had cared. Delia had cared passionately. What was it she used to say—flinging out of the house, leaving them all for the Cause, for this man? Justice, Liberty? She must go to her. This would be the end of all her dreams. She turned and hailed a cab.

She leant over the flaps of the cab looking out. The streets they were driving through were horribly poor; and not only poor, she thought, but vicious. Here was the vice, the obscenity, the reality of London. It was lurid in the mixed evening light. Lamps were being lit. Paper-boys were crying, Parnell . . . Parnell. He's dead, she said to herself, still conscious of the two worlds; one flowing in wide sweeps overhead, the other tip-tapping circumscribed upon the pavement. But here she was . . . She held up her hand. She stopped the cab opposite a little row of posts in an alley. She got out and made her way into the Square.

The sound of the traffic was dulled. It was very silent here. In the October afternoon, with dead leaves falling, the old faded Square looked dingy and decrepit and full of mist. The houses

were let out in offices, to societies, to people whose names were
pinned up on the door-posts. The whole neighbourhood
seemed to her foreign and sinister. She came to the old Queen
Anne doorway with its heavy carved eyebrows and pressed the
bell at the top of six or seven bells. Names were written over
them, sometimes only on visiting-cards. Nobody came. She
pushed the door open and went in; she mounted the wooden
stairs with carved bannisters, that seemed to have been degraded from their past dignity. Jugs of milk with bills under
them stood in the deep window-seats. Some of the panes were
broken. Outside Delia's door, at the top, there was a milk-jug
too, but it was empty. Her card was fixed by a drawing-pin to a
panel. She knocked and waited. There was no sound. She
turned the handle. The door was locked. She stood for a moment listening. A little window at the side gave on to the square.
Pigeons crooned on the tree-tops. The traffic hummed far off;
she could just hear paper-boys crying death . . . death . . . death.
The leaves were falling. She turned and went downstairs.

She strolled along the streets. Children had chalked the
pavement into squares; women leant from the upper windows,
raking the street with a rapacious, dissatisfied stare. Rooms were
let out to single gentlemen only. There were cards in them
which said "Furnished Apartments" or "Bed and Breakfast."
She guessed at the life that went on behind those thick yellow
curtains. This was the purlieus in which her sister lived, she
thought, turning; she must often come back this way at night
alone. Then she went back to the Square and climbed the stairs
and rattled at the door again. But there was no sound within.
She stood for a moment watching the leaves fall; she heard the
paper-boys crying and the pigeons crooning in the tree-tops.
Take two coos, Taffy, take two coos, Taffy, tak . . . Then a leaf
fell.

———

THE TRAFFIC at Charing Cross thickened as the afternoon
wore on. People on foot, people in cabs were being sucked in at
the gates of the station. Men swung along at a great pace as if
there were some demon in the station who would be enraged if
they kept him waiting. But even so they paused and snatched a
paper as they passed. The clouds parting and massing let the
light shine and then veiled it. The mud, now dark brown, now
liquid gold, was splashed up by the wheels and hooves, and in
the general churn and uproar the shrill chatter of the birds on
the eaves was silenced. The hansoms jingled and passed; jingled
and passed. At last among all the jingling cabs came one in
which sat a stout red-faced man holding a flower wrapped in
tissue-paper — the Colonel.

"HI!" HE CRIED as the cab passed the gates; and drove one
hand through the trap door in the roof. He leant out and a paper
was thrust up at him.

"Parnell!" he exclaimed, as he fumbled for his glasses.
"Dead, by Jove!"

The cab trotted on. He read the news two or three times
over. He's dead, he said, taking off his glasses. A shock of something like relief, of something that had a tinge of triumph in it,
went through him as he leant back in the corner. Well, he said
to himself, he's dead — that unscrupulous adventurer — that ag-
itator who had done all the mischief, that man . . . Some feeling
connected with his own daughter here formed in him; he could
not say exactly what, but it made him frown. Anyhow he's dead
now, he thought. How had he died? Had he killed himself? It
wouldn't be surprising. . . . Anyhow he was dead and that was an
end of it. He sat holding the paper crumpled in one hand, the
flower wrapped in tissue paper in the other, as the cab drove
down Whitehall. . . . One could respect him, he thought, as the
cab passed the House of Commons, which was more than could

be said for some of the other fellows . . . and there'd been a lot of nonsense talked about the divorce case. He looked out. The cab was driving near a certain street where he used to stop and look about him years ago. He turned and glanced down a street to the right. But a man in public life can't afford to do those things, he thought. He gave a little nod as the cab passed on. And now she's written to ask me for money, he thought. The other chap had turned out, as he knew he would, a bad egg. She'd lost all her looks, he was thinking; she had grown very stout. Well, he could afford to be generous. He put on his glasses again and read the City news.

It would make no difference, Parnell's death, coming now, he thought. Had he lived, had the scandal died down—he looked up. The cab was going the long way round as usual. "Left!" he shouted, "Left!" as the driver, as they always did, took the wrong turning.

IN THE RATHER dark basement at Browne Street, the Italian manservant was reading the paper in his shirt sleeves, when the housemaid waltzed in carrying a hat.

"Look what she's given me!" she cried. To atone for the mess in the drawing-room, Lady Pargiter had given her a hat. "Ain't I stylish?" she said, pausing in front of the glass with the great Italian hat that looked as if it were made of spun glass on one side of her head. And Antonio had to drop his paper and catch her round the waist from sheer gallantry, since she was no beauty, and her action was merely a parody of what he remembered in the hill towns of Tuscany. But a cab stopped in front of the railings; two legs stood still there, and he must detach himself, put on his jacket and go upstairs to answer the bell.

HE TAKES HIS TIME, the Colonel thought, as he stood on the doorstep waiting. The shock of the death had been absorbed almost; it still swept round in his system; but did not prevent him from thinking, as he stood there, that they had had the bricks re-pointed; but how had they money to spare, with the three boys to educate, and the two little girls? Eugénie was a clever woman of course; but he wished she would get a parlourmaid instead of these Italian dagoes who always seemed to be swallowing macaroni. Here the door opened, and as he went upstairs he thought he heard, from somewhere in the background, a shout of laughter.

He liked Eugénie's drawing-room, he thought, as he stood there waiting. It was very untidy. There was a litter of shavings from something that was being unpacked on the floor. They had been to Italy, he remembered. A looking-glass stood on the table. It was probably one of the things she had picked up there: the sort of thing that people did pick up in Italy; an old glass, covered with spots. He straightened his tie in front of it.

But I prefer a glass in which one can see oneself, he thought, turning away. There was the piano open; and the tea— he smiled—with the cup half full as usual; and branches stuck about the room, branches of withering red and yellow leaves. She liked flowers. He was glad he had remembered to bring her his usual gift. He held the flower wrapped in tissue paper in front of him. But why was the room so full of smoke? A gust blew in. Both windows in the back room were open, and the smoke was blowing in from the garden. Were they burning weeds, he wondered? He walked to the window and looked out. Yes, there they were—Eugénie and the two little girls. There was a bonfire. As he looked, Magdalena, the little girl who was his favourite, tossed a whole armful of dead leaves. She jerked them as high as she could, and the fire blazed up. A great fan of red flame flung out.

"That's dangerous!" he called out.

Eugénie pulled the children back. They were dancing with

excitement. The other little girl, Sara, ducked under her mother's arm, seized another armful of leaves and flung them again. A great fan of red flame flung out. Then the Italian servant came and mentioned his name. He tapped on the window. Eugénie turned and saw him. She held the children back with one hand and raised the other in welcome.

"Stay where you are!" she cried. "We're coming!"

A cloud of smoke blew straight at him; it made his eyes water, and he turned and sat down in the chair by the sofa. In another second she came, hurrying towards him with both her hands stretched out. He rose and took them.

"We're having a bonfire," she said. Her eyes were glowing; her hair was looping down. "That's why I'm all so blown-about," she added, putting her hand to her head. She was untidy, but extremely handsome all the same, Abel thought. A fine large woman, growing ample, he noted as she shook hands; but it suited her. He admired that type more than the pink-and-white pretty Englishwoman. The flesh flowed over her like warm yellow wax; she had great dark eyes like a foreigner, and a nose with a ripple in it. He held out his camellia; his customary gift. She made a little exclamation as she took the flower from the tissue paper and sat down.

"How very good of you!" she said, and held it for a moment in front of her, and then did what he had often seen her do with a flower—put the stalk between her lips. Her movements charmed him as usual.

"Having a bonfire for the birthday?" he asked. . . . "No, no, no," he protested, "I don't want tea."

She had taken her cup, and sipped the cold tea that was left in it. As he watched her, some memory of the East came back to him; so women sat in hot countries in their doorways in the sun. But it was very cold at the moment with the window open and the smoke blowing in. He still had his newspaper in his hand; he laid it on the table.

"Seen the news?" he asked.

She put down her cup and slightly opened her large dark eyes. Immense reserves of emotion seemed to dwell in them. As she waited for him to speak, she raised her hand as if in expectation.

"Parnell," said Abel briefly. "He's dead."

"Dead?" Eugénie echoed him. She let her hand fall dramatically.

"Yes. At Brighton. Yesterday."

"Parnell is dead!" she repeated.

"So they say," said the Colonel. Her emotion always made him feel more matter-of-fact; but he liked it. She took up the paper.

"Poor thing!" she exclaimed, letting it fall.

"Poor thing?" he repeated. Her eyes were full of tears. He was puzzled. Did she mean Kitty O'Shea? He hadn't thought of her.

"She ruined his career for him," he said with a little snort.

"Ah, but how she must have loved him!" she murmured.

She drew her hand over her eyes. The Colonel was silent for a moment. Her emotion seemed to him out of all proportion to its object; but it was genuine. He liked it.

"Yes," he said, rather stiffly. "Yes, I suppose so." Eugénie picked up the flower again and held it, twirling it. She was oddly absentminded now and then, but he always felt at his ease with her. His body relaxed. He felt relieved of some obstruction in her presence.

"How people suffer! . . ." she murmured, looking at the flower. "How they suffer, Abel!" she said. She turned and looked straight at him.

A great gust of smoke blew in from the other room.

"You don't mind the draught?" he asked, looking at the window. She did not answer at once; she was twirling her flower. Then she roused herself and smiled.

"Yes, yes. Shut it!" she said with a wave of her hand. He went and shut the window. When he turned round, she had got up and was standing at the looking-glass, arranging her hair.

"We've had a bonfire for Maggie's birthday," she murmured, looking at herself in the Venetian glass that was covered with spots. "That's why, that's why—" she smoothed her hair and fixed the camellia in her dress. "I'm so very—"

She put her head a little on one side as if to observe the effect of the flower in her dress. The Colonel sat down and waited. He glanced at his paper.

"They seem to be hushing things up," he said.

"You don't mean—" Eugénie was beginning; but here the door opened and the children came in. Maggie, the elder, came first; the other little girl, Sara, hung back behind her.

"Hullo!" the Colonel exclaimed. "Here they are!" He turned round. He was very fond of children. "Many happy returns of the day to you, Maggie!" He felt in his pocket for the necklace that Crosby had done up in a cardboard box. Maggie came up to him to take it. Her hair had been brushed, and she was dressed in a stiff clean frock. She took the parcel and undid it; she held the blue-and-gold necklace dangling from her finger. For a moment the Colonel doubted whether she liked it. It looked a little garish as she held it dangling in her hand. And she was silent. Her mother at once supplied the words she should have spoken.

"How lovely, Maggie! How perfectly lovely!" Maggie held the beads in her hand and said nothing.

"Thank Uncle Abel for the lovely necklace," her mother prompted her.

"Thank you for the necklace, Uncle Abel," said Maggie. She spoke directly and accurately, but the Colonel felt another twinge of doubt. A pang of disappointment out of all proportion to its object came over him. Her mother, however, fastened it round her neck. Then she turned away to her sister, who was peeping from behind a chair.

"Come, Sara," said her mother. "Come and say how-d'you-do."

She held out her hand partly to coax the little girl, partly, Abel guessed, in order to conceal the very slight deformity that always made him uncomfortable. She had been dropped when she was a baby; one shoulder was slightly higher than the other; it made him feel squeamish; he could not bear the least deformity in a child. It did not affect her spirits, however. She skipped up to him, whirling round on her toe, and kissed him lightly on the cheek. Then she tugged at her sister's frock, and they both rushed away into the back room laughing.

"They are going to admire your lovely present, Abel," said Eugénie. "How you spoil them!—and me too," she added, touching the camellia on her breast.

"I hope she liked it?" he asked. Eugénie did not answer him. She had taken up the cup of cold tea again and was sipping it in her indolent Southern manner.

"And now," she said, leaning back comfortably, "tell me all your news."

The Colonel, too, lay back in his chair. He pondered for a moment. What was his news? Nothing occurred to him on the spur of the moment. With Eugénie, too, he always wanted to make a little splash; she put a shine on things. While he hesitated, she began:

"We've been having a wonderful time in Venice! I took the children. That's why we're all so brown. We had rooms not on the Grand Canal—I hate the Grand Canal—but just off it.

Two weeks of blazing sun; and the colours"— she hesitated—
"marvellous!" she exclaimed, "marvellous!" She threw out her
hand. She had gestures of extraordinary significance. That's how
she rigs things up, he thought. But he liked her for it.

He had not been to Venice for years.

"Any pleasant people there?" he asked.

"Not a soul," she said. "Not a soul. No one except a dreadful Miss ———. One of those women who make one ashamed of
one's country," she said energetically.

"I know 'em," he chuckled.

"But coming back from the Lido in the evening," she resumed, "with the clouds above and the water below—we had a
balcony; we used to sit there." She paused.

"Was Digby with you?" the Colonel asked.

"No, poor Digby. He took his holiday earlier, in August. He
was up in Scotland with the Lasswades shooting. It does him
good, you know." There she goes, rigging things up again, he
thought.

But she resumed.

"Now tell me about the family. Martin and Eleanor, Hugh
and Milly, Morris and . . ." She hesitated; he suspected that she
had forgotten the name of Morris's wife.

"Celia," he said. He stopped. He wanted to tell her about
Mira. But he told her about the family: Hugh and Milly; Morris
and Celia. And Edward.

"They seem to think a lot of him at Oxford," he said
gruffly. He was very proud of Edward.

"And Delia?" said Eugénie. She glanced at the paper. The
Colonel at once lost his affability. He looked glum and formidable, like an old bull with his head down, she thought.

"Perhaps it will bring her to her senses," he said sternly.
They were silent for a moment. There were shouts of laughter
from the garden.

"Oh, those children!" she exclaimed. She rose and went to the window. The Colonel followed her. The children had stolen back into the garden. The bonfire was burning fiercely. A clear pillar of flame rose in the middle of the garden. The little girls were laughing and shouting as they danced round it. A shabby old man, something like a decayed groom to look at, stood there with a rake in his hand. Eugénie flung up the window and cried out. But they went on dancing. The Colonel leant out too; they looked like wild creatures with their hair flying. He would have liked to go down and jump over the bonfire, but he was too old. The flames leapt high—clear gold, bright red.

"Bravo!" he cried, clapping his hands. "Bravo!"

"Little demons!" said Eugénie. She was as much excited as they were, he observed. She leant out of the window and cried to the old man with the rake:

"Make it blaze! Make it blaze!"

But the old man was raking out the fire. The sticks were scattered. The flames had sunk.

The old man pushed the children away.

"Well, that's over," said Eugénie, heaving a sigh. She turned. Someone had come into the room.

"Oh, Digby, I never heard you!" she exclaimed. Digby stood there with a case in his hands.

"Hullo, Digby!" said Abel, shaking hands.

"What's all the smoke?" said Digby, looking round him.

He's aged a bit, Abel thought. There he stood in his frock coat with the top buttons undone. His coat was a little threadbare; his hair was white on top. But he was very handsome; beside him the Colonel felt large, weather-beaten and rough. He was a little ashamed that he had been caught leaning out of the window clapping his hands. He looks older, he thought, as they stood side by side; yet he's five years younger than I am. He was a distinguished man in his way; the top of his tree; a knight and all the rest of it. But he's not as rich as I am, he remembered with satisfaction; for he had always been the failure of the two.

"You look so tired, Digby!" Eugénie exclaimed, sitting down. "He ought to take a real holiday," she said, turning to Abel. "I wish you'd tell him so." Digby brushed away a white thread that had stuck to his trousers. He coughed slightly. The room was full of smoke.

"What's all the smoke for?" he asked his wife.

"We've been having a bonfire for Maggie's birthday," she said as if excusing herself.

"Oh, yes," he said. Abel was irritated; Maggie was his favourite; her father ought to have remembered her birthday.

"Yes," said Eugénie, turning to Abel again, "he lets everybody else take a holiday, but he never takes one himself. And then, when he's done a full day's work at the office, he comes back with his bag full of papers—" She pointed at the bag.

"You shouldn't work after dinner," said Abel. "That's a bad habit." Digby did look a bit off-colour, he thought. Digby brushed aside this feminine effusiveness.

"Seen the news?" he said to his brother, indicating the paper.

"Yes. By Jove!" said Abel. He liked talking politics with his brother, though he slightly resented his official airs as if he could say more but must not. And then it's all in the papers the day after, he thought. Still they always talked politics. Eugénie lying back in her corner always let them talk; she never interrupted. But at length she got up and began tidying the litter that had fallen from the packing-case. Digby stopped what he was saying and watched her. He was looking at the glass.

"Like it?" said Eugénie, with her hand on the frame.

"Yes," said Digby; but there was a hint of criticism in his voice. "Quite a pretty one."

"It's only for my bedroom," she said quickly. Digby watched her stuffing the bits of paper into the box.

"Remember," he said, "we're dining with the Chathams tonight."

"I know." She touched her hair again. "I shall have to make myself tidy," she said. Who were "the Chathams"? Abel wondered. Bigwigs, mandarins, he supposed half contemptuously. They moved a great deal in that world. He took it as a hint that he should go. They had come to the end of what they had to say to each other—he and Digby. He still hoped, however, that he might talk with Eugénie alone.

"About this African business—" he began, bethinking him of another question—when the children came in; they had come to say good-night. Maggie was wearing his necklace and it looked very pretty, he thought, or was it she who looked so pretty? But their frocks, their clean blue and pink frocks, were crumpled; they were smudged with the sooty London leaves that they had been holding in their arms.

"Grubby little ruffians!" he said, smiling at them. "Why d'you wear your best clothes to play in the garden?" said Sir Digby, as he kissed Maggie. He said it jokingly, but there was a hint of disapproval in his tones. Maggie made no answer. Her eyes were riveted on the camellia that her mother wore in the front of her dress. She went up and stood looking at her.

"And you—what a little sweep!" said Sir Digby, pointing to Sara.

"It's Maggie's birthday," said Eugénie, holding out her arm again as if to protect the little girl.

"That is a reason, I should have thought," said Sir Digby, surveying his daughters, "to—er—to—er—reform one's habits." He stumbled, trying to make his sentence sound playful; but it turned out as it generally did when he talked to the children, lame and rather pompous.

Sara looked at her father as if she were considering him.

"To — er — to — er — reform one's habits," she repeated. Emptied of all meaning, she had got the rhythm of his words exactly. The effect was somehow comic. The Colonel laughed; but Digby, he felt, was annoyed. He only patted Sara on the head when she came to say good-night; but he kissed Maggie as she passed him.

"Had a nice birthday?" he said, pulling her to him. Abel made it an excuse to go.

"But there is no need for you to go yet, Abel?" Eugénie protested as he held out his hand.

She kept hold of his hand as if to prevent him from going. What did she mean? Did she want him to stay, did she want him to go? Her eyes, her large dark eyes, were ambiguous.

"But you're dining out?" he said.

"Yes," she replied, letting his hand fall, and as she said no more there was nothing for it, he supposed — he must take himself off.

"Oh, I can find my way out alone," he said as he left the room.

He went downstairs rather slowly. He felt depressed and disappointed. He had not seen her alone; he had not told her anything. Perhaps he never would tell anybody anything. After all, he thought as he went downstairs, slowly, heavily, it was his own affair; it didn't matter to anybody else. One must burn one's own smoke, he thought as he took his hat. He glanced round.

Yes, . . . the house was full of pretty things. He looked vaguely at a great crimson chair with gilt claws that stood in the hall. He envied Digby his house, his wife, his children. He was getting old, he felt. All his children were grown-up; they had left him. He paused on the doorstep and looked out into the street. It was quite dark; lamps were lit; the autumn was drawing in; and as he marched up the dark windy street, now spotted with raindrops, a puff of smoke blew full in his face; and leaves were falling.

IT WAS midsummer; and the nights were hot. The moon, falling on water, made it white, inscrutable, whether deep or shallow. But where the moonlight fell on solid objects it gave them a burnish and a silver plating, so that even the leaves in country roads seemed varnished. All along the silent country roads leading to London carts plodded; the iron reins fixed in the iron hands, for vegetables, fruit, flowers travelled slowly. Heaped high with round crates of cabbage, cherries, carnations, they looked like caravans piled with the goods of tribes migrating in search of water, driven by enemies to seek new pasturage. On they plodded, down this road, that road, keeping close to the kerb. Even the horses, had they been blind, could have heard the hum of London in the distance; and the drivers, dozing, yet saw through half-shut eyes the fiery gauze of the eternally burning city. At dawn, at Covent Garden, they laid down their burdens; tables and trestles, even the cobbles were frilled as with some celestial laundry with cabbages, cherries and carnations.

All the windows were open. Music sounded. From behind crimson curtains, rendered semi-transparent and sometimes blowing wide, came the sound of the eternal waltz—After the ball is over, after the dance is done—like a serpent that swallowed its own tail, since the ring was complete from Hammersmith to Shoreditch. Over and over again it was repeated by trombones outside public houses; errand boys whistled it; bands inside private rooms where people were dancing played it. There they sat at little tables at Wapping in the romantic Inn that overhung the river, between timber warehouses where barges were moored; and here again in Mayfair. Each table had its lamp; its canopy of tight red silk, and the flowers that had sucked damp from the earth that noon relaxed and spread their petals in vases. Each table had its pyramid of strawberries, its pale plump quail; and Martin, after India, after Africa, found it exciting to talk to a girl with bare shoulders, to a woman iridescent with green beetles' wings in her hair in a manner that the waltz condoned and half concealed under its amorous blandishments. Did it matter what one said? For she looked over her shoulder, only half listening, as a man came in wearing decorations, and a lady, in black with diamonds, beckoned him to a private corner.

As the night wore on a tender blue light lay on the market carts still plodding close to the kerb, past Westminster, past the yellow round clocks, the coffee stalls and the statues that stood there in the dawn holding so stiffly their rods or rolls of paper. And the scavengers followed after, sluicing the pavements. Cigarette ends, little bits of silver paper, orange peel—all the litter of the day was swept off the pavement and still the carts plodded, and the cabs trotted, indefatigably, along the dowdy pavements of Kensington, under the sparkling lights of Mayfair, carrying ladies with high headdresses and gentlemen in white waistcoats along the hammered dry roads which looked in the moonlight as if they were plated with silver.

"Look!" said Eugénie as the cab trotted over the bridge in the summer twilight. "Isn't that lovely?"

She waved her hand at the water. They were crossing the Serpentine; but her exclamation was only an aside; she was listening to what her husband was saying. Their daughter Magdalena was with them; and she looked where her mother pointed. There was the Serpentine, red in the setting sun; the trees grouped together, sculptured, losing their detail; and the ghostly architecture of the little bridge, white at the end, composed the scene. The lights—the sunlight and the artificial light—were strangely mixed.

". . . of course it's put the Government in a fix," Sir Digby was saying. "But then that's what he wants."

"Yes . . . he'll make a name for himself, that young man," said Lady Pargiter.

The cab passed over the bridge. It entered the shadow of the trees. Now it left the Park and joined the long line of cabs, taking people in evening dress to plays, to dinner-parties, that was streaming towards the Marble Arch. The light grew more and more artificial; yellower and yellower. Eugénie leant across and touched something on her daughter's dress. Maggie looked up. She had thought that they were still talking politics.

"So," said her mother, arranging the flower in front of her dress. She put her head a little on one side and looked at her daughter approvingly. Then she gave a sudden laugh and threw her hand out. "D'you know what made me so late?" she said. "That imp, Sally . . ."

But her husband interrupted her. He had caught sight of an illuminated clock.

"We shall be late," he said.

"But eight-fifteen means eight-thirty," said Eugénie as they turned down a side street.

ALL WAS SILENT in the house at Browne Street. A ray from the street lamp fell through the fanlight and, rather capriciously, lit up a tray of glasses on the hall table; a top hat; and a chair with gilt paws. The chair, standing empty, as if waiting for someone, had a look of ceremony; as if it stood on the cracked floor of some Italian ante-room. But all was silent. Antonio, the man-servant, was asleep; Mollie, the housemaid, was asleep; down-stairs in the basement a door flapped to and fro — otherwise all was silent.

SALLY IN HER BEDROOM at the top of the house turned on her side and listened intently. She thought she heard the front door click. A burst of dance music came in through the open window and made it impossible to hear.

She sat up in bed and looked out through the slit of the blind. Through the gap she could see a slice of the sky; then roofs; then the tree in the garden; then the backs of houses op-posite standing in a long row. One of the houses was brilliantly lit and from the long open windows came dance music. They were waltzing. She saw shadows twirling across the blind. It was impossible to read; impossible to sleep. First there was the music; then a burst of talk; then people came out into the gar-den; voices chattered, then the music began again.

It was a hot summer's night, and though it was late, the whole world seemed to be alive; the rush of traffic sounded dis-tant but incessant.

A faded brown book lay on her bed; as if she had been read-ing. But it was impossible to read; impossible to sleep. She lay back on the pillow with her hands behind her head.

"And he says," she murmured, "the world is nothing but . . ." She paused. What did he say? Nothing but thought, was it? she asked herself as if she had already forgotten. Well, since it was impossible to read and impossible to sleep, she would let herself *be* thought. It was easier to act things than to think them. Legs, body, hands, the whole of her must be laid out passively to take part in this universal process of thinking which the man said was the world living. She stretched herself out. Where did thought begin?

In the feet? she asked. There they were, jutting out under the single sheet. They seemed separated, very far away. She closed her eyes. Then against her will something in her hardened. It was impossible to act thought. She became something; a root; lying sunk in the earth; veins seemed to thread the cold mass; the tree put forth branches; the branches had leaves.

"—the sun shines through the leaves," she said, waggling her finger. She opened her eyes in order to verify the sun on the leaves and saw the actual tree standing out there in the garden. Far from being dappled with sunlight, it had no leaves at all. She felt for a moment as if she had been contradicted. For the tree was black, dead black.

She leant her elbow on the sill and looked out at the tree. A confused clapping sound came from the room where they were having the dance. The music had stopped; people began to come down the iron staircase into the garden which was marked out with blue and yellow lamps dotted along the wall. The voices grew louder. More people came and more people came. The dotted square of green was full of the flowing pale figures of women in evening dress; of the upright black-and-white figures of men in evening dress. She watched them moving in and out. They were talking and laughing; but they were too far off for her to hear what they were saying. Sometimes a single word or a laugh rose above the rest, and then there was a confused babble of sound. In their own garden all was empty and silent. A cat slid stealthily along the top of a wall; stopped; and then went on again as if drawn on some secret errand. Another dance struck up.

"Over again, over and over again!" she exclaimed impatiently. The air, laden with the curious dry smell of London earth, puffed in her face, blowing the blind out. Stretched flat on her bed, she saw the moon; it seemed immensely high above her. Little vapours were moving across the surface. Now they parted and she saw engravings chased over the white disc. What were they, she wondered—mountains? valleys? And if valleys, she said to herself half closing her eyes, then white trees; then icy hollows, and nightingales, two nightingales calling to each other, calling and answering each other across the valleys. The waltz music took the words "calling and answering each other" and flung them out; but as it repeated the same rhythm again and again, it coarsened them, it destroyed them. The dance music interfered with everything. At first exciting, then it became boring and finally intolerable. Yet it was only twenty minutes to one.

Her lip raised itself, like that of a horse that is going to bite. The little brown book was dull. She reached her hand above her head and took down another book from the shelf of battered books without looking at it. She opened the book at random; but her eye was caught by one of the couples who were still sitting out in the garden though the others had gone in. What were they saying, she wondered? There was something gleaming in the grass, and, as far as she could see, the black-and-white figure stooped and picked it up.

"And as he picks it up," she murmured, looking out, "he says to the lady beside him: Behold, Miss Smith, what I have found on the grass—a fragment of my heart; of my broken heart, he says. I have found it in the grass; and I wear it on my breast"—she hummed the words in time to the melancholy waltz music—"my broken heart, this broken glass, for love—" she paused and glanced at the book. On the fly-leaf was written:

"Sara Pargiter from her Cousin Edward Pargiter."

". . . for love," she concluded, "is best."

She turned to the title-page.

"The Antigone of Sophocles, done into English verse by Edward Pargiter," she read.

Once more she looked out of the window. The couple had moved. They were going up the iron staircase. She watched them. They went into the ballroom. "And suppose in the middle of the dance," she murmured, "she takes it out; and looks at it and says, 'What is this?' and it's only a piece of broken glass— of broken glass. . . ." She looked down at the book again.

"The Antigone of Sophocles," she read. The book was brand-new; it cracked as she opened it; this was the first time she had opened it.

"The Antigone of Sophocles, done into English verse by Edward Pargiter," she read again. He had given it her in Oxford; one hot afternoon when they had been trailing through chapels and libraries. "Trailing and wailing," she hummed, turning over the pages, "and he said to me, getting up from the low armchair, and brushing his hand through his hair"—she glanced out of the window—"'my wasted youth, my wasted youth.'" The waltz was now at its most intense, its most melancholy. "Taking in his hand," she hummed in time to it, "this broken glass, this faded heart, he said to me . . ." Here the music stopped; there was a sound of clapping; the dancers once more came out into the garden.

She skipped through the pages. At first she read a line or two at random; then, from the litter of broken words, scenes rose, quickly, inaccurately, as she skipped. The unburied body of a murdered man lay like a fallen tree-trunk, like a statue, with one foot stark in the air. Vultures gathered. Down they flopped on the silver sand. With a lurch, with a reel, the top-heavy birds came waddling; with a flap of the grey throat swinging, they hopped—she beat her hand on the counterpane as she read— to that lump there. Quick, quick, quick with repeated jerks they struck the mouldy flesh. Yes. She glanced at the tree outside in the garden. The unburied body of the murdered man lay on the sand. Then in a yellow cloud came whirling—who? She turned the page quickly. Antigone? She came whirling out of the dust-cloud to where the vultures were reeling and flung white sand over the blackened foot. She stood there letting fall white dust over the blackened foot. Then behold! there were more clouds; dark clouds; the horsemen leapt down; she was seized; her wrists were bound with withies; and they bore her, thus bound—where?

There was a roar of laughter from the garden. She looked up. Where did they take her? she asked. The garden was full of people. She could not hear a word that they were saying. The figures were moving in and out.

"To the estimable court of the respected ruler?" she murmured, picking up a word or two at random, for she was still looking out into the garden. The man's name was Creon. He buried her. It was a moonlight night. The blades of the cactuses were sharp silver. The man in the loincloth gave three sharp taps with his mallet on the brick. She was buried alive. The tomb was a brick mound. There was just room for her to lie straight out. Straight out in a brick tomb, she said. And that's the end, she yawned, shutting the book.

She laid herself out, under the cold smooth sheets, and pulled the pillow over her ears. The one sheet and the one blanket fitted softly round her. At the bottom of the bed was a long stretch of cool fresh mattress. The sound of the dance music became dulled. Her body dropped suddenly; then reached ground. A dark wing brushed her mind, leaving a pause; a blank space. Everything—the music, the voices—became stretched and generalised. The book fell on the floor. She was asleep.

"It's a lovely night," said the girl who was going up the iron steps with her partner. She rested her hand on the balustrade. It felt very cold. She looked up; a slice of yellow light lay round the moon. It seemed to laugh round it. Her partner looked up too, and then mounted another step without saying anything for he was shy.

"Going to the match tomorrow?" he said stiffly, for they scarcely knew each other.

"If my brother gets off in time to take me," she said, and went up another step too. Then, as they entered the ballroom, he gave her a little bow and left her; for his partner was waiting.

The moon which was now clear of clouds lay in a bare space as if the light had consumed the heaviness of the clouds and left a perfectly clear pavement, a dancing ground for revelry. For some time the dappled iridescence of the sky remained unbroken. Then there was a puff of wind; and a little cloud crossed the moon.

THERE WAS a sound in the bedroom. Sara turned over.

"Who's that?" she murmured. She sat up and rubbed her eyes.

It was her sister. She stood at the door, hesitating. "Asleep?" she said in a low voice.

"No," said Sara. She rubbed her eyes. "I'm awake," she said, opening them.

Maggie came across the room and sat down on the edge of the bed. The blind was blowing out; the sheets were slipping off the bed. She felt dazed for a moment. After the ballroom, it looked so untidy. There was a tumbler with a toothbrush in it on the wash-stand; the towel was crumpled on the towel-horse; and a book had fallen on the floor. She stooped and picked up the book. As she did so, the music burst out down the street. She held back the blind. The women in pale dresses, the men in black and white, were crowding up the stairs into the ballroom. Snatches of talk and laughter were blown across the garden.

"Is there a dance?" she asked.

"Yes. Down the street," said Sara.

Maggie looked out. At this distance the music sounded romantic, mysterious, and the colours flowed over each other, neither pink nor white nor blue.

Maggie stretched herself and unpinned the flower that she was wearing. It was drooping; the white petals were stained with black marks. She looked out of the window again. The mixture of lights was very odd; one leaf was a lurid green; another was a bright white. The branches crossed each other at different levels. Then Sally laughed.

"Did anybody give you a piece of glass," she said, "saying to you, Miss Pargiter . . . my broken heart?"

"No," said Maggie, "why should they?" The flower fell off her lap onto the floor.

"I was thinking," said Sara. "The people in the garden . . ."

She waved her hand at the window. They were silent for a moment, listening to the dance music.

"And who did you sit next?" Sara asked after a time.

"A man in gold lace," said Maggie.

"In gold lace?" Sara repeated.

Maggie was silent. She was getting used to the room; the discrepancy between this litter and the shiny ballroom was leaving her. She envied her sister lying in bed with the window open and the breeze blowing in.

"Because he was going to a party," she said. She paused. Something had caught her eye. A branch swayed up and down in the little breeze. Maggie held the blind so that the window was uncurtained. Now she could see the whole sky, and the houses and the branches in the garden.

"It's the moon," she said. It was the moon that was making the leaves white. They both looked at the moon which shone like a silver coin, perfectly polished, very sharp and hard.

"But if they don't say O my broken heart," said Sara, "what do they say, at parties?"

Maggie flicked off a white fleck that had stuck to her arm from her gloves.

"Some people say one thing," she said, getting up, "and some people say another."

She picked up the little brown book which lay on the counterpane and smoothed out the bedclothes. Sara took the book out of her hand.

"This man," she said, tapping the ugly little brown volume, "says the world's nothing but thought, Maggie."

"Does he?" said Maggie, putting the book on the washstand. It was a device, she knew, to keep her standing there talking.

"D'you think it's true?" Sara asked.

"Possibly," said Maggie, without thinking what she was saying. She put out her hand to draw the curtain.

"The world's nothing but thought, does he say?" she repeated, holding the curtain apart.

She had been thinking something of the kind when the cab crossed the Serpentine; when her mother interrupted her. She had been thinking, Am I that, or am I this? Are we one, or are we separate—something of the kind.

"Then what about trees and colours?" she said, turning round.

"Trees and colours?" Sara repeated.

"Would there be trees if we didn't see them?" said Maggie.

"What's 'I'? . . . 'I' . . ." She stopped. She did not know what she meant. She was talking nonsense.

"Yes," said Sara. "What's 'I'?" She held her sister tight by the skirt, whether she wanted to prevent her from going, or whether she wanted to argue the question.

"What's 'I'?" she repeated.

But there was a rustling outside the door and their mother came in.

"OH, MY DEAR CHILDREN!" she exclaimed, "still out of bed? Still talking?"

She came across the room, beaming, glowing, as if she were still under the influence of the party. Jewels flashed on her neck and her arms. She was extraordinarily handsome. She glanced round her.

"And the flower's on the floor, and everything's so untidy," she said. She picked up the flower that Maggie had dropped and put it to her lips.

"Because I was reading, Mama, because I was waiting," said Sara. She took her mother's hand and stroked the bare arm. She imitated her mother's manner so exactly that Maggie smiled. They were the very opposite of each other—Lady Pargiter so sumptuous; Sally so angular. But it's worked, she thought to herself, as Lady Pargiter allowed herself to be pulled down onto the bed. The imitation had been perfect.

"But you must go to sleep, Sal," she protested. "What did the doctor say? Lie straight, lie still, he said." She pushed her back onto the pillows.

"I am lying straight and still," said Sara. "Now"—she looked up at her—"tell me about the party."

Maggie stood upright in the window. She watched the couples coming down the iron staircase. Soon the garden was full of pale whites and pinks, moving in and out. She half heard them behind her talking about the party.

"It was a very nice party," her mother was saying.

Maggie looked out of the window. The square of the garden was filled with differently tinted colours. They seemed to ripple one over the other until they entered the angle where the light from the house fell, when they suddenly turned to ladies and gentlemen in full evening dress.

"No fish-knives?" she heard Sara saying.

She turned.

"Who was the man I sat next?" she asked.

"Sir Matthew Mayhew," said Lady Pargiter.

"Who is Sir Matthew Mayhew?" said Maggie.

"A most distinguished man, Maggie!" said her mother, flinging her hand out.

"A most distinguished man," Sara echoed her.

"But he is," Lady Pargiter repeated, smiling at her daughter whom she loved perhaps because of her shoulder.

"It was a great honour to sit next him, Maggie," she continued. "A great honour," she said reprovingly. She paused, as if she saw a little scene. She looked up.

"And then," she resumed, "when Mary Palmer says to me, Which is your daughter? I see Maggie, miles away, at the other end of the room, talking to Martin, whom she might have met every day of her life in an omnibus!"

Her words were stressed so that they seemed to rise and fall. She emphasised the rhythm still further by tapping with her fingers on Sally's bare arm.

"But I don't see Martin every day," Maggie protested.

"I haven't seen him since he came back from Africa." Her mother interrupted her.

"But you don't go to parties, my dear Maggie, to talk to your own cousins. You go to parties to —"

Here the dance music crashed out. The first chords seemed possessed of frantic energy, as if they were summoning the dancers imperiously to return. Lady Pargiter stopped in the middle of her sentence. She sighed; her body seemed to become indolent and suave. The heavy lids lowered themselves slightly over her large dark eyes. She swayed her head slowly in time to the music.

"What's that they're playing?" she murmured. She hummed the tune, beating time with her hand. "Something I used to dance to."

"Dance it now, Mama," said Sara.

"Yes, Mama. Show us how you used to dance," Maggie urged her.

"But without a partner—?" Lady Pargiter protested.

Maggie pushed a chair away.

"Imagine a partner," Sara urged her.

"Well," said Lady Pargiter. She rose. "It was something like this," she said. She paused; she held her skirt out with one hand; she slightly crooked the other in which she held the flower; she twirled round and round in the space which Maggie had cleared. She moved with extraordinary stateliness. All her limbs seemed to bend and flow in the lilt and the curve of the music; which became louder and clearer as she danced to it. She circled in and out among the chairs and tables and then, as the music stopped, "There!" she exclaimed. Her body seemed to fold and close itself together as she sighed "There!" and sank all in one movement on the edge of the bed.

"Wonderful!" Maggie exclaimed. Her eyes rested on her mother with admiration.

"Nonsense," Lady Pargiter laughed, panting slightly. "I'm much too old to dance now; but when I was young; when I was your age—" She sat there panting.

"You danced out of the house onto the terrace and found a little note folded in your bouquet—" said Sara, stroking her mother's arm. "Tell us that story, Mama."

"Not tonight," said Lady Pargiter. "Listen—there's the clock striking!"

Since the Abbey was so near, the sound of the hour filled the room; softly, tumultuously, as if it were a flurry of soft sighs hurrying one on top of another, yet concealing something hard. Lady Pargiter counted. It was very late.

"I'll tell you the true story one of these days," she said as she bent to kiss her daughter good-night.

"Now! Now!" cried Sara, holding her fast.

"No, not now—not now!" Lady Pargiter laughed, snatching away her hand. "There's Papa calling me!"

They heard footsteps in the passage outside, and then Sir Digby's voice at the door.

"Eugénie! It's very late, Eugénie!" they heard him say.

"Coming!" she cried. "Coming!"

Sara caught her by the train of her dress. "You haven't told us the story of the bouquet, Mama!" she cried.

"Eugénie!" Sir Digby repeated. His voice sounded peremptory. "Have you locked—"

"Yes, yes, yes," said Eugénie. "I will tell you the true story another time," she said, freeing herself from her daughter's grasp. She kissed them both quickly and went out of the room.

"SHE WON'T TELL US," said Maggie, picking up her gloves. She spoke with some bitterness.

They listened to the voices talking in the passage. They could hear their father's voice. He was expostulating. His voice sounded querulous and cross.

"Pirouetting up and down with his sword between his legs; with his opera hat under his arm and his sword between his legs," said Sara, pummelling her pillows viciously.

The voices went further away, downstairs.

"Who was the note from, d'you think?" said Maggie. She paused, looking at her sister burrowing into her pillows.

"The note? What note?" said Sara. "Oh, the note in the bouquet. I don't remember," she said. She yawned.

Maggie shut the window and pulled the curtain but she left a chink of light.

"Pull it tight, Maggie," said Sara irritably. "Shut out that din."

She curled herself up with her back to the window. She had raised a hump of pillow against her head as if to shut out the dance music that was still going on. She pressed her face into a cleft of the pillows. She looked like a chrysalis wrapped round in the sharp white folds of the sheet. Only the tip of her nose was visible. Her hip and her feet jutted out at the end of the bed covered by a single sheet. She gave a profound sigh that was half a snore; she was asleep already.

MAGGIE WENT ALONG the passage. Then she saw that there were lights in the hall beneath. She stopped and looked down over the bannister. The hall was lit up. She could see the great Italian chair with the gilt claws that stood in the hall. Her mother had thrown her evening cloak over it, so that it fell in soft golden folds over the crimson cover. She could see a tray with whisky and a soda-water syphon on the hall table. Then she heard the voices of her father and mother as they came up the kitchen stairs. They had been down in the basement; there had been a burglary up the street; her mother had promised to have a new lock put on the kitchen door but had forgotten. She could hear her father say:

". . . they'd melt it down; we should never get it back again."

Maggie went on a few steps upstairs.

"I'm so sorry, Digby," Eugénie said as they came into the hall. "I will tie a knot in my handkerchief; I will go directly after breakfast tomorrow morning. . . . Yes," she said, gathering her cloak in her arms, "I will go myself, and I will say, 'I've had enough of your excuses, Mr. Toye. No, Mr. Toye, you have deceived me once too often. And after all these years!'"

Then there was a pause. Maggie could hear soda-water squirted into a tumbler; the chink of a glass; and then the lights went out.

1 9 0 8

IT WAS MARCH and the wind was blowing. But it was not "blowing." It was scraping, scourging. It was so cruel. So unbecoming. Not merely did it bleach faces and raise red spots on noses; it tweaked up skirts; showed stout legs; made trousers reveal skeleton shins. There was no roundness, no fruit in it. Rather it was like the curve of a scythe which cuts, not corn, usefully; but destroys, revelling in sheer sterility. With one blast it blew out colour—even a Rembrandt in the National Gallery, even a solid ruby in a Bond Street window: one blast and they were gone. Had it any breeding place it was in the Isle of Dogs among tin cans lying beside a workhouse drab on the banks of a polluted city. It tossed up rotten leaves, gave them another span of degraded existence; scorned, derided them, yet had nothing to put in the place of the scorned, the derided. Down they fell. Uncreative, unproductive, yelling its joy in destruction, its power to peel off the bark, the bloom, and show the bare bone, it paled every window; drove old gentlemen further and further into the leather-smelling recesses of clubs; and old ladies to sit eyeless, leather cheeked, joyless among the tassels and antimacassars of their bedrooms and kitchens. Triumphing in its wantonness it emptied the streets; swept flesh before it; and coming smack against a dust cart standing outside the Army and Navy Stores, scattered along the pavement a litter of old envelopes; twists of hair; papers already blood smeared, yellow smeared, smudged with print and sent them scudding to plaster legs, lamp posts, pillar boxes, and fold themselves frantically against area railings.

MATTY STILES, the caretaker, huddled in the basement of the house in Browne Street, looked up. There was a rattle of dust along the pavement. It worked its way under the doors, through the window frames; on to chests and dressers. But she didn't care. She was one of the unlucky ones. She had been thinking it was a safe job, sure to last the summer out anyhow. The lady was dead; the gentleman too. She had got the job through her son the policeman. The house with its basement would never let this side of Christmas—so they told her. She had only to show parties round who came with orders to view from the agent. And she always mentioned the basement—how damp it was. "Look at that stain on the ceiling." There it was, sure enough. All the same, the party from China took a fancy to it. It suited him, he said. He had business in the city. She was one of the unlucky ones—after three months to turn out and lodge with her son in Pimlico.

A bell rang. Let him ring, ring, ring, she growled. She wasn't going to open the door any more. There he was standing on the door-step. She could see a pair of legs against the railing. Let him ring as much as he liked. The house was sold. Couldn't he see the notice on the board? Couldn't he read it? Hadn't he eyes? She huddled closer to the fire, which was covered with pale ash. She could see his legs there, standing on the doorstep, between the canaries' cage and the dirty linen which she had been going to wash, but this wind made her shoulder ache cruel. Let him ring the house down, for all she cared.

———

MARTIN WAS standing there.

"Sold" was written on a strip of bright red paper pasted across the house-agent's board.

"Already!" said Martin. He had made a little circle to look at the house in Browne Street. And it was already sold. The red strip gave him a shock. It was sold already, and Digby had only been dead three months—Eugénie not much more than a year. He stood for a moment gazing at the black windows now grimed with dust. It was a house of character; built some time in the eighteenth century. Eugénie had been proud of it. And I used to like going there, he thought. But now an old newspaper was on the doorstep; wisps of straw had caught in the railings; and he could see, for there were no blinds, into an empty room. A woman was peering up at him from behind the bars of a cage in the basement. It was no use ringing. He turned away. A feeling of something extinguished came over him as he went down the street.

It's a grimy, it's a sordid end, he thought; I used to enjoy going there. But he disliked brooding over unpleasant thoughts. What's the good of it? he asked himself.

"The King of Spain's daughter," he hummed as he turned the corner, "came to visit me . . ."

"AND HOW MUCH LONGER," he asked himself, pressing the bell, as he stood on the doorstep of the house in Abercorn Terrace, "is old Crosby going to keep me waiting?" The wind was very cold.

He stood there, looking at the buff-coloured front of the large, architecturally insignificant, but no doubt convenient family mansion in which his father and sister still lived. "She takes her time nowadays," he thought, shivering in the wind. But here the door opened, and Crosby appeared.

"Hullo, Crosby!" he said.

She beamed on him so that her gold tooth showed. He was always her favourite, they said, and the thought pleased him today.

"How's the world treating you?" he asked, as he gave her his hat.

She was just the same—more shrivelled, more gnat-like, and her blue eyes were more prominent than ever.

"Feeling the rheumatics?" he asked, as she helped him off with his coat. She grinned, silently. He felt friendly; he was glad to find her much as usual. "And Miss Eleanor?" he asked, as he opened the drawing-room door. The room was empty. She was not there. But she had been there, for there was a book on the table. Nothing had been changed, he was glad to see. He stood in front of the fire and looked at his mother's picture. In the course of the past few years it had ceased to be his mother; it had become a work of art. But it was dirty.

There used to be a flower in the grass, he thought, peering into a dark corner: but now there was nothing but dirty brown paint. And what's she been reading? he wondered. He took the book that was propped up against the teapot and looked at it. "Renan," he read. "Why Renan?" he asked himself, beginning to read as he waited.

"MR. MARTIN, MISS," said Crosby, opening the study door. Eleanor looked round. She was standing by her father's chair with her hands full of long strips of newspaper cuttings, as if she had been reading them aloud. There was a chess-board in front of him; the chess-men were set out for a game; but he was lying back in his chair. He looked lethargic, and rather gloomy.

"Put 'em away. . . . Keep 'em safe somewhere," he said, jerking his thumb at the cuttings. That was a sign that he had grown very old, Eleanor thought—wanting newspaper cuttings kept. He had grown inert and ponderous after his stroke; there were red veins in his nose and in his cheeks. She too felt old, heavy and dull.

"Mr. Martin's called," Crosby repeated.

"Martin's come," Eleanor said. Her father seemed not to hear. He sat still with his head sunk on his breast. "Martin," Eleanor repeated. "Martin . . ."

Did he want to see him or did he not want to see him? She waited as if for some sluggish thought to rise. At last he gave a little grunt; but what it meant she was not certain.

"I'll send him in after tea," she said. She paused for a moment. He roused himself and began fumbling with his chessmen. He still had courage, she observed with pride. He still insisted upon doing things for himself.

SHE WENT into the drawing-room and found Martin standing in front of the placid, smiling picture of their mother. He held a book in his hand.

"Why Renan?" he said as she came in. He shut the book and kissed her. "Why Renan?" he repeated. She flushed slightly. It made her shy, for some reason, that he had found the book there, open. She sat down and laid the press cuttings on the tea-table.

"How's Papa?" he asked. She had lost something of her bright colour, he thought, glancing at her, and her hair had a tuft of grey in it.

"Rather gloomy," she said, glancing at the press cuttings. "I wonder," she added, "who writes that sort of thing?"

"What sort of thing?" said Martin. He picked up one of the crinkled strips and began reading it: "'. . . an exceptionally able public servant . . . a man of wide interests. . . .' Oh, Digby," he said. "Obituaries. I passed the house this afternoon," he added. "It's sold."

"Already?" said Eleanor.

"It looked very shut-up and desolate," he added. "There was a dirty old woman in the basement."

Eleanor took out a hair-pin and began fraying the wick of the kettle. Martin watched her for a moment in silence.

"I liked going there," he said at length. "I liked Eugénie," he added.

Eleanor paused.

"Yes . . ." she said doubtfully. She had never felt at her ease with her. "She exaggerated," she added.

"Well, of course," Martin laughed. He smiled, recalling some memory. "She had less sense of truth than . . . that's no sort of use, Nell," he broke off, irritated by her fumbling with the wick.

"Yes, yes," she protested. "It boils in time."

She paused. Stretching out towards the tea caddy, she measured the tea. "One, two, three, four," she counted.

She still used the nice old silver tea-caddy, he noticed, with the sliding lid. He watched her measuring the tea methodically—one, two, three, four. He was silent.

"We can't tell a lie to save our souls," he said abruptly.

What makes him say that? Eleanor wondered.

"When I was with them in Italy—" she said aloud. But here the door opened and Crosby came in carrying some sort of dish. She left the door ajar and a dog pushed in after her.

"I mean—" Eleanor added; but she could not say what she meant with Crosby in the room fidgeting about.

"It's time Miss Eleanor got a new kettle," said Martin, pointing to the old brass kettle, faintly engraved with a design of roses, which he had always hated.

"Crosby," said Eleanor, still poking with her pin, "doesn't hold with new inventions. Crosby won't trust herself in the Tube, will you, Crosby?"

Crosby grinned. They always spoke to her in the third person, because she never answered but only grinned. The dog snuffed at the dish she had just put down. "Crosby's letting that beast get much too fat," said Martin, pointing at the dog.

"That's what I'm always telling her," said Eleanor.

"If I were you, Crosby," said Martin, "I'd cut down his meals and take him for a brisk run round the park every morning." Crosby opened her mouth wide.

"Oh, Mr. Martin!" she protested, shocked by his brutality into speech.

The dog followed her out of the room.

"Crosby's the same as ever," said Martin.

Eleanor had lifted the lid of the kettle and was looking in. There were no bubbles on the water yet.

"Damn that kettle," said Martin. He took up one of the newspaper cuttings and began to make it into a spill.

"No, no, Papa wants them kept," said Eleanor. "But he wasn't like that," she said, laying her hand on the newspaper cuttings. "Not in the least."

"What was he like?" Martin asked.

Eleanor paused. She could see her uncle clearly in her mind's eye; he held his top-hat in his hand; he laid his hand on her shoulder as they stopped in front of some picture. But how could she describe him?

"He used to take me to the National Gallery," she said.

"Very cultivated, of course," said Martin. "But he was such a damned snob."

"Only on the surface," said Eleanor.

"And always finding fault with Eugénie about little things," Martin added.

"But think of living with her," said Eleanor.

"That manner—" She threw her hand out; but not as Eugénie threw her hand out, Martin thought.

"I liked her," he said. "I liked going there." He saw the untidy room; the piano open; the window open; a wind blowing the curtains, and his aunt coming forward with her arms open. "What a pleasure, Martin! what a pleasure!" she would say. What had her private life been, he wondered—her love affairs? She must have had them—obviously, obviously.

"Wasn't there some story," he began, "about a letter?" He wanted to say, Didn't she have an affair with somebody? But it was more difficult to be open with his sister than with other women, because she treated him as if he were a small boy still. Had Eleanor ever been in love, he wondered, looking at her.

"Yes," she said. "There was a story—"

But here the electric bell rang sharply. She stopped.

"Papa," she said. She half rose.

"No," said Martin. "I'll go." He got up. "I promised him a game of chess."

"Thanks, Martin. He'll enjoy that," said Eleanor with relief as he left the room, and she found herself alone.

SHE LEANT BACK in her chair. How terrible old age was, she thought; shearing off all one's faculties, one by one, but leaving something alive in the centre: leaving—she swept up the press cuttings—a game of chess, a drive in the park, and a visit from old General Arbuthnot in the evening.

It was better to die, like Eugénie and Digby, in the prime of life with all one's faculties about one. But he wasn't like that, she thought, glancing at the press cuttings. "A man of singularly handsome presence . . . shot, fished, and played golf." No, not like that in the least. He had been a curious man; weak; sensitive; liking titles, liking pictures; and often depressed, she guessed, by his wife's exuberance. She pushed the cuttings away and took up her book. It was odd how different the same person seemed to two different people, she thought. There was

Martin, liking Eugénie; and she, liking Digby. She began to
read.

She had always wanted to know about Christianity—how
it began; what it meant, originally. God is love, The kingdom of
Heaven is within us, sayings like that, she thought, turning over
the pages, what did they mean? The actual words were very
beautiful. But who said them—when? Then the spout of the
tea-kettle puffed steam at her and she moved it away. The wind
was rattling the windows in the back room; it was bending the
little bushes; they still had no leaves on them. It was what a man
said under a fig tree, on a hill, she thought. And then another
man wrote it down. But suppose that what that man says is just
as false as what this man—she touched the press cuttings with
her spoon—says about Digby? And here am I, she thought,
looking at the china in the Dutch cabinet, in this drawing-room,
getting a little spark from what someone said all those years
ago—here it comes (the china was changing from blue to livid)
skipping over all those mountains, all those seas. She found her
place and began to read.

But a sound in the hall interrupted her. Was someone coming in? She listened. No, it was the wind. The wind was terrific.
It pressed on the house; gripped it tight, then let it fall apart.
Upstairs a door slammed; a window must be open in the bedroom above. A blind was tapping. It was difficult to fix her mind
on Renan. She liked it, though. French she could read easily of
course; and Italian; and a little German. But what vast gaps
there were, what blank spaces, she thought, leaning back in her
chair, in her knowledge! How little she knew about anything.
Take this cup for instance; she held it out in front of her. What
was it made of? Atoms? And what were atoms, and how did
they stick together? The smooth hard surface of the china with
its red flowers seemed to her for a second a marvellous mystery.

But there was another sound in the hall. It was the wind, but it was also a voice, talking. It must be Martin. But who could he be talking to, she wondered? She listened, but she could not hear what he was saying because of the wind. And why, she asked herself, did he say, We can't tell a lie to save our souls? He was thinking about himself; one always knew when people were thinking about themselves by their tone of voice. Perhaps he was justifying himself for having left the Army. That had been courageous, she thought, but isn't it odd, she mused, listening to the voices, that he should be such a dandy too? He was wearing a new blue suit with white stripes on it. And he had shaved off his moustache. He ought never to have been a soldier, she thought; he was much too pugnacious. . . . They were still talking. She could not hear what he was saying, but from the sound of his voice it came over her that he must have a great many love affairs. Yes—it became perfectly obvious to her, listening to his voice through the door, that he had a great many love affairs. But who with? and why do men think love affairs so important? she asked as the door opened.

"HULLO, ROSE!" she exclaimed, surprised to see her sister come in too. "I thought you were in Northumberland!"

"You thought I was in Northumberland!" Rose laughed, kissing her. "But why? I said the eighteenth."

"But isn't today the eleventh?" said Eleanor.

"You're only a week behind the times, Nell," said Martin.

"Then I must have dated all my letters wrong!" Eleanor exclaimed. She glanced apprehensively at her writing-table. The walrus, with a worn patch in its bristles, no longer stood there.

"Tea, Rose?" she asked.

"No. It's a bath I want," said Rose. She threw off her hat and ran her fingers through her hair.

"You're looking very well," said Eleanor, thinking how handsome she looked. But she had a scratch on her chin.

"A positive beauty, isn't she?" Martin laughed at her.

Rose threw her head up rather like a horse. They always bickered, Eleanor thought—Martin and Rose. Rose was handsome, but she wished she dressed better. She was dressed in a green hairy coat and skirt with leather buttons, and she carried a shiny bag. She had been holding meetings in the North.

"I want a bath," Rose repeated. "I'm dirty. And what's all this?" she said, pointing to the press cuttings on the table. "Oh, Uncle Digby," she added casually, pushing them away. He had been dead some months now; they were already yellowish and curled.

"Martin says the house has been sold," said Eleanor.

"Has it?" she said indifferently. She broke off a piece of cake and began munching it. "Spoiling my dinner," she said. "But I had no time for lunch."

"What a woman of action she is!" Martin chaffed her.

"And the meetings?" Eleanor asked.

"Yes. What about the North?" said Martin.

They began to discuss politics. She had been speaking at a by-election. A stone had been thrown at her; she put her hand to her chin. But she had enjoyed it.

"I think we gave 'em something to think about," she said, breaking off another piece of cake.

She ought to have been the soldier, Eleanor thought. She was exactly like the picture of old Uncle Pargiter of Pargiter's Horse. Martin, now that he had shaved his moustache off and showed his lips, ought to have been—what? Perhaps an architect, she thought. He's so—she looked up. Now it was hailing. White rods came across the window in the back room. There was a great gust of wind; the little bushes blanched and bent under it. And a window banged upstairs in her mother's bedroom. Perhaps I ought to go and shut it, she thought. The rain must be coming in.

"Eleanor—" said Rose. "Eleanor"—she repeated.

Eleanor started.

"Eleanor's broody," said Martin.

"No, not at all—not at all," she protested. "What are you talking about?"

"I was asking you," said Rose. "Do you remember that row when the microscope was broken? Well, I met that boy—that horrid, ferret-faced boy—Erridge—up in the North."

"He wasn't horrid," said Martin.

"He was," Rose persisted. "A horrid little sneak. He pretended that it was I who broke the microscope and it was he who broke it. . . . D'you remember that row?" She turned to Eleanor.

"I don't remember that row," said Eleanor. "There were so many," she added.

"That was one of the worst," said Martin.

"It was," said Rose. She pursed her lips together. Some memory seemed to have come back to her. "And after it was over," she said, turning to Martin, "you came up into the nursery and asked me to go beetling with you in the Round Pond. D'you remember?"

She paused. There was something queer about the memory, Eleanor could see. She spoke with a curious intensity.

"And you said, 'I'll ask you three times; and if you don't answer the third time, I'll go alone.' And I swore, 'I'll let him go alone.'" Her blue eyes blazed.

"I can see you," said Martin. "Wearing a pink frock, with a knife in your hand."

"And you went," Rose said; she spoke with suppressed vehemence. "And I dashed into the bathroom and cut this

gash"—she held out her wrist. Eleanor looked at it. There was
a thin white scar just above the wrist joint.

When did she do that? Eleanor thought. She could not remember. Rose had locked herself into the bathroom with a
knife and cut her wrist. She had known nothing about it. She
looked at the white mark. It must have bled.

"Oh, Rose always was a firebrand!" said Martin. He got up.
"She always had the devil's own temper," he added. He stood
for a moment looking round the drawing-room, cluttered up
with several hideous pieces of furniture that he would have got
rid of had he been Eleanor, he thought, and forced to live there.
But perhaps she did not mind things like that.

"Dining out?" she said. He dined out every night. She
would like to have asked him where he was dining.

He nodded without saying anything. He met all sorts of
people she did not know, she reflected; and he did not want to
talk about them. He had turned to the fireplace.

"That picture wants cleaning," he said, pointing to the picture of their mother.

"It's a nice picture," he added, looking at it critically. "But
usen't there to be a flower in the grass?"

Eleanor looked at it. She had not looked at it, so as to see
it, for many years.

"Was there?" she said.

"Yes. A little blue flower," said Martin. "I can remember it
when I was a child. . . ."

He turned. Some memory from his childhood came over
him as he saw Rose sitting there at the tea table with her fist still
clenched. He saw her standing with her back to the schoolroom door; very red in the face, with her lips tight shut as they
were now. She had wanted him to do something. And he had
crumpled a ball of paper in his hand and shied it at her.

"What awful lives children live!" he said, waving his hand at her as he crossed the room. "Don't they, Rose?"

"Yes," said Rose. "And they can't tell anybody," she added.

There was another gust and the sound of glass crashing.

"Miss Pym's conservatory?" said Martin, pausing with his hand on the door.

"Miss Pym?" said Eleanor. "She's been dead these twenty years!"

IN THE country it was an ordinary day enough; one of the long reel of days that turned as the years passed from green to orange; from grass to harvest. It was neither hot nor cold, an English spring day, bright enough, but a purple cloud behind the hill might mean rain. The grasses rippled with shadow, and then with sunlight.

In London, however, the stricture and pressure of the season were already felt, especially in the West End, where flags flew; canes tapped; dresses flowed; and houses freshly painted had awnings spread and swinging baskets of red geraniums. The Parks too—St. James's, the Green Park, Hyde Park—were making ready. Already in the morning before there was a chance of a procession, the green chairs were ranged among the plump brown flower beds with their curled hyacinths, as if waiting for something to happen; for a curtain to rise; for Queen Alexandra to come, bowing through the gates. She had a face like a flower petal, and always wore her pink carnation.

Men lay flat on the grass reading newspapers with their shirts open; on the bald scrubbed space by the Marble Arch speakers congregated; nursemaids vacantly regarded them; and mothers, squatted on the grass, watched their children play. Down Park Lane and Piccadilly vans, cars, omnibuses ran along the streets as if the streets were slots; stopped and jerked; as if a puzzle were solved, and then broken, for it was the Season, and the streets were crowded. Over Park Lane and Piccadilly the clouds kept their freedom, wandering fitfully, staining windows gold, daubing them black, passed and vanished, though marble in Italy looked no more solid, gleaming in the quarries, veined with yellow, than the clouds over Park Lane.

IF THE BUS stopped here, Rose thought, looking down over the side, she would get up. The bus stopped, and she rose. It was a pity, she thought, as she stepped onto the pavement and caught a glimpse of her own figure in a tailor's window, not to dress better, not to look nicer. Always reach-me-downs, coats and skirts from Whiteley's. But they saved time, and the years after all — she was over forty — made one care very little what people thought. They used to say, why don't you marry? Why don't you do this or that, interfering. But not any longer.

She paused in one of the little alcoves that were scooped out in the bridge, from habit. People always stopped to look at the river. It was running fast, a muddy gold this morning with smooth breadths and ripples, for the tide was high. And there was the usual tug and the usual barges with black tarpaulins and corn showing. The water swirled round the arches. As she stood there, looking down at the water, some buried feeling began to arrange the stream into a pattern. The pattern was painful. She remembered how she had stood there on the night of a certain engagement, crying; her tears had fallen, her happiness, it seemed to her, had fallen. Then she had turned — here she turned — and had seen the churches, the masts and roofs of the city. There's *that*, she had said to herself. Indeed it was a splendid view. . . . She looked, and then again she turned. There were the Houses of Parliament. A queer expression, half frown, half smile, formed on her face and she threw herself slightly backwards, as if she were leading an army.

"Damned humbugs!" she said aloud, striking her fist on the balustrade. A clerk who was passing looked at her with surprise. She laughed. She often talked aloud. Why not? That too was one of the consolations, like her coat and skirt, and the hat she stuck on without giving a look in the glass. If people chose to laugh, let them. She strode on. She was lunching in Hyams Place with her cousins. She had asked herself on the spur of the moment, meeting Maggie in a shop. First she had heard a voice; then seen a hand. And it was odd, considering how little she knew them—they had lived abroad—how strongly, sitting there at the counter before Maggie saw her, simply from the sound of her voice, she had felt—she supposed it was affection?—some feeling bred of blood in common. She had got up and said May I come and see you? busy as she was, hating to break her day in the middle. She walked on. They lived in Hyams Place, over the river—Hyams Place, that little crescent of old houses with the name carved in the middle which she used to pass so often when she lived down here. She used to ask herself in those far off days Who was Hyam? But she had never solved the question to her satisfaction. She walked on, across the river.

The shabby street on the south side of the river was very noisy. Now and again a voice detached itself from the general clamour. A woman shouted to her neighbour; a child cried. A man trundling a barrow opened his mouth and bawled up at the windows as he passed. There were bedsteads, grates, pokers and odd pieces of twisted iron on his barrow. But whether he was selling old iron or buying old iron it was impossible to say; the rhythm persisted; but the words were almost rubbed out.

The swarm of sound, the rush of traffic, the shouts of the hawkers, the single cries and the general cries, came into the upper room of the house in Hyams Place where Sara Pargiter sat at the piano. She was singing. Then she stopped; she watched her sister laying the table.

"Go search the valleys," she murmured, as she watched her, "pluck up every rose." She paused. "That's very nice," she added, dreamily. Maggie had taken a bunch of flowers; had cut the tight little string which bound them, and had laid them side by side on the table; and was arranging them in an earthenware pot. They were differently coloured, blue, white and purple. Sara watched her arranging them. She laughed suddenly.

"What are you laughing at?" said Maggie absentmindedly. She added a purple flower to the bunch and looked at it.

"Dazed in a rapture of contemplation," said Sara, "shading her eyes with peacocks' feathers dipped in morning dew—" she pointed to the table. "Maggie said," she jumped up and pirouetted about the room, "three's the same as two, three's the same as two." She pointed to the table upon which three places had been laid.

"But we are three," said Maggie. "Rose is coming." Sara stopped. Her face fell.

"Rose is coming?" she repeated.

"I told you," said Maggie. "I said to you, Rose is coming to luncheon on Friday. It is Friday. And Rose is coming to luncheon. Any minute now," she said. She got up and began to fold some stuff that was lying on the floor.

"It is Friday, and Rose is coming to luncheon," Sara repeated.

"I told you," said Maggie. "I was in a shop. I was buying stuff. And somebody"—she paused to make her fold more accurately—"came out from behind a counter and said, 'I'm your cousin. I'm Rose,' she said. 'Can I come and see you? Any day, any time,' she said. So I said," she put the stuff on a chair, "lunch."

She looked round the room to see that everything was in readiness. Chairs were missing. Sara pulled up a chair.

"Rose is coming," she said, "and this is where she'll sit." She placed the chair at the table facing the window. "And she'll take off her gloves; and she'll lay one on this side, one on that. And she'll say, 'I've never been in this part of London before.'"

"And then?" said Maggie, looking at the table.

"You'll say, 'It's so convenient for the theatres.'"

"And then?" said Maggie.

"And then she'll say rather wistfully, smiling, putting her head on one side, 'D'you often go to the theatre, Maggie?'"

"No," said Maggie. "Rose has red hair."

"Red hair?" Sara exclaimed. "I thought it was grey—a little wisp straggling from under a black bonnet," she added.

"No," said Maggie. "She has a great deal of hair; and it's red."

"Red hair; red Rose," Sara exclaimed. She spun round on her toe.

"Rose of the flaming heart; Rose of the burning breast; Rose of the weary world—red, red Rose!"

A door slammed below; they heard footsteps mounting the stairs. "There she is," said Maggie.

The steps stopped. They heard a voice saying, "Still further up? On the very top? Thank you." Then the steps began mounting the stairs again.

"This is the worst torture . . ." Sara began, screwing her hands together and clinging to her sister, "that life . . ."

"Don't be such an ass," said Maggie, pushing her away, as the door opened.

ROSE CAME IN.

"It's ages since we met," she said, shaking hands.

She wondered what had made her come. Everything was different from what she expected. The room was rather poverty-stricken; the carpet did not cover the floor. There was a sewing-machine in the corner, and Maggie too looked different from what she had looked in the shop. But there was a crimson-and-gilt chair; she recognised it with relief.

"That used to stand in the hall, didn't it?" she said, putting her bag down on the chair.

"Yes," said Maggie.

"And that glass—" said Rose, looking at the old Italian glass blurred with spots that hung between the windows, "wasn't that there too?"

"Yes," said Maggie, "in my mother's bedroom."

There was a pause. There seemed to be nothing to say.

"What nice rooms you've found!" Rose continued, making conversation. It was a large room and the door-posts had little carvings on them. "But don't you find it rather noisy?" she continued.

The man was crying under the window. She looked out of the window. Opposite there was a row of slate roofs, like half-opened umbrellas; and, rising high above them, a great building which, save for thin black strokes across it, seemed to be made entirely of glass. It was a factory. The man bawled in the street underneath.

"Yes, it's noisy," said Maggie. "But very convenient."

"Very convenient for the theatres," said Sara, as she put down the meat.

"So I remember finding," said Rose, turning to look at her, "when I lived here myself."

"Did you live here?" said Maggie, beginning to help the cutlets.

"Not here," she said. "Round the corner. With a friend."

"We thought you lived in Abercorn Terrace," said Sara.

"Can't one live in more places than one?" Rose asked, feeling vaguely annoyed, for she had lived in many places, felt many passions, and done many things.

"I remember Abercorn Terrace," said Maggie. She paused.

"There was a long room; and a tree at the end; and a picture over the fireplace, of a girl with red hair?"

Rose nodded. "Mama when she was young," she said.

"And a round table in the middle?" Maggie continued.

Rose nodded.

"And you had a parlourmaid with very prominent blue eyes?"

"Crosby. She's still with us."

They ate in silence.

"And then?" said Sara, as if she were a child asking for a story.

"And then?" said Rose. "Well, then"—she looked at Maggie, thinking of her as a little girl who had come to tea.

She saw them sitting round a table; and a detail that she had not thought of for years came back to her—how Milly used to take her hair pin and fray the wick of the kettle. And she saw Eleanor sitting with her account books; and she saw herself go up to her and say: "Eleanor, I want to go to Lamley's."

Her past seemed to be rising above her present. And for some reason she wanted to talk about her past; to tell them something about herself that she had never told anybody— something hidden. She paused, gazing at the flowers in the middle of the table without seeing them. There was a blue knot in the yellow glaze she noticed.

"I remember Uncle Abel," said Maggie. "He gave me a necklace; a blue necklace with gold spots."

"He's still alive," said Rose.

They talked, she thought, as if Abercorn Terrace were a scene in a play. They talked as if they were speaking of people who were real, but not real in the way in which she felt herself to be real. It puzzled her; it made her feel that she was two different people at the same time; that she was living at two different times at the same moment. She was a little girl wearing a pink frock; and here she was in this room, now. But there was a great rattle under the windows. A dray went roaring past. The glasses jingled on the table. She started slightly, roused from her thoughts about her childhood, and separated the glasses.

"Don't you find it very noisy here?" she said.

"Yes. But very convenient for the theatres," said Sara.

Rose looked up. She had repeated herself. She thinks me an old fool, Rose thought, making the same remark twice over. She blushed slightly.

What is the use, she thought, of trying to tell people about one's past? What is one's past? She stared at the pot with the blue knot loosely tied in the yellow glaze. Why did I come, she thought, when they only laugh at me? Sally rose and cleared away the plates.

"And Delia—" Maggie began as they waited. She pulled the pot towards her, and began to arrange the flowers. She was not listening; she was thinking her own thoughts. She reminded Rose, as she watched her, of Digby—absorbed in the arrangement of a bunch of flowers, as if to arrange flowers, to put the white by the blue, were the most important thing in the world.

"She married an Irishman," she said aloud.

Maggie took a blue flower and placed it beside a white flower.

"And Edward?" she asked.

"Edward . . ." Rose was beginning, when Sally came in with the pudding.

"Edward!" she exclaimed, catching the word.

"Oh, blasted eyes of my deceased wife's sister—withered prop of my defunct old age . . ." She put down the pudding. "That's Edward," she said. "A quotation from a book he gave me. 'My wasted youth—my wasted youth' . . ." The voice was

Edward's; Rose could hear him say it. For he had a way of be-littling himself, when in fact he had a very good opinion of himself.

But it was not the whole of Edward. And she would not have him laughed at; for she was very fond of her brother and very proud of him.

"There's not much of 'my wasted youth' about Edward now," she said.

"I thought not," said Sara, taking her place opposite.

They were silent. Rose looked at the flower again. Why did I come? she kept asking herself. Why had she broken up her morning, and interrupted her day's work, when it was clear to her that they had not wished to see her?

"Go on, Rose," said Maggie, helping the pudding. "Go on telling us about the Pargiters."

"About the Pargiters?" said Rose. She saw herself running along the broad avenue in the lamplight.

"What could be more ordinary?" she said. "A large family, living in a large house . . ." And yet she felt that she had been herself very interesting. She paused. Sara looked at her.

"It's not ordinary," she said. "The Pargiters—" She was holding a fork in her hand, and she drew a line on the table-cloth. "The Pargiters," she repeated, "going on and on and on"—here her fork touched a salt-cellar—"until they come to a rock," she said; "and then Rose"—she looked at her again: Rose drew herself up slightly, "—Rose claps spurs to her horse, rides straight up to a man in a gold coat, and says, 'Damn your eyes!' Isn't that Rose, Maggie?" she said, looking at her sister as if she had been drawing her picture on the table-cloth.

That is true, Rose thought as she took her pudding. That is myself. Again she had the odd feeling of being two people at the same time.

"Well, that's done," said Maggie, pushing away her plate. "Come and sit in the armchair, Rose," she said.

She went over to the fireplace and pulled out an armchair, which had springs like hoops, Rose noticed, in the seat.

They were poor, Rose thought, glancing round her. That was why they had chosen this house to live in—because it was cheap. They cooked their own food—Sally had gone into the kitchen to make the coffee. She drew her chair up beside Maggie's.

"You make your own clothes?" she said, pointing to the sewing-machine in the corner. There was silk folded on it.

"Yes," said Maggie, looking at the sewing-machine.

"For a party?" said Rose. The stuff was silk, green, with blue rays on it.

"Tomorrow night," said Maggie. She raised her hand with a curious gesture to her face, as if she wanted to conceal something. She wants to hide herself from me, Rose thought, as I want to hide myself from her. She watched her; she had got up, had fetched the silk and the sewing-machine, and was threading the needle. Her hands were large and thin and strong, Rose noticed.

"I never could make my own clothes," she said, watching her arrange the silk smoothly under the needle. She was beginning to feel at her ease. She took off her hat and threw it on the floor. Maggie looked at her with approval. She was handsome, in a ravaged way; more like a man than a woman.

"But then," said Maggie, beginning to turn the handle rather cautiously, "you did other things." She spoke in the absorbed tones of someone who is using their hands.

The machine made a comfortable whirring sound as the needle pricked through the silk.

"Yes, I did other things," said Rose, stroking the cat that had stretched itself against her knee, "when I lived down here."

"But that was years ago," she added, "when I was young. I lived here with a friend," she sighed, "and taught little thieves."

Maggie said nothing; she was whirring the machine round and round.

"I always liked thieves better than other people," Rose added after a time.

"Yes," said Maggie.

"I never liked being at home," said Rose. "I liked being on my own much better."

"Yes," said Maggie.

Rose went on talking.

It was quite easy to talk, she found; quite easy. And there was no need to say anything clever; or to talk about one's self. She was talking about the Waterloo Road as she remembered it when Sara came in with the coffee.

"What was that about clinging to a fat man in the Campagna?" she asked, setting her tray down.

"The Campagna?" said Rose. "There was nothing about the Campagna."

"Heard through a door," said Sara, pouring out the coffee, "talk sounds very odd." She gave Rose her cup.

"I thought you were talking about Italy; about the Campagna, about the moonlight."

Rose shook her head. "We were talking about the Waterloo Road," she said. But what had she been talking about? Not simply about the Waterloo Road. Perhaps she had been talking nonsense. She had been saying the first thing that came into her head.

"All talk would be nonsense, I suppose, if it were written down," she said, stirring her coffee.

Maggie stopped the machine for a moment and smiled.

"And even if it isn't," she said.

"But it's the only way we have of knowing each other," Rose

protested. She looked at her watch. It was later than she thought. She got up.

"I must go," she said. "But why don't you come with me?" she added on the spur of the moment.

Maggie looked up at her. "Where?" she said.

Rose was silent. "To a meeting," she said at length. She wanted to conceal the thing that interested her most; she felt extraordinarily shy. And yet she wanted them to come. But why? she asked herself, as she stood there awkwardly waiting. There was a pause.

"You could wait upstairs," she said suddenly. "And you'd see Eleanor; you'd see Martin—the Pargiters in the flesh," she added. She remembered Sara's phrase, "the caravan crossing the desert," she said.

She looked at Sara. She was balancing herself on the arm of a chair, sipping her coffee and swinging her foot up and down.

"Shall I come?" she asked, vaguely, still swinging her foot up and down.

Rose shrugged her shoulders. "If you like," she said.

"But should I like it?" Sara continued, still swinging her foot. ". . . this meeting? What do you think, Maggie?" she said, appealing to her sister. "Shall I go, or shan't I? Shall I go, or shan't I?" Maggie said nothing.

Then Sara got up, went to the window and stood there for a moment humming a tune. "Go search the valleys; pluck up every rose," she hummed. The man was passing; he was crying, "Any old iron? Any old iron?" She turned round with a sudden jerk.

"I'll come," she said, as if she had made up her mind. "I'll fling on my clothes and come."

She sprang up and went into the bedroom. She's like one of those birds at the Zoo, Rose thought, that never flies but hops rapidly across the grass.

She turned to the window. It was a depressing little street, she thought. There was a public-house at the corner. The houses opposite looked very dingy, and it was very noisy. "Any old iron to sell?" the man was crying under the window, "any old iron?" Children were screaming in the road; they were playing a game with chalk-marks on the pavement. She stood there looking down on them.

"Poor little wretches!" she said. She picked up her hat and ran two bonnet-pins sharply through it. "Don't you find it rather unpleasant," she said, giving her hat a little pat on one side as she looked in the looking-glass, "coming home late at night sometimes with that public-house at the corner?"

"Drunken men, you mean?" said Maggie.

"Yes," said Rose. She buttoned the row of leather buttons on her tailor-made suit and gave herself a little pat here and there, as if she were making ready.

"And now what are you talking about?" said Sara, coming in carrying her shoes. "Another visit to Italy?"

"No," said Maggie. She spoke indistinctly because her mouth was full of pins. "Drunken men following one."

"Drunken men following one," said Sara. She sat down and began to put on her shoes.

"But they don't follow me," she said. Rose smiled. That was obvious. She was sallow, angular and plain. "I can walk over Waterloo Bridge at any hour of the day or night," she continued, tugging at her shoe-laces, "and nobody notices." The shoe-lace was in a knot; she fumbled with it. "But I can remember," she continued, "being told by a woman—a very beautiful woman—she was like—"

"Hurry up," Maggie interrupted. "Rose is waiting."

". . . Rose is waiting—well, the woman told me, when she went into Regent's Park to have an ice"—she stood up, trying to fit her shoe on to her foot—"to have an ice, at one of those little tables under the trees, one of those little round tables laid with a cloth under the trees"—she hopped about with one shoe off and one shoe on—"the eyes, she said, came through every leaf like the darts of the sun; and her ice was melted. . . . Her ice was melted!" she repeated, tapping her sister on the shoulder as she twirled round on her toe.

Rose held out her hand. "You're going to stay and finish your dress?" she said. "You won't come with us?" It was Maggie she wanted to come.

"No, I won't come," said Maggie, shaking hands. "I should hate it," she added, smiling at Rose with a candour that was baffling.

Did she mean me? thought Rose as she went down the stairs. Did she mean that she hated me? When I liked her so much?

IN THE ALLEY that led into the old square off Holborn an elderly man, battered and red-nosed, as if he had weathered out many years at street corners, was selling violets. He had his pitch by a row of posts. The bunches, tightly laced, each with a green frill of leaves round the rather withered flowers, lay in a row on the tray; for he had not sold many.

"Nice vilets, fresh vilets," he repeated automatically as the people passed. Most of them went by without looking. But he went on repeating his formula automatically. "Nice vilets, fresh vilets," as if he scarcely expected anyone to buy. Then two ladies came; and he held out his violets, and he said once more, "Nice vilets, fresh vilets." One of them slapped down two coppers on his tray; and he looked up. The other lady stopped, put her hand on the post, and said, "Here I leave you." Upon which the one who was short and stout, struck her on the shoulder and said, "Don't be such an ass!" And the tall lady gave a sudden cackle of laughter, took a bunch of violets from the tray as if she had paid for it; and off they walked. She's an odd customer, he thought—she took the violets though she hadn't paid for them. He watched them walking round the square; then he began muttering again, "Nice vilets, sweet vilets."

"Is THIS the place where you meet?" said Sara as they walked along the square.

It was very quiet. The noise of the traffic had ceased. The trees were not in full leaf yet, and pigeons were shuffling and crooning on the tree tops. Little bits of twig fell on the pavement as the birds fidgeted among the branches. A soft air puffed in their faces. They walked on round the square.

"That's the house over there," said Rose, pointing. She stopped when she reached a house with a carved doorway, and many names on the door-post. The windows on the ground floor were open; the curtains blew in and out, and through them they could see a row of heads, as if people were sitting round a table, talking.

Rose paused on the door-step.

"Are you coming in," she said, "or aren't you?"

Sara hesitated. She peered in. Then she brandished her bunch of violets in Rose's face and cried out, "All right!" she cried. "Ride on!"

MIRIAM PARRISH was reading a letter. Eleanor was blackening the strokes on her blotting-paper. I've heard all this, I've done all this so often, she was thinking. She glanced round the table. People's faces even seemed to repeat themselves. There's the Judd type, there's the Lazenby type, and there's Miriam, she thought, drawing on her blotting-paper. I know what he's going to say, I know what she's going to say, she thought, digging a little hole in the blotting-paper. Here Rose came in. But who's that with her, Eleanor asked? She did not recognise her. Whoever it was was waved by Rose to a seat in the corner, and the meeting went on. Why must we do it? Eleanor thought, drawing a spoke from the hole in the middle. She looked up. Someone was rattling a stick along the railings and whistling; the branches of a tree swung up and down in the garden outside. The leaves were already unfolding. . . . Miriam put down her papers; Mr. Spicer rose.

There's no other way, I suppose, she thought, taking up her pencil again. She made a note as Mr. Spicer spoke. She found that her pencil could take notes quite accurately while she herself thought of something else. She seemed able to divide herself into two. One person followed the argument—and he's putting it very well, she thought; while the other, for it was a fine afternoon, and she had wanted to go to Kew, walked down a green glade and stopped in front of a flowering tree. Is it a magnolia? she asked herself, or are they already over? Magnolias, she remembered, have no leaves, but masses of white blossom. . . . She drew a line on the blotting-paper.

Now Pickford . . . she said, looking up again. Mr. Pickford spoke. She drew more spokes; blackened them. Then she looked up, for there was a change in the tone of voice.

"I know Westminster very well," Miss Ashford was saying.

"So do I!" said Mr. Pickford. "I've lived there for forty years."

Eleanor was surprised. She had always thought he lived at Ealing. He lived at Westminster, did he? He was a clean-shaven, dapper little man, whom she had always seen in her mind's eye running to catch a train with a newspaper under his arm. But he lived at Westminster, did he? That was odd, she thought.

Then they went on arguing again. The cooing of the pigeons became audible. Take two coos, take two coos, tak . . . they were crooning. Martin was speaking. And he speaks very well, she thought . . . but he shouldn't be sarcastic; it puts people's backs up. She drew another stroke.

Then she heard the rush of a car outside; it stopped outside the window. Martin stopped speaking. There was a momentary pause. Then the door opened and in came a tall woman in evening dress. Everybody looked up.

"Lady Lasswade!" said Mr. Pickford, getting up and scraping back his chair.

"Kitty!" Eleanor exclaimed. She half rose, but she sat down again. There was a little stir. A chair was found for her. Lady Lasswade took her place opposite Eleanor.

"I'm so sorry," she apologised, "to be so late. And for coming in these ridiculous clothes," she added, touching her cloak. She did look strange, dressed in evening dress in the broad daylight. There was something shining in her hair.

"The Opera?" said Martin as she sat down beside him.

"Yes," she said briefly. She laid her white gloves in a businesslike way on the table. Her cloak opened and showed the gleam of a silver dress beneath. She did look odd compared with the others; but it's very good of her to come, Eleanor thought, looking at her, considering she's going on to the Opera. The meeting began again.

How long has she been married? Eleanor wondered. How long is it since we broke the swing together at Oxford? She drew another stroke on the blotting-paper. The dot was now surrounded with strokes.

". . . and we discussed the whole matter perfectly frankly," Kitty was saying. Eleanor listened. That's the manner I like, she thought. She had been meeting Sir Edward at dinner. . . . It's the great ladies' manner, Eleanor thought . . . authoritative, natural. She listened again. The great ladies' manner charmed Mr. Pickford; but it irritated Martin, she knew. He was pooh-poohing Sir Edward and his frankness. Then Mr. Spicer was off again; and Kitty had joined in. Now there was Rose. They were all at loggerheads. Eleanor listened. She became more and more irritated. All it comes to is: I'm right and you're wrong, she thought. This bickering merely wasted time. If we could only get at something, something deeper, deeper, she thought, prodding her pencil on the blotting-paper. Suddenly she saw the only point that was of any importance. She had the words on the tip of her tongue. She opened her mouth to speak. But just as she cleared her throat, Mr. Pickford swept his papers together and rose. Would they pardon him? he said. He had to be at the Law Courts. He rose and went.

The meeting dragged on. The ash-tray in the middle of the table became full of cigarette-stumps; the air became thick with smoke; then Mr. Spicer went; Miss Bodham went; Miss Ashford wound a scarf tightly round her neck, snapped her attaché-case to, and strode out of the room. Miriam Parrish took off her pince-nez and fixed them to a hook that was sewn onto the front of her dress. Everybody was going; the meeting was over. Eleanor got up. She wanted to speak to Kitty. But Miriam intercepted her.

"About coming to see you on Wednesday," she began.

"Yes," said Eleanor.

"I've just remembered I've promised to take a niece to the dentist," said Miriam.

"Saturday would suit me just as well," said Eleanor.

Miriam paused. She pondered.

"Would Monday do instead?" she said.

"I'll write," said Eleanor with an irritation that she could never conceal, saint though Miriam was, and Miriam fluttered away with a guilty air as if she were a little dog caught stealing.

ELEANOR TURNED. The others were still arguing.

"You'll agree with me one of these days," Martin was saying.

"Never! Never!" said Kitty, slapping her gloves on the table. She looked very handsome; at the same time rather absurd in her evening dress.

"Why didn't you speak, Nell?" she said, turning on her.

"Because—" Eleanor began, "I don't know," she added, rather feebly. She felt suddenly shabby and dowdy compared with Kitty, who stood there in full evening dress with something shining in her hair.

"Well," said Kitty, turning away, "I must be off. But can't I give anyone a lift?" she said, pointing to the window. There was her car.

"What a magnificent car!" said Martin, looking at it, with a sneer in his voice.

"It's Charlie's," said Kitty rather sharply.

"What about you, Eleanor?" she said, turning to her.

"Thanks," said Eleanor: "—one moment."

She had muddled her things up. She had left her gloves somewhere. Had she brought an umbrella, or hadn't she? She felt flustered and dowdy, as if she were a schoolgirl suddenly. There was the magnificent car waiting, and the chauffeur held the door open with a rug in his hand.

"Get in," said Kitty. And she got in and the chauffeur put the rug over her knees.

"We'll leave them," said Kitty, with a wave of her hand, "caballing." And the car drove off.

"WHAT A pig-headed set they are!" said Kitty, turning to Eleanor.

"Force is always wrong—don't you agree with me?—always wrong!" she repeated, drawing the rug over her knees. She was still under the influence of the meeting. Yet she wanted to talk to Eleanor. They met so seldom; she liked her so much. But she was shy, sitting there in her absurd clothes, and she could not jerk her mind out of the rut of the meeting in which it was running.

"What a pig-headed set they are!" she repeated. Then she began:

"Tell me. . . ."

There were many things that she wanted to ask; but the engine was so powerful; the car swept in and out of the traffic so smoothly; before she had time to say any of the things she wanted to say Eleanor had put her hand out because they had reached the Tube station.

"Would he stop here?" she said, rising.

"But must you get out?" Kitty began. She had wanted to talk to her. "I must, I must," said Eleanor. "Papa's expecting me." She felt like a child again beside this great lady and the chauffeur, who was holding the door open.

"Do come and see me — do let us meet again soon, Nell," said Kitty, taking her hand.

THE CAR STARTED on again. Lady Lasswade sat back in her corner. She wished she saw more of Eleanor, she thought; but she never could get her to come and dine. It was always "Papa's expecting me" or some other excuse, she thought rather bitterly. They had gone such different ways, they had lived such different lives, since Oxford. . . . The car slowed down. It had to take its place in the long line of cars that moved at a foot's pace, now stopping dead, now jerking on, down the narrow street, blocked by market carts, that led to the Opera House. Men and women in full evening dress were walking along the pavement. They looked uncomfortable and self-conscious as they dodged between costers' barrows, with their high-piled hair and their evening cloaks; with their button holes and their white waistcoats in the glare of the afternoon sun. The ladies tripped uncomfortably on their high-heeled shoes; now and then they put their hands to their heads. The gentlemen kept close beside them as though protecting them. It's absurd, Kitty thought; it's ridiculous to come out in full evening dress at this time of day. She leant back in her corner. Covent Garden porters, dingy little clerks in their ordinary working clothes, coarse-looking women in aprons stared in at her. The air smelt strongly of oranges and bananas. But the car was coming to a standstill. It drew up under the archway; she pushed through the glass doors and went in.

She felt at once a sense of relief. Now that the daylight was extinguished and the air glowed yellow and crimson, she no longer felt absurd. On the contrary, she felt appropriate. The ladies and gentlemen who were mounting the stairs were dressed exactly as she was. The smell of oranges and bananas had been replaced by another smell—a subtle mixture of clothes and gloves and flowers that affected her pleasantly. The carpet was thick beneath her feet. She went along the corridor till she came to her own box with the card on it. She went in and the whole Opera House opened in front of her. She was not late after all. The orchestra was still tuning up; the players were laughing, talking and turning round in their seats as they fiddled busily with their instruments. She stood looking down at the stalls. The floor of the house was in a state of great agitation. People were passing to their seats; they were sitting down and getting up again; they were taking off their cloaks and signalling to friends. They were like birds settling on a field. In the boxes white figures were appearing here and there; white arms rested on the ledges of boxes; white shirt-fronts shone beside them. The whole house glowed—red, gold, cream-coloured, and smelt of clothes and flowers, and echoed with the squeaks and trills of the instruments and with the buzz and hum of voices. She glanced at the programme that was laid on the ledge of her box. It was *Siegfried*—her favourite opera. In a little space within the highly decorated border the names of the cast were given. She stooped to read them; then a thought struck her and she glanced at the royal box. It was empty. As she looked the door opened and two men came in; one was her cousin Edward; the other a boy, a cousin of her husband's.

"They haven't put it off?" he said as he shook hands. "I was afraid they might." He was something in the Foreign Office; with a handsome Roman head.

They all looked instinctively at the royal box. Programmes lay along the edge; but there was no bouquet of pink carnations. The box was empty.

"The doctors have given him up," said the young man, looking very important. They all think they know everything, Kitty thought, smiling at his air of private information.

"But if he dies?" she said, looking at the royal box, "d'you think they'll stop it?"

The young man shrugged his shoulders. About that he could not be positive apparently. The house was filling up. Lights winked on ladies' arms as they turned; ripples of light flashed, stopped, and then flashed the opposite way as they turned their heads.

But now the conductor pushed his way through the orchestra to his raised seat. There was an outburst of applause; he turned, bowed to the audience; turned again, all the lights sank down; the overture had begun.

Kitty leant back against the wall of the box; her face was shaded by the folds of the curtain. She was glad to be shaded. As they played the overture she looked at Edward. She could only see the outline of his face in the red glow; it was heavier than it used to be; but he looked intellectual, handsome and a little remote as he listened to the overture. It wouldn't have done, she thought; I'm much too . . . she did not finish the sentence. He has never married, she thought; and she had. And I've three boys. I've been in Australia, I've been in India. . . . The music made her think of herself and her own life as she seldom did. It exalted her; it cast a flattering light over herself, her past. But why did Martin laugh at me for having a car? she thought. What's the good of laughing? she asked.

Here the curtain went up. She leant forward and looked at the stage. The dwarf was hammering at the sword. Hammer, hammer, hammer, he went with little short, sharp strokes. She listened. The music had changed. *He,* she thought, looking at the handsome boy, knows exactly what the music means. He was already completely possessed by the music. She liked the look of complete absorption that had swum up on top of his immaculate respectability, making him seem almost stern. . . . But here was Siegfried. She leant forward. Dressed in leopard-skins, very fat, with nut-brown thighs, leading a bear—here he was. She liked the fat bouncing young man in his flaxen wig: his voice was magnificent. Hammer, hammer, hammer he went. She leant back again. What did that make her think of? A young man who came into a room with shavings in his hair . . . when she was very young. In Oxford? She had gone to tea with them; had sat on a hard chair; in a very light room; and there was a sound of hammering in the garden. And then a boy came in with shavings in his hair. And she had wanted him to kiss her. Or was it the farm hand up at Carter's, when old Carter had loomed up suddenly leading a bull with a ring through its nose?

"That's the sort of life I like," she thought, taking up her opera-glasses. "That's the sort of person I am . . ." she finished her sentence.

Then she put the opera-glasses to her eyes. The scenery suddenly became bright and close; the grass seemed to be made of thick green wool; she could see Siegfried's fat brown arms glistening with paint. His face was shiny. She put down the glasses and leant back in her corner.

And old Lucy Craddock—she saw Lucy sitting at a table; with her red nose, and her patient, kind eyes. "So you've done no work this week again, Kitty!" she said reproachfully. How I loved her! Kitty thought. And then she had gone back to the Lodge; and there was the tree, with a prop in the middle; and her mother sitting bolt upright. . . . I wish I hadn't quarrelled so much with my mother, she thought, overcome with a sudden sense of the passage of time and its tragedy. Then the music changed.

She looked at the stage again. The Wanderer had come in. He was sitting on a bank in a long grey dressing-gown; and a patch wobbled uncomfortably over one of his eyes. On and on he went; on and on. Her attention flagged. She glanced round the dim red house; she could only see white elbows pointed on the ledges of boxes; here and there a sharp pinpoint of light showed as someone followed the score with a torch. Edward's fine profile again caught her eye. He was listening, critically, intently. It wouldn't have done, she thought, it wouldn't have done at all.

At last the Wanderer had gone. And now? she asked herself, leaning forward. Siegfried burst in. Dressed in his leopard-skins, laughing and singing, here he was again. The music excited her. It was magnificent. Siegfried took the broken pieces of the sword and blew on the fire and hammered, hammered, hammered. The singing, the hammering and the fire leaping all went on at the same time. Quicker and quicker, more and more rhythmically, more and more triumphantly he hammered, until at last up he swung the sword high above his head and brought it down—crack! The anvil burst asunder. And then he brandished the sword over his head and shouted and sang; and the music rushed higher and higher; and the curtain fell.

The lights opened in the middle of the house. All the colour came back. The whole Opera House leapt into life again with its faces and its diamonds and its men and women. They were clapping and waving their programmes. The whole house seemed to be fluttering with white squares of paper. The curtains fell apart and were held back by tall footmen in knee-breeches. Kitty stood up and clapped. Again the curtains closed; again they parted. The footmen were almost pulled off their feet by the heavy folds that they had to hold back. Again and again they held the curtain back; and even when they had let it fall and the singers had disappeared and the orchestra were leaving their seats, the audience still stood clapping and waving their programmes.

Kitty turned to the young man in her box. He was leaning over the ledge. He was still clapping. He was shouting "Bravo! Bravo!" He had forgotten her. He had forgotten himself.

"Wasn't that marvellous?" he said at last, turning round.

There was an odd look on his face as if he were in two worlds at once and had to draw them together.

"Marvellous!" she agreed. She looked at him with a pang of envy.

"And now," she said, gathering her things together, "let us have dinner."

At Hyams Place they had finished dinner. The table was cleared; only a few crumbs remained, and the pot of flowers stood in the middle of the table like a sentry. The only sound in the room was the stitching of a needle, pricking through silk, for Maggie was sewing. Sara sat hunched on the music stool, but she was not playing.

"Sing something," said Maggie suddenly. Sara turned and struck the notes.

"Brandishing, flourishing my sword in my hand . . ." she sang. The words were the words of some pompous eighteenth century march, but her voice was reedy and thin. Her voice broke. She stopped singing.

She sat silent with her hands on the notes. "What's the good of singing if one hasn't any voice?" she murmured. Maggie went on sewing.

"What did you do today?" she said at length, looking up abruptly.

"Went out with Rose," said Sara.

"And what did you do with Rose?" said Maggie. She spoke absent-mindedly. Sara turned and glanced at her. Then she began to play again. "Stood on the bridge and looked into the water," she murmured.

"Stood on the bridge and looked into the water," she hummed, in time to the music. "Running water; flowing water. May my bones turn to coral; and fish light their lanthorns; fish light their green lanthorns in my eyes." She half turned and looked round at Maggie. But she was not attending. Sara was silent. She looked at the notes again. But she did not see the notes, she saw a garden; flowers; and her sister; and a young man with a big nose who stooped to pick a flower that was gleaming in the dark. And he held the flower out in his hand in the moonlight . . . Maggie interrupted her.

"You went out with Rose," she said. "Where to?"

Sara left the piano and stood in front of the fireplace.

"We got into a bus and went to Holborn," she said. "And we walked along a street," she went on; "and suddenly," she jerked her hand out, "I felt a clap on my shoulder. 'Damned liar!' said Rose, and took me and flung me against a public-house wall!"

Maggie stitched on in silence.

"You got into a bus and went to Holborn," she repeated mechanically after a time. "And then?"

"Then we went into a room," Sara continued, "and there were people—multitudes of people. And I said to myself . . ." she paused.

"A meeting?" Maggie murmured. "Where?"

"In a room," Sara answered. "A pale greenish light. A woman hanging clothes on a line in the back garden; and someone went by rattling a stick on the railings."

"I see," said Maggie. She stitched on quickly.

"I said to myself," Sara resumed, "whose heads are those . . ." she paused.

"A meeting," Maggie interrupted her. "What for? What about?"

"There were pigeons cooing," Sara went on. "Take two coos, Taffy. Take two coos . . . Tak . . . And then a wing darkened the air, and in came Kitty clothed in starlight; and sat on a chair."

She paused. Maggie was silent. She went on stitching for a moment.

"Who came in?" she asked at length.

"Somebody very beautiful; clothed in starlight; with green in her hair," said Sara. "Whereupon"—here she changed her voice and imitated the tones in which a middle class man might be supposed to welcome a lady of fashion, "up jumps Mr. Pickford, and says, 'Oh, Lady Lasswade, won't you take this chair?'"

She pushed a chair in front of her.

"And then," she went on, flourishing her hands, "Lady Lasswade sits down; puts her gloves on the table"—she patted a cushion—"like that."

Maggie looked up over her sewing. She had a general impression of a room full of people; sticks rattling on the railings; clothes hanging out to dry, and someone coming in with beetles' wings in her hair.

"What happened then?" she asked.

"Then withered Rose, spiky Rose, tawny Rose, thorny Rose," Sara burst out laughing, "shed a tear."

"No, no," said Maggie. There was something wrong with the story; something impossible. She looked up. The light of a passing car slid across the ceiling. It was growing too dark to see. The lamp from the public-house opposite made a yellow glare in the room; the ceiling trembled with a watery pattern of fluctuating light. There was a sound of brawling in the street outside; a scuffling and trampling as if the police were hauling someone along the street against his will. Voices jeered and shouted after him.

"Another row?" Maggie murmured, sticking her needle in the stuff.

Sara got up and went to the window. A crowd had gathered outside the public-house. A man was being thrown out. There he came, staggering. He fell against a lamp-post to which he clung. The scene was lit up by the glare of the lamp over the public-house door. Sara stood for a moment at the window watching them. Then she turned; her face in the mixed light looked cadaverous and worn, as if she were no longer a girl, but an old woman worn out by a life of childbirth, debauchery and crime. She stood there hunched up, with her hands clenched together.

"In time to come," she said, looking at her sister, "people, looking into this room—this cave, this little antre, scooped out of mud and dung, will hold their fingers to their noses"—she held her fingers to her nose—"and say, 'Pah! They stink!'"

She fell down into a chair.

Maggie looked at her. Curled round, with her hair falling over her face and her hands screwed together she looked like some great ape, crouching there in a little cave of mud and dung. "Pah!" Maggie repeated to herself, "They stink" . . . She drove her needle through the stuff in a spasm of disgust. It was true, she thought; they were nasty little creatures, driven by uncontrollable lusts. The night was full of roaring and cursing; of violence and unrest, also of beauty and joy. She got up, holding the dress in her hands. The folds of silk fell down to the floor and she ran her hand over them.

"That's done. That's finished," she said, laying the dress on the table. There was nothing more she could do with her hands. She folded the dress up and put it away. Then the cat, which had been asleep, rose very slowly, arched its back and stretched itself to its full length.

"You want your supper, do you?" said Maggie. She went into the kitchen and came back with a saucer of milk. "There, poor puss," she said, putting the saucer down on the floor. She stood watching the cat lap up its milk, mouthful by mouthful; then it stretched itself out again with extraordinary grace.

Sara, standing at a little distance, watched her. Then she imitated her.

"There, poor puss, there, poor puss," she repeated. "As you rock the cradle, Maggie," she added.

Maggie raised her arms as if to ward off some implacable destiny; then let them fall. Sara smiled as she watched her; then tears brimmed, fell and ran slowly down her cheeks. But as she put up her hand to wipe them there was a sound of knocking; somebody was hammering on the door of the next house. The hammering stopped. Then it began again—hammer, hammer, hammer.

They listened.

"Upcher's come home drunk and wants to be let in," said Maggie. The knocking ceased. Then it began again.

Sara dried her eyes, roughly, energetically.

"Bring up your children on a desert island where the ships only come when the moon's full!" she exclaimed.

"Or have none?" said Maggie. A window was thrown open. A woman's voice was heard shrieking abuse at the man. He bawled back in a thick drunken voice from the doorstep. Then the door slammed.

They listened.

"Now he'll stagger against the wall and be sick," said Maggie. They could hear heavy footsteps lurching up the stairs in the next house. Then there was silence.

Maggie crossed the room to shut the window. The great windows of the factory opposite were all lit up; it looked like a palace of glass with thin black bars across it. A glaze of yellow light lit up the lower halves of the houses opposite; the slate roofs shone blue, for the sky hung down in a heavy canopy of yellow light. Footsteps tapped on the pavement, for people were still walking in the street. Far off a voice was crying hoarsely. Maggie leant out. The night was windy and warm.

"What's he crying?" she said.

The voice came nearer and nearer.

"Death . . . ?" she said.

"Death . . . ?" said Sara. They leant out. But they could not hear the rest of the sentence. Then a man who was wheeling a barrow along the street shouted up to them:

"The King's dead!"

1911

THE SUN was rising. Very slowly it came up over the horizon shaking out light. But the sky was so vast, so cloudless, that to fill it with light took time. Very gradually the clouds turned blue; leaves on forest trees sparkled; down below a flower shone; eyes of beasts—tigers, monkeys, birds—sparkled. Slowly the world emerged from darkness. The sea became like the skin of an innumerable scaled fish, glittering gold. Here in the South of France the furrowed vineyards caught the light; the little vines turned purple and yellow; and the sun coming through the slats of the blinds striped the white walls. Maggie, standing at the window, looked down on the courtyard, and saw her husband's book cracked across with shadow from the vine above; and the glass that stood beside him glowed yellow. Cries of peasants working came through the open window.

The sun, crossing the channel, beat vainly on the blanket of thick sea mist. Light slowly permeated the haze over London; struck on the statues in Parliament Square, and on the Palace where the flag flew though the King, borne under a white and blue Union Jack, lay in the caverns at Frogmore. It was hotter than ever. Horses' noses hissed as they drank from the troughs; their hoofs made ridges hard and brittle as plaster on the country roads. Fires tearing over the moors left charcoal twigs behind them. It was August, the holiday season. The glass roofs of the great railway stations were globes incandescent with light. Travellers watched the hands of the round yellow clocks as they followed porters, wheeling portmanteaus, with dogs on leashes. In all the stations trains were ready to bore their way through England; to the North, to the South, to the West. Now the guard standing with his hand raised dropped his flag and the tea-urn slid past. Off the trains swung through the public gardens with asphalt paths; past the factories; into open country. Men standing on bridges fishing looked up; horses cantered; women came to doors and shaded their eyes; the shadow of the smoke floated over the corn, looped down and caught a tree. And on they passed.

IN THE station yard at Wittering, Mrs. Chinnery's old victoria stood waiting. The train was late; it was very hot. William the gardener sat on the box in his buff-coloured coat with the plated buttons flicking the flies off. The flies were troublesome. They had gathered in little brown clusters on the horses' ears. He flicked his whip; the old mare stamped her hoofs; and shook her ears, for the flies had settled again. It was very hot. The sun beat down on the station yard, on the carts and flies and traps waiting for the train. At last the signal dropped; a puff of smoke blew over the hedge; and in a minute people came streaming out into the yard, and here was Miss Pargiter carrying her bag in her hand and a white umbrella. William touched his hat.

"Sorry to be so late," said Eleanor, smiling up at him, for she knew him; she came every year.

She put her bag on the seat and sat back under the shade of her white umbrella. The leather of the carriage was hot behind her back; it was very hot—hotter even than Toledo. They turned into the High Street; the heat seemed to make everything drowsy and silent. The broad street was full of traps and carts with the reins hanging loose and the horses' heads drooping.

But after the din of the foreign market places how quiet it seemed! Men in gaiters were leaning against the walls; the shops had their awnings out; the pavement was barred with shadow. They had parcels to fetch. At the fishmonger's they stopped; and a damp white parcel was handed out to them. At the iron-monger's they stopped; and William came back with a scythe. Then they stopped at the chemist's; but there they had to wait, because the lotion was not yet ready.

Eleanor sat back under the shade of her white umbrella. The air seemed to hum with the heat. The air seemed to smell of soap and chemicals. How thoroughly people wash in England, she thought, looking at the yellow soap, the green soap, and the pink soap in the chemist's window. In Spain she had hardly washed at all; she had dried herself with a pocket hand-kerchief standing among the white dry stones of the Guadal-quivir. In Spain it was all parched and shrivelled. But here — she looked down the High Street — every shop was full of vege-tables; of shining silver fish; of yellow-clawed, soft-breasted chickens; of buckets, rakes and wheel-barrows. And how friendly people were!

She noticed how often hats were touched; hands were grasped; people stopped, talking, in the middle of the road. But now the chemist came out with a large bottle wrapped in tissue paper. It was stowed away under the scythe.

"Midges very bad this year, William?" she asked, recognis-ing the lotion.

"Tarrible bad, miss, tarrible," he said, touching his hat. There hadn't been such a drought since the Jubilee she under-stood him to say; but his accent, his sing-song and Dorsetshire rhythm, made it difficult to catch what he said. Then he flicked his whip and they drove on; past the market cross; past the red brick town hall, with the arches under it; along a street of bow-

windowed eighteenth century houses, the residences of doctors
and solicitors; past the pond with chains linking white posts together and a horse drinking; and so out into the country. The
road was laid with soft white dust; the hedges, hung with
wreaths of travellers' joy, seemed also thick with dust. The old
horse settled down into his mechanical jog trot, and Eleanor lay
back under her white umbrella.

Every summer she came to visit Morris at his mother-in-
law's house. Seven times, eight times she had come, she
counted; but this year it was different. This year everything was
different. Her father was dead; her house was shut up; she had
no attachment at the moment anywhere. As she jolted through
the hot lanes she thought drowsily, What shall I do now? Live
there? she asked herself, as she passed a very respectable Georgian villa in the middle of a street. No, not in a village, she said
to herself; and they jogged through the village. What about that
house then, she said to herself, looking at a house with a verandah among some trees. But then she thought, I should turn into
a grey-haired lady cutting flowers with a pair of scissors and tapping at cottage doors. She did not want to tap at cottage doors.
And the clergyman—a clergyman was wheeling his bicycle up
the hill—would come to tea with her. But she did not want the
clergyman to come to tea with her. How spick and span it all is,
she thought; for they were passing through the village. The little
gardens were bright with red and yellow flowers. Then they
began to meet village people; a procession. Some of the women
carried parcels; there was a gleaming silver object on the quilt of
a perambulator; and one old man clasped a hairy-headed coconut to his breast. There had been a Fête she supposed; here
it was, returning. They drew to the side of the road as the carriage trotted past, and cast steady curious looks at the lady sitting under her white umbrella. Now they came to a white gate;

trotted briskly down a short avenue; and drew up with a flourish of the whip in front of two slender columns; door-scrapers
like bristling hedgehogs; and a wide open hall door.

She waited for a moment in the hall. Her eyes were dimmed
after the glare of the road. Everything seemed pale and frail and
friendly. The rugs were faded; the pictures were faded. Even the
Admiral in his cocked hat over the fireplace wore a curious look
of faded urbanity. In Greece one was always going back two
thousand years. Here it was always the eighteenth century. Like
everything English, she thought, laying down her umbrella on
the refectory table beside the china bowl, with dried rose leaves
in it, the past seemed near, domestic, friendly.

THE DOOR OPENED. "Oh, Eleanor!" her sister-in-law exclaimed, running into the hall in her fly-away summer clothes.
"How nice to see you! How brown you look! Come into the
cool!"

She led her into the drawing-room. The drawing-room piano
was strewn with white baby-linen; pink and green fruit glim-
mered in glass bottles.

"We're in such a mess," said Celia, sinking onto the sofa.
"Lady St. Austell has only just this minute gone, and the Bishop."

She fanned herself with a sheet of paper.

"But it's been a great success. We had the bazaar in the garden. They acted." It was a programme with which she was fan-
ning herself.

"A play?" said Eleanor.

"Yes, a scene from Shakespeare," said Celia. "*Midsummer-
Night? As You Like It?* I forget which. Miss Green got it up.
Happily it was so fine. Last year it poured. But how my feet are
aching!" The long window opened onto the lawn. Eleanor could
see people dragging tables.

"What an undertaking!" she said.

"It was!" Celia panted. "We had Lady St. Austell and the Bishop, coconut shies and a pig; but I think it all went off very well. They enjoyed it."

"For the Church?" Eleanor asked.

"Yes. The new steeple," said Celia.

"What a business!" said Eleanor again. She looked out onto the lawn. The grass was already scorched and yellow; the laurel bushes looked shrivelled. Tables were standing against the laurel bushes. Morris passed, dragging a table.

"Was it nice in Spain?" Celia was asking. "Did you see wonderful things?"

"Oh, yes!" Eleanor exclaimed. "I saw . . ." She stopped. She had seen wonderful things—buildings, mountains, a red city in a plain. But how could she describe it?

"You must tell me all about it afterwards," said Celia, getting up. "It's time we got ready. But I'm afraid," she said, toiling rather painfully up the broad staircase, "I must ask you to be careful, because we're very short of water. The well . . ." she stopped. The well, Eleanor remembered, always gave out in a hot summer. They walked together down the broad passage, past the old yellow globe which stood under the pleasant eighteenth-century picture of all the little Chinnerys in long drawers and nankeen trousers standing round their father and mother in the garden. Celia paused with her hand on the bedroom door. The sound of doves cooing came in through the open window.

"We're putting you in the Blue room this time," she said. Generally Eleanor had the Pink room. She glanced in. "I hope you've got everything—" she began.

"Yes, I'm sure I've got everything," said Eleanor, and Celia left her.

THE MAID had already unpacked her things. There they were— laid on the bed. Eleanor took off her dress, and stood in her white petticoat washing herself, methodically but carefully, since they were short of water. The English sun still made her face prickle all over where the Spanish sun had burnt it. Her neck had been cut off from her chest as if it had been painted brown, she thought, as she slipped on her evening dress in front of the looking-glass. She twisted her thick hair, with the grey strand in it, rapidly into a coil; hung the jewel, a red blob like congealed raspberry jam with a gold seed in the centre, round her neck; and gave one glance at the woman who had been for fifty-five years so familiar that she no longer saw her—Eleanor Pargiter. That she was getting old was obvious; there were wrinkles across her forehead; hollows and creases where the flesh used to be firm.

And what was my good point? she asked herself, running the comb once more through her hair. My eyes? Her eyes laughed back at her as she looked at them. My eyes, yes, she thought. Somebody had once praised her eyes. She made herself open them instead of screwing them together. Round each eye were several little white strokes, where she had crinkled them up to avoid the glare on the Acropolis, at Naples, at Granada and Toledo. But that's over, she thought, people praising my eyes, and finished her dressing.

She stood for a moment looking at the burnt, dry lawn. The grass was almost yellow; the elm trees were beginning to turn brown; red-and-white cows were munching on the far side of the sunk hedge. But England was disappointing, she thought; it was small; it was pretty; she felt no affection for her native land—none whatever. Then she went down, for she wanted if possible to see Morris alone.

BUT HE was not alone. He got up as she came in and introduced her to a stoutish, white-haired old man in a dinner-jacket.

"You know each other, don't you?" said Morris.

"Eleanor—Sir William Whatney." He put a little stress humorously upon the "Sir" which for a moment confused Eleanor.

"We used to know each other," said Sir William, coming forward and smiling as he took her hand.

She looked at him. Could it be William Whatney—old Dubbin—who used to come to Abercorn Terrace years ago? It was. She had not seen him since he went to India.

But are we all like that? she asked herself, looking from the grisled, crumpled, red-and-yellow face of the boy she had known—he was almost hairless—at her own brother Morris. He looked bald and thin; but surely he was in the prime of life, as she was herself? Or had they all suddenly become old fogies like Sir William? Then her nephew North and her niece Peggy came in with their mother and they went in to dinner. Old Mrs. Chinnery dined upstairs.

How has Dubbin become Sir William Whatney? she wondered, glancing at him as they ate the fish that had been brought up in the damp parcel. She had last seen him—in a boat on the river. They had gone for a picnic; they had supped on an island in the middle of the river. Maidenhead, was it?

They were talking about the Fête. Craster had won the pig; Mrs. Grice had won the silver-plated salver.

"That's what I saw on the perambulator," said Eleanor. "I met the Fête coming back," she explained. She described the procession. And they talked about the Fête.

"Don't you envy my sister-in-law?" said Celia, turning to Sir William. "She's just back from a tour in Greece."

"Indeed!" said Sir William. "Which part of Greece?"

"We went to Athens, then to Olympia, then to Delphi," Eleanor began, reciting the usual formula. They were on purely formal terms evidently—she and Dubbin.

"My brother-in-law, Edward," Celia explained, "takes these delightful tours."

"You remember Edward?" said Morris. "Weren't you up with him?"

"No, he was junior to me," said Sir William. "But I've heard of him, of course. He's—let me think—what is he—a great swell, isn't he?"

"Oh, he's at the top of his tree," said Morris.

He was not jealous of Edward, Eleanor thought; but there was a certain note in his voice which told her that he was comparing his career with Edward's.

"They loved him," she said. She smiled; she saw Edward lecturing troops of devout school mistresses on the Acropolis. Out came their notebooks and down they scribbled every word he said. But he had been very generous; very kind; he had looked after her all the time.

"Did you meet anyone at the Embassy?" Sir William asked her. Then he corrected himself. "Not an Embassy though, is it?"

"No. Athens is not an Embassy," said Morris. Here there was a diversion; what was the difference between an Embassy and a Legation? Then they began to discuss the situation in the Balkans.

"There's going to be trouble there in the near future," Sir William was saying. He turned to Morris; they discussed the situation in the Balkans.

Eleanor's attention wandered. What's he done? she wondered. Certain words and gestures brought him back to her as he had been thirty years ago. There were relics of the old Dubbin if one half-shut one's eyes. She half-shut her eyes. Suddenly she remembered—it was *he* who had praised her eyes. "Your sister has the brightest eyes I ever saw," he had said. Morris had told her. And she had hidden her face behind a newspaper in the train going home to conceal her pleasure. She looked at him again. He was talking. She listened. He seemed too big for the quiet, English dining-room; his voice boomed out. He wanted an audience.

He was telling a story. He spoke in clipped, nervous sentences as if there were a ring round them—a style she admired, but she had missed the beginning. His glass was empty.

"Give Sir William some more wine," Celia whispered to the nervous parlourmaid. There was some juggling with decanters on the sideboard. Celia frowned nervously. A girl from the village who doesn't know her job, Eleanor reflected. The story was reaching its climax; but she had missed several links.

". . . and I found myself in an old pair of riding-breeches standing under a peacock umbrella; and all the good people were crouching with their heads to the ground. 'Good Lord,' I said to myself, 'if they only knew what a bally ass I feel!'" He held out his glass to be filled. "That's how we were taught our job in those days," he added.

He was boasting, of course; that was natural. He came back to England after ruling a district "about the size of Ireland," as they always said; and nobody had ever heard of him. She had a feeling that she would hear a great many more stories that sailed serenely to his own advantage, during the week-end. But he talked very well. He had done a great many interesting things. She wished that Morris would tell stories too. She wished that he would assert himself instead of leaning back and passing his hand—the hand with the cut on it—over his forehead.

Ought I to have urged him to go to the Bar? she thought. Her father had been against it. But once it's done there it is; he married; the children came; he had to go on, whether he wanted to or not. How irrevocable things are, she thought. We make our experiments, then they make theirs. She looked at her nephew North and at her niece Peggy. They sat opposite her with the sun on their faces. Their perfectly healthy egg-shell faces looked extraordinarily young. Peggy's blue dress stuck out

like a child's muslin frock; North was still a brown-eyed cricketing boy. He was listening intently; Peggy was looking down at
her plate. She had the non-committal look which well-brought-
up children have when they listen to the talk of their elders. She
might be amused; or bored? Eleanor could not be sure which it
was.

"There he goes," Peggy said, suddenly looking up. "The
owl...," she said, catching Eleanor's eye. Eleanor turned to
look out of the window behind her. She missed the owl; she saw
the heavy trees, gold in the setting sun; and the cows slowly
moving as they munched their way across the meadow.

"You can time him," said Peggy, "he's so regular." Then
Celia made a move.

"Shall we leave the gentlemen to their politics," she said,
"and have our coffee on the terrace?" and they shut the door
upon the gentlemen and their politics.

"I'll fetch my glasses," said Eleanor, and she went upstairs.

She wanted to see the owl before it got too dark. She was
becoming more and more interested in birds. It was a sign of
old age, she supposed, as she went into her bedroom. An old
maid who washes and watches birds, she said to herself as she
looked in the glass. There were her eyes—they still seemed to
her rather bright, in spite of the lines round them—the eyes she
had shaded in the railway carriage because Dubbin praised
them. But now I'm labelled, she thought—an old maid who
washes and watches birds. That's what they think I am. But I'm
not—I'm not in the least like that, she said. She shook her
head, and turned away from the glass. It was a nice room; shady,
civilised, cool after the bedrooms in foreign inns, with marks on
the wall where someone had squashed bugs and men brawling
under the window. But where were her glasses? Put away in
some drawer? She turned to look for them.

———

"DID FATHER say Sir William was in love with her?" Peggy asked as they waited on the terrace.

"Oh, I don't know about that," said Celia. "But I wish they could have married. I wish she had children of her own. And then they could have settled here," she added. "He's such a delightful man."

Peggy was silent. There was a pause.

Celia resumed:

"I hope you were polite to the Robinsons this afternoon, dreadful as they are. . . ."

"They give ripping parties anyhow," said Peggy.

"'Ripping, ripping,'" her mother complained, half laughing. "I wish you wouldn't pick up all North's slang, my dear. . . . Oh, here's Eleanor," she broke off.

Eleanor came out onto the terrace with her glasses, and sat down beside Celia. It was still very warm; it was still light enough to see the hills in the distance.

"He'll be back in a minute," said Peggy, drawing up a chair. "He'll come along that hedge."

She pointed to the dark line of hedge that went across the meadow. Eleanor focused her glasses and waited.

"Now," said Celia, pouring out the coffee. "There are so many things I want to ask you." She paused. She always had a hoard of questions to ask; she had not seen Eleanor since April. In four months questions accumulated. Out they came drop by drop.

"In the first place," she began. "No. . . ." She rejected that question in favour of another.

"What's all this about Rose?" she asked.

"What?" said Eleanor absentmindedly, altering the focus of her glasses. "It's getting too dark," she said; the field was blurred.

"Morris says she's been had up in a police-court," said Celia. She dropped her voice slightly though they were alone.

"She threw a brick——" said Eleanor. She focused her glasses on the hedge again. She held them poised in case the owl should come that way again.

"Will she be put in prison?" Peggy asked quickly.

"Not this time," said Eleanor. "Next time—— Ah, here he comes!" she broke off. The blunt-headed bird came swinging along the hedge. He looked almost white in the dusk. Eleanor got him within the circle of her lens. He held a little black spot in front of him.

"He's got a mouse in his claws!" she exclaimed. "He's got a nest in the steeple," said Peggy. The owl swooped out of the field of vision.

"Now I can't see him any more," said Eleanor. She lowered her glasses. They were silent for a moment, sipping their coffee. Celia was thinking of her next question; Eleanor anticipated her.

"Tell me about William Whatney," she said. "When I last saw him he was a slim young man in a boat." Peggy burst out laughing.

"That must have been ages ago!" she said.

"Not so very long," said Eleanor. She felt rather nettled. "Well——" she reflected, "twenty years—twenty-five years perhaps."

It seemed a very short time to her; but then, she thought, it was before Peggy was born. She could only be sixteen or seventeen.

"Isn't he a delightful man?" Celia exclaimed. "He was in India, you know. Now he's retired, and we do hope he'll take a house here; but Morris thinks he'd find it too dull."

They sat silent for a moment, looking out over the meadow. The cows coughed now and then as they munched and moved a step further through the grass. A sweet scent of cows and grass was wafted up to them.

"It's going to be another hot day tomorrow," said Peggy. The sky was perfectly smooth; it seemed made of innumerable grey-blue atoms the colour of an Italian officer's cloak; until it reached the horizon where there was a long bar of pure green. Everything looked very settled; very still; very pure. There was not a single cloud, and the stars were not yet showing.

It was small; it was smug; it was petty after Spain, but still, now that the sun had sunk and the trees were massed together without separate leaves it had its beauty, Eleanor thought. The downs were becoming larger and simpler; they were becoming part of the sky.

"How lovely it is!" she exclaimed, as if she were making amends to England after Spain.

"If only Mr. Robinson doesn't build!" sighed Celia; and Eleanor remembered—they were the local scourge; rich people who threatened to build. "I did my best to be polite to them at the bazaar today," Celia continued. "Some people won't ask them; but I say one must be polite to neighbours in the country. . . ."

Then she paused. "There are so many things I want to ask you," she said. The bottle was tilted on its end again. Eleanor waited obediently.

"Have you had an offer for Abercorn Terrace yet?" Celia demanded. Drop, drop, drop, out her questions came.

"Not yet," said Eleanor. "The agent wants me to cut it up into flats."

Celia pondered. Then she hopped on again.

"And now about Maggie—when's her baby going to be born?"

"In November, I think," said Eleanor. "In Paris," she added.

"I hope it'll be all right," said Celia. "But I do wish it could have been born in England." She reflected again. "Her children will be French, I suppose?" she said.

"Yes; French, I suppose," said Eleanor. She was looking at the green bar; it was fading; it was turning blue. It was becoming night.

"Everybody says he's a very nice fellow," said Celia. "But René—René," her accent was bad, "—it doesn't sound like a man's name."

"You can call him Renny," said Peggy, pronouncing it in the English way.

"But that reminds me of Ronny; and I don't like Ronny. We had a stable-boy called Ronny."

"Who stole the hay," said Peggy. They were silent again. "It's such a pity—" Celia began. Then she stopped. The maid had come to clear away the coffee.

"It's a wonderful night, isn't it?" said Celia, adapting her voice to the presence of servants. "It looks as if it would never rain again. In which case I don't know . . ." And she went on prattling about the drought; about the lack of water. The well always ran dry. Eleanor, looking at the hills, hardly listened. "Oh, but there's quite enough for everybody at present," she heard Celia saying. And for some reason she held the sentence suspended without a meaning in her mind's ear, ". . . quite enough for everybody at present," she repeated. After all the foreign languages she had been hearing, it sounded to her pure English. What a lovely language, she thought, saying over to herself again the commonplace words, spoken by Celia quite simply, but with some indescribable burr in the r's, for the Chinnerys had lived in Dorsetshire since the beginning of time.

The maid had gone.

"What was I saying?" Celia resumed. "I was saying, It's such a pity. Yes. . . ." But there was a sound of voices; a scent of cigar smoke; the gentlemen were upon them. "Oh, here they are!" she broke off. And the chairs were pulled up and re-arranged.

They sat in a semi-circle looking across the meadows at the

fading hills. The broad bar of green that lay across the horizon had vanished. Only a tinge was left in the sky. It had become peaceful and cool; in them too something seemed to be smoothed out. There was no need to talk. The owl flew down the meadow again; they could just see the white of his wing against the dark of the hedge.

"There he goes," said North, puffing at a cigar which was his first, Eleanor guessed, Sir William's gift. The elm trees had become dead black against the sky. Their leaves hung in a fretted pattern like black lace with holes in it. Through a hole Eleanor saw the point of a star. She looked up. There was another.

"It's going to be a fine day tomorrow," said Morris, knocking out his pipe against his shoe. Far away on a distant road there was a rattle of cart-wheels; then a chorus of voices singing—country people going home. This is England, Eleanor thought to herself; she felt as if she were slowly sinking into some fine mesh made of branches shaking, hills growing dark, and leaves hanging like black lace with stars among them. But a bat swooped low over their heads.

"I hate bats!" Celia exclaimed, raising her hand to her head nervously.

"Do you?" said Sir William. "I rather like them." His voice was quiet and almost melancholy. Now Celia will say, They get into one's hair, Eleanor thought.

"They get into one's hair," Celia said.

"But I haven't any hair," said Sir William. His bald head, his large face, gleamed out in the darkness.

The bat swooped again, skimming the ground at their feet. A little cool air stirred at their ankles. The trees had become part of the sky. There was no moon, but the stars were coming out. There's another, Eleanor thought, gazing at a twinkling light ahead of her. But it was too low; too yellow; it was another house she realised, not a star. And then Celia began talking to Sir William, whom she wanted to settle near them; and Lady St. Austell had told her that the Grange was to let. Was that the Grange, Eleanor wondered, looking at a light, or a star? And they went on talking.

TIRED OF HER own company, old Mrs. Chinnery had come down early. There she sat in the drawing-room waiting. She had made a formal entry, but there was nobody there. Arrayed in her old ladies' dress of black satin, with a lace cap on her head, she sat waiting. Her hawk-like nose was curved in her shrivelled cheeks; a little red rim showed on one of her drooping eyelids.

"Why don't they come in?" she said peevishly to Ellen, the discreet black maid who stood behind her. Ellen went to the window and tapped on the pane.

Celia stopped talking and turned round. "That's Mama," she said. "We must go in." She got up and pushed back her chair.

After the dark, the drawing-room with its lamps lit had the effect of a stage. Old Mrs. Chinnery sitting in her wheeled chair with her ear trumpet seemed to sit there awaiting homage. She looked exactly the same; not a day older; as vigorous as ever. As Eleanor bent to give her the customary kiss, life once more took on its familiar proportions. So she had bent, night after night, over her father. She was glad to stoop down; it made her feel younger herself. She knew the whole procedure by heart. They, the middle-aged, deferred to the very old; the very old were courteous to them; and then came the usual pause. They had nothing to say to her; she had nothing to say to them. What happened next? Eleanor saw the old lady's eyes suddenly brighten. What made the eyes of an old woman of ninety turn blue? Cards? Yes. Celia had fetched the green baize table; Mrs. Chinnery had a passion for whist. But she too had her ceremony; she too had her manners.

"Not tonight," she said, making a little gesture as if to push away the table. "I am sure it will bore Sir William?" She gave a nod in the direction of the large man who stood there seeming a little outside the family party.

"Not at all. Not at all," he said with alacrity. "Nothing would please me more," he assured her.

You're a good fellow, Dubbin, Eleanor thought. And they drew up the chairs; and dealt the cards; and Morris chaffed his mother-in-law down her ear-trumpet and they played rubber after rubber. North read a book; Peggy strummed on the piano; and Celia, dozing over her embroidery, now and then gave a sudden start and put her hand over her mouth. At last the door opened stealthily. Ellen, the discreet black maid, stood behind Mrs. Chinnery's chair, waiting. Mrs. Chinnery pretended to ignore her, but the others were glad to stop. Ellen stepped forward and Mrs. Chinnery, submitting, was wheeled off to the mysterious upper chamber of extreme old age. Her pleasure was over.

Celia yawned openly.

"The bazaar," she said, rolling up her embroidery. "I shall go to bed. Come, Peggy. Come, Eleanor."

North jumped up with alacrity to open the door. Celia lit the brass candlesticks and began, rather heavily, to climb the stairs. Eleanor followed after. But Peggy lagged behind. Eleanor heard her whispering with her brother in the hall.

"Come along, Peggy," Celia called back over the bannister as she toiled upstairs. When she got to the landing at the top she stopped under the picture of the little Chinnerys and called back again rather sharply:

"Come, Peggy." There was a pause. Then Peggy came, reluctantly. She kissed her mother obediently; but she did not look in the least sleepy. She looked extremely pretty and rather flushed. She did not mean to go to bed, Eleanor felt sure.

———

SHE WENT into her room and undressed. All the windows were
open and she heard the trees rustling in the garden. It was so
hot still that she lay in her nightgown on top of the bed with
only the sheet over her. The candle burnt its little pear-shaped
flame on the table by her side. She lay listening vaguely to the
trees in the garden; and watched the shadow of a moth that
dashed round and round the room. Either I must get up and
shut the window or blow out the candle, she thought drowsily.
She did not want to do either. She wanted to lie still. It was a relief to lie in the semi-darkness after the talk, after the cards. She
could still see the cards falling; black, red and yellow; kings,
queens and knaves; on a green baize table. She looked drowsily
round her. A nice vase of flowers stood on the dressing-table;
there was the polished wardrobe and a china box by her
bedside. She lifted the lid. Yes; four biscuits and a pale piece
of chocolate — in case she should be hungry in the night. Celia
had provided books too, *The Diary of a Nobody, Ruff's Tour in
Northumberland* and an odd volume of Dante, in case she should
wish to read in the night. She took one of the books and laid it
on the counterpane beside her. Perhaps because she had been
travelling, it seemed as if the ship were still padding softly
through the sea; as if the train were still swinging from side to
side as it rattled across France. She felt as if things were moving
past her as she lay stretched on the bed under the single sheet.
But it's not the landscape any longer, she thought; it's people's
lives, their changing lives.

The door of the Pink bedroom shut. William Whatney
coughed next door. She heard him cross the room. Now he
was standing by the window, smoking a last cigar. What's he
thinking, she wondered — about India? — how he stood under
a peacock umbrella? Then he began moving about the room,
undressing. She could hear him take up a brush and put it down
again on his dressing-table. And it's to him, she thought, re-

membering the wide sweep of his chin and the floating stains of
pink and yellow that lay underneath it, that I owe that moment,
which had been more than pleasure, when she hid her face
behind the newspaper in the corner of the third-class railway
carriage.

Now there were three moths dashing round the ceiling.
They made a little tapping noise as they dashed round and
round from corner to corner. If she left the window open much
longer the room would be full of moths. A board creaked in the
passage outside. She listened. Peggy, was it, escaping, to join her
brother? She felt sure there was some scheme on foot. But she
could only hear the heavy-laden branches moving up and down
in the garden; a cow lowing; a bird chirping, and then, to her
delight, the liquid call of an owl going from tree to tree, looping them with silver.

She lay looking at the ceiling. A faint water mark appeared
there. It was like a hill. It reminded her of one of the great desolate mountains in Greece or in Spain, which looked as if nobody had ever set foot there since the beginning of time.

She opened the book that lay on the counterpane. She
hoped it was *Ruff's Tour,* or *The Diary of a Nobody;* but it was
Dante, and she was too lazy to change it. She read a few lines,
here and there. But her Italian was rusty; the meaning escaped
her. There was a meaning however; a hook seemed to scratch
the surface of her mind.

> chè per quanti si dice più lì nostro
> tanto possiede più di ben ciascuno.

What did that mean? She read the English translation.

> For by so many more there are who say 'ours'
> So much the more of good doth each possess.

Brushed lightly by her mind that was watching the moths on the
ceiling, and listening to the call of the owl as it looped from tree
to tree with its liquid cry, the words did not give out their full
meaning, but seemed to hold something furled up in the hard
shell of the archaic Italian. I'll read it one of these days, she
thought, shutting the book. When I've pensioned Crosby off,
when . . . Should she take another house? Should she travel?
Should she go to India, at last? Sir William was getting into bed
next door, his life was over; hers was beginning. No, I don't
mean to take another house, not another house, she thought,
looking at the stain on the ceiling. Again the sense came to her
of a ship padding softly through the waves; of a train swinging
from side to side down a railway-line. Things can't go on for
ever, she thought. Things pass, things change, she thought,
looking up at the ceiling. And where are we going? Where?
Where? . . . The moths were dashing round the ceiling; the book
slipped on to the floor. Craster won the pig, but who was it won
the silver salver? she mused; made an effort; turned round, and
blew out the candle. Darkness reigned.

1 9 1 3

It was January. Snow was falling; snow had fallen all day. The sky spread like a grey goose's wing from which feathers were falling all over England. The sky was nothing but a flurry of falling flakes. Lanes were levelled; hollows filled; the snow clogged the streams, obscured windows, and lay wedged against doors. There was a faint murmur in the air, a slight crepitation, as if the air itself were turning to snow; otherwise all was silent, save when a sheep coughed, snow flopped from a branch, or slipped in an avalanche down some roof in London. Now and again a shaft of light spread slowly across the sky as a car drove through the muffled roads. But as the night wore on, snow covered the wheel ruts; softened to nothingness the marks of the traffic, and coated monuments, palaces and statues with a thick vestment of snow.

It was still snowing when the young man came from the House Agents to see over Abercorn Terrace. The snow cast a hard white glare upon the walls of the bathroom, showed up the cracks on the enamel bath, and the stains on the wall. Eleanor stood looking out of the window. The trees in the back garden were heavily lined with snow; all the roofs were softly moulded with snow; it was still falling. She turned. The young man turned

too. The light was unbecoming to them both, yet the snow—
she saw it through the window at the end of the passage—was
beautiful, falling.

Mr. Grice turned to her, as they went downstairs.

"The fact is, our clients expect more lavatory accommoda-
tion nowadays," he said, stopping outside a bedroom door.

Why can't he say "baths" and have done with it, she thought.
Slowly she went downstairs. Now she could see the snow falling
through the panels of the hall door. As he went downstairs, she
noticed the red ears which stood out over his high collar; and
the neck which he had washed imperfectly in some sink at
Wandsworth. She was annoyed; as he went round the house,
sniffing and peering, he had indicted their cleanliness, their hu-
manity; and he used absurd long words. He was hauling himself
up into the class above him, she supposed, by means of long
words. Now he stepped cautiously over the body of the sleeping dog; took his hat from the hall table, and went down the
front door steps in his business man's buttoned boots, leaving
yellow footprints in the thick white cushion of snow. A four-
wheeler was waiting.

Eleanor turned. There was Crosby, dodging about in her
best bonnet and mantle. She had been following Eleanor about
the house like a dog all the morning; the odious moment could
no longer be put off. Her four-wheeler was at the door; they had
to say good-bye.

"Well, Crosby, it all looks very empty, doesn't it?" said
Eleanor, looking in at the empty drawing-room. The white light
of the snow glared in on the walls. It showed up the marks on
the walls where the furniture had stood, where the pictures had
hung.

"It does, Miss Eleanor," said Crosby. She stood looking too.
Eleanor knew that she was going to cry. She did not want her
to cry. She did not want to cry herself.

"I can still see you all sitting round that table, Miss Eleanor," said Crosby. But the table had gone. Morris had taken this; Delia had taken that; everything had been shared out and separated.

"And the kettle that wouldn't boil," said Eleanor. "D'you remember that?" She tried to laugh.

"Oh, Miss Eleanor," said Crosby, shaking her head, "I remember everything!" The tears were forming; Eleanor looked away into the further room.

There too were marks on the wall, where the bookcase had stood, where the writing-table had stood. She thought of herself sitting there, drawing a pattern on the blotting-paper; digging a hole, adding up tradesmen's books. . . . Then she turned. There was Crosby. Crosby was crying. The mixture of emotions was positively painful; she was so glad to be quit of it all, but for Crosby it was the end of everything.

She had known every cupboard, flagstone, chair and table in that large rambling house, not from five or six feet of distance as they had known it; but from her knees, as she scrubbed and polished; she had known every groove, stain, fork, knife, napkin and cupboard. They and their doings had made her entire world. And now she was going off, alone, to a single room at Richmond.

"I should think you'd be glad to be out of that basement anyhow, Crosby," said Eleanor, turning into the hall again. She had never realised how dark, how low it was, until, looking at it with "our Mr. Grice," she had felt ashamed.

"It was my home for forty years, Miss," said Crosby. The tears were running. For forty years! Eleanor thought with a start. She had been a little girl of thirteen or fourteen when Crosby came to them, looking so stiff and smart. Now her blue gnat's eyes protruded and her cheeks were sunk.

Crosby was stooping to put Rover on the chain.

"You're sure you want him?" said Eleanor, looking at the

rather smelly, wheezy and unattractive old dog. "We could easily find a nice home for him in the country."

"Oh, miss, don't ask me to give him up!" said Crosby. Tears checked her speech. Tears were running freely down her cheeks. For all Eleanor could do to prevent it, tears formed in her eyes too.

"Dear Crosby, good-bye," she said. She bent and kissed her. She had a curious dry quality of skin, she noticed. But her own tears were falling. Then Crosby, holding Rover on the chain, began to edge sideways down the slippery steps. Eleanor, holding the door open, looked after her. It was a dreadful moment; unhappy; muddled; altogether wrong. Crosby was so miserable; she was so glad. Yet as she held the door open her tears formed and fell. They had all lived here; she had stood here to wave Morris to school; there was the little garden in which they used to plant crocuses. And now Crosby with flakes of snow falling on her black bonnet, climbed into the four-wheeler, holding Rover in her arms. Eleanor shut the door and went in.

SNOW WAS FALLING as the cab trotted along the streets. There were long yellow ruts on the pavement where people, shopping, had pressed it into slush. It was beginning to thaw slightly; loads of snow slipped off the roofs and fell onto the pavement. Little boys, too, were snowballing; one of them threw a ball which struck the cab as it passed. But when it turned into Richmond Green the whole of the vast space was completely white. Nobody seemed to have crossed the snow there; everything was white. The grass was white; the trees were white; the railings were white; the only marks in the whole vista were the rooks, sitting huddled black on the tree tops. The cab trotted on.

The carts had churned the snow to a yellowish clotted mixture by the time the cab stopped in front of the little house off the Green. Crosby, carrying Rover in her arms lest his feet

should mark the stairs, went up the steps. There was Louisa
Burt standing to welcome her; and Mr. Bishop, the lodger from
the top floor who had been a butler. He lent a hand with the
luggage, and Crosby followed after, to her little room.

HER ROOM was at the top, and at the back, overlooking the garden. It was small, but when she had unpacked her things it was
comfortable enough. It had a look of Abercorn Terrace. Indeed
for many years she had been hoarding odds and ends with a
view to her retirement. Indian elephants, silver vases, the walrus
that she had found in the waste-paper basket one morning,
when the guns were firing for the old Queen's funeral—there
they all were. She ranged them askew on the mantelpiece, and
when she had hung the portraits of the family—some in
wedding-dress, some in wigs and gowns, and Mr. Martin in his
uniform in the middle because he was her favourite—it was
quite like home.

But whether it was the change to Richmond, or whether he
had caught cold in the snow, Rover sickened immediately. He refused his food. His nose was hot. His eczema broke out again.
When she tried to take him shopping with her next morning he
rolled over with his feet in the air as if he begged to be left alone.
Mr. Bishop had to tell Mrs. Crosby—for she wore the courtesy
title in Richmond—that in his opinion the poor old chap (here
he patted his head) was better out of the way.

"Come along with me, my dear," said Mrs. Burt, putting her
arm on Crosby's shoulder, "and let Bishop do it."

"He won't suffer, I can assure you," said Mr. Bishop, rising
from his knees. He had put her Ladyship's dogs to sleep scores
of time before this. "He'll just take one sniff"—Mr. Bishop had
his pocket-handkerchief in his hand—"and he'll be off in a jiffy."

"It'll be for his good, Annie," Mrs. Burt added, trying to
draw her away.

Indeed, the poor old dog looked very miserable. But Crosby shook her head. He had wagged his tail; his eyes were open. He was alive. There was a gleam of what she had long considered a smile on his face. He depended on her, she felt. She was not going to hand him over to strangers. She sat by his side for three days and nights; she fed him with a teaspoon on Brand's Essence; but at last he refused to open his lips; his body grew stiffer and stiffer; a fly walked across his nose without its twitching. This was in the early morning with the sparrows twittering on the trees outside.

"IT'S A MERCY she's got something to distract her," said Mrs. Burt as Crosby passed the kitchen window the day after the funeral in her best mantle and bonnet; for it was Thursday, when she fetched Mr. Pargiter's socks from Ebury Street. "But he ought to have been put down long ago," she added, turning back to the sink. His breath had smelt.

CROSBY TOOK the District Railway to Sloane Square and then she walked. She walked slowly, with her elbows jutting out from her sides as if to protect herself from the haphazardry of the streets. She still looked sad; but the change from Richmond to Ebury Street did her good. She felt more herself in Ebury Street than in Richmond. A common sort of people lived in Richmond, she always felt. Here the ladies and gentlemen had the same kind of way with them. She glanced approvingly into the shops as she passed. And General Arbuthnot, who used to visit the Master, lived in Ebury Street, she reflected as she turned into that gloomy thoroughfare. He was dead now; Louisa had shown her the notice in the papers. But when he was alive, he had lived here. She had reached Mr. Martin's lodgings. She paused on the steps and adjusted her bonnet. She always had a word with Martin when she came to fetch his socks; it was one of her pleasures; and she enjoyed a gossip with Mrs. Briggs, his landlady. Today she would have the pleasure of telling her of the death of Rover. Sidling cautiously down the area steps which were slippery with sleet she stood at the back door and rang the bell.

MARTIN SAT in his room reading his newspaper. The war in the Balkans was over; but there was more trouble brewing—that he was now quite sure. He turned the page. The room was very dark with the sleet falling. And he could never read while he was waiting. Crosby was coming; he could hear voices in the hall. How they gossiped! How they chattered! he thought impatiently. He threw the paper down and waited. Now she was coming; her hand was on the door. But what was he to say to her? he wondered, as he saw the handle turning. He put down the paper. He made use of the usual formula: "Well, Crosby, how's the world treating you?" as she came in.

She remembered Rover; and the tears started to her eyes.

Martin listened to the story; he wrinkled his brow sympathetically. Then he got up, went into his bedroom, and came back holding a pyjama jacket in his hand.

"What d'you call *that*, Crosby?" he said. He pointed to a hole under the collar, fringed with brown. Crosby adjusted her gold-rimmed spectacles.

"A burn, sir," she said with conviction.

"Brand new pyjamas; only worn them twice," said Martin, holding them extended. Crosby touched them. They were made of the finest silk, she could tell.

"Tut—tut—tut!" she said, shaking her head.

"Will you please take this pyjama to Mrs. What's-her-name," he went on, holding it out in front of him. He wanted to use a metaphor; but one had to be very literal and use only the simplest language, he remembered, when one talked to Crosby.

"Tell her to get another laundress," he concluded, "and send the old one to the devil."

Crosby gathered the injured pyjama tenderly to her breast; Mr. Martin never could abide wool next the skin, she remembered. Martin paused. One must pass the time of the day with Crosby, but the death of Rover had seriously limited their topics of conversation.

"How's the rheumatics?" he asked, as she stood very upright at the door of the room with the pyjamas on her arm. She had grown distinctly smaller, he thought. She shook her head. Richmond was very low compared with Abercorn Terrace, she said. Her face dropped. She was thinking of Rover, he supposed. He must get her mind off that; he could not bear tears.

"Seen Miss Eleanor's new flat?" he asked. Crosby had. But she did not like flats. In her opinion Miss Eleanor wore herself out.

"And the people's not worth it, sir," she said, referring to the Zwinglers, Paravicinis and Cobbs who used to come to the back door for cast-off clothing in the old days.

Martin shook his head. He could not think what to say next. He hated talking to servants; it always made him feel insincere. Either one simpers, or one's hearty, he was thinking. In either case it's a lie.

"And are you keeping pretty well yourself, Master Martin?" Crosby asked him, using the diminutive, which was a perquisite of her long service.

"Not married yet, Crosby," said Martin.

Crosby cast her eye round the room. It was a bachelor's apartment, with its leather chairs; its chessmen on top of a pile of books and its soda-water syphon on a tray. She ventured to say that she was sure that there were plenty of nice young ladies who would be very glad to take care of him.

"Ah, but I like lying in bed of a morning," said Martin.

"You always did, sir," she said, smiling. And then it was possible for Martin to take out his watch, step briskly to the window and exclaim as if he had suddenly remembered an appointment,

"By Jove, Crosby, I must be off!" and the door shut upon Crosby.

IT WAS A LIE. He had no engagement. One always lies to servants, he thought, looking out of the window. The mean outlines of the Ebury Street houses showed through the falling sleet. Everybody lies, he thought. His father had lied—after his death they had found letters from a woman called Mira tied up in his table-drawer. And he had seen Mira—a stout respectable lady who wanted help with her roof. Why had his father lied? What was the harm of keeping a mistress? And he had lied himself; about the room off the Fulham Road where he and Dodge and Erridge used to smoke cheap cigars and tell smutty stories. It was an abominable system, he thought; family life; Abercorn Terrace. No wonder the house would not let. It had one bathroom, and a basement; and there all those different people had lived, boxed up together, telling lies.

Then as he stood at the window looking at the little figures slinking along the wet pavement he saw Crosby come up the area steps with a parcel under her arm. She stood for a moment, like a frightened little animal, peering round her before she ventured to brave the dangers of the street. At last, off she trotted. He saw the snow falling on her black bonnet as she disappeared. He turned away.

It was a brilliant spring; the day was radiant. Even the air seemed to have a burr in it, as it touched the tree tops; it vibrated, it rippled. The leaves were sharp and green. In the country old church clocks rasped out the hour; the rusty sound went over fields that were red with clover, and up went the rooks as if flung by the bells. Round they wheeled; then settled on the tree tops.

In London all was gallant and strident; the Season was beginning; horns hooted; the traffic roared; flags flew taut as trout in a stream. And from all the spires of all the London churches—the fashionable saints of Mayfair, the dowdy saints of Kensington, the hoary saints of the city—the hour was proclaimed. The air over London seemed a rough sea of sound through which circles travelled. But the clocks were irregular, as if the saints themselves were divided. There were pauses, silences. . . . Then the clocks struck again.

Here in Ebury Street some distant frail-voiced clock was striking. It was eleven. Martin, standing at his window, looked down on the narrow street. The sun was bright; he was in the best of spirits; he was going to visit his stockbroker in the city. His affairs were turning out well. At one time, he was thinking, his father had made a lot of money; then he lost it; then he made it; but in the end he had done very well.

He stood at the window for a moment admiring a lady of fashion in a charming hat who was looking at a pot in the curiosity shop opposite. It was a blue pot on a Chinese stand with green brocade behind it. The sloping symmetrical body, the depth of blue, the little cracks in the glaze pleased him. And the lady looking at the pot was also charming.

He took his hat and stick and went out into the street. He would walk part of the way to the city. "The King of Spain's daughter," he hummed as he turned up Sloane Street, "came to visit me. All for the sake of . . ." He looked into the shop windows as he passed. They were full of summer dresses; charming confections of green and gauze, and there were flights of hats stuck on little rods. ". . . all for the sake of," he hummed as he walked on, "my silver nutmeg tree." But what was a silver nutmeg tree he wondered? An organ was fluting its merry little jig further down the street. The organ moved round and round, shifted this way and that, as if the old man who played it were half dancing to the tune. A pretty servant girl ran up the area steps and gave him a penny. His supple Italian face wrinkled all over as he whipped off his cap and bowed to her. The girl smiled and slipped back into the kitchen.

". . . all for the sake of my silver nutmeg tree," Martin hummed, peering down through the area railings into the kitchen where they were sitting. They looked very snug, with teapots and bread and butter on the kitchen table. His stick swung from side to side like the tail of a cheerful dog. Everybody seemed lighthearted and irresponsible, sallying out of their houses, flaunting along the streets with pennies for the organ grinders and pennies for the beggars. Everybody seemed to have money to spend. Women clustered round the plate-glass windows. He too stopped, looked at the model of a toy boat; at dressing-cases, shining yellow with rows of silver bottles. But who wrote that song, he wondered, as he strolled on, about the King of Spain's daughter, the song that Pippy used to sing him, as she wiped his ears with a piece of slimy flannel? She used to take him on her knee and croak out in her wheezy rattle of a voice, "The King of Spain's daughter came to visit me, all for the sake of . . ." And then suddenly her knee gave, and down he was tumbled onto the floor.

Here he was at Hyde Park Corner. The scene was extremely animated. Vans, motor-cars, motor omnibuses were streaming down the hill. The trees in the Park had little green leaves on them. Cars with gay ladies in pale dresses were already passing in at the gates. Everybody was going about their business. And somebody, he observed, had written the words "God is Love" in pink chalk on the gates of Apsley House. That must need some pluck, he thought, to write "God is Love" on the gates of Apsley House when at any moment a policeman might nab you. But here came his bus; and he climbed on top.

"To St. Paul's," he said, handing the conductor his coppers.

THE OMNIBUSES swirled and circled in a perpetual current round the steps of St. Paul's. The statue of Queen Anne seemed to preside over the chaos and to supply it with a centre, like the hub of a wheel. It seemed as if the white lady ruled the traffic with her sceptre; directed the activities of the little men in bowler hats and round coats; of the women carrying attaché cases; of the vans, the lorries and the motor omnibuses. Now and then single figures broke off from the rest and went up the steps into the church. The doors of the Cathedral kept opening and shutting. Now and again a blast of faint organ music was blown out into the air. The pigeons waddled; the sparrows fluttered. Soon after midday a little old man carrying a paper bag took up his station half-way up the steps and proceeded to feed the birds. He held out a slice of bread. His lips moved. He seemed to be wheedling and coaxing them. Soon he was haloed by a circle of fluttering wings. Sparrows perched on his head and his hands. Pigeons waddled close to his feet. A little crowd gathered to watch him feeding the sparrows. He tossed his bread round him in a circle. Then there was a ripple in the air. The great clock, all the clocks of the city, seemed to be gathering their forces together; they seemed to be whirring a preliminary warning. Then the stroke struck. "One" blared out. All the sparrows fluttered up into the air; even the pigeons were frightened; some of them made a little flight round the head of Queen Anne.

As THE last ripple of the stroke died away, Martin came out in the open space in front of the Cathedral.

He crossed over and stood with his back against a shop window looking up at the great dome. All the weights in his body seemed to shift. He had a curious sense of something moving in his body in harmony with the building; it righted itself: it came to a full stop. It was exciting—this change of proportion. He wished he had been an architect. He stood with his back pressed against the shop trying to get the whole of the cathedral clear. But it was difficult with so many people passing. They knocked against him and brushed in front of him. It was the rush hour, of course, when City men were making for their luncheons. They were taking short cuts across the steps. The pigeons were swirling up and then settling down again. The doors were opening and shutting as he mounted the steps. The pigeons were a nuisance, he thought, making a mess on the steps. He climbed up slowly.

"And who's that?" he thought, looking at someone who was standing against one of the pillars. "Don't I know her?"

Her lips were moving. She was talking to herself.

"It's Sally!" he thought. He hesitated; should he speak to her, or should he not? But she was company; and he was tired of his own.

"A penny for your thoughts, Sal!" he said, tapping her on the shoulder.

She turned; her expression changed instantly. "Just as I was thinking of you, Martin!" she exclaimed.

"What a lie!" he said, shaking hands.

"When I think of people, I always see them," she said. She gave her queer little shuffle as if she were a bird, a somewhat di-shevelled fowl, for her cloak was not in the fashion. They stood for a moment on the steps, looking down at the crowded street beneath. A gust of organ music came out from the Cathedral behind them as the doors opened and shut. The faint ecclesias-tical murmur was vaguely impressive, and the dark space of the Cathedral seen through the door.

"What were you thinking . . . ?" he began. But he broke off. "Come and lunch," he said. "I'll take you to a City chop house," and he shepherded her down the steps, along a narrow alley, blocked by carts, into which packages were being shot from the warehouses. They pushed through the swing doors into the chop house.

"Very full today, Alfred," said Martin affably, as the waiter took his coat and hat and hung them on the rack. He knew the waiter; he often lunched there; the waiter knew him too.

"Very full, Captain," he said.

"Now," he said, sitting down, "what shall we have?"

A vast brownish-yellow joint was being trundled from table to table on a lorry.

"That," said Sara, waving her hand at it.

"And drink?" said Martin. He took the wine-list and con-sulted it.

"Drink——" said Sara, "drink, I leave to you." She took off her gloves and laid them on a small reddish-brown book that was obviously a prayer-book.

"Drink you leave to me," said Martin. Why, he wondered, do prayer-books always have their leaves gilt with red and gold? He chose the wine.

"And what were you doing," he said, dismissing the waiter, "at St. Paul's?"

"Listening to the service," she said. She looked round her. The room was very hot and crowded. The walls were covered with gold leaves encrusted on a brown surface. People were passing them and coming in and out all the time. The waiter brought the wine. Martin poured her out a glass.

"I didn't know you went to services," he said, looking at her prayer-book.

She did not answer. She kept looking round her, watching the people come in and go out. She sipped her wine. The colour was coming into her cheeks. She took up her knife and fork and began to eat the admirable mutton. They ate in silence for a moment.

He wanted to make her talk.

"And what, Sal," he said, touching the little book, "d'you make of it?"

She opened the prayer-book at random and began to read:

"The father incomprehensible; the son incomprehensible——" she spoke in her ordinary voice.

"Hush!" he stopped her. "Somebody's listening."

In deference to him she assumed the manner of a lady lunching with a gentleman in a city restaurant.

"And what were you doing," she asked, "at St. Paul's?"

"Wishing I'd been an architect," he said. "But they sent me into the Army instead, which I loathed." He spoke emphatically.

"Hush," she whispered. "Somebody's listening."

He looked round quickly; then he laughed. The waiter was setting their tart in front of them. They ate in silence. He filled her glass again. Her cheeks were flushed; her eyes were bright. He envied her the generalised sensation of universal well-being that he used to get from a glass of wine. Wine was good—it broke down barriers. He wanted to make her talk.

"I didn't know you went to services," he said, looking at her prayer-book. "And what do you think of it?" She looked at it too. Then she tapped it with her fork.

"What do *they* think of it, Martin?" she asked. "The woman praying and the man with a long white beard?"

"Much what Crosby thinks when she comes to see me," he said. He thought of the old woman standing at the door of his room with the pyjama jacket over her arm, and the devout look on her face.

"I'm Crosby's God," he said, helping her to Brussels sprouts.

"Crosby's God! Almighty, all-powerful Mr. Martin!" She laughed.

She raised her glass to him. Was she laughing at him? he wondered. He hoped she did not think him very old. "You remember Crosby, don't you?" he said. "She's retired, and her dog's dead."

"Retired and her dog's dead?" she repeated. She looked again over her shoulder. Conversation in a restaurant was impossible; it was broken into little fragments. City men in their neat striped suits and bowler hats were brushing past them all the time.

"It's a fine church," she said, turning round. She had hopped back to St. Paul's, he supposed.

"Magnificent," he replied. "Were you looking at the monuments?"

Somebody had come in whom he recognised: Erridge, the

stockbroker. He raised a finger and beckoned. Martin rose and went to speak to him. When he came back she had filled her glass again. She was sitting there, looking at the people, as if she were a child that he had taken to a pantomime.

"And what are you doing this afternoon?" he asked.

"The Round Pond at four," she said. She drummed on the table. "The Round Pond at four." Now she had passed, he guessed, into the drowsy benevolence which waits on a good dinner and a glass of wine.

"Meeting somebody?" he asked.

"Yes, Maggie," she said.

They ate in silence. Fragments of other people's talk reached them in broken sentences. Then the man to whom Martin had spoken touched him on the shoulder as he went out.

"Wednesday at eight," he said.

"Right you are," said Martin. He made a note in his pocket-book.

"And what are you doing this afternoon?" she asked.

"Ought to see my sister in prison," he said, lighting a cigarette.

"In prison?" she asked.

"Rose. For throwing a brick," he said.

"Red Rose, tawny Rose," she began, reaching out her hand for the wine again, "wild Rose, thorny Rose—"

"No," he said, putting his hand over the mouth of the bottle, "you've had enough." A little excited her. He must damp her excitement. There were people listening.

"A damned unpleasant thing," he said, "being in prison."

She drew back her glass and sat gazing at it, as if the engine of the brain were suddenly cut off. She was very like her mother—except when she laughed.

He would have liked to talk to her about her mother. But it was impossible to talk. Too many people were listening, and they were smoking. Smoke mixed with the smell of meat made the air heavy. He was thinking of the past when she exclaimed:

"Sitting on a three-legged stool having meat crammed down her throat!"

He roused himself. She was thinking of Rose, was she?

"Crash came a brick!" she laughed, flourishing her fork.

"'Roll up the map of Europe,' said the man to the flunkey. 'I don't believe in force'!" She brought down her fork. A plum-stone jumped. Martin looked round. People were listening. He got up.

"Shall we go?" he said, "— if you've had enough?"

She got up and looked for her cloak.

"Well, I've enjoyed it," she said, taking her cloak. "Thanks, Martin, for my good lunch."

He beckoned to the waiter who came with alacrity and totted up the bill. Martin laid a sovereign on the plate. Sara began to thrust her arms into the sleeves of her cloak.

"Shall I come with you," he said, helping her, "to the Round Pond at four?"

"Yes!" she said, spinning round on her heel. "To the Round Pond at four!"

She walked off, a little unsteadily he observed, past the City men who were still eating.

Here the waiter came up with the change and Martin began to slip it in his pocket. He kept back one coin for the tip. But as he was about to give it, he was struck by something shifty in Alfred's expression. He flicked up the flap of the bill; a two-shilling piece lay beneath. It was the usual trick. He lost his temper.

"What's this?" he said angrily.

"Didn't know it was there, sir," the waiter stammered.

Martin felt his blood rise to his ears. He felt exactly like his father in a rage; as if he had white spots above his temples. He pocketed the coin that he had been going to give the waiter; and marched past him, brushing aside his hand. The man slunk back with a murmur.

"Let's be off," he said, hustling Sara along the crowded room. "Let's get out of this."

He hurried her into the street. The fug, the warm meaty smell of the City chop house, had suddenly become intolerable.

"How I hate being cheated!" he said as he put on his hat.

"Sorry, Sara," he apologised. "I oughtn't to have taken you there. It's a beastly hole."

He drew in a breath of fresh air. The street noises, the unconcerned, business-like look of things, were refreshing after the hot steamy room. There were the carts waiting, drawn up along the street; and the packages sliding down into them from the warehouses. Again they came out in front of St. Paul's. He looked up. There was the same old man still feeding the sparrows. And there was the Cathedral. He wished he could feel again the sense of weights changing in his body and coming to a stop; but the queer thrill of some correspondence between his own body and the stone no longer came to him. He felt nothing except anger. Also, Sara distracted him. She was about to cross the crowded road. He put out his hand to stop her. "Take care," he said. Then they crossed.

"Shall we walk?" he asked. She nodded. They began to walk along Fleet Street. Conversation was impossible. The pavement was so narrow that he had to step on and off in order to keep beside her. He still felt the discomfort of anger, but the anger itself was cooling. What ought I to have done? he thought, seeing himself brush past the waiter without giving him a tip. Not that; he thought, no, not that. People pressing against him made him step off the pavement. After all, the poor devil had to make a living. He liked being generous: he liked to leave people smiling; and two shillings meant nothing to him. But what's the use, he thought, now it's done? He began to hum his little song—and then stopped, remembering that he was with someone.

"Look at that, Sal," he said, clutching at her arm. "Look at that!"

He pointed at the splayed-out figure at Temple Bar; it looked as ridiculous as usual—something between a serpent and a fowl.

"Look at that!" he repeated, laughing. They paused for a moment to look at the little flattened figures lodged so uncomfortably against the pediment of Temple Bar: Queen Victoria: King Edward. Then they walked on. It was impossible to talk because of the crowd. Men in wigs and gowns hurried across the street: some carried red bags, others blue bags.

"The Law Courts," he said, pointing at the cold mass of decorated stone. It looked very gloomy and funereal, ". . . where Morris spends his time," he said aloud.

He still felt uncomfortable at having lost his temper. But the feeling was passing. Only a little ridge of roughness remained in his mind.

"D'you think I ought to have been . . ." he began, a barrister he meant; but also Ought I to have done that—lost his temper with the waiter.

"Ought to have been—ought to have done?" she asked, bending towards him. She had not caught his meaning in the roar of the traffic. It was impossible to talk; but at any rate the feeling that he had lost his temper was diminishing. That little sting was being successfully smoothed over. Then back it came because he saw a beggar selling violets. And that poor devil, he thought, had to go without his tip because he cheated me. . . . He fixed his eyes on a pillar-box. Then he looked at a car. It was odd how soon one got used to cars without horses, he thought.

They used to look ridiculous. They passed the woman selling violets. She wore a hat over her face. He dropped a sixpence in
her tray to make amends to the waiter. He shook his head. No
violets, he meant; and indeed they were faded. But he caught
sight of her face. She had no nose; her face was seamed with
white patches; there were red rims for nostrils. She had no
nose — she had pulled her hat down to hide that fact.

"Let's cross," he said, abruptly. He took Sara's arm and
made her cross between the omnibuses. She must have seen
such sights often; he had, often; but not together — that made
a difference. He hurried her on to the further pavement.

"We'll get a bus," he said. "Come along."

He took her by the elbow to make her step out briskly. But
it was impossible; a cart blocked the way; there were people
passing. They were approaching Charing Cross. It was like the
piers of a bridge; men and women were sucked in instead of
water. They had to stop. Newspaper boys held placards against
their legs. Men were buying papers: some loitered; others
snatched them. Martin bought one and held it in his hand.

"We'll wait here," he said. "The bus'll come." An old straw
hat with a purple ribbon round it, he thought, opening his
paper. The sight persisted. He looked up. "The station clock's
always fast," he assured a man who was hurrying to catch a
train. Always fast, he said to himself as he opened the paper. But
there was no clock. He turned to read the news from Ireland.
Omnibus after omnibus stopped, then swooped off again. It
was difficult to concentrate on the news from Ireland; he
looked up.

"This is ours," he said, as the right bus came. They climbed
on top and sat side by side overlooking the driver.

"Two to Hyde Park Corner," he said, producing a handful
of silver, and looked through the pages of the evening paper;
but it was only an early edition.

"Nothing in it," he said, stuffing the paper under the seat. "And now—" he began, filling his pipe. They were running smoothly down the incline of Piccadilly. "—where my old father used to sit," he broke off, waving his pipe at Club windows. ". . . and now"—he lit a match, "—and now, Sally, you can say whatever you like. Nobody's listening. Say something," he added, throwing his match overboard, "very profound."

He turned to her. He wanted her to speak. Down they dipped; up they swooped again. He wanted her to speak; or he must speak himself. And what could he say? He had buried his feeling. But some emotion remained. He wanted her to speak it: but she was silent. No, he thought, biting the stem of his pipe. I won't say it. If I did she'd think me . . .

He looked at her. The sun was blazing on the windows of St. George's Hospital. She was looking at it with rapture. But why with rapture? he wondered, as the bus stopped and he got down.

THE SCENE since the morning had changed slightly. Clocks in the distance were just striking three. There were more cars; more women in pale summer dresses; more men in tail-coats and grey top-hats. The procession through the gates into the Park was beginning. Everyone looked festive. Even the little dressmakers' apprentices with band-boxes looked as if they were taking part in some ceremonial. Green chairs were drawn up at the edge of the Row. They were full of people looking about them as if they had taken seats at a play. Riders cantered to the end of the Row; pulled up their horses; turned and cantered the other way. The wind, coming from the west, moved white clouds grained with gold across the sky. The windows of Park Lane shone with blue and gold reflections.

Martin stepped out briskly.

"Come along," he said; "come—come!" He walked on.

I'm young, he thought; I'm in the prime of life. There was a tang of earth in the air; even in the Park there was some faint smell of spring, of the country.

"How I like—" he said aloud. He looked round. He had spoken to the empty air. Sara had lagged behind; there she was, tying her shoe-lace. But he felt as if he had missed a step going downstairs.

"What a fool one feels when one talks aloud to oneself," he said as she came up. She pointed.

"But look," she said, "they all do it."

A middle-aged woman was coming towards them. She was talking to herself. Her lips moved; she was gesticulating with her hand.

"It's the spring," he said, as she passed them.

"No. Once in winter I came here," she said, "and there was a negro, laughing aloud in the snow."

"In the snow," said Martin. "A negro." The sun was bright on the grass; they were passing a bed in which the many-coloured hyacinths were curled and glossy.

"Don't let's think of the snow," he said. "Let's think—" A young woman was wheeling a perambulator; a sudden thought came into his head. "Maggie," he said. "Tell me. I haven't seen her since her baby was born. And I've never met the French-man—what d'you call him?—René?"

"Renny," she said. She was still under the influence of the wine; of the wandering airs; of the people passing. He too felt the same distraction; but he wanted to end it.

"Yes. What's he like, this man René; Renny?"

He pronounced the word first in the French way; then as she did, in the English. He wanted to wake her. He took her arm.

"Renny!" Sara repeated. She threw her head back and laughed. "Let me see," she said. "He wears a red tie with white spots. And has dark eyes. And he takes an orange—suppose we're at dinner, and says, looking straight at you, 'This orange, Sara—'" She rolled her *r*'s. She paused.

"There's another person talking to himself," she broke off. A young man came past them in a closely buttoned-up coat as if he had no shirt. He was muttering as he walked. He scowled at them as he passed them.

"But Renny?" said Martin.

"We were talking about Renny," he reminded her. "He takes an orange—"

". . . and pours himself out a glass of wine," she resumed. "'Science is the religion of the future!'" she exclaimed, waving her hand as if she held a glass of wine.

"Of wine?" said Martin. Half listening, he had visualised an earnest French professor—a little picture to which now he must add inappropriately a glass of wine.

"Yes, wine," she repeated. "His father was a merchant," she continued. "A man with a black beard; a merchant at Bordeaux. And one day," she continued, "when he was a little boy, playing in the garden, there was a tap on the window. 'Don't make so much noise. Play further away,' said a woman in a white cap. His mother was dead. . . . And he was afraid to tell his father that the horse was too big to ride . . . and they sent him to England. . . ."

She was skipping over railings.

"And then what happened?" said Martin, joining her. "They became engaged?"

She was silent. He waited for her to explain—why they had married—Maggie and Renny. He waited, but she said no more. Well, she married him and they're happy, he thought. He was jealous for a moment. The Park was full of couples walking together. Everything seemed fresh and full of sweetness. The air puffed soft in their faces. It was laden with murmurs; with the stir of branches; the rush of wheels; dogs barking, and now and again the intermittent song of a thrush.

Here a lady passed them, talking to herself. As they looked at her she turned and whistled, as if to her dog. But the dog she had whistled was another person's dog. It bounded off in the opposite direction. The lady hurried on pursing her lips together.

"People don't like being looked at," said Sara, "when they're talking to themselves." Martin roused himself.

"Look here," he said. "We've gone the wrong way." Voices floated out to them.

They had been walking in the wrong direction. They were near the bald rubbed space where the speakers congregate. Meetings were in full swing. Groups had gathered round the different orators. Mounted on their platforms, or sometimes only on boxes, the speakers were holding forth. The voices became louder, louder and louder as they approached.

"Let's listen," said Martin. A thin man was leaning forward holding a slate in his hand. They could hear him say, "Ladies and gentlemen . . ." They stopped in front of him. "Fix your eyes on me," he said. They fixed their eyes on him. "Don't be afraid," he said, crooking his finger. He had an ingratiating manner. He turned his slate over. "Do I look like a Jew?" he asked. Then he turned his slate and looked on the other side. And they heard him say that his mother was born in Bermondsey, as they strolled on, and his father in the Isle of— The voice died away.

"What about this chap?" said Martin. Here was a large man, banging on the rail of his platform.

"Fellow citizens!" he was shouting. They stopped. The crowd of loafers, errand-boys and nursemaids gaped up at him with their mouths falling open and their eyes gazing blankly. His hand raked in the line of cars that was passing with a superb gesture of scorn. His shirt appeared under his waistcoat.

"Joostice and liberty," said Martin, repeating his words, as the fist thumped on the railing. They waited. Then it all came over again.

"But he's a jolly good speaker," said Martin, turning. The voice died away. "And now, what's the old lady saying?" They strolled on.

The old lady's audience was extremely small. Her voice was hardly audible. She held a little book in her hand and she was saying something about sparrows. But her voice tapered off into a thin frail pipe. A chorus of little boys imitated her.

They listened for a moment. Then Martin turned again. "Come along, Sal," he said, putting his hand on her shoulder.

The voices grew fainter, fainter and fainter. Soon they ceased altogether. They strolled on across the smooth slope that rose and fell like a breadth of green cloth striped with straight brown paths in front of them. Great white dogs were gambolling; through the trees shone the waters of the Serpentine, set here and there with little boats. The urbanity of the Park, the gleam of the water, the sweep and curve and composition of the scene, as if somebody had designed it, affected Martin agreeably.

"Joostice and liberty," he said half to himself, as they came to the water's edge and stood a moment, watching the gulls cut the air into sharp white patterns with their wings.

"Did you agree with him?" he asked, taking Sara's arm to rouse her; for her lips were moving; she was talking to herself. "That fat man," he explained, "who flung his arm out." She started.

"Oi, oi, oi!" she exclaimed, imitating his cockney accent.

Yes, thought Martin, as they walked on. Oi, oi, oi, oi, oi, oi. It's always that. There wouldn't be much justice or liberty for the likes of him if the fat man had his way—or beauty either.

"And the poor old lady whom nobody listened to?" he said, "talking about the sparrows. . . ."

He could still see in his mind's eye the thin man persuasively crooking his finger; the fat man who flung his arms out so that his braces showed; and the little old lady who tried to make her voice heard above the catcalls and whistles. There was a mixture of comedy and tragedy in the scene.

But they had reached the gate into Kensington Gardens. A long row of cars and carriages was drawn up by the kerb. Striped umbrellas were open over the little round tables where people were already sitting, waiting for their tea. Waitresses were hurrying in and out with trays; the Season had begun. The scene was very gay.

A lady, fashionably dressed with a purple feather dipping down on one side of her hat, sat there sipping an ice. The sun dappled the table and gave her a curious look of transparency, as if she were caught in a net of light; as if she were composed of lozenges of floating colours. Martin half thought that he knew her; he half raised his hat. But she sat there looking in front of her; sipping her ice. No, he thought; he did not know her, and he stopped for a moment to light his pipe. What would the world be, he said to himself—he was still thinking of the fat man brandishing his arm—without "I" in it? He lit the match. He looked at the flame that had become almost invisible in the sun. He stood for a second drawing at his pipe. Sara had walked on. She too was netted with floating lights from between the leaves. A primal innocence seemed to brood over the scene. The birds made a fitful sweet chirping in the branches; the roar of London encircled the open space in a ring of distant but complete sound. The pink and white chestnut blossoms rode up and down as the branches moved in the breeze. The sun dappling the leaves gave everything a curious look of insubstantiality as if it were broken into separate points of light. He too, himself, seemed dispersed. His mind for a moment was a blank. Then he roused himself, threw away his match, and caught up Sally.

"Come along!" he said. "Come along. . . . The Round Pond at four!"

They walked on arm in arm in silence, down the long avenue with the Palace and the phantom church at the end of its
vista. The size of the human figure seemed to have shrunk. Instead of full-grown people, children were now in the majority.
Dogs of all sorts abounded. The air was full of barking and sudden shrill cries. Coveys of nursemaids pushed perambulators
along the paths. Babies lay fast asleep in them like images of
faintly tinted wax; their perfectly smooth eyelids fitted over their
eyes as if they sealed them completely. He looked down; he liked
children. Sally had looked like that the first time he saw her,
asleep in her perambulator in the hall in Browne Street.

He stopped short. They had reached the Pond.

"Where's Maggie?" he said. "There—is that her?" He
pointed to a young woman who was lifting a baby out of its perambulator under a tree.

"Where?" said Sara. She looked in the wrong direction.

He pointed.

"There, under that tree."

"Yes," she said, "that's Maggie."

They walked in that direction.

"But is it?" said Martin. He was suddenly doubtful; for she
had the unconsciousness of a person who is unaware that she is
being looked at. It made her unfamiliar. With one hand she held
the child; with the other she arranged the pillows of the perambulator. She too was dappled with lozenges of floating light.

"Yes," he said, noticing something about her gesture, "that's
Maggie."

She turned and saw them.

She held up her hand as if to warn them to approach quietly.
She put a finger to her lips. They approached silently. As they
reached her, the distant sound of a clock striking was wafted on
the breeze. One, two, three, four it struck. . . . Then it ceased.

———

"WE MET at St. Paul's," said Martin in a whisper. He dragged up two chairs and sat down. They were silent for a moment. The child was not asleep. Then Maggie bent over and looked at the child.

"You needn't talk in a whisper," she said aloud. "He's asleep."

"We met at St. Paul's," Martin repeated in his ordinary voice. "I'd been seeing my stockbroker." He took off his hat and laid it on the grass. "And when I came out," he resumed, "there was Sally. . . ." He looked at her. She had never told him, he remembered, what it was that she was thinking, as she stood there, with her lips moving, on the steps of St. Paul's.

Now she was yawning. Instead of taking the little hard green chair which he had pulled up for her, she had thrown herself down on the grass. She had folded herself like a grasshopper with her back against the tree. The prayer-book, with its red and gold leaves, was lying on the ground tented over with trembling blades of grass. She yawned; she stretched. She was already half asleep.

He drew his chair beside Maggie's; and looked at the scene in front of them.

It was admirably composed. There was the white figure of Queen Victoria against a green bank; beyond, was the red brick of the old palace; the phantom church raised its spire, and the Round Pond made a pool of blue. A race of yachts was going forward. The boats leant on their sides so that the sails touched the water. There was a nice little breeze.

"And what did you talk about?" said Maggie.

Martin could not remember. "She was tipsy," he said, pointing to Sara. "And now she's going to sleep." He felt sleepy himself. The sun for the first time was almost hot on his head.

Then he answered her question.

"The whole world," he said. "Politics; religion; morality." He yawned. Gulls were screaming as they rose and sank over a lady who was feeding them. Maggie was watching them. He looked at her.

"I haven't seen you," he said, "since your baby was born." It's changed her, having a child, he thought. It's improved her, he thought. But she was watching the gulls; the lady had thrown a handful of fish. The gulls swooped round and round her head.

"D'you like having a child?" he said.

"Yes," she said, rousing herself to answer him. "It's a tie though."

"But it's nice having ties, isn't it?" he enquired. He was fond of children. He looked at the sleeping baby with its eyes sealed and its thumb in its mouth.

"D'you want them?" she asked.

"Just what I was asking myself," he said, "before—"

Here Sara made a click at the back of her throat; he dropped his voice to a whisper. "Before I met her at St. Paul's," he said. They were silent. The baby was asleep; Sara was asleep; the presence of the two sleepers seemed to enclose them in a circle of privacy. Two of the racing yachts were coming together as if they must collide; but one passed just ahead of the other. Martin watched them. Life had resumed its ordinary proportions. Everything once more was back in its place. The boats were sailing; the men walking; the little boys dabbled in the pond for minnows; the waters of the pond rippled bright blue. Everything was full of the stir, the potency, the fecundity of spring.

Suddenly he said aloud:

"Possessiveness is the devil."

Maggie looked at him. Did he mean himself—herself and the baby? No. There was a tone in his voice that told her he was thinking not of her.

"What are you thinking?" she asked.

"About the woman I'm in love with," he said. "Love ought to stop on both sides, don't you think, simultaneously?" He spoke without any stress on the words, so as not to wake the sleepers. "But it won't—that's the devil," he added in the same undertone.

"Bored, are you?" she murmured.

"Stiff," he said. "Bored stiff." He stooped and disinterred a pebble in the grass.

"And jealous?" she murmured. Her voice was very low and soft.

"Horribly," he whispered. It was true, now that she referred to it. Here the baby half woke and stretched out its hand. Maggie rocked the perambulator. Sara stirred. Their privacy was imperilled. It would be destroyed at any moment, he felt; and he wanted to talk.

He glanced at the sleepers. The baby's eyes were shut, and Sara's too. Still they seemed encircled in a ring of solitude. Speaking in a low voice without accent, he told her his story; the story of the lady; how she wanted to keep him, and he wanted to be free. It was an ordinary story, but painful—mixed. As he told it, however, the sting was drawn. They sat silent, looking in front of them.

Another race was starting; men crouched at the edge of the pond, each with his stick resting on a toy boat. It was a charming scene, gay, innocent and a trifle ridiculous. The signal was given; off the boats went. And will he, Martin thought, looking at the sleeping baby, go through the same thing too? He was thinking of himself—of his jealousy.

"My father," he said suddenly, but softly, "had a lady. . . . She called him 'Bogy.'" And he told her the story of the lady who kept a boarding house at Putney—the very respectable lady, grown stout, who wanted help with her roof. Maggie laughed, but very gently, so as not to wake the sleepers. Both were still sleeping soundly.

"Was he in love," Martin asked her, "with your mother?"

She was looking at the gulls, cutting patterns on the blue

distance with their wings. His question seemed to sink through what she was seeing; then suddenly it reached her.

"Are we brother and sister?" she asked; and laughed out loud. The child opened its eyes, and uncurled its fingers.

"We've woken him," said Martin. The child began to cry. Maggie had to soothe him. Their privacy was over. The child cried; and the clocks began striking. The sound came wafted gently towards them on the breeze. One, two, three, four, five. . . .

"It's time to go," said Maggie, as the last stroke died away. She laid the baby back on its pillow, and turned. Sara was still asleep. She lay crumpled up with her back to the tree. Martin stooped and threw a twig at her. She opened her eyes but shut them again.

"No, no," she protested, stretching her arms over her head.

"It's time," said Maggie. Sara pulled herself up. "Time is it?" she sighed. "How strange . . . !" she murmured. She sat up and rubbed her eyes.

"Martin!" she exclaimed. She looked at him as he stood over her in his blue suit holding his stick in his hand. She looked at him as if she were bringing him back to the field of vision.

"Martin!" she said again.

"Yes, Martin!" he replied. "Did you hear what we've been saying?" he asked her.

"Voices," she yawned, shaking her head. "Only voices."

He paused for a moment, looking down at her. "Well, I'm off," he said, taking up his hat, "to dine with a cousin in Grosvenor Square," he added. He turned and left them.

He looked back at them after he had gone a little distance. They were still sitting by the perambulator under the trees. He walked on. Then he looked back again. The ground sloped, and the trees were hidden. A very stout lady was being tugged along the path by a small dog on a chain. He could see them no longer.

———

THE SUN was setting as he drove across the Park, an hour or two later. He was thinking that he had forgotten something; but what, he did not know. Scene passed over scene; one obliterated another. Now he was crossing the bridge over the Serpentine. The water glowed with sunset light; twisted poles of lamp light lay on the water, and there, at the end the white bridge composed the scene. The cab entered the shadow of the trees, and joined the long line of cabs that was streaming towards the Marble Arch. People in evening dress were going to plays and parties. The light became yellower and yellower. The road was beaten to a metallic silver. Everything looked festive.

But I'm going to be late, he thought, for the cab was held up in a block by the Marble Arch. He looked at his watch—it was just on eight-thirty. But eight-thirty means eight-forty-five, he thought, as the cab moved on. Indeed as it turned into the square there was a car at the door, and a man getting out. So I'm just on time, he thought, and paid the driver.

THE DOOR opened almost before he touched the bell, as if he had trod on a spring. The door opened, and two footmen started forward to take his things directly he entered the black-and-white paved hall. He followed another man up the imposing staircase of white marble, sweeping in a curve. A succession of large, dark pictures hung on the wall, and at the top outside the door was a yellow-and-blue picture of Venetian palaces and pale green canals.

"Canaletto or the school of?" he thought, pausing to let the other man precede him. Then he gave his name to the footman.

"Captain Pargiter," the man boomed out; and there was Kitty standing at the door. She was formal; fashionable; with a dash of red on her lips. She gave him her hand; but he moved on for other guests were arriving. "A saloon?" he said to himself, for the room with its chandeliers, yellow panels, and sofas and chairs dotted about had the air of a grandiose waiting-room. Seven or eight people were already there. It's not going to work this time, he said to himself as he chatted with his host, who had been racing. His face shone as if it had only that moment been taken out of the sun. One almost expected, Martin thought, as he stood talking, to see a pair of glasses slung round his shoulders, just as there was a red mark across his forehead where his hat had been. No, it's not going to work, Martin thought as they talked about horses. He heard a paper boy calling in the street below, and the hooting of horns. He preserved clearly his sense of the identity of different objects, and their differences. When a party worked all things, all sounds merged into one. He looked at an old lady with a wedge-shaped stone-coloured face sitting ensconced on a sofa. He glanced at Kitty's portrait by a fashionable portrait painter as he chatted, standing first on this foot, then on that, to the grizzled man with the bloodhound eyes and the urbane manner whom Kitty had married instead of Edward. Then she came up and introduced him to a girl all in white who was standing alone with her hand on the back of a chair.

"Miss Ann Hillier," she said. "My cousin, Captain Pargiter."

She stood for a moment beside them as if to facilitate their introduction. But she was a little stiff always; she did nothing but flick her fan up and down.

"Been to the races, Kitty?" Martin said, because he knew that she hated racing, and he always felt a wish to tease her.

"I? No; I don't go to races," she replied rather shortly. She turned away because somebody else had come in—a man in gold lace with a star.

I should have been better off, Martin thought, reading my book.

"Have you been to the races?" he said aloud to the girl whom he was to take down to dinner. She shook her head. She had white arms; a white dress; and a pearl necklace. Purely virginal, he said to himself; and only an hour ago I was lying stark naked in my bath in Ebury Street, he thought.

"I've been watching polo," she said. He looked down at his shoes, and noticed that they had creases across them; they were old; he had meant to buy a new pair, but had forgotten. That was what he had forgotten, he thought, seeing himself again in the cab, crossing the bridge over the Serpentine.

But they were going down to dinner. He gave her his arm. As they went down the stairs, and he watched the ladies' dresses in front of them trail from step to step, he thought, What on earth am I going to say to her? Then they crossed the black-and-white squares and went into the dining-room. It was harmoniously shrouded; pictures with hooded bars of light under them shone out; and the dinner table glowed; but no light shone directly on their faces. If this doesn't work, he thought, looking at the portrait of a nobleman with a crimson cloak and a star that hung luminous in front of him, I'll never do it again. Then he braced himself to talk to the virginal girl who sat beside him. But he had to reject almost everything that occurred to him—she was so young.

"I've thought of three subjects to talk about," he began straight off, without thinking how the sentence was to end. "Racing; the Russian ballet; and"—he hesitated for a moment—"Ireland. Which interests you?" He unfolded his napkin.

"Please," she said, bending slightly towards him, "say that again."

He laughed. She had a charming way of putting her head on one side and bending towards him.

"Don't let's talk of any of them," he said. "Let's talk of something interesting. Do you enjoy parties?" he asked her. She was dipping her spoon in her soup. She looked up at him as she lifted it with eyes that seemed like bright stones under a film of water. They're like drops of glass under water, he thought. She was extraordinarily pretty.

"But I've only been to three parties in my life!" she said. She gave a charming little laugh.

"You don't say so!" he exclaimed. "This is the third, then; or is it the fourth?"

He listened to the sounds in the street. He could just hear the cars hooting; but they had gone far away; they made a continuous rushing noise. It was beginning to work. He held out his glass. He would like her to say, he thought, as his glass was filled, "What a charming man I sat next!" when she went to bed that night.

"This is my third *real* party," she said, stressing the word "real" in a way that seemed to him slightly pathetic. She must have been in the nursery three months ago, he thought, eating bread and butter.

"And I was thinking as I shaved," he said, "that I would never go to a party again." It was true; he had seen a hole in the bookcase. Who's taken my life of Wren? he had thought, holding his razor out; and had wanted to stay and read, alone. But now . . . what little piece of his vast experience could he break off and give to her, he wondered?

"Do you live in London?" she asked.

"Ebury Street," he told her. And she knew Ebury Street, because it was on the way to Victoria; she often went to Victoria, because they had a house in Sussex.

"And now tell me," he said, feeling that they had broken the ice—when she turned her head to answer some remark of the man on the other side. He was annoyed. The whole fabric that he had been building, like a game of spillikins in which one frail little bone is hooked on top of another, was dashed to the ground. Ann was talking as if she had known the other man all her life; he had hair that looked as if a rake had been drawn through it; he was very young. Martin sat silent. He looked at the great portrait opposite. A footman was standing beneath it; a row of decanters obscured the folds of the cloak on the floor. That's the third Earl, or the fourth? he asked himself. He knew his eighteenth century; it was the fourth Earl who had made the great marriage. But after all, he thought, looking at Kitty at the head of the table, the Rigbys are a better family than they are. He smiled; he checked himself. I only think of "better families" when I dine in this sort of place, he thought. He looked at another picture; a lady in sea green; the famous Gainsborough. But here Lady Margaret, the woman on his left, turned to him.

"I'm sure you'll agree with me," she said, "Captain Pargiter"—he noticed that she swept her eyes over the name on his card before she spoke it, although they had met often before—"that it's a devilish thing to have done?"

She spoke so pouncingly that the fork she held upright seemed like a weapon with which she was about to pinion him. He threw himself into their conversation. It was about politics of course, about Ireland. "Tell me—what's your opinion?" she asked, with her fork poised. For a moment he had the illusion that he too was behind the scenes. The screen was down; the lights were up; and he too was behind the scenes. It was an illusion of course; they were only throwing him scraps from their larder; but it was an agreeable sensation while it lasted. He listened. Now she was holding forth to a distinguished old man at the end of the table. He watched him. He had let down a mask of infinitely wise tolerance over his face as she harangued them. He was arranging three crusts of bread by the side of his plate as if he were playing a mysterious little game of profound significance. "So," he seemed to be saying, "So," as if they were fragments of human destiny, not crusts, that he held in his fingers. The mask might conceal anything—or nothing? Anyhow it was a mask of great distinction. But here Lady Margaret pinioned him too with her fork; and he raised his eyebrows and moved one of the crusts a little to one side before he spoke. Martin leant forward to listen.

"When I was in Ireland," he began, "in 1880 . . ." He spoke very simply; he was offering them a memory; he told his story perfectly; it held its meaning without spilling a single drop. And he had played a great part. Martin listened attentively. Yes, it was absorbing. Here we are, he thought, going on and on and on. . . . He leant forward trying to catch every word. But he was conscious of some interruption; Ann had turned to him.

"Do tell me"— she was asking him —"who *he* is?" She bent her head to the right. She was under the impression that he knew everybody, apparently. He was flattered. He looked along the table. Who was it? Somebody he had met; somebody, he guessed, who was not quite at his ease.

"I know him," he said. "I know him —" He had a rather white, fat face; he was talking away at a great rate. And the young married woman to whom he was talking was saying, "I see; I see," with little nods of her head. But there was a slight look of strain on her face. You needn't put yourself to all that trouble, my good fellow, Martin felt inclined to say to him. She doesn't understand a word you're saying.

"I can't put a name to him," he said aloud. "But I've met him —let me see—where? In Oxford or Cambridge?"

A faint look of amusement came into Ann's eyes. She had spotted the difference. She coupled them together. They were not her world—no.

"Have you seen the Russian dancers?" she was saying. She had been there with her young man, it seemed. And what's your world, Martin thought, as she rapped out her slender stock of adjectives—"heavenly," "amazing," "marvellous," and so on. Is

it *"the"* world? he mused. He looked down the table. Anyhow no
other world had a chance against it, he thought. And it's a good
world too, he added; large; generous; hospitable. And very nice-
looking. He glanced from face to face. Dinner was drawing
to an end. They all looked as if they had been rubbed with wash
leather, like precious stones; yet the bloom seemed ingrained;
it went through the stone. And the stone was clear-cut; there
was no blur, no indecision. Here a footman's white-gloved hand
removing dishes knocked over a glass of wine. A red splash
trickled onto the lady's dress. But she did not move a muscle;
she went on talking. Then she straightened the clean napkin that
had been brought her, nonchalantly, over the stain.

That's what I like, Martin thought. He admired that. She
would have blown her fingers on her nose like an applewoman
if she wanted to, he thought. But Ann was talking.

"And when he gives that leap!" she exclaimed—she raised
her hand with a lovely gesture in the air—"and then comes
down!" She let her hand fall in her lap.

"Marvellous!" Martin agreed. He had got the very accent,
he thought; he had got it from the young man whose hair
looked as if a rake had gone through it.

"Yes: Nijinsky's marvellous," he agreed. "Marvellous," he
repeated.

"And my aunt has asked me to meet him at a party," said
Ann.

"Your aunt?" he said aloud.

She mentioned a well-known name.

"Oh, she's your aunt, is she?" he said. He placed her. So *that*
was her world. He wanted to ask her—for he found her charming in her youth, her simplicity—but it was too late. Ann was
rising.

"I hope—" he began. She bent her head towards him as if

she longed to stay, catch his last word, his least word; but could not, since Lady Lasswade had risen; and it was time for her to go.

Lady Lasswade had risen; everybody rose. All the pink, grey, sea-coloured dresses lengthened themselves, and for a moment the tall women standing by the table looked like the famous Gainsborough hanging on the wall. The table, strewn with napkins and wine-glasses, had a derelict air as they left it. For a moment the ladies clustered at the door; then the little old woman in black hobbled past them with remarkable dignity; and Kitty, coming last, put her arm round Ann's shoulder and led her out. The door shut on the ladies.

KITTY PAUSED for a moment.

"I hope you liked my old cousin?" she said to Ann as they walked upstairs together. She put her hand to her dress and straightened something as they passed a looking-glass.

"I thought him charming!" Ann exclaimed. "And what a lovely tree!" She spoke of Martin and the tree in exactly the same tone. They paused for a moment to look at a tree that was covered with pink blossoms in a china tub standing at the door. Some of the flowers were fully out; others were still unopened. As they looked a petal dropped.

"It's cruel to keep it here," said Kitty, "in this hot air."

They went in. While they dined the servants had opened the folding doors and lit lights in a further room so that it seemed as if they came into another room freshly made ready for them. There was a great fire blazing between two stately fire-dogs; but it seemed cordial and decorative rather than hot. Two or three of the ladies stood before it, opening and shutting their fingers as they spread them to the blaze; but they turned to make room for their hostess.

"How I love that picture of you, Kitty!" said Mrs. Aislabie, looking up at the portrait of Lady Lasswade as a young woman. Her hair had been very red in those days; she was toying with a basket of roses. Fiery but tender, she looked, emerging from a cloud of white muslin.

Kitty glanced at it and then turned away.

"One never likes one's own picture," she said.

"But it's the image of you!" said another lady.

"Not now," said Kitty, laughing off the compliment rather awkwardly. Always after dinner women paid each other compliments about their clothes or their looks, she thought. She did not like being alone with women after dinner; it made her shy. She stood there, upright among them, while footmen went round with trays of coffee.

"By the way, I hope the wine —" she paused and helped herself to coffee, "the wine didn't stain your frock, Cynthia?" she said to the young married woman who had taken the disaster so coolly.

"And such a lovely frock," said Lady Margaret, fondling the folds of golden satin between her finger and thumb.

"D'you like it?" said the young woman.

"It's perfectly lovely! I've been looking at it the whole evening!" said Mrs. Treyer, an Oriental-looking woman, with a feather floating back from her head in harmony with her nose, which was Jewish.

Kitty looked at them admiring the lovely frock. Eleanor would have found herself out of it, she thought. She had refused her invitation to dinner. That annoyed her.

"Do tell me," Lady Cynthia interrupted, "who was the man I sat next? One always meets such interesting people at your house," she added.

"The man you sat next?" said Kitty. She considered a moment. "Tony Ashton," she said.

"Is that the man who's been lecturing on French poetry at

Mortimer House?" chimed in Mrs. Aislabie. "I longed to go to those lectures. I heard they were wonderfully interesting."

"Mildred went," said Mrs. Treyer.

"Why should we all stand?" said Kitty. She made a movement with her hands towards the seats. She did things like that so abruptly that they called her, behind her back, "The Grenadier." They all moved this way and that, and she herself, after seeing how the couples sorted themselves, sat down by old Aunt Warburton, who was enthroned in the great chair.

"Tell me about my delightful godson," the old lady began. She meant Kitty's second son, who was with the fleet at Malta.

"He's at Malta—" she began. She sat down on a low chair and began answering her questions. But the fire was too hot for Aunt Warburton. She raised her knobbed old hand.

"Priestley wants to roast us all alive," said Kitty. She got up and went to the window. The ladies smiled as she strode across the room and jerked up the top of the long window. Just for a moment, as the curtains hung apart, she looked at the square outside. There was a spatter of leaf-shadow and lamplight on the pavement; the usual policeman was balancing himself as he patrolled; the usual little men and women, foreshortened from this height, hurried along by the railings. So she saw them hurrying, the other way, when she brushed her teeth in the morning. Then she came back and sat down on a low stool beside old Aunt Warburton. The worldly old woman was honest, in her way.

"And the little red-haired ruffian whom I love?" she asked. He was her favourite; the little boy at Eton.

"He's been in trouble," said Kitty. "He's been swished." She smiled. He was her favourite too.

The old lady grinned. She liked boys who got into trouble. She had a wedge-shaped yellow face with an occasional bristle on her chin; she was over eighty; but she sat as if she were riding a hunter, Kitty thought, glancing at her hands. They were coarse hands, with big finger-joints; red and white sparks flashed from her rings as she moved them.

"And you, my dear," said the old lady, looking at her shrewdly under her bushy eyebrows, "busy as usual?"

"Yes. Much as usual," said Kitty, evading the shrewd old eyes; for she did things on the sly that they—the ladies over there—did not approve.

They were chattering together. Yet animated as it sounded, to Kitty's ear the talk lacked substance. It was a battledore and shuttlecock talk, to be kept going until the door opened and the gentlemen came in. Then it would stop. They were talking about a by-election. She could hear Lady Margaret telling some story that was rather coarse presumably, in the eighteenth-century way, since she dropped her voice.

"—turned her upside down and slapped her," she could hear her say. There was a twitter of laughter.

"I'm so delighted he got in in spite of them," said Mrs. Treyer. They dropped their voices.

"I'm a tiresome old woman," said Aunt Warburton, raising one of her knobbed hands to her shoulder. "But now I'm going to ask you to shut that window." The draught was getting at her rheumatic joint.

Kitty strode to the window. "Damn these women!" she said to herself. She laid hold of the long stick with a beak at the end that stood in the window and poked; but the window stuck. She would have liked to fleece them of their clothes, of their jewels, of their intrigues, of their gossip. The window went up with a jerk. There was Ann standing about with nobody to talk to.

"Come and talk to us, Ann," she said, beckoning to her. Ann drew up a footstool and sat down at Aunt Warburton's feet. There was a pause. Old Aunt Warburton disliked young girls; but they had relations in common.

"Where's Timmy, Ann?" she asked.

"Harrow," said Ann.

"Ah, you've always been to Harrow," said Aunt Warburton. And then the old lady, with the beautiful breeding that simulated at least human charity, flattered the girl, likening her to her grandmother, a famous beauty.

"How I should love to have known her!" Ann exclaimed. "Do tell me—what was she like?"

The old lady began making a selection from her memoirs; it was only a selection; an edition with asterisks; for it was a story that could hardly be told to a girl in white satin. Kitty's mind wandered. If Charles stayed much longer downstairs, she thought, glancing at the clock, she would miss her train. Could Priestley be trusted to whisper a message in his ears? She would give them another ten minutes; she turned to Aunt Warburton again.

"She must have been wonderful!" Ann was saying. She sat with her hands clasped round her knees looking up into the face of the hairy old dowager. Kitty felt a moment's pity. Her face will be like their faces, she thought, looking at the little group at the other side of the room. Their faces looked harassed, worried; their hands moved restlessly. Yet they're brave, she thought; and generous. They gave as much as they took. Had Eleanor after all any right to despise them? Had she done more with her life than Margaret Marrable? And I? she thought. And I? . . . Who's right? she thought. Who's wrong? . . . Here mercifully the door opened.

The gentlemen came in. They came in reluctantly, rather slowly, as if they had just stopped talking, and had to get their bearings in the drawing-room. They were a little flushed and still laughing, as if they had stopped in the middle of what they were saying. They filed in; and the distinguished old man moved across the room with the air of a ship making port, and all the ladies stirred without rising. The game was over; the battledores and shuttlecocks put away. They were like gulls settling on fish, Kitty thought. There was a rising and a fluttering. The great man let himself slowly down into a chair beside his old friend Lady Warburton. He put the tips of his fingers together and began, "Well . . . ?" as if he were continuing a conversation left unfinished the night before. Yes, she thought, there was something—was it human? civilised? she could not find the word she wanted—about the old couple, talking, as they had talked for the past fifty years. . . . They were all talking. They had all settled in to add another sentence to the story that was just ending, or in the middle, or about to begin.

But there was Tony Ashton standing by himself without a sentence to add to the story. She went up to him therefore.

"Have you seen Edward lately?" he asked her as usual.

"Yes, today," she said. "I lunched with him. We walked in the Park. . . ." She stopped. They had walked in the Park. A thrush had been singing; they had stopped to listen. "That's the wise thrush that sings each song twice over . . ." he had said. "Does he?" she had asked innocently. And it had been a quotation.

She had felt foolish; Oxford always made her feel foolish. She disliked Oxford; yet she respected Edward and Tony too, she thought, looking at him. A snob on the surface; underneath a scholar. . . . They had a standard. . . . But she roused herself.

He would like to talk to some smart woman—Mrs. Aislabie, or Margaret Marrable. But they were both engaged—both were adding sentences with considerable vivacity. There was a pause. She was not a good hostess, she reflected; this sort of hitch always happened at her parties. There was Ann; Ann about to be captured by a youth she knew. But Kitty beckoned. Ann came instantly and submissively.

"Come and be introduced," she said, "to Mr. Ashton. He's been lecturing at Mortimer House," she explained, "about—" She hesitated.

"Mallarmé," he said with his odd little squeak, as if his voice had been pinched off.

KITTY TURNED AWAY. Martin came up to her.

"A very brilliant party, Lady Lasswade," he said with his usual tiresome irony.

"This? Oh, not at all," she said brusquely. This wasn't a party. Her parties were never brilliant. Martin was trying to tease her as usual. She looked down and saw his shabby shoes.

"Come and talk to me," she said, feeling the old family affection return. She noticed with amusement that he was a little flushed, a little, as the nurses used to say, "above himself." How many "parties" would it need, she wondered, to turn her satirical, uncompromising cousin into an obedient member of society?

"Let's sit down and talk sense," she said, sinking on to a little sofa. He sat down beside her.

"Tell me, what's Nell doing?" she asked.

"She sent her love," said Martin. "She told me to say how much she wanted to see you."

"Then why wouldn't she come tonight?" said Kitty. She felt hurt. She could not help it.

"She hasn't the right kind of hairpin," he said with a laugh, looking down at his shoes. Kitty looked down at them too.

"My shoes, you see, don't matter," he said. "But then I'm a man."

"It's such nonsense . . ." Kitty began. "What does it matter . . ."

But he was looking round him at the groups of beautifully dressed women; then at the picture.

"That's a horrid daub of you over the mantelpiece," he said, looking at the red-haired girl. "Who did it?"

"I forget . . . Don't let's look at it," she said.

"Let's talk . . ." Then she stopped.

He was looking round the room. It was crowded; there were little tables with photographs; ornate cabinets with vases of flowers; and panels of yellow brocade let into the walls. She felt that he was criticising the room and herself too.

"I always want to take a knife and scrape it all off," she said. But what's the use, she thought? If she moved a picture, "Where's Uncle Bill on the old cob?" her husband would say, and back it had to go again.

"Like a hotel, isn't it?" she continued.

"A saloon," he remarked. He did not know why he wanted to hurt her; but he did; it was a fact.

"I was asking myself," he dropped his voice, "Why have a picture like that"—he nodded his head at the portrait—"when they've a Gainsborough . . ."

"And why," she dropped her voice, imitating his tone that was half sneering, half humorous, "come and eat their food when you despise them?"

"I don't! Not a bit!" he exclaimed. "I'm enjoying myself immensely. I like seeing you, Kitty," he added. It was true—he always liked her. "You haven't dropped your poor relations. That's very nice of you."

"It's they who've dropped me," she said.

"Oh, Eleanor," he said. "She's a queer old bird."

"It's all so . . ." Kitty began. But there was something wrong about the disposition of her party; she stopped in the middle of her sentence. "You've got to come and talk to Mrs. Treyer," she said, getting up.

Why does one do it? he wondered as he followed her. He had wanted to talk to Kitty; he had nothing to say to that

Oriental-looking harpy with a pheasant's feather floating at the back of her head. Still, if you drink the good wine of the noble countess, he said, bowing, you have to entertain her less desirable friends. He led her off.

Kitty went back to the fireplace. She dealt the coal a blow, and the sparks went volleying up the chimney. She was irritable; she was restless. Time was passing; if they stayed much longer she would miss her train. Surreptitiously she noted that the hands of the clock were close on eleven. The party was bound to break up soon; it was only the prelude to another party. Yet they were all talking, and talking, as if they would never go. She glanced at the groups that seemed immovable. Then the clock chimed a succession of petulant little strokes, on the last of which the door opened and Priestley advanced. With his inscrutable butler's eyes and crooked forefinger he summoned Ann Hillier.

"That's Mama fetching me," said Ann, advancing down the room with a little flutter.

"She's taking you on?" said Kitty. She held her hand for a moment. Why? she asked herself, looking at the lovely face, empty of meaning, or character, like a page on which nothing has been written but youth. She held her hand for a moment.

"Must you go?" she said.

"I'm afraid I must," said Ann, withdrawing her hand.

There was a general rising and movement, like the flutter of white-winged gulls.

"Coming with us?" Martin heard Ann say to the youth through whose hair the rake seemed to have been passed. They turned to leave together. As she passed Martin, who stood with his hand out, Ann gave him the least bend of her head, as if his image had been already swept from her mind. He was dashed; his feeling was out of all proportion to its object. He felt a

strong desire to go with them, wherever it was. But he had not
been asked; Ashton had; he was following in their wake.

"What a toady!" he thought to himself with a bitterness that
surprised him. It was odd how jealous he felt for a moment.
They were all "going on," it seemed. He hung about a little awkwardly. Only the old fogies were left—no, even the great man
was going on, it seemed. Only the old lady was left. She was
hobbling across the room on Lasswade's arm. She wanted to
confirm something that she had been saying about a miniature.
Lasswade had taken it off the wall; he held it under a lamp so
that she could pronounce her verdict. Was it Grandpapa on the
cob, or was it Uncle William?

"Sit down, Martin, and let us talk," said Kitty. He sat down:
but he had a feeling that she wanted him to go. He had seen her
glance at the clock. They chatted for a moment. Now the old
lady came back; she was proving, beyond a doubt, from her un-
exampled store of anecdotes, that it must be Uncle William on
the cob; not Grandpapa. She was going. But she took her time.
Martin waited till she was fairly in the doorway, leaning on her
nephew's arm. He hesitated; they were alone now; should he
stay, or should he go? But Kitty was standing up. She was holding out her hand.

"Come again soon and see me alone," she said. She had dismissed him, he felt.

That's what people always say, he said to himself as he made
his way slowly downstairs behind Lady Warburton. Come again:
but I don't know that I shall. . . . Lady Warburton went downstairs like a crab, holding on to the banisters with one hand, to
Lasswade's arm with the other. He lingered behind her. He
looked at the Canaletto once more. A nice picture: but a copy,
he said to himself. He peered over the banisters and saw the
black-and-white slabs on the hall beneath.

It did work, he said to himself, descending step by step into the hall. Off and on; by fits and starts. But was it worth it? he asked himself, letting the footman help him into his coat. The double doors stood wide open into the street. One or two people were passing; they peered in curiously, looking at the footmen, at the bright big hall; and at the old lady who paused for a moment on the black-and-white squares. She was robing herself. Now she was accepting her cloak with a violet slash in it; now her furs. A bag dangled from her wrist. She was hung about with chains; her fingers were knobbed with rings. Her sharp stone-coloured face, riddled with lines and wrinkled into creases, looked out from its soft nest of fur and laces. The eyes were still bright.

The nineteenth century going to bed, Martin said to himself as he watched her hobble down the steps on the arm of her footman. She was helped into her carriage. Then he shook hands with that good fellow his host, who had had quite as much wine as was good for him, and walked off through Grosvenor Square.

UPSTAIRS in the bedroom at the top of the house Kitty's maid Baxter was looking out of the window, watching the guests drive off. There—that was the old lady going. She wished they would hurry; if the party went on much longer her own little jaunt would be done for. She was going up the river tomorrow with her young man. She turned and looked round her. She had everything ready—her ladyship's coat, skirt, and the bag with the ticket in it. It was long past eleven. She stood at the dressing-table waiting. The three-folded mirror reflected silver pots, powder puffs, combs and brushes. Baxter stooped down and smirked at herself in the glass—that was how she would look when she went up the river—then she drew herself up; she heard footsteps in the passage. Her ladyship was coming. Here she was.

Lady Lasswade came in, slipping the rings from her fingers. "Sorry to be so late, Baxter," she said. "Now I must hurry."

Baxter, without speaking, unhooked her dress; slipped it dexterously to her feet, and bore it away. Kitty sat down at her dressing-table and kicked off her shoes. Satin shoes were always too tight. She glanced at the clock on her dressing-table. She just had time.

Baxter was handing her coat. Now she was handing her bag.

"The ticket's in there, m'lady," she said, touching the bag.

"Now my hat," said Kitty. She stooped to settle it in front of the mirror. The little tweed travelling-hat poised on the top of her hair made her look quite a different person; the person she liked being. She stood in her travelling-dress, wondering if she had forgotten anything. Her mind was a perfect blank for a moment. Where am I? she wondered. What am I doing? Where am I going? Her eyes fixed themselves on the dressing-table; vaguely she remembered some other room, and some other time when she was a girl. At Oxford was it?

"The ticket, Baxter?" she said perfunctorily.

"In your bag, m'lady," Baxter reminded her. She was holding it in her hand.

"So that's everything," said Kitty, glancing round her.

She felt a moment's compunction.

"Thanks, Baxter," she said. "I hope you'll enjoy your . . ."— she hesitated: she did not know what Baxter did on her day off—". . . your play," she said at a venture. Baxter gave a queer little bitten-off smile. Maids bothered Kitty with their demure politeness; with their inscrutable, pursed-up faces. But they were very useful.

"Good-night!" she said to Baxter at the door of the bedroom; for there Baxter turned back as if her responsibility for her mistress ended. Somebody else had charge of the stairs.

Kitty looked in at the drawing-room, in case her husband

should be there. But the room was empty. The fire was still blazing; the chairs, drawn out in a circle, still seemed to hold the skeleton of the party in their empty arms. But the car was waiting for her at the door.

"Plenty of time?" she said to the chauffeur as he laid the rug across her knees. Off they started.

IT WAS a clear still night and every tree in the Square was visible; some were black, others were sprinkled with strange patches of green artificial light. Above the arc lamps rose shafts of darkness. Although it was close on midnight, it scarcely seemed to be night; but rather some etherial disembodied day, for there were so many lamps in the streets; cars passing; men in white mufflers with their light overcoats open walking along the clean dry pavements, and many houses were still lit up, for everyone was giving parties. The town changed as they drew smoothly through Mayfair. The public-houses were closing; here was a group clustered round a lamp-post at the corner. A drunken man was bawling out some loud song; a tipsy girl with a feather bobbing in her eyes was swaying as she clung to the lamp-post . . . but Kitty's eyes alone registered what she saw. After the talk, the effort and the hurry, she could add nothing to what she saw. And they swept on quickly. Now they had turned, and the car was gliding at full speed up a long bright avenue of great shuttered shops. The streets were almost empty. The yellow station clock showed that they had five minutes to spare.

Just in time, she said to herself. The usual exhilaration mounted in her as she walked along the platform. Diffused light poured down from a great height. Men's cries and the clangour of shunting carriages echoed in the immense vacancy. The train was waiting; travellers were making ready to start. Some were standing with one foot on the step of the carriage drinking out of thick cups as if they were afraid to go far from their seats. She looked down the length of the train and saw the engine sucking water from a hose. It seemed all body, all muscle; even the neck had been consumed into the smooth barrel of the body. This was "the" train; the others were toys in comparison. She snuffed up the sulphurous air, which left a slight tinge of acid at the back of the throat, as if it already had a tang of the north.

The guard had seen her and was coming towards her with his whistle in his hand.

"Good evening, m'lady," he said.

"Good evening, Purvis. Run it rather fine," she said as he unlocked the door of her carriage.

"Yes, m'lady. Only just in time," he replied.

He locked the door. Kitty turned and looked round the small lighted room in which she was to spend the night. Everything was ready; the bed was made; the sheets were turned down; her bag was on the seat. The guard passed the window, holding his flag in his hand. A man who had only just caught the train ran across the platform with his arms spread out. A door slammed.

"Just in time," Kitty said to herself as she stood there. Then the train gave a gentle tug. She could hardly believe that so great a monster could start so gently on so long a journey. Then she saw the tea-urn sliding past.

"We're off," she said to herself, sinking back onto the seat. "We're off!"

All the tension went out of her body. She was alone; and the train was moving. The last lamp on the platform slid away. The last figure on the platform vanished.

"What fun!" she said to herself, as if she were a little girl who had run away from her nurse and escaped. "We're off!"

SHE SAT STILL for a moment in her brightly lit compartment; then she tugged the blind and it sprang up with a jerk. Elongated

lights slid past; lights in factories and warehouses; lights in obscure back streets. Then there were asphalt paths; more lights in
public gardens; and then bushes and a hedge in a field. They
were leaving London behind them; leaving that blaze of light
which seemed, as the train rushed into the darkness, to contract
itself into one fiery circle. The train rushed with a roar through
a tunnel. It seemed to perform an act of amputation; now she
was cut off from that circle of light.

She looked round the narrow little compartment in which
she was isolated. Everything shook slightly. There was a perpetual faint vibration. She seemed to be passing from one world to
another; this was the moment of transition. She sat still for a
moment; then undressed and paused with her hand on the
blind. The train had got into its stride now; it was rushing at full
speed through the country. A few distant lights twinkled here
and there. Black clumps of trees stood in the grey summer
fields; the fields were full of summer grasses. The light from the
engine lit up a quiet group of cows; and a hedge of hawthorn.
They were in open country now.

She pulled down the blind and climbed into her bed. She
laid herself out on the rather hard shelf with her back to the carriage wall, so that she felt a faint vibration against her head. She
lay listening to the humming noise which the train made, now
that it had got into its stride. Smoothly and powerfully she was
being drawn through England to the north. I need do nothing,
she thought, nothing, nothing, but let myself be drawn on. She
turned and pulled the blue shade over the lamp. The sound of
the train became louder in the darkness; its roar, its vibration,
seemed to fall into a regular rhythm of sound, raking through
her mind, rolling out her thoughts.

Ah, but not all of them, she thought, turning restlessly on
her shelf. Some still jutted up. One's not a child, she thought,
staring at the light under the blue shade, any longer. The years

changed things; destroyed things; heaped things up—worries
and bothers; here they were again. Fragments of talk kept coming back to her; sights came before her. She saw herself raise the
window with a jerk; and the bristles on Aunt Warburton's chin.
She saw the women rising, and the men filing in. She sighed
as she turned on her ledge. All their clothes are the same,
she thought; all their lives are the same. And which is right? she
thought, turning restlessly on her shelf. Which is wrong? She
turned again.

The train rushed her on. The sound had deepened; it had
become a continuous roar. How could she sleep? How could
she prevent herself from thinking? She turned away from the
light. *Now* where are we, she said to herself. Where is the train
at this moment? *Now,* she murmured, shutting her eyes, we are
passing the white house on the hill; *now* we are going through
the tunnel; *now* we are crossing the bridge over the river. . . . A
blank intervened; her thoughts became spaced; they became
muddled. Past and present became jumbled together. She saw
Margaret Marrable pinching the dress in her fingers, but she was
leading a bull with a ring through its nose. . . . This is sleep, she
said to herself, half opening her eyes; thank goodness, she said
to herself, shutting them again, this is sleep. And she resigned
herself to the charge of the train, whose roar now became dulled
and distant.

THERE WAS a tap at her door. She lay for a moment, wondering why the room shook so; then the scene settled itself; she was
in the train; she was in the country; they were nearing the station. She got up.

She dressed rapidly and stood in the corridor. It was still
early. She watched the fields galloping past. They were the bare
fields, the angular fields of the north. The spring was late here;
the trees were not fully out yet. The smoke looped down and

caught a tree in its white cloud. When it lifted, she thought how fine the light was; clear and sharp, white and grey. The land had none of the softness, none of the greenness of the land in the south. But here was the junction; here was the gasometer; they were running into the station. The train slowed down, and all the lamp-posts on the platform gradually came to a standstill.

She got out and drew in a deep breath of the cold raw air. The car was waiting for her; and directly she saw it she remembered—it was the new car; a birthday present from her husband. She had never driven in it yet. Cole touched his hat.

"Let's have it open, Cole," she said, and he opened the stiff new hood, and she got in beside him. Very slowly, for the engine seemed to beat intermittently, starting and stopping and then starting again, they moved off. They drove through the town; all the shops were still shut; women were on their knees scrubbing doorsteps; blinds were still drawn in bedrooms and sitting-rooms; there was very little traffic about. Only milk-carts rattled past. Dogs roamed down the middle of the street on private errands of their own. Cole had to hoot again and again.

"They'll learn in time, m'lady," he said as a great brindled cur slunk out of their way. In the town he drove carefully; but once they were outside he speeded up. Kitty watched the needle jump forward on the speedometer.

"She does it easily?" she asked, listening to the soft purr of the engine.

Cole lifted his foot to show how lightly it touched the accelerator. Then he touched it again and the car sped on. They were driving too fast, Kitty thought; but the road—she kept her eye on it—was still empty. Only two or three lumbering farm waggons passed them; the men went to the horses' heads and held them as they went by. The road stretched pearl-white in front of them; the hedges were decked with the little pointed leaves of early spring.

"Spring's very late up here," said Kitty; "cold winds I suppose?"

Cole nodded. He had none of the servile ways of the London flunkey; she was at her ease with him; she could be silent. The air seemed to have different grades of warmth and chill in it; now sweet; now—they were passing a farmyard—strong-smelling, acrid from the sour smell of manure. She leant back, holding her hat to her head as they rushed a hill. "You won't get her up this on top, Cole," she said. The pace slackened a little; they were climbing the familiar Crabbs hill, with the yellow streaks where carters had put on their brakes. In the old days, when she drove horses, they used to get out here and walk. Cole said nothing. He was going to show off his engine, she suspected. The car swept up finely. But the hill was long; there was a level stretch; then the road mounted again. The car faltered. Cole coaxed her on. Kitty saw him jerk his body slightly backwards and forwards as if he were encouraging horses. She felt the tension of his muscles. They slowed—they almost stopped. No, now they were on the crest of the hill. She had done it on top!

"Well done!" she exclaimed. He said nothing; but he was very proud, she knew.

"We couldn't have done that on the old car," she said.

"Ah, but it wasn't her fault," said Cole.

He was a very humane man; the kind of man she liked, she reflected—silent, reserved. On they swept again. Now they were passing the grey stone house where the mad lady lived alone with her peacocks and her bloodhounds. They had passed it. Now the woods were on their right hand and the air came singing through them. It was like the sea, Kitty thought, looking, as they passed, down a dark green drive patched with yellow sunlight. On they went again. Now heaps of ruddy brown leaves lay by the roadside staining the puddles red.

"It's been raining?" she said. He nodded. They came out on the high ridge with woods beneath and there, in a clearing among the trees, was the grey tower of the Castle. She always looked for it and greeted it as if she were raising a hand to a friend. They were on their own land now. Gateposts were branded with their initials; their arms swung above the doorways of inns; their crest was mounted over cottage doors. Cole looked at the clock. The needle leapt again.

Too fast, too fast! Kitty said to herself. But she liked the rush of the wind in her face. Now they reached the Lodge gate; Mrs. Preedy was holding it open with a white-haired child on her arm. They rushed through the Park. The deer looked up and hopped away lightly through the fern.

"Two minutes under the quarter, m'lady," said Cole as they swept in a circle and drew up at the door. Kitty stood for a moment looking at the car. She laid her hand on the bonnet. It was hot. She gave it a little pat. "She did it beautifully, Cole," she said. "I'll tell his Lordship." Cole smiled; he was happy.

She went in. Nobody was about; they had arrived earlier than was expected. She crossed the great stone-flagged hall, with the armour and the busts, and went into the morning-room where breakfast was laid.

The green light dazzled her as she went in. It was as if she stood in the hollow of an emerald. All was green outside. The statues of grey French ladies stood on the terrace, holding their baskets; but the baskets were empty. In summer flowers would burn there. Green turf fell down in broad swathes between clipped yews; dipped to the river; and then rose again to the hill that was crested with woods. There was a curl of mist on the woods now—the light mist of early morning. As she gazed a bee buzzed in her ear; she thought she heard the murmur of the river over the stones; pigeons crooned in the tree tops. It was the voice of early morning, the voice of summer. But the door opened. Here was breakfast.

She breakfasted; she felt warm, stored, and comfortable as she lay back in her chair. And she had nothing to do — nothing whatever. The whole day was hers. It was fine too. The sunlight suddenly quickened in the room, and laid a broad bar of light across the floor. The sun was on the flowers outside. A tortoise-shell butterfly flaunted across the window; she saw it settle on a leaf, and there it sat, opening its wings and shutting them, opening and shutting them, as if it feasted on the sunlight. She watched it. The down was soft rust-red on its wings. Off it flaunted again. Then, admitted by an invisible hand, the chow stalked in; came straight up to her; sniffed at her skirt, and flung himself down in a bright patch of sunlight.

Heartless brute! she thought, but his indifference pleased her. He asked nothing of her either. She stretched her hand for a cigarette. And what would Martin say, she wondered, as she took the enamel box that turned from green to blue, as she opened it. Hideous? Vulgar? Possibly — but what did it matter what people said? Criticism seemed light as smoke this morning. What did it matter what he said, what they said, what anybody said, since she had a whole day to herself? — since she was alone? And there they are, still asleep, in their houses, she thought, standing at the window, looking at the green-grey grass, after their dances, after their parties ... The thought pleased her. She threw away her cigarette and went upstairs to change her clothes.

The sun was much stronger when she came down again. The garden had already lost its look of purity; the mist was off the woods. She could hear the squeak of the lawn mower as she stepped out of the window. The rubber-shoed pony was pacing up and down the lawns leaving a pale wake in the grass behind him. The birds were singing in their scattered way. The starlings in their bright mail were feeding on the grass. Dew shone, red, violet, gold on the trembling tips of the grass blades. It was a perfect May morning.

She sauntered slowly along the terrace. As she passed she glanced in at the long windows of the library. Everything was shrouded and shut up. But the long room looked more than usually stately, its proportions seemly; and the brown books in their long rows seemed to exist silently, with dignity, by themselves, for themselves. She left the terrace and strolled down the long grass path. The garden was still empty; only a man in his shirt sleeves was doing something to a tree; but she need speak to nobody. The chow stalked after her; he too was silent. She walked on past the flower beds to the river. There she always stopped, on the bridge, with the cannon balls at intervals. The water always fascinated her. The quick northern river came down from the moors; it was never smooth and green, never deep and placid like southern rivers. It raced; it hurried. It splayed itself, red, yellow and clear brown over the pebbles on the bed. Resting her elbows on the balustrade, she watched it eddy round the arches; she watched it make diamonds and sharp arrow streaks over the stones. She listened. She knew the different sounds it made in summer and winter; now it hurried, it raced.

But the chow was bored; he marched on. She followed him. She went up the green ride towards the snuffer-shaped monument on the crest of the hill. Every path through the woods had its name. There was Keepers' Path, Lovers' Walk, Ladies' Mile, and here was the Earl's Ride. But before she went into the woods, she stopped and looked back at the house. Times out of number she had stopped here; the Castle looked grey and stately; asleep this morning, with the blinds drawn, and no flag on the flagstaff. Very noble it looked, and ancient, and enduring. Then she went on into the woods.

The wind seemed to rise as she walked under the trees. It sang in their tops, but it was silent beneath. The dead leaves crackled under foot; among them sprang up the pale spring flowers, the loveliest of the year—blue flowers and white flowers, trembling on cushions of green moss. Spring was sad always, she thought; it brought back memories. All passes, all changes, she thought, as she climbed up the little path between the trees. Nothing of this belonged to her; her son would inherit; his wife would walk here after her. She broke off a twig; she picked a flower and put it to her lips. But she was in the prime of life; she was vigorous. She strode on. The ground rose sharply; her muscles felt strong and flexible as she pressed her thick-soled shoes to the ground. She threw away her flower. The trees thinned as she strode higher and higher. Suddenly she saw the sky between two striped tree trunks extraordinarily blue. She came out on the top. The wind ceased; the country spread wide all round her. Her body seemed to shrink; her eyes to widen. She threw herself on the ground, and looked over the billowing land that went rising and falling, away and away, until somewhere far off it reached the sea. Uncultivated, uninhabited, existing by itself, for itself, without towns or houses it looked from this height. Dark wedges of shadow, bright breadths of light lay side by side. Then, as she watched, light moved and dark moved; light and shadow went travelling over the hills and over the valleys. A deep murmur sang in her ears—the land itself, singing to itself, a chorus, alone. She lay there listening. She was happy, completely. Time had ceased.

1917

A VERY cold winter's night, so silent that the air seemed frozen, and, since there was no moon, congealed to the stillness of glass spread over England. Ponds and ditches were frozen; the puddles made glazed eyes in the roads, and on the pavement the frost had raised slippery knobs. Darkness pressed on the windows; towns had merged themselves in open country. No light shone, save when a searchlight rayed round the sky, and stopped, here and there, as if to ponder some fleecy patch.

"IF THAT is the river," said Eleanor, pausing in the dark street outside the station, "Westminster must be there." The omnibus in which she had come, with its silent passengers looking cadaverous in the blue light, had already vanished. She turned.

She was dining with Renny and Maggie, who lived in one of the obscure little streets under the shadow of the Abbey. She walked on. The further side of the street was almost invisible. The lamps were shrouded in blue. She flashed her torch on to a name on a street corner. Again she flashed her torch. Here it lit up a brick wall; there a dark green tuft of ivy. At last the number thirty, the number she was looking for, shone out. She knocked and rang at the same moment, for the darkness seemed to muffle sound as well as sight. Silence weighed on her as she stood there waiting. Then the door opened and a man's voice said, "Come in!"

He shut the door behind him, quickly, as if to shut out the light. It looked strange after the streets—the perambulator in the hall; the umbrellas in the stand; the carpet, the pictures: they all seemed intensified.

"Come in!" said Renny again, and led her into the sitting-room ablaze with light. Another man was standing in the room, and she was surprised because she had expected to find them alone. But the man was somebody whom she did not know.

For a moment they stared at each other; then Renny said, "You know Nicholas . . ." but he did not speak the surname distinctly, and it was so long that she could not catch it. A foreign name, she thought. A foreigner. He was clearly not English. He shook hands with a bow like a foreigner, and he went on talking, as if he were in the middle of a sentence that he wished to finish . . . "we are talking about Napoleon . . ." he said, turning to her.

"I see," she said. But she had no notion what he was saying. They were in the middle of an argument, she supposed. But it came to an end without her understanding a word of it, except that it had to do with Napoleon. She took off her coat and laid it down. They stopped talking.

"I will go and tell Maggie," said Renny. He left them abruptly.

"You were talking about Napoleon?" Eleanor said. She looked at the man whose surname she had not heard. He was very dark; he had a rounded head and dark eyes. Did she like him or not? She did not know.

I've interrupted them, she felt, and I've nothing whatever to say. She felt dazed and cold. She spread her hands over the fire. It was a real fire; wood blocks were blazing; the flame ran along the streaks of shiny tar. A little trickle of feeble gas was all that was left her at home.

"Napoleon," she said, warming her hands. She spoke without any meaning.

"We were considering the psychology of great men," he said. "By the light of modern science," he added with a little laugh. She wished the argument had been more within her reach.

"That's very interesting," she said shyly.

"Yes—if we knew anything about it," he said.

"If we knew anything about it . . ." she repeated. There was a pause. She felt numb all over—not only her hands, but her brain.

"The psychology of great men—" she said, for she did not wish him to think her a fool, ". . . was that what you were discussing?"

"We were saying—" He paused. She guessed that he found it difficult to sum up their argument—they had evidently been talking for some time, judging by the newspapers lying about and the cigarette-ends on the table.

"I was saying," he went on, "I was saying we do not know ourselves, ordinary people; and if we do not know ourselves, how then can we make religions, laws, that—" he used his hands as people do who find language obdurate, "that—"

"That fit—that fit," she said, supplying him with a word that was shorter, she felt sure, than the dictionary word that foreigners always used.

"—that fit, that fit," he said, taking the word and repeating it as if he were grateful for her help.

". . . that fit," she repeated. She had no idea what they were talking about. Then suddenly, as she bent to warm her hands over the fire, words floated together in her mind and made one intelligible sentence. It seemed to her that what he had said was,

"We cannot make laws and religions that fit because we do not know ourselves."

"How odd that you should say that!" she said, smiling at him, "because I've so often thought it myself!"

"Why is that odd?" he said. "We all think the same things; only we do not say them."

"Coming along in the omnibus tonight," she began, "I was thinking about this war—I don't feel this, but other people do . . ." She stopped. He looked puzzled; probably she had misunderstood what he had said; she had not made her own meaning plain.

"I mean," she began again, "I was thinking as I came along in the bus—"

But here Renny came in.

He was carrying a tray with bottles and glasses.

"It is a great thing," said Nicholas, "being the son of a wine merchant."

It sounded like a quotation from the French grammar.

The son of the wine merchant, Eleanor repeated to herself, looking at his red cheeks, dark eyes and large nose. The other man must be Russian, she thought. Russian, Polish, Jewish?— she had no idea what he was, who he was.

She drank; the wine seemed to caress a knob in her spine. Here Maggie came in.

"Good evening," she said, disregarding the foreigner's bow as if she knew him too well to greet him.

"Papers," she protested, looking at the litter on the floor, "papers, papers." The floor was strewn with papers.

"We dine in the basement," she continued, turning to Eleanor, "because we've no servants." She led the way down the steep little stairs.

"But, Magdalena," said Nicholas, as they stood in the little low-ceilinged room in which dinner was laid, "Sara said, 'We shall meet tomorrow night at Maggie's . . .' She is not here."

He stood; the others had sat down.

"She will come in time," said Maggie.

"I shall ring her up," said Nicholas. He left the room.

"Isn't it much nicer," said Eleanor, taking her plate, "not having servants . . ."

"We have a woman to do the washing-up," said Maggie.

"And we are extremely dirty," said Renny.

He took up a fork and examined it between the prongs.

"No, this fork, as it happens, is clean," he said, and put it down again.

Nicholas came back into the room. He looked perturbed. "She is not there," he said to Maggie. "I rang her up, but I could get no answer."

"Probably she's coming," said Maggie. "Or she may have forgotten. . . ."

She handed him his soup. But he sat looking at his plate without moving. Wrinkles had come on his forehead; he made no attempt to hide his anxiety. He was without self-consciousness. "There!" he suddenly exclaimed, interrupting them as they talked. "She is coming!" he added. He put down his spoon and waited. Someone was coming slowly down the steep stairs.

The door opened and Sara came in. She looked pinched with the cold. Her cheeks were white here and red there, and she blinked as if she were still dazed from her walk through the blue-shrouded streets. She gave her hand to Nicholas and he kissed it. But she wore no engagement ring, Eleanor observed.

"Yes, we are dirty," said Maggie, looking at her; she was in her day clothes. "In rags," she added, for a loop of gold thread hung down from her own sleeve as she helped the soup.

"I was thinking how beautiful . . ." said Eleanor, for her

eyes had been resting on the silver dress with gold threads in it. "Where did you get it?"

"In Constantinople, from a Turk," said Maggie.

"A turbaned and fantastic Turk," Sara murmured, stroking the sleeve as she took her plate. She still seemed dazed.

"And the plates," said Eleanor, looking at the purple birds on her plate. "Don't I remember them?" she asked.

"In the cabinet in the drawing-room at home," said Maggie. "But it seemed silly—keeping them in a cabinet."

"We break one every week," said Renny.

"They'll last the war," said Maggie.

Eleanor observed a curious mask-like expression come down over Renny's face as she said "the war." Like all the French, she thought, he cares passionately for his country. But contradictorily, she felt, looking at him. He was silent. His silence oppressed her. There was something formidable about his silence.

"And why were you so late?" said Nicholas, turning to Sara. He spoke gently, reproachfully, rather as if she were a child. He poured her out a glass of wine.

Take care, Eleanor felt inclined to say to her; the wine goes to one's head. She had not drunk wine for months. She was feeling already a little blurred; a little light-headed. It was the light after the dark; talk after silence; the war, perhaps, removing barriers.

But Sara drank. Then she burst out:

"Because of that damned fool."

"Damned fool?" said Maggie. "Which?"

"Eleanor's nephew," said Sara. "North. Eleanor's nephew, North." She held her glass towards Eleanor, as if she were addressing her. "North . . ." Then she smiled. "There I was, sitting alone. The bell rang. 'That's the wash,' I said. Footsteps came up the stairs. There was North—North," she raised her hand to her head as if in salute, "cutting a figure like this. . . . 'What the devil's that for?' I asked. 'I leave for the Front tonight,' he said, clicking his heels together. 'I'm a lieutenant in ——' whatever it was— Royal Regiment of Rat-catchers or something. . . . And he hung his cap on the bust of our grandfather. And I poured out tea. 'How many lumps of sugar does a lieutenant in the Royal Rat-catchers require?' I asked. 'One. Two. Three. Four. . . .'"

She dropped pellets of bread on to the table. As each fell, it seemed to emphasise her bitterness. She looked older, more worn; though she laughed, she was bitter.

"Who is North?" Nicholas asked. He pronounced the word "North" as if it were a point on the compass.

"My nephew. My brother Morris's son," Eleanor explained.

"There he sat," Sara resumed, "in his mud-coloured uniform, with his switch between his legs, and his ears sticking out on either side of his pink, foolish face, and whatever I said, 'Good,' he said, 'Good,' 'Good,' until I took up the poker and tongs," she took up her knife and fork, "and played 'God save the King, Happy and Glorious, Long to reign over us—'" She held her knife and fork as if they were weapons.

I'm sorry he's gone, Eleanor thought. A picture came before her eyes—the picture of a nice cricketing boy smoking a cigar on a terrace. I'm sorry. . . . Then another picture formed. She was sitting on the same terrace; but now the sun was setting; a maid came out and said, "The soldiers are guarding the line with fixed bayonets!" That was how she had heard of the war—three years ago. And she had thought, putting down her coffee-cup on a little table, Not if I can help it! overcome by an absurd but vehement desire to protect those hills; she had looked at the hills across the meadow. . . . Now she looked at the foreigner opposite.

"How unfair you are," Nicholas was saying to Sara. "Prejudiced; narrow; unfair," he repeated, tapping her hand with his finger.

He was saying what Eleanor felt herself.

"Yes. Isn't it natural . . ." she began. "Could you allow the Germans to invade England and do nothing?" she said, turning to Renny. She was sorry she had spoken; and the words were not the ones she had meant to use. There was an expression of suffering, or was it anger? on his face.

"I?" he said. "I help them to make shells."

Maggie stood behind him. She had brought in the meat. "Carve," she said. He was staring at the meat which she had put down in front of him. He took up the knife and began to carve mechanically.

"Now, Nurse," she reminded him. He cut another helping.

"Yes," said Eleanor awkwardly as Maggie took away the plate. She did not know what to say. She spoke without thinking. "Let's end it as quickly as possible and then . . ." She looked at him. He was silent. He turned away. He had turned to listen to what the others were saying, as if to take refuge from speaking himself.

"Poppycock, poppycock . . . don't talk such damned poppycock—that's what you really said," Nicholas was saying. His hands were large and clean and the finger-nails were trimmed very close, Eleanor noticed. He might be a doctor, she thought.

"What's 'poppy-cock'?" she asked, turning to Renny. For she did not know the word.

"American," said Renny. "He's an American," he said, nodding at Nicholas.

"No," said Nicholas, turning round, "I am a Pole."

"His mother was a Princess," said Maggie as if she were teasing him. That explains the seal on his chain, Eleanor thought. He wore a large old seal on his chain.

"She was," he said quite seriously. "One of the noblest families in Poland. But my father was an ordinary man—a man of the people. . . . You should have had more self-control," he added, turning again to Sara.

"So I should," she sighed. "But then he gave his bridle reins a shake and said, 'Adieu for evermore, adieu for evermore!'" She stretched out her hand and poured herself another glass of wine.

"You shall have no more to drink," said Nicholas, moving away the bottle. "She saw herself," he explained, turning to Eleanor, "on top of a tower, waving a white handkerchief to a knight in armour."

"And the moon was rising over a dark moor," Sara murmured, touching a pepper-pot.

The pepper-pot's a dark moor, Eleanor thought, looking at it. A little blur had come round the edges of things. It was the wine; it was the war. Things seemed to have lost their skins; to be freed from some surface hardness; even the chair with gilt claws, at which she was looking, seemed porous; it seemed to radiate out some warmth, some glamour, as she looked at it.

"I remember that chair," she said to Maggie. "And your mother . . ." she added. But she always saw Eugénie not sitting but in movement.

". . . dancing," she added.

"Dancing . . ." Sara repeated. She began drumming on the table with her fork.

"When I was young, I used to dance," she hummed.

"All men loved me when I was young. . . . Roses and syringas hung, when I was young, when I was young. D'you remember, Maggie?" She looked at her sister as if they both remembered the same thing.

Maggie nodded. "In the bedroom. A waltz," she said.

"A waltz . . ." said Eleanor. Sara was drumming a waltz

rhythm on the table. Eleanor began to hum in time to it: "Hoity te, toity te, hoity te. . . ."

A long-drawn hollow sound wailed out.

"No, no!" she protested, as if somebody had given her the wrong note. But the sound wailed again.

"A fog horn?" she said. "On the river?"

But as she said it she knew what it was.

The siren wailed again.

"The Germans!" said Renny. "Those damned Germans!" He put down his knife and fork with an exaggerated gesture of boredom.

"Another raid," said Maggie, getting up. She left the room. Renny followed her.

"THE GERMANS . . ." said Eleanor as the door shut. She felt as if some dull bore had interrupted an interesting conversation. The colours began to fade. She had been looking at the red chair. It lost its radiance as she looked at it, as if a light had gone out.

They heard the rush of wheels in the street. Everything seemed to be going past very quickly. There was the sound of feet tapping on the pavement. Eleanor got up and drew the curtains slightly apart. The basement was sunk beneath the pavement, so that she only saw people's legs and skirts as they went past the area railings. Two men came by walking very quickly; then an old woman, with her skirt swinging from side to side, walked past.

"Oughtn't we to ask people in?" she said, turning round. But when she looked back the old woman had disappeared. So had the men. The street was now quite empty. The houses opposite were completely curtained. She drew their own curtain carefully. The table, with the gay china and the lamp, seemed ringed in a circle of bright light as she turned back.

She sat down again. "D'you mind air raids?" Nicholas asked, looking at her with his inquisitive expression. "People differ so much."

"Not at all," she said. She would have crumbled a piece of bread to show him that she was at her ease; but as she was not afraid, the action seemed to her unnecessary.

"The chances of being hit oneself are so small," she said. "What were we saying?" she added.

It seemed to her that they had been saying something extremely interesting; but she could not remember what. They sat silent for a moment. Then they heard a shuffling on the stairs.

"The children . . ." said Sara. They heard the dull boom of a gun in the distance.

Here Renny came in.

"Bring your plates," he said.

"In here." He led them into the cellar. It was a large cellar. With its crypt-like ceiling and stone walls it had a damp ecclesiastical look. It was used partly for coal, partly for wine. The light in the centre shone on glittering heaps of coal; bottles of wine wrapped in straw lay on their sides on stone shelves. There was a mouldy smell of wine, straw and damp. It was chilly after the dining-room. Sara came in carrying quilts and dressing-gowns which she had fetched from upstairs. Eleanor was glad to wrap herself in a blue dressing-gown; she wrapped it round her and sat holding her plate on her knees. It was cold.

"And now?" said Sara, holding her spoon erect.

They all looked as if they were waiting for something to happen. Maggie came in carrying a plum pudding.

"We may as well finish our dinner," she said. But she spoke too sensibly; she was anxious about the children, Eleanor guessed. They were in the kitchen. She had seen them as she passed.

"Are they asleep?" she asked.

"Yes. But if the guns . . ." she began, helping the pudding. Another gun boomed out. This time it was distinctly louder.

"They've got through the defences," said Nicholas.

They began to eat their pudding.

A gun boomed again. This time there was a bark in its boom.

"Hampstead," said Nicholas. He took out his watch. The silence was profound. Nothing happened. Eleanor looked at the blocks of stone arched over their heads. She noticed a spider's web in one corner. Another gun boomed. A sigh of air rushed up with it. It was right on top of them this time.

"The Embankment," said Nicholas. Maggie put down her plate and went into the kitchen.

There was profound silence. Nothing happened. Nicholas looked at his watch as if he were timing the guns. There was something queer about him, Eleanor thought; medical, priestly? He wore a seal that hung down from his watch-chain. The number on the box opposite was 1397. She noticed everything. The Germans must be overhead now. She felt a curious heaviness on top of her head. One, two, three, four, she counted, looking up at the greenish-grey stone. Then there was a violent crack of sound, like the split of lightning in the sky. The spider's web oscillated.

"On top of us," said Nicholas, looking up. They all looked up. At any moment a bomb might fall. There was dead silence. In the silence they heard Maggie's voice in the kitchen.

"That was nothing. Turn round and go to sleep." She spoke very calmly and soothingly.

One, two, three four, Eleanor counted. The spider's web was swaying. That stone may fall, she thought, fixing a certain stone with her eyes. Then a gun boomed again. It was fainter— further away.

"That's over," said Nicholas. He shut his watch with a click. And they all turned and shifted on their hard chairs as if they had been cramped.

MAGGIE CAME IN.

"Well, that's over," she said. ("He woke for a moment, but he went off to sleep again," she said in an undertone to Renny, "but the baby slept right through.") She sat down and took the plate that Renny was holding for her.

"Now let's finish our pudding," she said, speaking in her natural voice.

"Now we will have some wine," said Renny. He examined one bottle; then another; finally he took a third and wiped it carefully with the tail of his dressing-gown. He placed the bottle on a wooden case and they sat round in a circle.

"It didn't come to much, did it?" said Sara. She was tilting back her chair as she held out her glass.

"Ah, but we were frightened," said Nicholas. "Look—how pale we all are."

They looked at each other. Draped in their quilts and dressing-gowns, against the grey-green walls, they all looked whitish, greenish.

"It's partly the light," said Maggie. "Eleanor," she said, looking at her, "looks like an abbess."

The deep-blue dressing-gown which hid the foolish little ornaments, the tabs of velvet and lace on her dress, had improved her appearance. Her middle-aged face was crinkled like an old glove that has been creased into a multitude of fine lines by the gestures of a hand.

"Untidy, am I?" she said, putting her hand to her hair.

"No. Don't touch it," said Maggie.

"And what were we talking about before the raid?" Eleanor asked. Again she felt that they had been in the middle of saying something very interesting when they were interrupted. But there had been a complete break; none of them could remember what they had been saying.

"Well, it's over now," said Sara. "So let's drink a health— Here's to the New World!" she exclaimed. She raised her glass with a flourish. They all felt a sudden desire to talk and laugh.

"Here's to the New World!" they all cried, raising their glasses, and clinking them together.

The five glasses filled with yellow liquid came together in a bunch.

"To the New World!" they cried and drank. The yellow liquid swayed up and down in their glasses.

"Now, Nicholas," said Sara, setting her glass down with a tap on the box, "a speech! A speech!"

"Ladies and gentlemen!" he began, flinging his hand out like an orator. "Ladies and gentlemen . . ."

"We don't want speeches," Renny interrupted him.

Eleanor was disappointed. She would have liked a speech. But he seemed to take the interruption good-humouredly; he sat there nodding and smiling.

"Let's go upstairs," said Renny, pushing away the box.

"And leave this cellar," said Sara, stretching her arms out, "this cave of mud and dung. . . ."

"Listen!" Maggie interrupted. She held up her hand. "I thought I heard the guns again. . . ."

They listened. The guns were still firing, but far away in the distance. There was a sound like the breaking of waves on a shore far away.

"They're only killing other people," said Renny savagely. He kicked the wooden box.

But you must let us think of something else, Eleanor protested. The mask had come down over his face.

"And what nonsense, what nonsense Renny talks," said

Nicholas, turning to her privately. "Only children letting off
fireworks in the back garden," he muttered as he helped her out
of her dressing-gown. They went upstairs.

ELEANOR CAME into the drawing-room. It looked larger than
she remembered it, and very spacious and comfortable. Papers
were strewn on the floor; the fire was burning brightly; it was
warm; it was cheerful. She felt very tired. She sank down into
an armchair. Sara and Nicholas had lagged behind. The others
were helping the nurse to carry the children up to bed, she supposed. She lay back in the chair. Everything seemed to become
quiet and natural again. A feeling of great calm possessed her.
It was as if another space of time had been issued to her, but,
robbed by the presence of death of something personal, she
felt—she hesitated for a word—"immune?" Was that what she
meant? Immune, she said, looking at a picture without seeing it.
Immune, she repeated. It was a picture of a hill and a village perhaps in the South of France; perhaps in Italy. There were olive
trees; and white roofs grouped against a hillside. Immune, she
repeated, looking at the picture.

She could hear a gentle thudding on the floor above; Maggie and Renny were settling the children into their beds again,
she supposed. There was a little squeak, like a sleepy bird chirping in its nest. It was very private and peaceful after the guns.
But here the others came in.

"Did they mind it?" she said, sitting up, "—the children?"

"No," said Maggie. "They slept through it."

"But they may have dreamt," said Sara, pulling up a chair.
Nobody spoke. It was very quiet. The clocks that used to boom
out the hour in Westminster were silent.

Maggie took the poker and struck the wood blocks. The
sparks went volleying up the chimney in a shower of gold eyes.

"How that makes me . . ." Eleanor began.

She stopped.

"Yes?" said Nicholas.

". . . think of my childhood," she added.

She was thinking of Morris and herself, and old Pippy; but had she told them nobody would know what she meant. They were silent. Suddenly a clear flute-like note rang out in the street below.

"What's that?" said Maggie. She started; she looked at the window; she half rose.

"The bugles," said Renny, putting out his hand to stop her.

The bugles blew again beneath the window. Then they heard them further down the street; then further away still down the next street. Almost directly the hooting of cars began again, and the rushing of wheels as if the traffic had been released and the usual night life of London had begun again.

"It's over," said Maggie. She lay back in her chair; she looked very tired for a moment. Then she pulled a basket towards her and began to darn a sock.

"I'm glad I'm alive," said Eleanor. "Is that wrong, Renny?" she asked. She wanted him to speak. It seemed to her that he hoarded immense supplies of emotion that he could not express. He did not answer. He was leaning on his elbow, smoking a cigar and looking into the fire.

"I have spent the evening sitting in a coal cellar while other people try to kill each other above my head," he said suddenly. Then he stretched out and took up a paper.

"Renny, Renny, Renny," said Nicholas, as if he were expostulating with a naughty child. Renny went on reading. The rush of wheels and the hooting of motor cars had run themselves into one continuous sound.

As Renny was reading and Maggie was darning there was

silence in the room. Eleanor watched the fire run along veins of
tar and blaze and sink.

"What are you thinking, Eleanor?" Nicholas interrupted
her. He calls me Eleanor, she thought; that's right.

"About the New World . . ." she said aloud. "D'you think
we're going to improve?" she asked.

"Yes, yes," he said, nodding his head.

He spoke quietly as if he did not wish to rouse Renny who
was reading, or Maggie who was darning, or Sara who was lying
back in her chair half asleep. They seemed to be talking, privately, together.

"But how . . ." she began, ". . . how can we improve ourselves . . . live more . . ." she dropped her voice as if she were
afraid of waking sleepers, ". . . live more naturally . . . better . . .
How can we?"

"It is only a question," he said—he stopped. He drew himself close to her—"of learning. The soul . . ." Again he stopped.

"Yes—the soul?" she prompted him.

"The soul—the whole being," he explained. He hollowed
his hands as if to enclose a circle. "It wishes to expand; to adventure; to form—new combinations?"

"Yes, yes," she said, as if to assure him that his words were
right.

"Whereas now,"—he drew himself together; put his feet
together; he looked like an old lady who is afraid of mice —"this
is how we live, screwed up into one hard little, tight little —
knot?"

"Knot, knot—yes, that's right," she nodded.

"Each is his own little cubicle; each with his own cross or
holy books; each with his fire, his wife . . ."

"Darning socks," Maggie interrupted.

Eleanor started. She had seemed to be looking into the future. But they had been overheard. Their privacy was ended.

Renny threw down his paper. "It's all damned rot!" he said. Whether he referred to the paper, or to what they were saying, Eleanor did not know. But talk in private was impossible.

"Why d'you buy them then?" she said, pointing to the papers.

"To light fires with," said Renny.

Maggie laughed and threw down the sock she was mending. "There!" she exclaimed. "Mended. . . ."

Again they sat silent, looking at the fire. Eleanor wished that he would go on talking—the man she called Nicholas. When, she wanted to ask him, when will this New World come? When shall we be free? When shall we live adventurously, wholly, not like cripples in a cave? He seemed to have released something in her; she felt not only a new space of time, but new powers, something unknown within her. She watched his cigarette moving up and down. Then Maggie took the poker and struck the wood and again a shower of red-eyed sparks went volleying up the chimney. We shall be free, we shall be free, Eleanor thought.

"And what have you been thinking all this time?" said Nicholas, laying his hand on Sara's knee. She started. "Or have you been asleep?" he added.

"I heard what you were saying," she said.

"What were we saying?" he asked.

"The soul flying upwards like sparks up the chimney," she said. The sparks were flying up the chimney.

"Not such a bad shot," said Nicholas.

"Because people always say the same thing," she laughed. She roused herself and sat up. "There's Maggie—she says nothing. There's Renny—he says 'What damned rot!' Eleanor says, 'That's just what I was thinking.' . . . And Nicholas, Nicholas,"—she patted him on the knee—"who ought to be in prison, says, 'Oh, my dear friends, let us improve the soul!'"

"Ought to be in prison?" said Eleanor, looking at him.

"Because he loves," Sara explained. She paused. "—the other sex, the other sex, you see," she said lightly, waving her hand in the way that was so like her mother's.

For a second a sharp shiver of repugnance passed over Eleanor's skin as if a knife had sliced it. Then she realised that it touched nothing of importance. The sharp shiver passed. Underneath was—what? She looked at Nicholas. He was watching her.

"Does that," he said, hesitating a little, "make you dislike me, Eleanor?"

"Not in the least! Not in the least!" she exclaimed spontaneously. All the evening, off and on, she had been feeling about him; this, that, and the other; but now all the feelings came together and made one feeling, one whole—liking. "Not in the least," she said again. He gave her a little bow. She returned it with a little bow. But the clock on the mantelpiece was striking. Renny was yawning. It was late. She got up. She went to the window and parted the curtains and looked out. All the houses were still curtained. The cold winter's night was almost black. It was like looking into the hollow of a dark-blue stone. Here and there a star pierced the blue. She had a sense of immensity and peace—as if something had been consumed. . . .

"Shall I get you a cab?" Renny interrupted.

"No, I'll walk," she said, turning. "I like walking in London."

"We will come with you," said Nicholas. "Come, Sara," he said. She was lying back in her chair swinging her foot up and down.

"But I don't want to come," she said, waving him away. "I want to stay; I want to talk; I want to sing—a hymn of praise—a song of thanksgiving. . . ."

"Here is your hat; here is your bag," said Nicholas, giving them to her.

"Come," he said, taking her by the shoulder and pushing her out of the room. "Come."

Eleanor went up to say good-night to Maggie.

"I should like to stay too," she said. "There are so many things I should like to talk about—"

"But I want to go to bed—I want to go to bed," Renny protested. He stood there with his hands stretched above his head, yawning.

Maggie rose. "So you shall," she laughed at him.

"Don't bother to come downstairs," Eleanor protested as he opened the door for her. But he insisted. He is very rude and at the same time very polite, she thought, as she followed him down the stairs. A man who feels many different things, and all passionately, all at the same time, she thought. . . . But they had reached the hall. Nicholas and Sara were standing there.

"Cease to laugh at me for once, Sara," Nicholas was saying as he put on his coat.

"And cease to lecture me," she said, opening the front door.

Renny smiled at Eleanor as they stood for a moment by the perambulator.

"Educating themselves!" he said.

"Good-night," she said, smiling as she shook hands. That is the man, she said to herself, with a sudden rush of conviction, as she came out into the frosty air, that I should like to have married. She recognised a feeling which she had never felt. But he's twenty years younger than I am, she thought, and married to my cousin. For a moment she resented the passage of time and the accidents of life which had swept her away—from all that, she said to herself. And a scene came before her; Maggie and Renny sitting over the fire. A happy marriage, she thought, that's what I was feeling all the time. A happy marriage. She looked up as she walked down the dark little street behind the others. A broad fan of light, like the sail of a windmill, was sweeping slowly across the sky. It seemed to take what she was feeling and to express it broadly and simply, as if another voice were speaking in another language. Then the light stopped and examined a fleecy patch of sky, a suspected spot.

The raid! she said to herself. I'd forgotten the raid!

The others had come to the crossing; there they stood.

"I'd forgotten the raid!" she said aloud as she came up with them. She was surprised but it was true.

They were in Victoria Street. The street curved away, looking wider and darker than usual. Little figures were hurrying along the pavement; they emerged for a moment under a lamp, then vanished into darkness again. The street was very empty.

"Will the omnibuses be running as usual?" Eleanor asked as they stood there.

They looked round them. Nothing was coming along the street at the moment.

"I shall wait here," said Eleanor.

"Then I shall go," said Sara abruptly. "Good-night!"

She waved her hand and walked away. Eleanor took it for granted that Nicholas would go with her.

"I shall wait here," she repeated.

But he did not move. Sara had already vanished. Eleanor looked at him. Was he angry? Was he unhappy? She did not know. But here a great form loomed up through the darkness; its lights were shrouded with blue paint. Inside silent people sat huddled up; they looked cadaverous and unreal in the blue light. "Good-night," she said, shaking hands with Nicholas. She looked back and saw him still standing on the pavement. He still held his hat in his hand. He looked tall, impressive and solitary standing there alone, while the searchlights wheeled across the sky.

———

THE OMNIBUS moved on. She found herself staring at an old man in the corner who was eating something out of a paper bag. He looked up and caught her staring at him.

"Like to see what I've got for supper, lady?" he said, cocking one eyebrow over his rheumy, twinkling old eyes. And he held out for her inspection a hunk of bread on which was laid a slice of cold meat or sausage.

1918

A VEIL of mist covered the November sky; a many-folded veil, so fine meshed that it made one density. It was not raining, but here and there the mist condensed on the surface into dampness; moistened the country roads and made pavements greasy. Here and there on a grass blade or on a hedge leaf a drop hung motionless. It was windless and calm. Sounds coming through the veil—the bleat of sheep, the croak of rooks—were deadened. The uproar of the traffic merged into one growl. Now and then as if a door opened and shut, or the veil parted and closed, the roar boomed and faded.

"DIRTY BRUTE," Crosby muttered as she hobbled along the asphalt path across Richmond Green. Her legs were paining her. It was not actually raining, but the great open space was full of mist; and there was nobody near, so that she could talk aloud.

"Dirty brute," she muttered again. She had got into the habit of talking aloud. There was nobody in sight; the end of the path was lost in mist. It was very silent. Only the rooks gathered on the tree-tops now and then let fall a queer little croak, and a leaf, spotted with black, fell to the ground. Her face twitched as she walked, as if her muscles had got into the habit of protesting, involuntarily, against the spites and obstacles that tormented her. She had aged greatly during the past four years. She looked so small and hunched that it seemed doubtful if she could make her way across the wide open space shrouded in white mist. But she had to go to the High Street to do her shopping.

"The dirty brute," she muttered again. She had had some words that morning with Mrs. Burt about the Count's bath. He spat in it, and Mrs. Burt had told her to clean it.

"Count indeed—he's no more Count than you are," she continued. She was talking to Mrs. Burt now. "I'm quite willing to oblige you," she went on. Even out here, in the mist, where she was free to say what she liked, she adopted a conciliatory tone, because she knew that they wanted to be rid of her. She gesticulated with the hand that was not carrying the bag as she told Louisa that she was quite ready to oblige her. She hobbled on. "And I shouldn't mind going either," she added bitterly, but this was spoken to herself only. It was no pleasure to her to live in the house any more; but there was nowhere else for her to go; the Burts knew that very well.

"And I'm quite ready to oblige you," she added aloud, as indeed she had said to Louisa herself. But the truth was that she was no longer able to work as she had done. Her legs pained her. It took all the strength out of her to do her own shopping, let alone to clean the bath. But it was all take-it-or-leave-it now. In the old days she would have sent the whole lot packing.

"Drabs . . . hussies," she muttered. She was now addressing the red-haired servant girl who had flung out of the house yesterday without warning. *She* could easily get another job. It didn't matter to her. So it was left to Crosby to clean the Count's bath.

"Dirty brute, dirty brute," she repeated; her pale-blue eyes glared impotently. She saw once more the blob of spittle that the Count had left on the side of his bath—the Belgian who called himself a Count. "I've been used to work for gentlefolk, not for dirty foreigners like you," she told him as she hobbled.

The roar of traffic sounded louder as she approached the ghostly line of trees. She could see houses now beyond the trees. Her pale-blue eyes peered forward through the mist as she made her way towards the railings. Her eyes alone seemed to express an unconquerable determination; she was not going to give in; she was bent on surviving. The soft mist was slowly lifting. Leaves lay damp and purple on the asphalt path. The rooks croaked and shuffled on the tree-tops. Now a dark line of railings emerged from the mist. The roar of traffic in the High Street sounded louder and louder. Crosby stopped and rested her bag on the railing before she went on to battle with the crowd of shoppers in the High Street. She would have to shove and push, be jostled this way and that; and her feet pained her. They didn't mind if you bought or not, she thought; and often she was pushed out of her place by some bold-faced drab. She thought of the red-haired girl again, as she stood there, panting slightly, with her bag on the railing. Her legs pained her. Suddenly the long-drawn note of a siren floated out its melancholy wail of sound; then there was a dull explosion.

"Them guns again," Crosby muttered, looking up at the pale-grey sky with peevish irritation. The rooks, scared by the gun-fire, rose and wheeled round the tree-tops. Then there was another dull boom. A man on a ladder who was painting the windows of one of the houses paused with his brush in his hand and looked round. A woman who was walking along carrying a loaf of bread that stuck half out of its paper wrapping stopped too. They both waited as if for something to happen. A topple of smoke drifted over and flopped down from the chimneys. The guns boomed again. The man on the ladder said something to the woman on the pavement. She nodded her head. Then he dipped his brush in the pot and went on painting. The woman walked on. Crosby pulled herself together and tottered across the road into the High Street. The guns went on booming and the sirens wailed. The war was over—so somebody told her as she took her place at the counter of the grocer's shop. The guns went on booming and the sirens wailed.

PRESENT DAY

IT WAS a summer evening; the sun was setting; the sky was blue still, but tinged with gold, as if a thin veil of gauze hung over it, and here and there in the gold-blue amplitude an island of cloud lay suspended. In the fields the trees stood majestically caparisoned, with their innumerable leaves gilt. Sheep and cows, pearl white and parti-coloured, lay recumbent or munched their way through the half-transparent grass. An edge of light surrounded everything. A red-gold fume rose from the dust on the roads. Even the little red brick villas on the high roads had become porous, incandescent with light, and the flowers in cottage gardens, lilac and pink like cotton dresses, shone veined as if lit from within. Faces of people standing at cottage doors or padding along pavements showed the same red glow as they fronted the slowly sinking sun.

ELEANOR CAME OUT of her flat and shut the door. Her face was lit up by the glow of the sun as it sank over London, and for a moment she was dazzled and looked out over the roofs and spires that lay beneath. There were people talking inside her room, and she wanted to have a word with her nephew alone. North, her brother Morris's son, had just come back from Africa, and she had scarcely seen him alone. So many people had dropped in that evening—Miriam Parrish; Ralph Pickersgill; Antony Wedd; her niece Peggy, and on top of them all, that very talkative man, her friend Nicholas Pomjalovsky, whom they called Brown for short. She had scarcely had a word with North alone. For a moment they stood in the bright square of sunshine that fell on the stone floor of the passage. Voices were still talking within. She put her hand on his shoulder.

"It's so nice to see you," she said. "And you haven't changed . . ." She looked at him. She still saw traces of the brown-eyed cricketing boy in the massive man, who was so burnt, and a little grey too over the ears. "We sha'n't let you go back," she continued, beginning to walk downstairs with him, "to that horrid farm."

He smiled. "And you haven't changed either," he said.

She looked very vigorous. She had been in India. Her face was tanned with the sun. With her white hair and her brown cheeks she scarcely looked her age, but she must be well over seventy, he was thinking. They walked downstairs arm-in-arm. There were six flights of stone steps to descend, but she insisted upon coming all the way down with him, to see him off.

"And, North," she said, when they reached the hall, "you will be careful. . . ." She stopped on the doorstep. "Driving in London," she said, "isn't the same as driving in Africa."

There was his little sports car outside; a man was going past the door in the evening sunlight crying "Old chairs and baskets to mend."

He shook his head; his voice was drowned by the voice of the man crying. He glanced at a board that hung in the hall with names on it. Who was in and who was out was signified with a care that amused him slightly, after Africa. The voice of the man crying, "Old chairs and baskets to mend," slowly died away.

"Well, good-bye, Eleanor," he said, turning. "We shall meet later." He got into his car.

"Oh, but, North—" she cried, suddenly remembering something she wanted to say to him. But he had turned on the engine; he did not hear her voice. He waved his hand to her— there she stood at the top of the steps with her hair blowing in the wind. The car started off with a jerk. She gave another wave of her hand to him as he turned the corner.

Eleanor is just the same, he thought: more erratic perhaps. With a room full of people—her little room had been crowded— she had insisted upon showing him her new shower-bath. "You press that knob," she had said, "and look—" Innumerable needles of water shot down. He laughed aloud. They had sat on the edge of the bath together.

But the cars behind him hooted persistently; they hooted and hooted. What at? he asked. Suddenly he realised that they were hooting at him. The light had changed; it was green now, he had been blocking the way. He started off with a violent jerk. He had not mastered the art of driving in London.

The noise of London still seemed to him deafening, and the speed at which people drove was terrifying; but it was exciting after Africa. The shops even, he thought, as he shot past rows of plate-glass windows, were marvellous. Along the kerb, too, there were barrows of fruit and flowers. Everywhere there was profusion; plenty . . . Again the red light shone out; he pulled up.

He looked about him. He was somewhere in Oxford Street; the pavement was crowded with people; jostling each other; swarming round the plate-glass windows which were still lit up. The gaiety, the colour, the variety, were amazing after Africa. All these years, he thought to himself, looking at a floating banner of transparent silk, he had been used to raw goods; hides and fleeces; here was the finished article. A dressing-case, of yellow leather fitted with silver bottles, caught his eye. But the light was green again. On he jerked.

He had only been back ten days, and his mind was a jumble of odds and ends. It seemed to him that he had never stopped talking: shaking hands; saying How-d'you-do? People sprang up everywhere; his father; his sister; old men got up from arm-chairs and said, You don't remember me? Children he had left in the nursery were grown-up men at college; girls with pigtails were now married women. He was still confused by it all; they talked so fast; they must think him very slow, he thought. He had to withdraw into the window and say, "What, what, what do they mean by it?"

For instance, this evening at Eleanor's there was a man there with a foreign accent who squeezed lemon into his tea. Who might he be, he wondered? "One of Nell's dentists," said his sister Peggy, wrinkling her lip. For they all had lines cut; phrases ready-made. But that was the silent man on the sofa. It was the other one he meant—squeezing lemon in his tea. "We call him Brown," she murmured. Why Brown if he's a foreigner, he wondered. Anyhow they all romanticized solitude and sav-agery—"I wish I'd done what you did," said a little man called Pickersgill—except this man Brown, who had said something that interested him. "If we do not know ourselves, how can we know other people?" he had said. They had been discussing dic-tators; Napoleon; the psychology of great men. But there was the green light—"GO." He shot on again. And then the lady with the ear-rings gushed about the beauties of Nature. He glanced at the name of the street on the left. He was going to dine with Sara but he had not much notion how to get there. He had only heard her voice on the telephone saying, "Come and dine with me—Milton Street, fifty-two, my name's on the door." It was near the Prison Tower. But this man Brown—it was difficult to place him at once. He talked, spreading his fin-gers out with the volubility of a man who will in the end be-come a bore. And Eleanor wandered about, holding a cup,

telling people about her shower-bath. He wished they would
stick to the point. Talk interested him. Serious talk on abstract
subjects. "Was solitude good; was society bad?" That was interesting; but they hopped from thing to thing. When the large
man said, "Solitary confinement is the greatest torture we inflict," the meagre old woman with the wispy hair at once piped
up, laying her hand on her heart, "It ought to be abolished!" She
visited prisons, it seemed.

"Where the dickens am I now?" he asked, peering at the
name on the street corner. Somebody had chalked a circle on
the wall with a jagged line in it. He looked down the long vista.
Door after door, window after window, repeated the same pattern. There was a red-yellow glow over it all, for the sun was
sinking through the London dust. Everything was tinged with
a warm yellow haze. Barrows full of fruit and flowers were
drawn up at the kerb. The sun gilt the fruit; the flowers had a
blurred brilliance; there were roses, carnations and lilies too. He
had half a mind to stop and buy a bunch to take to Sally. But
the cars were hooting behind him. He went on. A bunch of
flowers, he thought, held in the hand would soften the awk-
wardness of meeting and the usual things that had to be said.
"How nice to see you—you've filled out," and so on. He had
only heard her voice on the telephone, and people changed
after all these years. Whether this was the right street or not, he
could not be sure; he filtered slowly round the corner. Then
stopped; then went on again. This was Milton Street, a dusky
street, with old houses, now let out as lodgings; but they had
seen better days.

"The odds on that side; the evens on this," he said. The
street was blocked with vans. He hooted. He stopped. He
hooted again. A man went to the horse's head, for it was a coal-
cart, and the horse slowly plodded on. Fifty-two was just along
the road. He dribbled up to the door. He stopped.

A voice pealed out across the street, the voice of a woman singing scales.

"What a dirty," he said, as he sat still in the car for a moment—here a woman crossed the street with a jug under her arm—"sordid," he added, "low-down street to live in." He cut off his engine; got out, and examined the names on the door. Names mounted one above another; here on a visiting-card, here engraved on brass—Foster; Abrahamson; Roberts; S. Pargiter was near the top, punched on a strip of aluminum. He rang one of the many bells. No one came. The woman went on singing scales, mounting slowly. The mood comes, the mood goes, he thought. He used to write poetry; now the mood had come again as he stood there waiting. He pressed the bell two or three times sharply. But no one answered. Then he gave the door a push; it was open. There was a curious smell in the hall; of vegetables cooking; and the oily brown paper made it dark. He went up the stairs of what had once been a gentleman's residence. The bannisters were carved; but they had been daubed over with some cheap yellow varnish. He mounted slowly and stood on the landing, uncertain which door to knock at. He was always finding himself now outside the doors of strange houses. He had a feeling that he was no one and nowhere in particular. From across the road came the voice of the singer deliberately ascending the scale, as if the notes were stairs; and here she stopped indolently, languidly, flinging out the voice that was nothing but pure sound. Then he heard somebody inside, laughing.

That's her voice, he said. But there is somebody with her. He was annoyed. He had hoped to find her alone. The voice was speaking and did not answer when he knocked. Very cautiously he opened the door and went in.

"Yes, yes, yes," Sara was saying. She was kneeling at the telephone talking; but there was nobody there. She raised her hand

when she saw him and smiled at him; but she kept her hand
raised as if the noise he had made caused her to lose what she
was trying to hear.

"What?" she said, speaking into the telephone. "What?"
He stood silent, looking at the silhouettes of his grandparents
on the mantelpiece. There were no flowers, he observed. He
wished he had brought her some. He listened to what she was
saying; he tried to piece it together.

"Yes, now I can hear. . . . Yes, you're right. Someone has
come in. . . . Who? North. My cousin from Africa. . . ."

That's me, North thought. "My cousin from Africa." That's
my label.

"You've met him?" she was saying. There was a pause.
"D'you think so?" she said. She turned and looked at him. They
must be discussing him, he thought. He felt uncomfortable.

"Good-bye," she said, and put down the telephone.

"He says he met you tonight," she said, going up to him and
taking his hand. "And liked you," she added, smiling.

"Who was that?" he asked, feeling awkward; but he had no
flowers to give her.

"A man you met at Eleanor's," she said.

"A foreigner?" he asked.

"Yes. Called Brown," she said, pushing up a chair for him.

He sat down on the chair she had pushed out for him, and
she curled up opposite with her foot under her. He remembered
the attitude; she came back in sections; first the voice; then the
attitude; but something remained unknown.

"You've not changed," he said—the face he meant. A plain
face scarcely changed; whereas beautiful faces wither. She
looked neither young nor old; but shabby; and the room, with
the pampas grass in a pot in the corner, was untidy. A lodging-
house room tidied in a hurry, he guessed.

"And you—" she said, looking at him. It was as if she were

trying to put two different versions of him together; the one on the telephone perhaps and the one on the chair. Or was there some other? This half knowing people, this half being known, this feeling of the eye on the flesh, like a fly crawling—how uncomfortable it was, he thought; but inevitable, after all these years. The tables were littered; he hesitated, holding his hat in his hand. She smiled at him, as he sat there, holding his hat uncertainly.

"Who's the young Frenchman," she said, "with the top hat in the picture?"

"What picture?" he asked.

"The one who sits looking puzzled with his hat in his hand," she said. He put his hat on the table, but awkwardly. A book fell to the floor.

"Sorry," he said. She meant, presumably, when she compared him to the puzzled man in the picture, that he was clumsy; he always had been.

"This isn't the room where I came last time?" he asked.

He recognised a chair—a chair with gilt claws; there was the usual piano.

"No—that was on the other side of the river," she said, "when you came to say good-bye."

He remembered. He had come to her the evening before he left for the war; and he had hung his cap on the bust of their grandfather—that had vanished. And she had mocked him.

"How many lumps of sugar does a lieutenant in His Majesty's Royal Regiment of Rat-catchers require?" she had sneered. He could see her now dropping lumps of sugar into his tea. And they had quarrelled. And he had left her. It was the night of the raid, he remembered. He remembered the dark night; the searchlights that slowly swept over the sky; here and there they stopped to ponder a fleecy patch; little pellets of shot fell; and people scudded along the empty blue-shrouded streets. He had been going to Kensington to dine with his family; he had said good-bye to his mother; he had never seen her again.

The voice of the singer interrupted. "Ah—h-h, oh-h-h, ah—h-h, oh—h-h," she sang, languidly climbing up and down the scale on the other side of the street.

"Does she go on like that every night?" he asked. Sara nodded. The notes coming through the humming evening air sounded slow and sensuous. The singer seemed to have endless leisure; she could rest on every stair.

And there was no sign of dinner, he observed; only a dish of fruit on the cheap lodging-house table-cloth, already yellowed with some gravy stain.

"Why d'you always choose slums—" he was beginning, for children were screaming in the street below, when the door opened and a girl came in carrying a bunch of knives and forks. The regular lodging-house skivvy, North thought; with red hands, and one of those jaunty white caps that girls in lodging-houses clap on top of their hair when the lodger has a party. In her presence they had to make conversation. "I've been seeing Eleanor," he said. "That was where I met your friend Brown. . . ."

The girl made a clatter laying the table with the knives and forks she held in a bunch.

"Oh, Eleanor," said Sara. "Eleanor—" But she watched the girl going clumsily round the table; she breathed rather hard as she laid it.

"She's just back from India," he said. He too watched the girl laying the table. Now she stood a bottle of wine among the cheap lodging-house crockery.

"Gallivanting round the world," Sara murmured.

"And entertaining the oddest set of old fogies," he added. He thought of the little man with the fierce blue eyes, who wished he had been in Africa; and the wispy woman with beads, who visited prisons, it seemed.

". . . and that man, your friend—" he began. Here the girl went out of the room, but she left the door open, a sign that she was about to come back.

"Nicholas," said Sara, finishing his sentence. "The man you call Brown."

There was a pause. "And what did you talk about?" she asked.

He tried to remember.

"Napoleon; the psychology of great men; if we don't know ourselves how can we know other people . . ." He stopped. It was difficult to remember accurately what had been said even one hour ago.

"And then," she said, holding out one hand and touching a finger exactly as Brown had done, ". . . how can we make laws, religions, that fit, that fit, when we don't know ourselves?"

"Yes! Yes!" he exclaimed. She had caught his manner exactly; the slight foreign accent; the repetition of the little word "fit," as if he were not quite sure of the shorter words in English.

"And Eleanor," Sara continued, "says . . . 'Can we improve— can we improve ourselves?' sitting on the edge of the sofa?"

"Of the bath," he laughed, correcting her.

"You've had that talk before," he said. That was precisely what he was feeling. They had talked before. "And then," he continued, "we discussed . . ."

But here the girl burst in again. She had plates in her hand this time; blue-ringed plates, cheap lodging-house plates: "—society or solitude; which is best," he finished his sentence.

Sara kept looking at the table. "And which," she asked, in the distracted way of someone who with their surface senses watches what is being done, but at the same time thinks of

something else "—which did you say? You who've been alone
all these years," she said. The girl left the room again. "—among
your sheep, North." She broke off; for now a trombone player
had struck up in the street below, and as the voice of the woman
practising her scales continued, they sounded like two people
trying to express completely different views of the world in general at one and the same time. The voice ascended; the trombone wailed. They laughed.

". . . Sitting on the verandah," she resumed, "looking at the
stars."

He looked up: was she quoting something? He remembered
he had written to her when he first went out. "Yes, looking at
the stars," he said.

"Sitting on the verandah in the silence," she added. A
van went past the window. All sounds were for the moment
obliterated.

"And then . . ." she said as the van rattled away—she paused
as if she were referring to something else that he had written.

"—then you saddled a horse," she said, "and rode away!"

She jumped up, and for the first time he saw her face in the
full light. There was a smudge on the side of her nose.

"D'you know," he said, looking at her, "that you've a
smudge on your face?"

She touched the wrong cheek.

"Not that side—the other," he said.

She left the room without looking in the glass. From which
we deduce the fact, he said to himself, as if he were writing a
novel, that Miss Sara Pargiter has never attracted the love of
men. Or had she? He did not know. These little snapshot pictures of people left much to be desired, these little surface pictures that one made, like a fly crawling over a face, and feeling,
here's the nose, here's the brow.

———

HE STROLLED to the window. The sun must be setting, for the brick of the house at the corner blushed a yellowish pink. One or two high windows were burnished gold. The girl was in the room, and she distracted him; also the noise of London still bothered him. Against the dull background of traffic noises, of wheels turning and brakes squeaking, there rose near at hand the cry of a woman suddenly alarmed for her child; the monotonous cry of a man selling vegetables; and far away a barrel-organ was playing. It stopped; it began again. I used to write to her, he thought, late at night, when I felt lonely, when I was young. He looked at himself in the glass. He saw his sunburnt face with the broad cheek bones and the little brown eyes.

The girl had been sucked down into the lower portion of the house. The door stood open. Nothing seemed to be happening. He waited. He felt an outsider. After all these years, he thought, everyone was paired off; settled down; busy with their own affairs. You found them telephoning, remembering other conversations; they went out of the room; they left one alone. He took up a book and read a sentence.

"A shadow like an angel with bright hair . . ."

NEXT MOMENT she came in. But there seemed to be some hitch in the proceedings. The door was open; the table laid; but nothing happened. They stood together, waiting, with their backs to the fireplace.

"How strange it must be," she resumed, "coming back after all these years—as if you'd dropped from the clouds in an aeroplane." She pointed to the table as if that were the field in which he had landed.

"On to an unknown land," said North. He leant forward and touched a knife on the table.

"—and finding people talking," she added.

"—talking, talking," he said, "about money and politics,"

he added, giving the fender behind him a vicious little kick with his heel.

Here the girl came in. She wore an air of importance derived apparently from the dish she carried, for it was covered with a great metal cover. She raised the cover with a certain flourish. There was a leg of mutton underneath. "Let's dine," Sara said.

"I'm hungry," he added.

They sat down and she took the carving-knife and made a long incision. A thin trickle of red juice ran out; it was under-done. She looked at it.

"Mutton oughtn't to be like that," she said. "Beef—but not mutton."

They watched the red juice running down into the well of the dish.

"Shall we send it back," she said, "or eat it as it is?"

"Eat it," he said. "I've eaten far worse joints than this," he added.

"In Africa . . ." she said, lifting the lids of the vegetable dishes. There was a slabbed-down mass of cabbage in one oozing green water; in the other, yellow potatoes that looked hard.

". . . in Africa, in the wilds of Africa," she resumed, helping him to cabbage, "in that farm you were on, where no one came for months at a time, and you sat on the verandah listening—"

"To sheep," he said. He was cutting his mutton into strips. It was tough.

"And there was nothing to break the silence," she went on, helping herself to potatoes, "but a tree falling, or a rock break-ing from the side of a distant mountain—" She looked at him as if to verify the sentences that she was quoting from his letters.

"Yes," he said. "It was very silent."

"And hot," she added. "Blazing hot at midday: an old tramp tapped on your door . . . ?"

He nodded. He saw himself again, a young man, and very lonely.

"And then—" she began again. But a great lorry came crashing down the street. Something rattled on the table. The walls and the floor seemed to tremble. She parted two glasses that were jingling together. The lorry passed; they heard it rumbling away in the distance.

"And the birds," she went on. "The nightingales, singing in the moonlight?"

He felt uncomfortable at the vision she called up. "I must have written you a lot of nonsense!" he exclaimed. "I wish you'd torn them up—those letters!"

"No! They were beautiful letters! Wonderful letters!" she exclaimed, raising her glass. A thimbleful of wine always made her tipsy, he remembered. Her eyes shone; her cheeks glowed.

"And then you had a day off," she went on, "and jolted along a rough white road in a springless cart to the next town—"

"Sixty miles away," he said.

"And went to a bar; and met a man from the next—ranch?" She hesitated as if the word might be the wrong one.

"Ranch, yes, ranch," he confirmed her. "I went to the town and had a drink at the bar—"

"And then?" she said. He laughed. There were some things he had not told her. He was silent.

"Then you stopped writing," she said. She put her glass down.

"When I forgot what you were like," he said, looking at her.

"You gave up writing too," he said.

"Yes, I too," she said.

The trombone had moved his station and was wailing lugubriously under the window. The doleful sound, as if a dog had thrown back its head and were baying the moon, floated up to them. She waved her fork in time to it.

"Our hearts full of tears, our lips full of laughter, we passed on the stairs"—she dragged her words out to fit the wail of the trombone—"we passed on the stair-r-r-s"—but here the trombone changed its measure to a jig. "He to sorrow, I to bliss," she jigged with it, "he to bliss and I to sorrow, we passed on the stair-r-r-s."

She set her glass down.

"Another cut off the joint?" she asked.

"No, thank you," he said, looking at the rather stringy disagreeable object which was still bleeding into the well. The willow-pattern plate was daubed with gory streaks. She stretched her hand out and rang the bell. She rang; she rang a second time. No one came.

"Your bells don't ring," he said.

"No," she smiled. "The bells don't ring, and the taps don't run." She thumped on the floor. They waited. No one came. The trombone wailed outside.

"But there was one letter you wrote me," he continued as they waited. "An angry letter; a cruel letter."

He looked at her. She had lifted her lip like a horse that is going to bite. That, too, he remembered.

"Yes?" she said.

"The night you came in from the Strand," he reminded her.

Here the girl came in with the pudding. It was an ornate pudding, semi-transparent, pink, ornamented with blobs of cream.

"I remember," said Sara, sticking her spoon into the quivering jelly, "a still autumn night; the lights lit; and people padding along the pavement with wreaths in their hands?"

"Yes," he nodded. "That was it."

"And I said to myself," she paused, "this is Hell. We are the damned?" He nodded.

She helped him to pudding.

"And I," he said, as he took his plate, "was among the damned." He stuck his spoon into the quivering mass that she had given him.

"Coward; hypocrite, with your switch in your hand; and your cap on your head—" He seemed to quote from a letter that she had written him. He paused. She smiled at him.

"But what was the word—the word I used?" she asked, as if she were trying to remember.

"Poppycock!" he reminded her. She nodded.

"And then I went over the bridge," she resumed, raising her spoon half-way to her mouth, "and stopped in one of those little alcoves, bays, what d'you call 'em?—scooped out over the water, and looked down—" She looked down at her plate.

"When you lived on the other side of the river," he prompted her.

"Stood and looked down," she said, looking at her glass which she held in front of her, "and thought: 'Running water, flowing water, water that crinkles up the lights; moonlight; starlight—'" She drank and was silent.

"Then the car came," he prompted her.

"Yes; the Rolls-Royce. It stopped in the lamplight and there they sat—"

"Two people," he reminded her.

"Two people. Yes," she said. "He was smoking a cigar. An upper-class Englishman with a big nose, in a dress suit. And she, sitting beside him, in a fur-trimmed cloak, took advantage of the pause under the lamplight to raise her hand"—she raised her hand—"and polish that spade, her mouth."

She swallowed her mouthful.

"And the peroration?" he prompted her.

She shook her head.

They were silent. North had finished his pudding. He took out his cigarette-case. Save for a dish of rather fly-blown fruit, apples and bananas, there was no more to eat apparently.

"We were very foolish when we were young, Sal," he said, as he lit his cigarette, "writing purple passages . . ."

"At dawn with the sparrows chirping," she said, pulling the plate of fruit towards her. She began peeling a banana, as if she were unsheathing some soft glove. He took an apple and peeled it. The curl of apple-skin lay on his plate, coiled up like a snake's skin, he thought; and the banana-skin was like the finger of a glove that had been ripped open.

The street was now quiet. The woman had stopped singing. The trombone-player had moved off. The rush hour was over and nothing went down the street. He looked at her, biting little bits off her banana.

When she came to the fourth of June, he remembered, she wore her skirt the wrong way round. She was crooked in those days too; and they had laughed at her—he and Peggy. She had never married; he wondered why not. He swept up the broken coils of apple peel on his plate.

"What does he do," he said suddenly, "—that man who throws his hands out?"

"Like this?" she said. She threw her hands out.

"Yes," he nodded. That was the man—one of those voluble foreigners with a theory about everything. Yet he had liked him—he gave off an aroma; a whirr; his flexible supple face worked amusingly; he had a round forehead; good eyes; and was bald.

"What does he do?" he repeated.

"Talks," she replied, "about the soul." She smiled. Again he felt an outsider; so many talks there must have been between them; such intimacy.

"About the soul," she continued, taking a cigarette. "Lectures," she added, lighting it. "Ten and six for a seat in the front row." She puffed her smoke out. "There's standing room at half a crown; but then," she puffed, "you don't hear so well. You only catch half the lesson of the Teacher, the Master," she laughed.

She was sneering at him now; she conveyed the impression that he was a charlatan. Yet Peggy had said that they were very intimate—she and this foreigner. The vision of the man at Eleanor's had changed slightly, like an air ball blown aside.

"I thought he was a friend of yours," he said aloud.

"Nicholas?" she exclaimed. "I love him!"

Her eyes certainly glowed. They fixed themselves upon a salt cellar with a look of rapture that made North feel once more puzzled.

"You love him . . ." he began. But here the telephone rang.

"There he is!" she exclaimed. "That's him! That's Nicholas!"

She spoke with extreme irritation.

The telephone rang again. "I'm not here!" she said. The telephone rang again. "Not here! Not here! Not here!" she repeated in time to the bell. She made no attempt to answer it. He could stand the stab of her voice and the bell no longer. He went over to the telephone. There was a pause as he stood with the receiver in his hand.

"Tell him I'm not here!" she said.

"Hullo," he said, answering the telephone. But there was a pause. He looked at her sitting on the edge of her chair, swinging her foot up and down. Then a voice spoke.

"I'm North," he answered the telephone. "I'm dining with Sara. . . . Yes, I'll tell her. . . ." He looked at her again. "She is sitting on the edge of her chair," he said, "with a smudge on her face, swinging her foot up and down."

ELEANOR STOOD holding the telephone. She smiled, and for a moment after she had put the receiver back stood there, still smiling, before she turned to her niece Peggy who had been dining with her.

"North is dining with Sara," she said, smiling at the little telephone picture of two people at the other end of London, one of whom was sitting on the edge of her chair with a smudge on her face.

"He's dining with Sara," she said again. But her niece did not smile, for she had not seen the picture, and she was slightly irritated because, in the middle of what they were saying, Eleanor suddenly got up and said, "I'll just remind Sara."

"Oh, is he?" she said casually.

Eleanor came and sat down.

"We were saying—" she began.

"You've had it cleaned," said Peggy simultaneously. While Eleanor telephoned, she had been looking at the picture of her grandmother over the writing-table.

"Yes." Eleanor glanced back over her shoulder. "Yes. And do you see there's a flower fallen on the grass?" she said. She turned and looked at the picture. The face, the dress, the basket of flowers all shone softly melting into each other, as if the paint were one smooth coat of enamel. There was a flower—a little sprig of blue—lying in the grass.

"It was hidden by the dirt," said Eleanor. "But I can just re-member it, when I was a child. That reminds me, if you want a good man to clean pictures—"

"But was it like her?" Peggy interrupted.

Somebody had told her that she was like her grandmother: and she did not want to be like her. She wanted to be dark and aquiline: but in fact she was blue-eyed and round-faced—like her grandmother.

"I've got the address somewhere," Eleanor went on.

"Don't bother—don't bother," said Peggy, irritated by her

aunt's habit of adding unnecessary details. It was age coming on, she supposed: age that loosened screws and made the whole apparatus of the mind rattle and jingle.

"Was it like her?" she asked again.

"Not as I remember her," said Eleanor, glancing once more at the picture. "When I was a child perhaps—no, I don't think even as a child. What's so interesting," she continued, "is that what they thought ugly—red hair for instance—we think pretty; so that I often ask myself," she paused, puffing at her cheroot, "'What is pretty?'"

"Yes," said Peggy. "That's what we were saying."

For when Eleanor suddenly took it into her head that she must remind Sara of the party, they had been talking about Eleanor's childhood—how things had changed; one thing seemed good to one generation, another to another. She liked getting Eleanor to talk about her past; it seemed to her so peaceful and so safe.

"Is there any standard, d'you think?" she said, wishing to bring her back to what they were saying.

"I wonder," said Eleanor absentmindedly. She was thinking of something else.

"How annoying!" she exclaimed suddenly. "I had it on the tip of my tongue—something I want to ask you. Then I thought of Delia's party: then North made me laugh—Sally sitting on the edge of her chair with a smudge on her nose; and that's put it out of my head." She shook her head.

"D'you know the feeling when one's been on the point of saying something, and been interrupted; how it seems to stick *here*," she tapped her forehead, "so that it stops everything else? Not that it was anything of importance," she added. She wandered about the room for a moment. "No, I give it up; I give it up," she said, shaking her head.

"I shall go and get ready now, if you'll call a cab."

She went into the bedroom. Soon there was the sound of running water.

Peggy lit another cigarette. If Eleanor were going to wash, as seemed likely from the sounds in the bedroom, there was no need to hurry about the cab. She glanced at the letters on the mantelpiece. An address stuck out on the top of one of them—"Mon Repos, Wimbledon." One of Eleanor's dentists, Peggy thought to herself. The man she went botanising with on Wimbledon Common perhaps. A charming man. Eleanor had described him. "He says every tooth is quite unlike every other tooth. And he knows all about plants. . . ." It was difficult to get her to stick to her childhood.

She crossed to the telephone; she gave the number. There was a pause. As she waited she looked at her hands holding the telephone. Efficient, shell-like, polished but not painted, they're a compromise, she thought, looking at her finger nails, between science and . . . But here a voice said, "Number please," and she gave it.

Again she waited. As she sat where Eleanor had sat she saw the telephone picture that Eleanor had seen—Sally sitting on the edge of her chair with a smudge on her face. What a fool, she thought bitterly, and a thrill ran down her thigh. Why was she bitter? For she prided herself upon being honest—she was a doctor—and that thrill she knew meant bitterness. Did she envy her because she was happy, or was it the croak of some ancestral prudery—did she disapprove of these friendships with men who did not love women? She looked at the picture of her grandmother as if to ask her opinion. But she had assumed the immunity of a work of art; she seemed as she sat there, smiling at her roses, to be indifferent to our right and wrong.

"Hullo," said a gruff voice, which suggested sawdust and a shelter, and she gave the address and put down the telephone

just as Eleanor came in—she was wearing a red-gold Arab
cloak with a silver veil over her hair.

"One of these days d'you think you'll be able to see things
at the end of the telephone?" Peggy said, getting up. Eleanor's
hair was her beauty, she thought; and her silver-washed dark
eyes—a fine old prophetess, a queer old bird, venerable and
funny at one and the same time. She was burnt from her travels so that her hair looked whiter than ever.

"What's that?" said Eleanor, for she had not caught her remark about the telephone. Peggy did not repeat it. They stood
at the window waiting for the cab. They stood there side by side,
silent, looking out, because there was a pause to fill up, and the
view from the window, which was so high over the roofs, over
the squares and angles of back gardens to the blue line of hills
in the distance served, like another voice speaking, to fill up the
pause. The sun was setting; one cloud lay curled like a red
feather in the blue. She looked down. It was queer to see cabs
turning corners, going round this street and down the other, and
not to hear the sound they made. It was like a map of London;
a section laid beneath them. The summer day was fading; lights
were being lit, primrose lights, still separate, for the glow of the
sunset was still in the air. Eleanor pointed at the sky.

"That's where I saw my first aeroplane—there between
those chimneys," she said. There were high chimneys, factory
chimneys, in the distance; and a great building—Westminster
Cathedral was it?—over there riding above the roofs.

"I was standing here, looking out," Eleanor went on.
"It must have been just after I'd got into the flat, a summer's
day, and I saw a black spot in the sky, and I said to whoever it
was—Miriam Parrish, I think, yes, for she came to help me to
get into the flat—I hope Delia, by the way, remembered to ask
her—" . . . that's old age, Peggy noted, bringing in one thing
after another.

"You said to Miriam——" she prompted her.

"I said to Miriam, 'Is it a bird? No, I don't think it can be a bird. It's too big. Yet it moves.' And suddenly it came over me, that's an aeroplane! And it was! You know they'd flown the Channel not so very long before. I was staying with you in Dorset at the time: and I remember reading it out in the paper, and someone——your father, I think——said: 'The world will never be the same again!'"

"Oh, well——" Peggy laughed. She was about to say that aeroplanes hadn't made all that difference, for it was her line to disabuse her elders of their belief in science, partly because their credulity amused her, partly because she was daily impressed by the ignorance of doctors——when Eleanor sighed.

"Oh, dear," she murmured.

She turned away from the window.

Old age again, Peggy thought. Some gust blew open a door: one of the many millions in Eleanor's seventy-odd years; out came a painful thought; which she at once concealed——she had gone to her writing-table and was fidgeting with papers——with the humble generosity, the painful humility of the old.

"What, Nell——?" Peggy began.

"Nothing, nothing," said Eleanor. She had seen the sky; and that sky was laid with pictures——she had seen it so often; any one of which might come uppermost when she looked at it. Now, because she had been talking to North, it brought back the war; how she had stood there one night, watching the search-lights. She had come home, after a raid; she had been dining in Westminster with Renny and Maggie. They had sat in a cellar; and Nicholas——it was the first time she had met him——had said that the war was of no importance. "We are children playing with fireworks in the back garden" ... she remembered his phrase; and how, sitting round a wooden packing case, they had drunk to a new world. "A new world——a new world!" Sally had cried, drumming with her spoon on top of the packing case. She turned to her writing-table, tore up a letter and threw it away.

"Yes," she said, fumbling among her papers, looking for something. "Yes—I don't know about aeroplanes, I've never been up in one; but motor cars—I could do without motor cars. I was almost knocked down by one, did I tell you? In the Brompton Road. All my own fault—I wasn't looking. . . . And wireless—that's a nuisance—the people downstairs turn it on after breakfast; but on the other hand—hot water; electric light; and those new—" She paused. "Ah, there it is!" she exclaimed. She pounced upon some paper that she had been hunting for. "If Edward's there tonight, do remind me—I'll tie a knot in my handkerchief. . . ."

She opened her bag, took out a silk handkerchief, and proceeded solemnly to tie it into a knot . . . "to ask him about Runcorn's boy."

The bell rang.

"The taxi," she said.

She glanced about to make sure that she had forgotten nothing. She stopped suddenly. Her eye had been caught by the evening paper, which lay on the floor with its broad bar of print and its blurred photograph. She picked it up.

"What a face!" she exclaimed, flattening it out on the table.

As far as Peggy could see, but she was short-sighted, it was the usual evening paper's blurred picture of a fat man gesticulating.

"Damned—" Eleanor shot out suddenly, "bully!" She tore the paper across with one sweep of her hand and flung it on the floor. Peggy was shocked. A little shiver ran over her skin as the paper tore. The word "damned" on her aunt's lips had shocked her.

Next moment she was amused; but still she had been shocked. For when Eleanor, who used English so reticently, said "damned" and then "bully," it meant much more than the words she and her friends used. And her gesture, tearing the paper . . . What a queer set they are, she thought, as she followed Eleanor down the stairs. Her red-gold cloak trailed from step to step. So she had seen her father crumple *The Times* and sit trembling with rage because somebody had said something in a newspaper. How odd!

And the way she tore it! she thought, half laughing, and she flung out her hand as Eleanor had flung hers. Eleanor's figure still seemed erect with indignation. It would be simple, she thought, it would be satisfactory, she thought, following her down flight after flight of stone steps, to be like that. The little knob on her cloak tapped on the stairs. They descended rather slowly.

"Take my aunt," she said to herself, beginning to arrange the scene into an argument she had been having with a man at the hospital, "take my aunt, living alone in a sort of workman's flat at the top of six flights of stairs . . ." Eleanor stopped.

"Don't tell me," she said, "that I left the letter upstairs— Runcorn's letter that I want to show Edward, about the boy?" She opened her bag. "No: here it is." There it was in her bag. They went on downstairs.

Eleanor gave the address to the cabman and sat down with a jerk in her corner. Peggy glanced at her out of the corner of her eye.

It was the force that she had put into the words that impressed her, not the words. It was as if she still believed with passion—she, old Eleanor—in the things that man had destroyed. A wonderful generation, she thought, as they drove off. Believers . . .

"You see," Eleanor interrupted, as if she wanted to explain her words, "it means the end of everything we cared for."

"Freedom?" said Peggy perfunctorily.

"Yes," said Eleanor. "Freedom and justice."

The cab drove off down the mild respectable little streets where every house had its bow window, its strip of garden, its private name. As they drove on, into the big main street, the scene in the flat composed itself in Peggy's mind as she would tell it to the man in the hospital. "Suddenly she lost her temper," she said, "took the paper and tore it across — my aunt, who's over seventy." She glanced at Eleanor to verify the details. Her aunt interrupted her.

"That's where we used to live," she said. She waved her hand towards a long lamp-starred street on the left. Peggy, looking out, could just see the imposing unbroken avenue with its succession of pale pillars and steps. The repeated columns, the orderly architecture, had even a pale pompous beauty as one stucco column repeated another stucco column all down the street.

"Abercorn Terrace," said Eleanor; ". . . the pillar-box," she murmured as they drove past. Why the pillar-box? Peggy asked herself. Another door had been opened. Old age must have endless avenues, stretching away and away down its darkness, she supposed, and now one door opened and then another.

"Aren't people —" Eleanor began. Then she stopped. As usual, she had begun in the wrong place.

"Yes?" said Peggy. She was irritated by this inconsequence.

"I was going to say — the pillar-box made me think," Eleanor began; then she laughed. She gave up the attempt to account for the order in which her thoughts came to her. There was an order, doubtless; but it took so long to find it, and this rambling, she knew, annoyed Peggy, for young people's minds worked so quickly.

"That's where we used to dine," she broke off, nodding at a big house at the corner of a square. "Your father and I. The man he used to read with. What was his name? He became a

Judge. . . . We used to dine there, the three of us. Morris, my father and I. . . . They had very large parties in those days. Always
legal people. And he collected old oak. Mostly shams," she
added with a little chuckle.

"You used to dine . . ." Peggy began. She wished to get her
back to her past. It was so interesting; so safe; so unreal—that
past of the 'eighties; and to her, so beautiful in its unreality.

"Tell me about your youth . . ." she began.

"But your lives are much more interesting than ours were,"
said Eleanor. Peggy was silent.

They were driving along a bright crowded street; here
stained ruby with the light from picture palaces; here yellow
from shop windows gay with summer dresses, for the shops,
though shut, were still lit up, and people were still looking at
dresses, at flights of hats on little rods, at jewels.

When my Aunt Delia comes to town, Peggy continued the
story of Eleanor that she was telling her friend at the hospital,
she says, We must have a party. Then they all flock together.
They love it. As for herself, she hated it. She would far rather
have stayed at home or gone to the pictures. It's the sense of the
family, she added, glancing at Eleanor as if to collect another
little fact about her to add to her portrait of a Victorian spinster. Eleanor was looking out of the window. Then she turned.

"And the experiment with the guinea-pig—how did that go
off?" she asked. Peggy was puzzled.

Then she remembered and told her.

"I see. So it proved nothing. So you've got to begin all over
again. That's very interesting. Now I wish you'd explain to
me . . ." There was another problem that puzzled her.

The things she wants explained, Peggy said to her friend at
the Hospital, are either as simple as two and two make four, or
so difficult that nobody in the world knows the answer. And if
you say to her, "What's eight times eight?"—she smiled at the

profile of her aunt against the window—she taps her forehead and says . . . but again Eleanor interrupted her.

"It's so good of you to come," she said, giving her a little pat on the knee. (But did I show her, Peggy thought, that I hate coming?)

"It's a way of seeing people," Eleanor continued. "And now that we're all getting on—not you, us—one doesn't like to miss chances."

They drove on. And how does one get *that* right? Peggy thought, trying to add another touch to the portrait. "Sentimental" was it? Or, on the contrary, was it good to feel like that . . . natural . . . right? She shook her head. I'm no use at describing people, she said to her friend at the Hospital. They're too difficult. . . . She's not like that—not like that at all, she said, making a little dash with her hand as if to rub out an outline that she had drawn wrongly. As she did so, her friend at the Hospital vanished.

She was alone with Eleanor in the cab. And they were passing houses. Where does she begin, and where do I end? she thought. . . . On they drove. They were two living people, driving across London; two sparks of life enclosed in two separate bodies; and those sparks of life enclosed in two separate bodies are at this moment, she thought, driving past a picture palace. But what is this moment; and what are we? The puzzle was too difficult for her to solve it. She sighed.

"You're too young to feel that," said Eleanor.

"What?" Peggy asked with a little start.

"About meeting people. About not missing chances of seeing them."

"Young?" said Peggy. "I shall never be as young as you are!" She patted her aunt's knee in her turn. "Gallivanting off to India . . ." she laughed.

"Oh, India. India's nothing nowadays," said Eleanor.

"Travel's so easy. You just take a ticket; just get on board ship. . . . But what I want to see before I die," she continued, "is something different. . . ." She waved her hand out of the window. They were passing public buildings; offices of some sort. ". . . another kind of civilisation. Tibet, for instance. I was reading a book by a man called—now what was he called?"

She paused, distracted by the sights in the street. "Don't people wear pretty clothes nowadays?" she said, pointing to a girl with fair hair and a young man in evening dress.

"Yes," said Peggy perfunctorily, looking at the painted face and the bright shawl; at the white waistcoat and the smoothed-back hair. Anything distracts Eleanor, everything interests her, she thought.

"Was it that you were suppressed when you were young?" she said aloud, recalling vaguely some childish memory; her grandfather with the shiny stumps instead of fingers; and a long dark drawing-room. Eleanor turned. She was surprised.

"Suppressed?" she repeated. She so seldom thought about herself now that she was surprised.

"Oh, I see what you mean," she added after a moment. A picture—another picture—had swum to the surface. There was Delia standing in the middle of the room; Oh, my God! Oh, my God! she was saying; a hansom cab had stopped at the house next door; and she herself was watching Morris—was it Morris?—going down the street to post a letter. . . . She was silent. I do not want to go back into my past, she was thinking. I want the present.

"Where's he taking us?" she said, looking out. They had reached the public part of London; the illuminated. The light fell on broad pavements; on white brilliantly lit-up public offices; on a pallid, hoary-looking church. Advertisements popped in and out. Here was a bottle of beer: it poured: then stopped: then poured again. They had reached the theatre quarter. There was the usual garish confusion. Men and women in evening dress were walking in the middle of the road. Cabs were wheeling and stopping. Their own taxi was held up. It stopped dead under a statue: the lights shone on its cadaverous pallor.

"Always reminds me of an advertisement of sanitary towels," said Peggy, glancing at the figure of a woman in nurse's uniform holding out her hand.

Eleanor was shocked for a moment. A knife seemed to slice her skin, leaving a ripple of unpleasant sensation; but what was solid in her body it did not touch, she realised after a moment. That she said because of Charles, she thought, feeling the bitterness in her tone — her brother, a nice dull boy who had been killed.

"The only fine thing that was said in the war," she said aloud, reading the words cut on the pedestal.

"It didn't come to much," said Peggy sharply.

The cab remained fixed in the block.

The pause seemed to hold them in the light of some thought that they both wished to put away.

"Don't people wear pretty clothes nowadays?" said Eleanor, pointing to another girl with fair hair in a long bright cloak and another young man in evening dress.

"Yes," said Peggy briefly.

But why don't you enjoy yourself more? Eleanor said to herself. Her brother's death had been very sad, but she had always found North much the more interesting of the two. The cab threaded its way through the traffic and passed into a back street. He was stopped now by a red light. "It's nice, having North back again," Eleanor said.

"Yes," said Peggy. "He says we talk of nothing but money and politics," she added. She finds fault with him because he was not the one to be killed; but that's wrong, Eleanor thought.

"Does he?" she said. "But then . . ." A newspaper placard,

with large black letters, seemed to finish her sentence for her. They were approaching the square in which Delia lived. She began to fumble with her purse. She looked at the metre which had mounted rather high. The man was going the long way round.

"He'll find his way in time," she said. They were gliding slowly round the square. She waited patiently, holding her purse in her hand. She saw a breadth of dark sky over the roofs. The sun had sunk. For a moment the sky had the quiet look of the sky that lies above fields and woods in the country.

"He'll have to turn, that's all," she said. "I'm not despondent," she added, as the taxi turned. "Travelling, you see: when one has to mix up with all sorts of other people on board ship, or in one of those little places where one has to stay—off the beaten track—" The taxi was sliding tentatively past house after house—"You ought to go there, Peggy," she broke off; "you ought to travel: the natives are so beautiful you know; half naked: going down to the river in the moonlight;—that's the house over there—" She tapped on the window—the taxi slowed down. "What was I saying? I'm not despondent, no, because people are so kind, so good at heart. . . . So that if only ordinary people, ordinary people like ourselves . . ."

The cab drew up at the house whose windows were lit up. Peggy leant forward and opened the door. She jumped out and paid the driver. Eleanor bundled out after her. "No, no, no, Peggy," she began.

"It's my cab. It's my cab," Peggy protested.

"But I insist on paying my share," said Eleanor, opening her purse.

"THAT'S ELEANOR," said North. He left the telephone and turned to Sara. She was still swinging her foot up and down.

"She told me to tell you to come to Delia's party," he said.

"To Delia's party? Why to Delia's party?" she asked.

"Because they're old and want you to come," he said, standing over her.

"Old Eleanor; wandering Eleanor; Eleanor with the wild eyes . . ." she mused. "Shall I, shan't I, shall I, shan't I?" she hummed, looking up at him. "No," she said, putting her feet to the ground, "I shan't."

"You must," he said. For her manner irritated him—Eleanor's voice was still in his ears.

"I must, must I?" she said, making the coffee.

"Then," she said, giving him his cup and picking up the book at the same time, "read until we must go."

She curled herself up again, holding her cup in her hand.

It was still early, it was true. But why, he thought as he opened the book again, and turned over the pages, won't she come? Is she afraid? he wondered. He looked at her crumpled in her chair. Her dress was shabby. He looked at the book again, but he could hardly see to read. She had not lit the lamp.

"I can't see to read without a light," he said. It grew dark soon in this street; the houses were so close. Now a car passed and a light slid across the ceiling.

"Shall I turn on the light?" she asked.

"No," he said. "I'll try to remember something." He began to say aloud the only poem he knew by heart. As he spoke the words out into the semi-darkness they sounded extremely beautiful, he thought, because they could not see each other, perhaps.

He paused at the end of the verse.

"Go on," she said.

He began again. The words going out into the room seemed like actual presences, hard and independent; yet as she was listening they were changed by their contact with her. But as he reached the end of the second verse —

> Society is all but rude —
> To this delicious solitude . . .

he heard a sound. Was it in the poem or outside of it, he wondered? Inside, he thought, and was about to go on, when she raised her hand. He stopped. He heard heavy footsteps outside the door. Was someone coming in? Her eyes were on the door.

"The Jew," she murmured.

"The Jew?" he said. They listened. He could hear quite distinctly now. Somebody was turning on taps; somebody was having a bath in the room opposite.

"The Jew having a bath," she said.

"The Jew having a bath?" he repeated.

"And tomorrow there'll be a line of grease round the bath," she said.

"Damn the Jew!" he exclaimed. The thought of a line of grease from a strange man's body on the bath next door disgusted him.

"Go on —" said Sara: "Society is all but rude," she repeated the last lines, "to this delicious solitude."

"No," he said.

They listened to the water running. The man was coughing and clearing his throat as he sponged.

"Who is this Jew?" he asked.

"Abrahamson, in the tallow trade," she said.

They listened.

"Engaged to a pretty girl in a tailor's shop," she added.

They could hear the sounds through the thin walls very distinctly.

He was snorting as he sponged himself.

"But he leaves hairs in the bath," she concluded.

North felt a shiver run through him. Hairs in food, hairs on basins, other people's hairs made him feel physically sick.

"D'you share a bath with him?" he asked.

She nodded.

He made a noise like "Pah!"

"'Pah.' That's what I said," she laughed. "'Pah!'—when I went into the bathroom on a cold winter's morning—'Pah!'"—she threw her hand out—"'Pah!'" She paused.

"And then—?" he asked.

"And then," she said, sipping her coffee, "I came back into the sitting-room. And breakfast was waiting. Fried eggs and a bit of toast. Lydia with her blouse torn and her hair down. The unemployed singing hymns under the window. And I said to myself—" She flung her hand out, "'Polluted city, unbelieving city, city of dead fish and worn-out frying-pans'—thinking of a river's bank, when the tide's out," she explained.

"Go on," he nodded.

"So I put on my hat and coat and rushed out in a rage," she continued, "and stood on the bridge, and said, 'Am I a weed, carried this way, that way, on a tide that comes twice a day without a meaning?'"

"Yes?" he prompted her.

"And there were people passing; the strutting; the tiptoeing; the pasty; the ferret-eyed; the bowler-hatted, servile innumerable army of workers. And I said, 'Must I join your conspiracy? Stain the hand, the unstained hand,'"—he could see her hand gleam as she waved it in the half-light of the sitting-room, "'—and sign on, and serve a master; all because of a Jew in my bath, all because of a Jew?'"

She sat up and laughed, excited by the sound of her own voice which had run into a jog-trot rhythm.

"Go on, go on," he said.

"But I had a talisman, a glowing gem, a lucent emerald"—
she picked up an envelope that lay on the floor—"a letter of
introduction. And I said to the flunkey in peach-blossom
trousers, 'Admit me, sirrah,' and he led me along corridors piled
with purple till I came to a door, a mahogany door, and
knocked; and a voice said, 'Enter.' And what did I find?" She
paused. "A stout man with red cheeks. On his table three or-
chids in a vase. Pressed into your hand, I thought, as the car
crunches the gravel by your wife at parting. And over the fireplace the usual picture—"

"Stop!" North interrupted her. "You have come to an office." He tapped the table. "You are presenting a letter of introduction—but to whom?"

"Oh, to whom?" she laughed. "To a man in sponge-bag
trousers. 'I knew your father at Oxford,' he said, toying with the
blotting-paper, ornamented in one corner with a cartwheel. But
what do *you* find insoluble, I asked him, looking at the mahogany man, the clean-shaven, rosy-gilled, mutton-fed man—"

"The man in a newspaper office," North checked her, "who
knew your father. And then?"

"There was a humming and a grinding. The great machines
went round; and little boys popped in with elongated sheets;
black sheets; smudged; damp with printer's ink. 'Pardon me a
moment,' he said, and made a note in the margin. But the Jew's
in my bath, I said—the Jew . . . the Jew. . . ." She stopped suddenly and emptied her glass.

Yes, he thought, there's the voice; there's the attitude; and
the reflection in other people's faces; but then there's something
true—in the silence perhaps. But it was not silent. They could
hear the Jew thudding in the bathroom; he seemed to stagger
from foot to foot as he dried himself. Now he unlocked the
door, and they heard him go upstairs. The pipes began to give
forth hollow gurgling sounds.

"How much of that was true?" he asked her. But she had lapsed into silence. The actual words he supposed—the actual words floated together and formed a sentence in his mind—meant that she was poor; that she must earn her living, but the excitement with which she had spoken, due to wine perhaps, had created yet another person; another semblance, which one must solidify into one whole.

The house was quiet now, save for the sound of the bath water running away. A watery pattern fluctuated on the ceiling. The street lamps jiggering up and down outside made the houses opposite a curious pale red. The uproar of the day had died away; no carts were rattling down the street. The vegetable-sellers, the organ-grinders, the woman practising her scales, the man playing the trombone, had all trundled away their barrows, pulled down their shutters, and closed the lids of their pianos. It was so still that for a moment North thought he was in Africa, sitting on the verandah in the moonlight; but he roused himself. "What about this party?" he said. He got up and threw away his cigarette. He stretched himself and looked at his watch. "It's time to go," he said. "Go and get ready," he urged her. For if one went to a party, he thought, it was absurd to go just as people were leaving. And the party must have begun.

"WHAT WERE you saying—what were you saying, Nell?" said Peggy, in order to distract Eleanor from paying her share of the cab, as they stood on the doorstep. "Ordinary people—ordinary people ought to do what?" she asked.

Eleanor was still fumbling with her purse and did not answer.

"No, I can't allow that," she said. "Here, take this—"

But Peggy brushed aside the hand, and the coins rolled on the doorstep. They both stooped simultaneously and their heads collided.

"Don't bother," said Eleanor as a coin rolled away. "It was all my fault." The maid was holding the door open.

"And where do we take our cloaks off?" she said. "In here?"

They went into a room on the ground floor which, though an office, had been arranged so that it could be used as a cloakroom. There was a looking-glass on the table: and in front of it trays of pins and combs and brushes. She went up to the glass and gave herself one brief glance.

"What a gipsy I look!" she said, and ran a comb through her hair. "Burnt as brown as a nigger!" Then she gave way to Peggy and waited.

"I wonder if this was the room . . ." she said.

"What room?" said Peggy abstractedly: she was attending to her face.

". . . where we used to meet," said Eleanor. She looked about her. It was still used as an office apparently; but now there were house-agents' placards on the wall.

"I wonder if Kitty'll come tonight," she mused.

Peggy was gazing into the glass and did not answer.

"She doesn't often come to town now. Only for weddings and christenings and so on," Eleanor continued.

Peggy was drawing a line with a tube of some sort round her lips.

"Suddenly you meet a young man six-foot-two and you realise this is the baby," Eleanor went on.

Peggy was still absorbed in her face.

"D'you have to do that fresh every time?" said Eleanor.

"I should look a fright if I didn't," said Peggy. The tightness round her lips and eyes seemed to her visible. She had never felt less in the mood for a party.

"Oh, how kind of you . . ." Eleanor broke off. The maid had brought in a sixpence.

"Now, Peggy," said she, proffering the coin, "let me pay my share."

"Don't be an ass," said Peggy, brushing away her hand.

"But it was my cab," Eleanor insisted. Peggy walked on. "Because I hate going to parties," Eleanor continued, following her, still holding out the coin, "on the cheap. You don't remember your grandfather? He always said, 'Don't spoil a good ship for a ha'porth of tar.' If you went shopping with him," she went on as they began mounting the stairs, " 'Show me the very best thing you've got,' he'd say."

"I remember him," said Peggy.

"Do you?" said Eleanor. She was pleased that anyone should remember her father. "They've lent these rooms, I suppose," she added as they walked upstairs. Doors were open. "That's a solicitor's," she said, looking at some deed-boxes with white names painted on them.

"Yes, I see what you mean about painting—making-up," she continued, glancing at her niece. "You do look nice. You look lit-up. I like it on young people. Not for myself. I should feel bedizened—bedizzened?—how d'you pronounce it? And what am I to do with these coppers if you won't take them? I ought to have left them in my bag downstairs." They mounted higher and higher. "I suppose they've opened all these rooms," she continued—they had now reached a strip of red carpet— "so that if Delia's little room gets too full—but of course the party's hardly begun yet. We're early. Everybody's upstairs. I hear them talking. Come along. Shall I go first?"

A babble of voices sounded behind a door. A maid intercepted them.

"Miss Pargiter," said Eleanor.

"Miss Pargiter!" the maid called out, opening the door.

————

"GO AND GET READY," said North. He crossed the room and fumbled with the switch.

He touched the switch, and the electric light in the middle of the room came on. The shade had been taken off, and a cone of greenish paper had been twisted round it.

"Go and get ready," he repeated. Sara did not answer. She had pulled a book towards her and pretended to read it.

"He's killed the king," she said. "So what'll he do next?" She held her finger between the pages of the book and looked up at him; a device, he knew, to put off the moment of action. He did not want to go either. Still, if Eleanor wanted them to go — he hesitated, looking at his watch.

"What'll he do next?" she repeated.

"Comedy," he said briefly. "Contrast," he said, remembering something he had read. "The only form of continuity," he added at a venture.

"Well, go on reading," she said, handing him the book.

He opened it at random.

"The scene is a rocky island in the middle of the sea," he said. He paused.

Always before reading he had to arrange the scene; to let this sink; that come forward. A rocky island in the middle of the sea, he said to himself—there were green pools, tufts of silver grass, sand, and far away the soft sigh of waves breaking. He opened his mouth to read. Then there was a sound behind him; a presence—in the play or in the room? He looked up.

"Maggie!" Sara exclaimed. There she was standing at the open door in evening dress.

"WERE YOU ASLEEP?" she said, coming into the room. "We've been ringing and ringing."

She stood smiling at them, amused, as if she had wakened sleepers.

"Why d'you trouble to have a bell when it's always broken?" said a man who stood behind her.

North rose. At first he scarcely remembered them. The surface sight was strange on top of his memory of them, as he had seen them years ago.

"The bells don't ring, and the taps don't run," he said, awkwardly. "Or they don't stop running," he added, for the bath water was still gurgling in the pipes.

"Luckily the door was open," said Maggie. She stood at the table looking at the broken apple peel and the dish of fly-blown fruit. Some beauty, North thought, withers; some, he looked at her, grows more beautiful with age. Her hair was grey; her children must be grown up now, he supposed. But why do women purse their lips up when they look in the glass? he wondered. She was looking in the glass. She was pursing her lips. Then she crossed the room, and sat down in the chair by the fireplace.

"And why has Renny been crying?" said Sara. North looked at him. There were wet marks on either side of his large nose.

"Because we've been to a very bad play," he said, "and should like something to drink," he added.

Sara went to the cupboard and began clinking glasses. "Were you reading?" said Renny, looking at the book which had fallen on the floor.

"We were on a rocky island in the middle of the sea," said Sara, putting the glasses on the table. Renny began to pour out whisky.

Now I remember him, North thought. Last time they had met was before he went to the war. It was in a little house in Westminster. They had sat in front of the fire. And a child had played with a spotted horse. And he had envied them their happiness. And they had talked about science. And Renny had said, "I help them to make shells," and a mask had come down over his face. A man who made shells; a man who loved peace; a man of science; a man who cried. . . .

"Stop!" cried Renny. "Stop!" Sara had spurted the soda water over the table.

"When did you get back?" Renny asked him, taking his glass and looking at him with eyes still wet with tears.

"About a week ago," he said.

"You've sold your farm?" said Renny. He sat down with his glass in his hand.

"Yes, sold it," said North. "Whether I shall stay, or go back," he said, taking his glass and raising it to his lips, "I don't know."

"Where was your farm?" said Renny, bending towards him. And they talked about Africa.

MAGGIE LOOKED at them drinking and talking. The twisted cone of paper over the electric light was oddly stained. The mottled light made their faces look greenish. The two grooves on each side of Renny's nose were still wet. His face was all peaks and hollows; North's face was round and snub-nosed and rather blueish about the lips. She gave her chair a little push so that she got the two heads in relation side by side. They were very different. And as they talked about Africa their faces changed, as if some twitch had been given to the fine network under the skin and the weights fell into different sockets. A thrill ran through her as if the weights in her own body had changed too. But there was something about the light that puzzled her. She looked round. A lamp must be flaring in the street outside. Its light, flickering up and down, mixed with the electric light under the greenish cone of mottled paper. It was that which. . . . She started; a voice had reached her.

"To Africa?" she said, looking at North.

"To Delia's party," he said. "I asked if you were coming. . . ." She had not been listening.

"One moment . . ." Renny interrupted. He held up his hand
like a policeman stopping traffic. And again they went on, talking about Africa.

Maggie lay back in her chair. Behind their heads rose the
curve of the mahogany chair back. And behind the curve of the
chair back was a crinkled glass with a red lip; then there was
the straight line of the mantelpiece with little black-and-white
squares on it; and then three rods ending in soft yellow plumes.
She ran her eye from thing to thing. In and out it went, collect-
ing, gathering, summing up into one whole, when, just as she
was about to complete the pattern, Renny exclaimed:

"We must—we must!"

He had got up. He had pushed away his glass of whisky.
He stood there like somebody commanding a troop, North
thought; so emphatic was his voice, so commanding his gesture. Yet it was only a question of going round to an old
woman's party. Or was there always, he thought, as he too rose
and looked for his hat, something that came to the surface, inappropriately, unexpectedly, from the depths of people, and
made ordinary actions, ordinary words, expressive of the whole
being, so that he felt, as he turned to follow Renny to Delia's
party, as if he were riding to the relief of a besieged garrison
across a desert?

He stopped with his hand on the door. Sara had come in
from the bedroom. She had changed; she was in evening dress;
there was something odd about her—perhaps it was the effect
of the evening dress estranging her?

"I am ready," she said, looking at them.

She stooped and picked up the book that North had let fall.

"We must go —" she said, turning to her sister.

She put the book on the table; she gave it a sad little pat as she shut it.

"We must go," she repeated, and followed them down the stairs.

Maggie rose. She gave one more look at the cheap lodging-house room. There was the pampas grass in its terra-cotta pot; the green vase with the crinkled lip; and the mahogany chair. On the dinner table lay the dish of fruit; the heavy sensual apples lay side by side with the yellow spotted bananas. It was an odd combination—the round and the tapering, the rosy and the yellow. She switched off the light. The room now was almost dark, save for a watery pattern fluctuating on the ceiling. In this phantom evanescent light only the outlines showed; ghostly apples, ghostly bananas, and the spectre of a chair. Colour was slowly returning, as her eyes grew used to the darkness, and substance. . . . She stood there for a moment looking. Then a voice shouted:

"Maggie! Maggie!"

"I'm coming!" she cried, and followed them down the stairs.

"AND YOUR name, miss?" said the maid to Peggy as she hung back behind Eleanor.

"Miss Margaret Pargiter," said Peggy.

"Miss Margaret Pargiter!" the maid called out into the room.

There was a babble of voices; lights opened brightly in front of her, and Delia came forward. "Oh, Peggy!" she exclaimed. "How nice of you to come!"

She went in; but she felt plated, coated over with some cold skin. They had come too early—the room was almost empty. Only a few people stood about, talking too loudly, as if to fill the room. Making believe, Peggy thought to herself as she shook hands with Delia and passed on, that something pleasant is about to happen. She saw with extreme clearness the Persian rug and the carved fireplace, but there was an empty space in the middle of the room.

What is the tip for this particular situation? she asked herself, as if she were prescribing for a patient. Take notes, she added. Do them up in a bottle with a glossy green cover, she thought. Take notes and the pain goes. Take notes and the pain goes, she repeated to herself as she stood there alone. Delia hurried past her. She was talking, but talking at random.

"It's all very well for you people who live in London—" she was saying. But the nuisance of taking notes of what people say, Peggy went on as Delia passed her, is that they talk such nonsense . . . such complete nonsense, she thought, drawing herself back against the wall. Here her father came in. He paused at the door; put his head up as if he were looking for someone, and advanced with his hand out.

And what's this? she asked, for the sight of her father in his rather worn shoes had given her a direct spontaneous feeling. This sudden warm spurt? she asked, examining it. She watched him cross the room. His shoes always affected her strangely. Part sex; part pity, she thought. Can one call it "love"? But she forced herself to move. Now that I have drugged myself into a state of comparative insensibility, she said to herself, I will walk across the room boldly; I will go to Uncle Patrick, who is standing by the sofa picking his teeth, and I will say to him—what shall I say?

A sentence suggested itself for no rhyme or reason as she crossed the room: "How's the man who cut his toes off with the hatchet?"

"How's the man who cut his toes off with the hatchet?" she said, speaking the words exactly as she thought them. The handsome old Irishman bent down, for he was very tall, and hollowed his hand, for he was hard of hearing.

"Hacket? Hacket?" he repeated. She smiled. The steps from brain to brain must be cut very shallow, if thought is to mount them, she noted.

"Cut his toes off with the hatchet when I was staying with you," she said. She remembered how when she last stayed with them in Ireland, the gardener had cut his foot with a hatchet.

"Hacket? Hacket?" he repeated. He looked puzzled. Then understanding dawned.

"Oh, the Hackets!" he said. "Dear old Peter Hacket—yes." It seemed that there were Hackets in Galway, and the mistake, which she did not trouble to explain, was all to the good, for it set him off, and he told her stories about the Hackets as they sat side by side on the sofa.

A grown woman, she thought, crosses London to talk to a deaf old man about the Hackets, whom she's never heard of, when she meant to ask after the gardener who cut his toes off with a hatchet. But does it matter? Hackets or hatchets? She laughed, happily in time with a joke, so that it seemed appropriate. But one wants somebody to laugh with, she thought. Pleasure is increased by sharing it. Does the same hold good of pain? she mused. Is that the reason why we all talk so much of ill-health—because sharing things lessens things? Give pain, give pleasure an outer body, and by increasing the surface diminish them. . . . But the thought slipped. He was off telling his old stories. Gently, methodically, like a man setting in motion some still serviceable but rather weary nag he was off remembering old days, old dogs, old memories that slowly shaped themselves, as he warmed, into little figures of country house life. She fancied as she half listened that she was looking at a faded snapshot of cricketers; of shooting parties on the many steps of some country mansion.

How many people, she wondered, listen? This "sharing," then, is a bit of a farce. She made herself attend.

"Ah, yes, those were fine old days!" he was saying. The light came into his faded eyes.

She looked once more at the snapshot of the men in gaiters, and the women in flowing skirts on the broad white steps with the dogs curled up at their feet. But he was off again.

"Did you ever hear from your father of a man called Roddy Jenkins who lived in the little white house on the right-hand side as you go along the road?" he asked. "But you must know that story?" he added.

"No," she said, screwing up her eyes as if she referred to the files of memory. "Tell me."

And he told her the story.

I'm good, she thought, at fact-collecting. But what makes up a person—(she hollowed her hand), the circumference,— no, I'm not good at that. There was her Aunt Delia. She watched her moving quickly about the room. What do I know about her? That she's wearing a dress with gold spots; has wavy hair, that was red, is white; is handsome; ravaged; with a past. But what past? She married Patrick. . . . The long story that Patrick was telling her kept breaking up the surface of her mind like oars dipping into water. Nothing could settle. There was a lake in the story too, for it was a story about duck-shooting.

She married Patrick, she thought, looking at his battered weather-worn face with the single hairs on it. Why did Delia marry Patrick? she wondered. How do they manage it—love, childbirth? The people who touch each other and go up in a cloud of smoke: red smoke? His face reminded her of the red skin of a gooseberry with the little stray hairs. But none of the lines on his face was sharp enough, she thought, to explain how they came together and had three children. They were lines that came from shooting; lines that came from worry; for the old days were over, he was saying. They had to cut things down.

"Yes, we're all finding that," she said perfunctorily. She

turned her wrist cautiously so that she could read her watch. Fifteen minutes only had passed. But the room was filling with people she did not know. There was an Indian in a pink turban.

"Ah, but I'm boring you with these old stories," said her uncle, wagging his head. He was hurt, she felt.

"No, no, no!" she said, feeling uncomfortable. He was off again, but out of good manners this time, she felt. Pain must outbalance pleasure by two parts to one, she thought; in all social relations. Or am I the exception, the peculiar person? she continued, for the others seemed happy enough. Yes, she thought, looking straight ahead of her, and feeling again the stretched skin round her lips and eyes tight from the tiredness of sitting up late with a woman in childbirth, I'm the exception; hard; cold; in a groove already; merely a doctor.

Getting out of grooves is damned unpleasant, she thought, before the chill of death has set in, like bending frozen boots. . . . She bent her head to listen. To smile, to bend, to make believe you're amused when you're bored, how painful it is, she thought. All ways, every way's painful, she thought, staring at the Indian in the pink turban.

"Who's that fellow?" Patrick asked, nodding his head in his direction.

"One of Eleanor's Indians, I expect," she said aloud, and thought, If only the merciful powers of darkness would obliterate the external exposure of the sensitive nerve and I could get up and . . . There was a pause.

"But I mustn't keep you here, listening to my old stories," said Uncle Patrick. His weather-beaten nag with the broken knees had stopped.

"But tell me, does old Biddy still keep the little shop," she asked, "where we used to buy sweets?"

"Poor old body—" he began. He was off again. All her patients said that, she thought. Rest—rest—let me rest. How to deaden; how to cease to feel; that was the cry of the woman bearing children; to rest, to cease to be. In the Middle Ages, she thought, it was the cell; the monastery; now it's the laboratory; the professions; not to live; not to feel; to make money, always money, and in the end, when I'm old and worn like a horse, no, it's a cow . . .—for part of old Patrick's story had imposed itself upon her mind: ". . . for there's no sale for the beasts at all," he was saying, "no sale at all. Ah, there's Julia Cromarty—" he exclaimed, and waved his hand, his large loose-jointed hand, at a charming compatriot.

She was left sitting alone on the sofa. For her uncle rose and went off with both hands outstretched to greet the bird-like old woman who had come in chattering.

She was left alone. She was glad to be alone. She had no wish to talk. But next moment somebody stood beside her. It was Martin. He sat down beside her. She changed her attitude completely.

"Hullo, Martin!" she greeted him cordially.

"Done your duty by the old mare, Peggy?" he said. He referred to the stories that old Patrick always told them.

"Did I look very glum?" she asked.

"Well," he said, glancing at her, "not exactly enraptured."

"One knows the end of his stories by now," she excused herself, looking at Martin. He had taken to brushing his hair up like a waiter's. He never looked her fully in the face. He never felt entirely at his ease with her. She was his doctor; she knew that he dreaded cancer. She must try to distract him from thinking, Does she see any symptoms?

"I was wondering how they came to marry," she said. "Were they in love?" She spoke at random to distract him.

"Of course he was in love," he said. He looked at Delia. She was standing by the fireplace talking to the Indian. She was still a very handsome woman, with her presence, with her gestures.

"We were all in love," he said, glancing sideways at Peggy. The younger generation were so serious.

"Oh, of course," she said, smiling. She liked his eternal pursuit of one love after another love—his gallant clutch upon the flying tail, the slippery tail of youth—even he, even now.

"But you," he said, stretching his feet out, hitching up his trousers, "your generation I mean—you miss a great deal . . . you miss a great deal," he repeated. She waited.

"Loving only your own sex," he added.

He liked to assert his own youth in that way, she thought; to say things that he thought up to date.

"I'm not that generation," she said.

"Well, well, well," he chuckled, shrugging his shoulders and glancing at her sideways. He knew very little about her private life. But she looked serious; she looked tired. She works too hard, he thought.

"I'm getting on," said Peggy. "Getting into a groove. So Eleanor told me tonight."

Or was it she, on the other hand, who had told Eleanor she was "suppressed"? One or the other.

"Eleanor's a gay old dog," he said. "Look!" He pointed.

There she was, talking to the Indian in her red cloak.

"Just back from India," he added. "A present from Bengal, eh?" he said, referring to the cloak.

"And next year she's off to China," said Peggy.

"But Delia—" she asked; Delia was passing them. "Was she in love?" (What you in your generation called "in love," she added to herself.)

He wagged his head from side to side and pursed his lips. He always liked his little joke, she remembered.

"I don't know—I don't know about Delia," he said. "There was the cause, you know—what she called in those days The

Cause." He screwed his face up. "Ireland, you know. Parnell. Ever heard of a man called Parnell?" he asked.

"Yes," said Peggy.

"And Edward?" she added. He had come in; he looked very distinguished, too, in his elaborate, if conscious simplicity.

"Edward—yes," said Martin. "Edward was in love. Surely you know that old story—Edward and Kitty?"

"The one who married—what was his name?—Lasswade?" Peggy murmured as Edward passed them.

"Yes, she married the other man—Lasswade. But he was in love—he was very much in love," Martin murmured. "But you—" He gave her a quick little glance. There was something in her that chilled him. "Of course, you have your profession," he added. He looked at the ground. He was thinking of his dread of cancer, she supposed. He was afraid that she had noted some symptom.

"Oh, doctors are great humbugs," she threw out at random.

"Why? People live longer than they used, don't they?" he said. "They don't die so painfully anyhow," he added.

"We've learnt a few little tricks," she conceded. He stared ahead of him with a look that moved her pity.

"You'll live to be eighty—if you want to live to be eighty," she said. He looked at her.

"Of course I'm all in favour of living to be eighty!" he exclaimed. "I want to go to America. I want to see their buildings. I'm on that side, you see. I enjoy life." He did, enormously.

He must be over sixty himself, she supposed. But he was wonderfully got up; as sprig and spruce as a man of forty, with his canary-coloured lady in Kensington.

"I don't know," she said aloud.

"Come, Peggy, come," he said. "Don't tell me you don't enjoy—here's Rose."

Rose came up. She had grown very stout.

"Don't you want to be eighty?" he said to her. He had to say it twice over. She was deaf.

"I do. Of course I do!" she said when she understood him. She faced them. She made an odd angle with her head thrown back, Peggy thought, as if she were a military man.

"Of course I do," she said, sitting down abruptly on the sofa beside them.

"Ah, but then——" Peggy began. She paused. Rose was deaf, she remembered. She had to shout. "People hadn't made such fools of themselves in your day," she shouted. But she doubted if Rose heard.

"I want to see what's going to happen," said Rose. "We live in a very interesting world," she added.

"Nonsense," Martin teased her. "You want to live," he bawled in her ear, "because you enjoy living."

"And I'm not ashamed of it," she said. "I like my kind——on the whole."

"What you like is fighting them," he bawled.

"D'you think you can get a rise out of me at this time o' day?" she said, tapping him on the arm.

Now they'll talk about being children; climbing trees in the back garden, thought Peggy, and how they shot somebody's cats. Each person had a certain line laid down in their minds, she thought, and along it came the same old sayings. One's mind must be criss-crossed like the palm of one's hand, she thought, looking at the palm of her hand.

"She always was a spitfire," said Martin, turning to Peggy.

"And they always put the blame on me," Rose said. "*He* had the school-room. Where was I to sit? 'Oh, run away and play in the nursery!'" She waved her hand.

"And so she went into the bathroom and cut her wrist with a knife," Martin jeered.

"No, that was Erridge: that was about the microscope," she corrected him.

It's like a kitten catching its tail, Peggy thought; round and round they go in a circle. But it's what they enjoy, she thought; it's what they come to parties for. Martin went on teasing Rose.

"And where's your red ribbon?" he was asking.

Some decoration had been given her, Peggy remembered, for her work in the war.

"Aren't we worthy to see you in your war paint?" he teased her.

"This fellow's jealous," she said, turning to Peggy again. "He's never done a stroke of work in his life."

"I work—I work," Martin insisted. "I sit in an office all day long—"

"Doing what?" said Rose.

Then they became suddenly silent. That turn was over— the old-brother-and-sister turn. Now they could only go back and repeat the same thing over again.

"Look here," said Martin, "we must go and do our duty." He rose. They parted.

"DOING WHAT?" Peggy repeated, as she crossed the room. "Doing what?" she repeated. She was feeling reckless; nothing that she did mattered. She walked to the window and twitched the curtain apart. There were the stars pricked in little holes in the blue-black sky. There was a row of chimney-pots against the sky. Then the stars. Inscrutable, eternal, indifferent—those were the words; the right words. But I don't feel it, she said, looking at the stars. So why pretend to? What they're really like, she thought, screwing up her eyes to look at them, is little bits of frosty steel. And the moon—there it was—is a polished dish-cover. But she felt nothing, even when she had reduced moon and stars to that. Then she turned and found herself face to face with a young man she thought she knew but could not put a name to. He had a fine brow, but a receding chin, and he was pale, pasty.

"How-d'you-do?" she said. Was his name Leacock or Laycock?

"Last time we met," she said, "was at the races." She connected him, incongruously, with a Cornish field, stone walls, farmers and rough ponies jumping.

"No, that's Paul," he said. "My brother Paul." He was tart about it. What did he do, then, that made him superior in his own esteem to Paul?

"You live in London?" she said.

He nodded.

"You write?" she hazarded. But why, because he was a writer—she remembered now seeing his name in the papers—throw your head back when you say "Yes"? She preferred Paul; he looked healthy; this one had a queer face; knit up; nerve-drawn; fixed.

"Poetry?" she said.

"Yes." But why bite off that word as if it were a cherry on the end of a stalk? she thought. There was nobody coming; they were bound to sit down side by side, on chairs by the wall.

"How do you manage, if you're in an office?" she said. Apparently in his spare time.

"My uncle," he began. ". . . You've met him?"

Yes, a nice commonplace man; he had been very kind to her about a passport once. This boy, of course, though she only half listened, sneered at him. Then why go into his office? she asked herself. My people, he was saying . . . hunted. Her attention wandered. She had heard it all before. I, I, I—he went on. It was like a vulture's beak pecking, or a vacuum-cleaner sucking, or a telephone bell ringing. I, I, I. But he couldn't help it, not with that nerve-drawn egotist's face, she thought, glancing at

him. He could not free himself, could not detach himself. He
was bound on the wheel with tight iron hoops. He had to ex-
pose, had to exhibit. But why let him? she thought, as he went
on talking. For what do I care about his "I, I, I"? Or his poetry?
Let me shake him off then, she said to herself, feeling like a person whose blood has been sucked, leaving all the nerve-centres
pale. She paused. He noted her lack of sympathy. He thought
her stupid, she supposed.

"I'm tired," she apologised. "I've been up all night," she explained. "I'm a doctor—"

The fire went out of his face when she said "I." That's done
it—now he'll go, she thought. He can't be "you"—he must be
"I." She smiled. For up he got and off he went.

SHE TURNED round and stood at the window. Poor little
wretch, she thought; atrophied, withered; cold as steel; hard as
steel; bald as steel. And I too, she thought, looking at the sky.
The stars seemed pricked haphazard in the sky, except that
there, to the right over the chimney-pots, hung that phantom
wheel-barrow—what did they call it? The name escaped her. I
will count them, she thought, returning to her notebook, and
had begun one, two, three, four . . . when a voice exclaimed behind her: "Peggy! Aren't your ears tingling?" She turned. It was
Delia of course, with her genial ways, her imitation Irish flattery:
"—because they ought to be," said Delia, laying a hand on her
shoulder, "considering what *he's* been saying"—she pointed to
a grey-haired man—"what praises he's been singing of you."

Peggy looked where she pointed. There was her teacher
over there, her master. Yes, she knew he thought her clever. She
was, she supposed. They all said so. Very clever.

"He's been telling me—" Delia began. But she broke off.

"Just help me open this window," she said. "It's getting
hot."

"Let me," said Peggy. She gave the window a jerk, but it stuck, for it was old and the frames did not fit.

"Here, Peggy," said somebody, coming behind her. It was her father. His hand was on the window, his hand with the scar. He pushed; the window went up.

"Thanks, Morris, that's better," said Delia. "I was telling Peggy her ears ought to be tingling," she began again: "'My most brilliant pupil!' That's what *he* said," Delia went on. "I assure you I felt quite proud. 'But she's my niece,' I said. He hadn't known it—"

There, said Peggy, that's pleasure. The nerve down her spine seemed to tingle as the praise reached her father. Each emotion touched a different nerve. A sneer rasped the thigh; pleasure thrilled the spine; and also affected the sight. The stars had softened; they quivered. Her father brushed her shoulder as he dropped his hand; but neither of them spoke.

"D'you want it open at the bottom too?" he said.

"No, that'll do," said Delia. "The room's getting hot," she said. "People are beginning to come. They must use the rooms downstairs," she said. "But who's that out there?" she pointed. Opposite the house against the railings of the square was a group in evening dress.

"I think I recognise one of them," said Morris, looking out. "That's North, isn't it?"

"Yes, that's North," said Peggy, looking out.

"Then why don't they come in?" said Delia, tapping on the window.

"BUT YOU must come and see it for yourselves," North was saying. They had asked him to describe Africa. He had said that there were mountains and plains; it was silent, he had said, and birds sang. He stopped; it was difficult to describe a place to people who had not seen it. Then curtains in the house opposite parted, and three heads appeared at the window. They looked at the heads outlined on the window opposite them. They were standing with their backs to the railings of the square. The trees hung dark showers of leaves over them. The trees had become part of the sky. Now and then they seemed to shift and shuffle slightly as a breeze went through them. A star shone among the leaves. It was silent too; the murmur of the traffic was run together into one far hum. A cat slunk past; for a second they saw the luminous green of the eyes; then it was extinguished. The cat crossed the lighted space and vanished. Someone tapped again on the window and cried, "Come in!"

"Come!" said Renny, and threw his cigar into the bushes behind him. "Come. We must."

THEY WENT UPSTAIRS, past the doors of offices, past long windows that opened on to back gardens that lay behind houses. Trees in full leaf stretched their branches across at different levels; the leaves, here bright green in the artificial light, here dark in shadow, moved up and down in the little breeze. Then they came to the private part of the house, where the red carpet was laid; and a roar of voices sounded from behind a door as if a flock of sheep were penned there. Then music, a dance, swung out.

"Now," said Maggie, pausing for a moment, outside the door. She gave their names to the servant.

"And you, sir?" said the maid to North, who hung behind.

"Captain Pargiter," said North, touching his tie.

"And Captain Pargiter!" the maid called out.

DELIA WAS upon them instantly. "And Captain Pargiter!" she exclaimed, as she came hurrying across the room. "How very nice of you to come!" she exclaimed. She took their hands at random, here a left hand, there a right hand, in her left hand, in her right hand.

"I thought it was you," she exclaimed, "standing in the square. I thought I could recognise Renny—but I wasn't sure about North. Captain Pargiter!" she wrung his hand, "you're quite a stranger—but a very welcome one! Now who d'you know? Who don't you know?"

She glanced round, twitching her shawl rather nervously.

"Let me see, there's all your uncles and aunts; and your cousins; and your sons and daughters—yes, Maggie, I saw your lovely couple not long ago. They're somewhere. . . . Only all the generations in our family are so mixed; cousins and aunts, uncles and brothers—but perhaps it's a good thing."

She stopped rather suddenly as if she had used up that vein. She twitched her shawl.

"They're going to dance," she said, pointing at the young man who was putting another record on the gramophone. "It's all right for dancing," she added, referring to the gramophone. "Not for music." She became simple for a moment. "I can't bear music on the gramophone. But dance music—that's another thing. And young people—don't you find that?—must dance. It's right they should. Dance or not—just as you like." She waved her hand.

"Yes, just as you like," her husband echoed her. He stood beside her, dangling his hands in front of him like a bear on which coats are hung in a hotel.

"Just as you like," he repeated, shaking his paws.

"Help me to move the tables, North," said Delia. "If they're going to dance, they'll want everything out of the way—and the rugs rolled up." She pushed a table out of the way. Then she ran across the room to whisk a chair against the wall.

Now one of the vases was upset, and a stream of water flowed across the carpet.

"Don't mind it, don't mind it—it doesn't matter at all!" Delia exclaimed, assuming the manner of a harum-scarum Irish hostess. But North stooped and swabbed up the water.

"And what are you going to do with that pocket handkerchief?" Eleanor asked him; she had joined them in her flowing red cloak.

"Hang it on a chair to dry," said North, walking off.

"And you, Sally?" said Eleanor, drawing back against the wall since they were going to dance. "Going to dance?" she asked, sitting down.

"I?" said Sara, yawning. "I want to sleep." She sank down on a cushion beside Eleanor.

"But you don't come to parties," Eleanor laughed, looking down at her, "to sleep, do you?" Again she saw the little picture she had seen at the end of the telephone. But she could not see her face; only the top of her head.

"Dining with you, wasn't he?" she said, as North passed them with his handkerchief.

"And what did you talk about?" she asked. She saw her, sitting on the edge of a chair, swinging her foot up and down, with a smudge on her nose.

"Talk about?" said Sara. "You, Eleanor." People were passing them all the time; they were brushing against their knees; they were beginning to dance. It made one feel a little dizzy, Eleanor thought, sinking back in her chair.

"Me?" she said. "What about me?"

"Your life," said Sara.

"My life?" Eleanor repeated. Couples began to twist and turn slowly past them. It was a fox-trot that they were dancing, she supposed.

My life, she said to herself. That was odd, it was the second time that evening that somebody had talked about her life. And I haven't got one, she thought. Oughtn't a life to be something you could handle and produce?—a life of seventy odd years. But I've only the present moment, she thought. Here she was alive, now, listening to the fox-trot. Then she looked round. There was Morris; Rose; Edward with his head thrown back talking to a man she did not know. I'm the only person here, she thought, who remembers how he sat on the edge of my bed that night, crying—the night Kitty's engagement was announced. Yes, things came back to her. A long strip of life lay behind her. Edward crying, Mrs. Levy talking; snow falling; a sunflower with a crack in it; the yellow omnibus trotting along the Bayswater Road. And I thought to myself, I'm the youngest person in this omnibus; now I'm the oldest. . . . Millions of things came back to her. Atoms danced apart and massed themselves. But how did they compose what people called a life? She clenched her hands and felt the hard little coins she was holding. Perhaps there's "I" at the middle of it, she thought; a knot; a centre; and again she saw herself sitting at her table drawing on the blotting-paper, digging little holes from which spokes radiated. Out and out they went; thing followed thing, scene obliterated scene. And then they say, she thought, "We've been talking about you!"

"My life . . ." she said aloud, but half to herself.

"Yes?" said Sara, looking up.

Eleanor stopped. She had forgotten her. But there was somebody listening. Then she must put her thoughts into order; then she must find words. But no, she thought, I can't find words; I can't tell anybody.

"Isn't that Nicholas?" she said, looking at a rather large man who stood in the doorway.

"Where?" said Sara. But she looked in the wrong direction. He had disappeared. Perhaps she had been mistaken. My life's been other people's lives, Eleanor thought—my father's; Morris's; my friends' lives; Nicholas's. . . . Fragments of a conversation with him came back to her. Either I'd been lunching with him or dining with him, she thought. It was in a restaurant. There was a parrot with a pink feather in a cage on the counter. And they had sat there talking—it was after the war—about the future; about education. And he wouldn't let me pay for the wine, she suddenly remembered, though it was I who ordered it. . . .

Here somebody stopped in front of her. She looked up. "Just as I was thinking of you!" she exclaimed.

It was Nicholas.

"Good-evening, madame!" he said, bending over her in his foreign way.

"Just as I was thinking of you!" she repeated. Indeed it was like a part of her, a sunk part of her, coming to the surface. "Come and sit beside me," she said, and pulled up a chair.

"D'YOU KNOW who that chap is, sitting by my aunt?" said North to the girl he was dancing with. She looked round; but vaguely.

"I don't know your aunt," she said. "I don't know anybody here."

The dance was over and they began walking towards the door.

"I don't even know my hostess," she said. "I wish you'd point her out to me."

"There—over there," he said. He pointed to Delia in her black dress with the gold spangles.

"Oh, that," she said, looking at her. "That's my hostess, is it?" He had not caught the girl's name, and she knew none of them either. He was glad of it. It made him seem different to himself—it stimulated him. He shepherded her towards the door. He wanted to avoid his relations. In particular he wanted to avoid his sister Peggy; but there she was, standing alone by the door. He looked the other way; he conveyed his partner out of the door. There must be a garden or a roof somewhere, he thought, where they could sit, alone. She was extraordinarily pretty and young.

"Come along," he said, "downstairs."

"AND WHAT were you thinking about me?" said Nicholas, sitting down beside Eleanor.

She smiled. There he was in his rather ill-assorted dress-clothes, with the seal engraved with the arms of his mother the princess, and his swarthy wrinkled face that always made her think of some loose-skinned, furry animal, savage to others but kind to herself. But what was she thinking about him? She was thinking of him in the lump; she could not break off little fragments. The restaurant had been smoky she remembered.

"How we dined together once in Soho," she said. ". . . d'you remember?"

"All the evenings with you I remember, Eleanor," he said. But his glance was a little vague. His attention was distracted. He was looking at a lady who had just come in; a well-dressed lady, who stood with her back to the bookcase equipped for every emergency. If I can't describe my own life, Eleanor thought, how can I describe him? For what he was she did not know; only that it gave her pleasure when he came in; relieved her of the need of thinking; and gave her mind a little jog. He was looking at the lady. She seemed upheld by their gaze; vibrating under it. And suddenly it seemed to Eleanor that it had all happened before. So a girl had come in that night in the restaurant; had stood, vibrating, in the door. She knew exactly what he was going to say. He had said it before, in the restaurant. He is going to say, She is like a ball on the top of a fishmonger's fountain. As she thought it, he said it. Does everything then come over again a little differently? she thought. If so, is there a pattern; a theme, recurring, like music; half remembered, half foreseen? . . . a gigantic pattern, momentarily perceptible? The thought gave her extreme pleasure: that there was a pattern. But who makes it? Who thinks it? Her mind slipped. She could not finish her thought.

"Nicholas . . ." she said. She wanted him to finish it; to take her thought and carry it out into the open unbroken; to make it whole, beautiful, entire.

"Tell me, Nicholas . . ." she began; but she had no notion how she was going to finish her sentence, or what it was that she wanted to ask him. He was talking to Sara. She listened. He was laughing at her. He was pointing at her feet.

". . . coming to a party," he was saying, "with one stocking that is white, and one stocking that is blue."

"The Queen of England asked me to tea," Sara hummed in time to the music, "and which shall it be; the gold or the rose; for all are in holes, my stockings, said she." This is their love-making, Eleanor thought, half listening to their laughter, to their bickering. Another inch of the pattern, she thought, still using her half-formulated idea to stamp the immediate scene. And if this love-making differs from the old, still it has its charm; it was "love," different from the old love, perhaps, but worse, was it? Anyhow, she thought, they are aware of each other; they live in each other; what else is love, she asked, listening to their laughter.

". . . Can you never act for yourself?" he was saying. "Can you never even choose stockings for yourself?"

"Never! Never!" Sara was laughing.

". . . Because you have no life of your own," he said. "She lives in dreams," he added, turning to Eleanor, "alone."

"The professor preaching his little sermon," Sara sneered, laying her hand on his knee.

"Sara singing her little song," Nicholas laughed, pressing her hand.

But they are very happy, Eleanor thought. They laugh at each other.

"Tell me, Nicholas . . ." she began again. But another dance was beginning. Couples came flocking back into the room. Slowly, intently, with serious faces, as if they were taking part in some mystic rite which gave them immunity from other feelings, the dancers began circling past them, brushing against their knees, almost treading on their toes. And then someone stopped in front of them.

"Oh, here's North," said Eleanor, looking up.

"North!" Nicholas exclaimed. "North! We met this evening," he stretched out his hand to North, "—at Eleanor's."

"We did," said North warmly. Nicholas crushed his fingers; he felt them separate again when the hand was removed. It was effusive; but he liked it. He was feeling effusive himself. His eyes shone. He had lost his puzzled look completely. His adventure had turned out well. The girl had written her name in his pocket-book. "Come and see me tomorrow at six," she had said.

"Good-evening again, Eleanor," he said, bowing over her hand. "You're looking very young. You're looking extraordinarily handsome. I like you in those clothes," he said, looking at her Indian cloak.

"The same to you, North," she said. She looked up at him. She thought she had never seen him look so handsome, so vigorous.

"Aren't you going to dance?" she asked. The music was in full swing.

"Not unless Sally will honour me," he said, bowing to her with exaggerated courtesy. What has happened to him? Eleanor thought. He looks so handsome, so happy. Sally rose. She gave her hand to Nicholas.

"I will dance with you," she said. They stood for a moment waiting; and then they circled away.

"WHAT AN odd-looking couple!" North exclaimed. He screwed his face up into a grin as he watched them. "They don't know how to dance!" he added. He sat down by Eleanor in the chair that Nicholas had left empty.

"Why don't they marry?" he asked.

"Why should they?" she said.

"Oh, everybody ought to marry," he said. "And I like him, though he's a bit of a—shall we say 'bounder'?" he suggested, as he watched them circling rather awkwardly in and out.

"'Bounder?'" Eleanor echoed him.

"Oh, it's his fob, you mean," she added, looking at the gold seal which swung up and down as Nicholas danced.

"No, not a bounder," she said aloud. "He's—"

But North was not attending. He was looking at a couple at the further end of the room. They were standing by the fireplace. Both were young; both were silent; they seemed held still in that position by some powerful emotion. As he looked at them, some emotion about himself, about his own life, came over him, and he arranged another background for them or for himself—not the mantelpiece and the bookcase, but cataracts roaring, clouds racing, and they stood on a cliff above a torrent. . . .

"Marriage isn't for everyone," Eleanor interrupted.

He started. "No. Of course not," he agreed. He looked at her. She had never married. Why not? he wondered. Sacrificed to the family, he supposed—old Grandpapa without any fingers. Then some memory came back to him of a terrace, a cigar and William Whatney. Was not that her tragedy, that she had loved him? He looked at her with affection. He felt fond of everyone at the moment.

"What luck to find you alone, Nell!" he said, laying his hand on her knee.

She was touched; the feel of his hand on her knee pleased her.

"Dear North!" she exclaimed. She felt his excitement through her dress; he was like a dog on a leash; straining forward with all his nerves erect, she felt, as he laid his hand on her knee.

"But don't marry the wrong woman!" she said.

"I?" he asked. "What makes you say that?" Had she seen him, he wondered, shepherding the girl downstairs?

"Tell me —" she began. She wanted to ask him, coolly and sensibly, what his plans were, now that they were alone; but as she spoke she saw his face change; an exaggerated expression of horror came over it.

"Milly!" he muttered. "Damn her!"

ELEANOR GLANCED quickly over her shoulder. Her sister Milly, voluminous in draperies proper to her sex and class, was coming towards them. She had grown very stout. In order to disguise her figure, veils with beads on them hung down over her arms. They were so fat that they reminded North of asparagus; pale asparagus tapering to a point.

"Oh, Eleanor!" she exclaimed. For she still kept relics of a younger sister's doglike devotion.

"Oh, Milly!" said Eleanor, but not so cordially.

"How nice to see you, Eleanor!" said Milly, with her little old-woman's chuckle; yet there was something deferential in her manner. "And you too, North!"

She gave him her fat little hand. He noticed how the rings were sunk in her fingers, as if the flesh had grown over them. Flesh grown over diamonds disgusted him.

"How very nice that you're back again!" she said, settling

slowly down into her chair. Everything, he felt, became dulled. She cast a net over them; she made them all feel one family; he had to think of their relations in common; but it was an unreal feeling.

"Yes, we're staying with Connie," she said; they had come up for a cricket match.

He sunk his head. He looked at his shoes.

"And I've not heard a word about your travels, Nell," she went on. They fall and fall, and cover all, he went on, as he listened to the damp falling patter of his aunt's little questions. But he was in such a superfluity of high spirits that he could still make her words jingle. Did the tarantulas bite, she was asking him, and were the stars bright? And where shall I spend tomorrow night? he added, for the card in his waistcoat pocket rayed out of its own accord without regard for the context scenes which obliterated the present moment. They were staying with Connie, she went on, who was expecting Jimmy, who was home from Uganda . . . his mind slipped a few words, for he was seeing a garden, a room, and the next word he heard was "adenoids"—which is a good word, he said to himself, separating it from its context; wasp-waisted; pinched in the middle; with a hard, shining, metallic abdomen, useful to describe the appearance of an insect—but here a vast bulk approached; chiefly white waistcoat, lined with black; and Hugh Gibbs stood over them. North sprang up to offer him his chair.

"My dear boy, you don't expect me to sit on *that?*" said Hugh, deriding the rather spindly seat that North offered him.

"You must find me something—" he looked about him, holding his hands to the sides of his white waistcoat, "more substantial."

North pulled a stuffed seat towards him. He lowered himself cautiously.

"Chew, chew, chew," he said as he sat down.

And Milly said, "Tut-tut-tut," North observed.

That was what it came to—thirty years of being husband
and wife—tut-tut-tut—and chew-chew-chew. It sounded like
the half-inarticulate munchings of animals in a stall. Tut-tut-tut,
and chew-chew-chew—as they trod out the soft steamy straw in
the stable; as they wallowed in the primeval swamp, prolific, pro-
fuse, half-conscious, he thought; listening vaguely to the good-
humoured patter, which suddenly fastened itself upon him.

"What d'you weigh, North?" his uncle was asking, sizing
him up. He looked him up and down as if he were a horse.

"We must get you to fix a date," Milly added, "when the
boys are home."

They were inviting him to stay with them at the Towers in
September for cub-hunting. The men shot, and the women—
he looked at his aunt as if she might be breaking into young
even there, on that chair—the women broke off into innumerable babies. And those babies had other babies; and the other
babies had—adenoids. The word recurred; but it now suggested nothing. He was sinking; he was falling under their
weight; the name in his pocket even was fading. Could nothing
be done about it? he asked himself. Nothing short of revolution,
he thought. The idea of dynamite, exploding dumps of heavy
earth, shooting earth up in a tree-shaped cloud, came to his
mind, from the War. But that's all poppy-cock, he thought; war's
poppy-cock, poppy-cock. Sara's word "poppy-cock" returned.
So what remains? Peggy caught his eye, where she stood talking
to an unknown man. You doctors, he thought, you scientists,
why don't you drop a little crystal into a tumbler, something
starred and sharp, and make them swallow it? Common sense;
reason; starred and sharp. But would they swallow it? He looked
at Hugh. He had a way of blowing his cheeks in and out, as he
said tut-tut-tut and chew-chew-chew. Would you swallow it? he
said silently to Hugh.

Hugh turned to him again.

"And I hope you're going to stay in England now, North," he said, "though I dare say it's a fine life out there?"

And so they turned to Africa and the paucity of jobs. His exhilaration was oozing. The card no longer rayed out pictures. The damp leaves were falling. They fall and fall and cover all, he murmured to himself and looked at his aunt, colourless save for a brown stain on her forehead; and her hair colourless save for a stain like the yolk of egg on it. All over he suspected she must be soft and discoloured like a pear that has gone sleepy. And Hugh himself—his great hand was on his knee—was bound round with raw beef-steak. He caught Eleanor's eye. There was a strained look in it.

"Yes, how they've spoilt it," she was saying.

But the resonance had gone out of her voice.

"Brand new villas everywhere," she was saying. She had been down in Dorsetshire apparently.

"Little red villas all along the road," she went on.

"Yes, that's what strikes me," he said, rousing himself to help her, "how you've spoilt England while I've been away."

"But you won't find many changes in our part of the world, North," said Hugh. He spoke with pride.

"No. But then we're lucky," said Milly. "We have several large estates. We're very lucky," she repeated. "Except for Mr. Phipps," she added. She gave a tart little laugh.

North woke up. She meant that, he thought. She spoke with an acerbity that made her real. Not only did she become real, but the village, the great house, the little house, the church and the circle of old trees also appeared before him in complete reality. He would stay with them.

"That's our parson," Hugh explained. "Quite a good chap in his way; but high—very high. Candles—that sort of thing."

"And his wife . . ." Milly began.

Here Eleanor sighed. North looked at her. She was dropping off to sleep. A glazed look, a fixed expression, had come
over her face. She looked terribly like Milly for a moment; sleep
brought out the family likeness. Then she opened her eyes wide;
by an effort of will she kept them open. But obviously she saw
nothing.

"You must come down and see what you make of us,"
Hugh said. "What about the first week in September, eh?" He
swayed from side to side as if his benevolence rolled about in
him. He was like an old elephant who may be going to kneel.
And if he does kneel, how will he ever get up again, North asked
himself? And if Eleanor falls sound asleep and snores, what am
I going to do, left sitting here between the knees of the elephant?

He looked round for an excuse to go.

There was Maggie coming along, not looking where she
was going. They saw her. He felt a strong desire to cry out,
"Take care! Take care!" for she was in the danger zone. The long
white tentacles that amorphous bodies leave floating so that
they can catch their food, would suck her in. Yes, they saw her:
she was lost.

"HERE'S MAGGIE!" Milly exclaimed, looking up.

"Haven't seen you for an age!" said Hugh, trying to heave
himself up.

She had to stop; to put her hand into that shapeless paw.
Using the last ounce of energy that remained to him, from the
address in his waistcoat pocket, North rose. He would carry her
off. He would save her from the contamination of family life.

But she ignored him. She stood there, answering their greet-
ings with perfect composure as if using an outfit provided for
emergencies. Oh, Lord, North said to himself, she's as bad as

they are. She was glazed; insincere. They were talking about *her*
children now.

"Yes. That's the baby," she was saying, pointing to a boy
who was dancing with a girl.

"And your daughter, Maggie?" Milly asked, looking round.

North fidgeted. This is the conspiracy, he said to himself;
this is the steam roller that smooths, obliterates; rounds into
identity; rolls into balls. He listened. Jimmy was in Uganda; Lily
was in Leicestershire; *my* boy—*my* girl . . . they were saying. But
they're not interested in other people's children, he observed.
Only in their own; their own property; their own flesh and
blood, which they would protect with the unsheathed claws of
the primeval swamp, he thought, looking at Milly's fat little
paws, even Maggie, even she. For she too was talking about my
boy, my girl. How then can we be civilised, he asked himself?

ELEANOR SNORED. She was nodding off, shamelessly, help-
lessly. There was an obscenity in unconsciousness, he thought.
Her mouth was open; her head was on one side.

But now it was his turn. Silence gaped. One has to egg it
on, he thought; somebody has to say something, or human society would cease. Hugh would cease; Milly would cease; and he
was about to apply himself to find something to say, something
with which to feed the immense vacancy of that primeval maw,
when Delia, either from the erratic desire of a hostess always to
interrupt, or divinely inspired by human charity—which he
could not say—came beckoning.

"The Ludbys!" she exclaimed. "The Ludbys!"

"Oh, where? The dear Ludbys!" said Milly, and up they
heaved and off they went, for the Ludbys, it appeared, seldom
left Northumberland.

———

"WELL, MAGGIE?" said North, turning to her—but here
Eleanor made a little click at the back of her throat. Her head
pitched forward. Sleep, now that she slept soundly, had given
her dignity. She looked peaceful, far from them, rapt in the calm
which sometimes gives the sleeper the look of the dead. They
sat silent, for a moment, alone together, in private.

"Why—why—why—" he said at last, making a gesture as
if he were plucking tufts of grass from the carpet.

"Why?" Maggie asked. "Why what?"

"The Gibbses," he murmured. He jerked his head at them,
where they stood talking by the fireplace. Gross, obese, shapeless, they looked to him like a parody, a travesty, an excrescence
that had overgrown the form within, the fire within.

"What's wrong?" he asked. She looked too. But she said
nothing. Couples came dancing slowly past them. A girl
stopped, and her gesture as she raised her hand, unconsciously,
had the seriousness of the very young anticipating life in its
goodness which touched him.

"Why—?" he jerked his thumb in the direction of the
young, "when they're so lovely—"

She too looked at the girl, who was fastening a flower that
had come undone in the front of her frock. She smiled. She said
nothing. Then half consciously she echoed his question without
a meaning in her echo, "Why?"

He was dashed for a moment. It seemed to him that she refused to help him. And he wanted her to help him. Why should
she not take the weight off his shoulders and give him what he
longed for—assurance, certainty? Because she too was deformed like the rest of them? He looked down at her hands.
They were strong hands; fine hands; but if it were a question, he
thought, watching the fingers curl slightly, of "my" children, of
"my" possessions, it would be one rip down the belly; or teeth
in the soft fur of the throat. We cannot help each other, he

thought, we are all deformed. Yet, disagreeable as it was to him to remove her from the eminence upon which he placed her, perhaps she was right, he thought, and we who make idols of other people, who endow this man, that woman, with power to lead us, only add to the deformity, and stoop ourselves.

"I'm going to stay with them," he said aloud.

"At the Towers?" she asked.

"Yes," he said. "For cubbing in September."

She was not listening. Her eyes were on him. She was getting him into relation with something else, he felt. It made him uneasy. She was looking at him as if he were not himself but somebody else. He felt again the discomfort that he had felt when Sally described him on the telephone.

"I know," he said, stiffening the muscles of his face, "I'm like the picture of a Frenchman holding his hat."

"Holding his hat?" she asked.

"And getting fat," he added.

". . . HOLDING A HAT . . . who's holding a hat?" said Eleanor, opening her eyes.

She glanced about her in bewilderment. Since her last recollection, and it seemed only a second ago, was of Milly talking of candles in a church, something must have happened. Milly and Hugh had been there; but they were gone. There had been a gap—a gap filled with the golden light of lolling candles, and some sensation which she could not name.

She woke up completely.

"What nonsense are you talking?" she said. "North's not holding a hat! And he's not fat," she added. "Not at all, not at all," she repeated, patting him affectionately on the knee.

She felt extraordinarily happy. Most sleep left some dream in one's mind—some scene or figure remained when one woke up. But this sleep, this momentary trance, in which the candles had lolled and lengthened themselves, had left her with nothing but a feeling; a feeling, not a dream.

"He's not holding a hat," she repeated.

They both laughed at her.

"You've been dreaming, Eleanor," said Maggie.

"Have I?" she said. A deep gulf had been cut in the talk, it was true. She could not remember what they had been saying. There was Maggie; but Milly and Hugh had gone.

"Only a second's nap," she said. "But what are you going to do, North? What are your plans?" she said, speaking rather quickly.

"We mustn't let him go back, Maggie," she said. "Not to that horrid farm."

She wished to appear extremely practical, partly to prove that she had not slept, partly to protect the extraordinary feeling of happiness that still remained with her. Covered up from observation it might survive, she felt.

"You've saved enough, haven't you?" she said aloud.

"Saved enough?" he said. Why, he wondered, did people who had been asleep always want to make out that they were extremely wide-awake? "Four or five thousand," he added at random.

"Well, that's enough," she insisted. "Five per cent; six per cent—" She tried to do the sum in her head. She appealed to Maggie for help. "Four or five thousand—how much would that be, Maggie? Enough to live on, wouldn't it?"

"Four or five thousand," repeated Maggie.

"At five or six per cent . . ." Eleanor put in. She could never do sums in her head at the best of times; but for some reason it seemed to her very important to bring things back to facts. She opened her bag, found a letter, and produced a stubby little pencil.

"There—work it out on that," she said. Maggie took the

paper and drew a few lines with the pencil as if to test it. North glanced over her shoulder. Was she solving the problem before her—was she considering his life, his needs? No. She was drawing, apparently a caricature—he looked—of a big man opposite in a white waistcoat. It was a farce. It made him feel slightly ridiculous.

"Don't be so silly," he said.

"That's my brother," she said, nodding at the man in the white waistcoat. "He used to take us for rides on an elephant...." She added a flourish to the waistcoat.

"And we're being very sensible," Eleanor protested.

"If you want to live in England, North—if you want—"

He cut her short.

"I don't know what I want," he said.

"Oh, I see!" she said. She laughed. Her feeling of happiness returned to her, her unreasonable exaltation. It seemed to her that they were all young, with the future before them. Nothing was fixed; nothing was known; life was open and free before them.

"Isn't that odd?" she exclaimed. "Isn't that queer? Isn't that why life's a perpetual—what shall I call it?—miracle? ... I mean," she tried to explain, for he looked puzzled, "old age they say is like this; but it isn't. It's different; quite different. So when I was a child; so when I was a girl; it's been a perpetual discovery, my life. A miracle." She stopped. She was rambling on again. She felt rather light-headed, after her dream.

"There's Peggy!" she exclaimed, glad to attach herself to something solid. "Look at her! Reading a book!"

PEGGY, marooned when the dance started, over by the bookcase, stood as close to it as she could. In order to cover her loneliness she took down a book. It was bound in green leather; and had, she noted as she turned it in her hands, little gilt stars tooled upon it. Which is all to the good, she thought, turning it over, because then it'll seem as if I were admiring the binding. . . . But I can't stand here admiring the binding, she thought. She opened it. He'll say what I'm thinking, she thought as she did so. Books opened at random always did.

"La médiocrité de l'univers m'étonne et me révolte," she read. That was it. Precisely. She read on. *". . . la petitesse de toutes choses m'emplit de dégoût . . ."* She lifted her eyes. They were treading on her toes. *". . . la pauvreté des êtres humains m'anéantit."* She shut the book and put it back on the shelf.

Precisely, she said.

She turned her watch on her wrist and looked at it surreptitiously. Time was getting on. An hour is sixty minutes, she said to herself; two hours are one hundred and twenty minutes. How many have I still to stay here? Could she go yet? She saw Eleanor beckoning. She put the book back on the shelf. She went towards them.

"COME, PEGGY, come and talk to us," Eleanor called out, beckoning.

"D'you know what time it is, Eleanor?" said Peggy, coming up to them. She pointed to her watch. "Don't you think it's time to be going?" she said.

"I'd forgotten the time," said Eleanor.

"But you'll be so tired tomorrow," Peggy protested, standing beside her.

"How like a doctor!" North twitted her. "Health, health, health!" he exclaimed. "But health's not an end in itself," he said, looking up at her.

She ignored him.

"D'you mean to stay to the end?" she said to Eleanor. "This'll go on all night." She looked at the twisting couples gyrating in time to the tune on the gramophone, as if some animal were dying in a slow but exquisite anguish.

"But we're enjoying ourselves," said Eleanor. "Come and enjoy yourself too."

She pointed to the floor at her side. Peggy let herself down onto the floor at her side. Give up brooding, thinking, analysing, Eleanor meant, she knew. Enjoy the moment—but could one? she asked, pulling her skirts round her feet as she sat down. Eleanor bent over and tapped her on the shoulder.

"I want you to tell me," she said, drawing her into the conversation, since she looked so glum, "you're a doctor—you know these things—what do dreams mean?"

Peggy laughed. Another of Eleanor's questions. Does two and two make four—and what is the nature of the universe?

"I don't mean dreams exactly," Eleanor went on. "Feelings—feelings that come when one's asleep?"

"My dear Nell," said Peggy, glancing up at her, "how often have I told you? Doctors know very little about the body; absolutely nothing about the mind." She looked down again.

"I always said they were humbugs!" North exclaimed.

"What a pity!" said Eleanor. "I was hoping you'd be able to explain to me—" She was bending down. There was a flush on her cheek, Peggy noted; she was excited; but what was there to be excited about?

"Explain—what?" she asked.

"Oh, nothing," said Eleanor. Now I've snubbed her, Peggy thought.

She looked at her again. Her eyes were bright; her cheeks were flushed, or was it only the tan from her voyage to India? And a little vein stood out on her forehead. But what was there to be excited about? She leant back against the wall. From her seat on the floor she had a queer view of people's feet; feet pointing this way, feet pointing that way; patent leather pumps; satin slippers, silk stockings and socks. They were dancing rhythmically, insistently, to the tune of the fox-trot. And what about the cocktail and the tea, said he to me, said he to me — the tune seemed to repeat over and over again. And voices went on over her head. Odd little gusts of inconsecutive conversations reached her . . . down in Norfolk where my brother-in-law has a boat . . . Oh, a complete washout, yes, I agree. . . . People talked nonsense at parties. And beside her Maggie was talking; North was talking; Eleanor was talking. Suddenly Eleanor swept her hand out.

"There's Renny!" she was saying. "Renny, whom I never see. Renny, whom I love. . . . Come and talk to us, Renny." And a pair of pumps crossed Peggy's field of vision and stopped in front of her. He sat down beside Eleanor. She could just see the line of his profile; the big nose; the thin cheek. And what about the cocktails and the tea, said he to me, said he to me, the music ground out; the couples danced past. But the little group on the chairs above her were talking; they were laughing.

"I know you'll agree with me . . ." Eleanor was saying. Through her half-shut eyes Peggy could see Renny turn towards her. She saw his thin cheek; his big nose; his nails, she noticed, were very close cut.

"Depends what you were saying . . ." he said.

"What were we saying?" Eleanor pondered. She's forgotten already, Peggy suspected.

". . . That things have changed for the better," she heard Eleanor's voice.

"Since you were a girl?" That, she thought, was Maggie's voice.

Then a voice from a skirt with a pink bow on the hem interrupted. ". . . I don't know how it is but the heat doesn't affect

me as much as it used to do. . . ." She looked up. There were fifteen pink bows on the dress, accurately stitched, and wasn't that
Miriam Parrish's little saint-like, sheep-like head on top?

"What I mean is, we've changed in ourselves," Eleanor was
saying. "We're happier—we're freer. . . ."

What does she mean by "happiness," by "freedom," Peggy
asked herself, lapsing against the wall again.

"Take Renny and Maggie," she heard Eleanor saying. And
then she stopped. And then she went on again:

"D'you remember, Renny, the night of the raid? When I
met Nicholas for the first time . . . when we sat in the cellar? . . .
Going downstairs I said to myself, That's a happy marriage. . . ."
There was another pause. "I said to myself," she continued, and
Peggy saw her hand laid on Renny's knee, "If I'd known Renny
when I was young . . ." She stopped. Does she mean she would
have fallen in love with him? Peggy wondered. Again the music
interrupted . . . said he to me, said he to me. . . .

"No, never . . ." she heard Eleanor say. "No, never. . . ." Was
she saying she had never been in love, never wanted to marry?
Peggy wondered. They were laughing.

"Why, you look like a girl of eighteen!" she heard North say.

"And I feel like one!" Eleanor exclaimed. But you'll be a
wreck tomorrow morning, Peggy thought, looking at her. She
was flushed, the veins stood out on her forehead.

"I feel . . ." she stopped. She put her hand to her head: "as
if I'd been in another world! So happy!" she exclaimed.

"Tosh, Eleanor, tosh," said Renny.

I thought he'd say that, Peggy said to herself with some
queer satisfaction. She could see his profile as he sat on the
other side of her aunt's knee. The French are logical; they are
sensible, she thought. Still, she added, why not let Eleanor have
her little flutter if she enjoys it?

"Tosh? What d'you mean by 'tosh'?" Eleanor was asking. She was leaning forward; she held her hand up as if she wanted him to speak.

"Always talking of the other world," he said. "Why not this one?"

"But I meant this world!" she said. "I meant, happy in this world—happy with living people." She waved her hand as if to embrace the miscellaneous company, the young, the old, the dancers, the talkers; Miriam with her pink bows, and the Indian in his turban. Peggy sank back against the wall. Happy in this world, she thought, happy with living people!

The music stopped. The young man who had been putting records on the gramophone had walked off. The couples broke apart and began to push their way through the door. They were going to eat perhaps; they were going to stream out into the back garden and sit on hard sooty chairs. The music which had been cutting grooves in her mind had ceased. There was a lull— a silence. Far away she heard the sounds of the London night; a horn hooted; a siren wailed on the river. The far-away sounds, the suggestion they brought in of other worlds, indifferent to this world, of people toiling, grinding, in the heart of darkness, in the depths of night, made her say over Eleanor's words, Happy in this world, happy with living people. But how can one be "happy," she asked herself, in a world bursting with misery? On every placard at every street corner was Death; or worse— tyranny; brutality; torture; the fall of civilisation; the end of freedom. We here, she thought, are only sheltering under a leaf, which will be destroyed. And then Eleanor says the world is better, because two people out of all those millions are "happy." Her eyes had fixed themselves on the floor; it was empty now save for a wisp of muslin torn from some skirt. But why do I notice everything? she thought. She shifted her position. Why must I think? She did not want to think. She wished that there were blinds like those in railway carriages that came down over the light and hooded the mind. The blue blind that one pulls down on a night journey, she thought. Thinking was torment; why not give up thinking, and drift and dream? But the misery of the world, she thought, forces me to think. Or was that a pose? Was she not seeing herself in the becoming attitude of one who points to his bleeding heart? to whom the miseries of the world are misery, when in fact, she thought, I do not love my kind. Again she saw the ruby-splashed pavement, and faces mobbed at the door of a picture palace; apathetic, passive faces; the faces of people drugged with cheap pleasures; who had not even the courage to be themselves, but must dress up, imitate, pretend. And here, in this room, she thought, fixing her eyes on a couple. . . . But I will not think, she repeated; she would force her mind to become a blank and lie back, and accept quietly, tolerantly, whatever came.

She listened. Scraps reached her from above. ". . . flats in Highgate have bathrooms," they were saying. ". . . Your mother . . . Digby. . . . Yes, Crosby's still alive. . . ." It was family gossip, and they were enjoying it. But how can I enjoy it? she said to herself. She was too tired; the skin round her eyes felt taut; a hoop was bound tight over her head; she tried to think herself away into the darkness of the country. But it was impossible; they were laughing. She opened her eyes, exacerbated by their laughter.

That was Renny laughing. He held a sheet of paper in his hand; his head was flung back; his mouth was wide open. From it came a sound like Ha! Ha! Ha! That is laughter, she said to herself. That is the sound people make when they are amused.

She watched him. Her muscles began to twitch involuntarily. She could not help laughing too. She stretched out her hand and Renny gave her the paper. It was folded; they had been playing a game. Each of them had drawn a different part

of a picture. On top there was a woman's head like Queen
Alexandra, with a fuzz of little curls; then a bird's neck; the body
of a tiger; and stout elephant's legs dressed in child's drawers
completed the picture.

"I drew that—I drew that!" said Renny, pointing to the legs
from which a long trail of ribbon depended. She laughed,
laughed, laughed; she could not help laughing.

"The face that launched a thousand ships!" said North,
pointing to another part of the monster's person. They all
laughed again. She stopped laughing; her lips smoothed themselves out. But her laughter had had some strange effect on her.
It had relaxed her, enlarged her. She felt, or rather she saw, not
a place, but a state of being, in which there was real laughter,
real happiness, and this fractured world was whole; whole, vast,
and free. But how could she say it?

"Look here . . ." she began. She wanted to express something that she felt to be very important; about a world in which
people were whole, in which people were free . . . But they were
laughing; she was serious. "Look here . . ." she began again.

Eleanor stopped laughing.

"Peggy wants to say something," she said. The others
stopped talking, but they had stopped at the wrong moment.
She had nothing to say when it came to the point, and yet she
had to speak.

"Here," she began again, "here you all are—talking about
North—" He looked up at her in surprise. It was not what she
had meant to say, but she must go on, now that she had begun.
Their faces gaped at her like birds with their mouths open.
". . . How he's to live, where he's to live," she went on. ". . . But
what's the use, what's the point of saying that?"

She looked at her brother. A feeling of animosity possessed
her. He was still smiling, but his smile smoothed itself out as she
looked at him.

"What's the use?" she said, facing him. "You'll marry. You'll have children. What'll you do then? Make money. Write little books to make money. . . ."

She had got it wrong. She had meant to say something impersonal, but she was being personal. It was done now however; she must flounder on now.

"You'll write one little book, and then another little book," she said viciously, "instead of living . . . living differently, differently."

She stopped. There was the vision still, but she had not grasped it. She had broken off only a little fragment of what she meant to say, and she had made her brother angry. Yet there it hung before her, the thing she had seen, the thing she had not said. But as she fell back with a jerk against the wall, she felt relieved of some oppression; her heart thumped; the veins on her forehead stood out. She had not said it, but she had tried to say it. Now she could rest; now she could think herself away under the shadow of their ridicule, which had no power to hurt her, into the country. Her eyes half shut; it seemed to her that she was on a terrace, in the evening; an owl went up and down, up and down; its white wing showed on the dark of the hedge; and she heard country people singing and the rattle of wheels on a road.

Then gradually the blur became distinct; she saw the line of the bookcase opposite; the wisp of muslin on the floor; and two large feet, in tight shoes, so that the bunions showed, stopped in front of her.

FOR A MOMENT nobody moved; nobody spoke. Peggy sat still. She did not want to move, or to speak. She wanted to rest, to lean, to dream. She felt very tired. Then more feet stopped, and the hem of a black skirt.

"Aren't you people coming down to supper?" said a chuckling

little voice. She looked up. It was her aunt Milly, with her husband by her side.

"Supper's downstairs," said Hugh. "Supper's downstairs." And they passed on.

"How prosperous they've grown!" said North's voice, laughing at them.

"Ah, but they're so good to people . . ." Eleanor protested. The sense of the family again, Peggy noted.

Then the knee against which she was sheltering herself moved.

"We must go," said Eleanor. Wait, wait, Peggy wanted to implore her. There was something she wanted to ask her; something she wanted to add to her outburst, since nobody had attacked her, and nobody had laughed at her. But it was useless; the knees straightened themselves; the red cloak elongated itself; Eleanor had risen. She was hunting for her bag or her handkerchief; she was ferreting in the cushions of her chair. As usual, she had lost something.

"I'm sorry to be such an old muddler," she apologised. She shook a cushion; coins rolled out onto the floor. A sixpenny bit spun on its edge across the carpet, reached a pair of silver shoes on the floor, and fell flat.

"There!" Eleanor exclaimed. "There! . . . But that's Kitty! isn't it?" she exclaimed.

Peggy looked up. A handsome elderly woman, with curled white hair and something shining in her hair was standing in the doorway looking round her, as if she had just come in and were looking for her hostess, who was not there. It was at her feet that the sixpence had fallen.

"Kitty!" Eleanor repeated. She went towards her with her hands stretched out. They all got up. Peggy got up. Yes, it was over; it was destroyed, she felt. Directly something got together, it broke. She had a feeling of desolation. And then you have to pick up the pieces, and make something new, something different, she thought, and crossed the room, and joined the foreigner, the man she called Brown, whose real name was Nicholas Pomjalovsky.

"WHO IS THAT LADY," Nicholas asked her, "who appears to come into a room as if the whole world belonged to her?"

"That's Kitty Lasswade," said Peggy. As she stood in the door, they could not pass.

"I'm afraid I'm dreadfully late," they heard her saying in her clear, authoritative tones. "But I've been to the ballet."

That's Kitty, is it? North said to himself, looking at her. She was one of those well-set-up rather masculine old ladies who repelled him slightly. He thought he remembered that she was the wife of one of our governors; or was it the Viceroy of India? He could see her, as she stood there, doing the honours of Government House. "Sit here. Sit there. And you, young man, I hope you take plenty of exercise?" He knew the type. She had a short straight nose and blue eyes very wide apart. She might have looked very dashing in the eighties, he thought; in a tight riding-habit; worn a small hat, with a cock's feather in it; perhaps had an affair with an aide-de-camp; and then settled down, become dictatorial, and told stories about her past. He listened.

"Ah, but he's not a patch on Nijinsky!" she was saying.

The sort of thing she would say, he thought. He examined the books in the bookcase. He took one out and held it upside down. One little book, and then another little book—Peggy's taunt returned to him. The words had stung him out of all proportion to their surface meaning. She had turned on him with such violence, as if she despised him; she had looked as if she were going to burst into tears. He opened the little book. Latin, was it? He broke off a sentence and let it swim in his mind. There the words lay, beautiful, yet meaningless, yet composed in a pattern—*nox est perpetua una dormienda.* He remembered his master saying, Mark the long word at the end of the sentence. There the words floated; but just as they were about to give out their meaning, there was a movement at the door. Old Patrick had come ambling up, had given his arm gallantly to the widow of the Governor-General, and they were proceeding with a curious air of antiquated ceremony down the stairs. The others began to follow them. The younger generation following in the wake of the old, North said to himself as he put the book back on the shelf and followed. Only, he observed, they were not so very young; Peggy—there were white hairs on Peggy's head— she must be thirty-seven, thirty-eight?

"Enjoying yourself, Peg?" he said as they hung back behind the others. He had a vague feeling of hostility towards her. She seemed to him bitter, disillusioned, and very critical of everyone, especially of himself.

"You go first, Patrick," they heard Lady Lasswade boom out in her genial loud voice. "These staircases are not adapted . . ." she paused, as she advanced what was probably a rheumatic leg, "for old people who . . ." there was another pause as she descended another step, " 've been kneeling on damp grass killing slugs."

North looked at Peggy and laughed. He had not expected the sentence to end like that, but the widows of viceroys, he thought, always have gardens, always kill slugs. Peggy smiled too. But he felt uncomfortable with her. She had attacked him. There they stood, however, side by side.

"Did you see old William Whatney?" she said, turning to him.

"No!" he exclaimed. "*He* still alive? That old white walrus with the whiskers?"

"Yes—that's him," she said. There was an old man in a white waistcoat standing in the door.

"The old Mock Turtle," he said. They had to fall back on childish slang, on childish memories, to cover their distance, their hostility.

"D'you remember . . ." he began.

"The night of the row?" she said. "The night I let myself out of the window by a rope."

"And we picnicked in the Roman camp," he said.

"We should never have been found out if that horrid little scamp hadn't told on us," she said, descending a step.

"A little beast with pink eyes," said North.

They could think of nothing else to say, as they stood blocked, waiting for the others to move on, side by side. And he used to read her his poetry in the apple-loft, he remembered, and as they walked up and down by the rose bushes. And now they had nothing to say to each other.

"Perry," he said, descending another step, suddenly remembering the name of the pink-eyed boy who had seen them coming home that morning and had told on them.

"Alfred," she added.

She still knew certain things about him, he thought; they still had something very profound in common. That was why, he thought, she had hurt him by what she had said, before the others, about his "writing little books." It was their past condemning his present. He glanced at her.

Damn women, he thought, they're so hard; so unimaginative. Curse their little inquisitive minds. What did their "education" amount to? It only made her critical, censorious. Old Eleanor, with all her rambling and stumbling, was worth a dozen of Peggy any day. She was neither one thing nor the other, he thought, glancing at her; neither in the fashion nor out of it.

She felt him look at her and look away. He was finding fault
with something about her, she knew. Her hands? Her dress? No,
it was because she criticised him, she thought. Yes, she thought
as she descended another step, now I'm going to be trounced;
now I'm going to be paid back for telling him he'd write "little
books." It takes from ten to fifteen minutes, she thought, to get
an answer; and then it'll be something off the point but disagreeable—very, she thought. The vanity of men was immea-
surable. She waited. He looked at her again. And now he's
comparing me with the girl I saw him talking to, she thought,
and saw again the lovely, hard face. He'll tie himself up with a
red-lipped girl, and become a drudge. He must, and I can't, she
thought. No, I've a sense of guilt always. I shall pay for it, I shall
pay for it, I kept saying to myself even in the Roman camp, she
thought. She would have no children, and he would produce
little Gibbses, more little Gibbses, she thought, looking in at the
door of a solicitor's office, unless she leaves him at the end of
the year for some other man. . . . The solicitor's name was Al-
ridge, she noted. But I will take no more notes; I will enjoy myself, she thought suddenly. She put her hand on his arm.

"Met anybody amusing tonight?" she said.

He guessed that she had seen him with the girl.

"One girl," he said briefly.

"So I saw," she said.

She looked away.

"I thought her lovely," she said, carefully observing a tinted
picture of a bird with a long beak that hung on the stairs.

"Shall I bring her to see you?" he asked.

So he cared for her opinion, did he? Her hand was still on
his arm; she felt something hard and taut beneath the sleeve,
and the touch of his flesh, bringing back to her the nearness of
human beings and their distance, so that if one meant to help
one hurt, yet they depended on each other, produced in her

such a tumult of sensation that she could scarcely keep herself from crying out, North! North! North! But I mustn't make a fool of myself again, she said to herself.

"Any evening after six," she said aloud, carefully descending another step, and they reached the bottom of the stairs.

A roar of voices sounded from behind the door of the supper room. She withdrew her hand from his arm. The door burst open.

"SPOONS! spoons! spoons!" cried Delia, brandishing her arms in a rhetorical manner as if she were still declaiming to someone inside. She caught sight of her nephew and niece. "Be an angel, North, and fetch spoons!" she cried, throwing her hands out towards him.

"Spoons for the widow of the Governor-General!" North cried, catching her manner, imitating her dramatic gesture.

"In the kitchen, in the basement!" Delia cried, waving her arm at the kitchen stairs. "Come, Peggy, come," she said, catching Peggy's hand in hers, "we're all sitting down to supper." She burst into the room where they were having supper. It was crowded. People were sitting on the floor, on chairs, on office stools. Long office tables, little typewriting tables, had been pressed into use. They were strewn with flowers, frilled with flowers. Carnations, roses, daisies, were flung down higgledy-piggledy. "Sit on the floor, sit anywhere," Delia commanded, waving her hand promiscuously.

"Spoons are coming," she said to Lady Lasswade, who was drinking her soup out of a mug.

"But I don't want a spoon," said Kitty. She tilted the mug and drank.

"No, you wouldn't," said Delia, "but other people do."

North brought in a bunch of spoons and she took them from him.

"Now who wants a spoon and who doesn't?" she said, brandishing the bunch of spoons in front of her. Some people do and some don't, she thought.

Her sort of people, she thought, did not want spoons; the others—the English—did. She had been making that distinction between people all her life.

"A spoon? A spoon?" she said, looking round her at the crowded room with some complacency. All sorts of people were there, she noted. That had always been her aim; to mix people; to do away with the absurd conventions of English life. And she had done it tonight, she thought. There were nobles and commoners; people dressed and people not dressed; people drinking out of mugs, and people waiting with their soup getting cold for a spoon to be brought to them.

"A spoon for me," said her husband, looking up at her.

She wrinkled her nose. For the thousandth time he had dashed her dream. Thinking to marry a wild rebel, she had married the most King-respecting, Empire-admiring of country gentlemen, and for that very reason partly—because he was, even now, such a magnificent figure of a man. "A spoon for your Uncle," she said dryly, and sent North off with the bunch. Then she sat down beside Kitty, who was gulping her soup like a child at a school treat. She set down her mug empty, among the flowers.

"Poor flowers," she said, taking up a carnation that lay on the table-cloth and putting it to her lips. "They'll die, Delia— they want water."

"Roses are cheap today," said Delia. "Twopence a bunch off a barrow in Oxford Street," she said. She took up a red rose and held it under the light, so that it shone, veined, semi-transparent.

"What a rich country England is!" she said, laying it down again. She took up her mug.

"What I'm always telling you," said Patrick, wiping his

mouth. "The only civilised country in the whole world," he added.

"I thought we were on the verge of a smash," said Kitty. "Not that it looked much like it at Covent Garden tonight," she added.

"Ah, but it's true," he sighed, going on with his own thoughts. "I'm sorry to say it—but we're savages compared with you."

"He won't be happy till he's got Dublin Castle back again," Delia twitted him.

"You don't enjoy your freedom?" said Kitty, looking at the queer old man whose face always made her think of a hairy gooseberry. But his body was magnificent.

"It seems to me that our new freedom is a good deal worse than our old slavery," said Patrick, fumbling with his toothpick.

Politics as usual, money and politics, North thought, over-hearing them, as he went round with the last of his spoons.

"You're not going to tell me that all that struggle has been in vain, Patrick?" said Kitty.

"Come to Ireland and see for yourself, m'lady," he said grimly.

"It's too early—too early to tell," said Delia.

Her husband looked past her with the sad innocent eyes of an old sporting dog whose hunting days are over. But they could not keep their fixity for long. "Who's this chap with the spoons?" he said, resting his eyes on North, who stood just behind them, waiting.

"North," said Delia. "Come and sit by us, North."

"Good-evening to you, Sir," said Patrick. They had met already, but he had already forgotten.

"What, Morris's son?" said Kitty, turning round abruptly. She shook hands cordially. He sat down and took a gulp of soup.

"He's just back from Africa. He's been on a farm there," said Delia.

"And how does the old country strike you?" said Patrick, leaning towards him genially.

"Very crowded," he said, looking round the room. "And you all talk," he added, "about money and politics." That was his stock phrase. He had said it twenty times already.

"You were in Africa?" said Lady Lasswade. "And what made you give up your farm?" she demanded. She looked him in the eyes and spoke just as he expected she would speak: too imperiously for his liking. What business is that of yours, old lady? he asked himself.

"I'd had about enough of it," he said aloud.

"And I'd have given anything to be a farmer!" she exclaimed. That was a little out of the picture, North thought. So were her eyes; she ought to have worn a pince-nez; but she did not.

"But in my youth," she said, rather fiercely—her hands were rather stubby, and the skin was rough, but she gardened, he remembered—"that wasn't allowed."

"No," said Patrick. "And it's my belief," he continued, drumming on the table with a fork, "that we should all be very glad, very glad, to go back to things as they were. What's the War done for us, eh? Ruined me for one." He wagged his head with melancholy tolerance from side to side.

"I'm sorry to hear that," said Kitty. "But speaking for myself, the old days were bad days, wicked days, cruel days. . . ." Her eyes turned blue with passion.

What about the aide-de-camp, and the hat with a cock's feather in it? North asked himself.

"Don't you agree with me, Delia?" said Kitty, turning to her.

But Delia was talking across her, using her rather exaggerated Irish sing-song to someone at the next table. Don't I re-

member this room, Kitty thought; a meeting; an argument. But
what was it about? Force . . .

"My dear Kitty," Patrick interrupted, patting her hand with
his great paw. "That's another instance of what I'm telling you.
Now these ladies have got the vote," he said, turning to North,
"are they any better off?"

Kitty looked fierce for a moment; then she smiled.

"We won't argue, my old friend," she said, giving him a little
pat on the hand.

"And it's just the same with the Irish," he went on. North
saw that he was bent on treading out the round of his familiar
thoughts like an old broken-winded horse. "They'd be glad
enough to join the Empire again, I assure you. I come of a family," he said to North, "that has served its king and country for
three hundred—"

"English settlers," said Delia, rather shortly, returning to her
soup. That's what they quarrel about when they're alone, North
thought.

"We've been three hundred years in the country," old
Patrick continued, padding out his round—he laid a hand on
North's arm, "and what strikes an old fellow like me, an old
fogy like me—"

"Nonsense, Patrick," Delia struck in, "I've never seen you
look younger. Might be fifty, mightn't he, North?"

But Patrick shook his head.

"I shan't see seventy again," he said simply. ". . . But what
strikes an old fellow like me," he continued, patting North's
arm, "is with such a lot of good feeling about," he nodded
rather vaguely at a placard that was pinned to the wall—"and
nice things too,"—he referred perhaps to the flowers, but his
head jerked involuntarily as he talked—"what do these fellows
want to be shooting each other for? I don't join any societies; I
don't sign any of these"—he pointed to the placard—"what

d'you call 'em? manifestoes—I just go to my friend Mike, or it
may be Pat—they're all good friends of mine, and we—"

He stooped and pinched his foot.

"Lord, these shoes!" he complained.

"Tight, are they?" said Kitty. "Kick 'em off."

Why had the poor old boy been brought over here, North
wondered, and stuck into those tight shoes? He was clearly talking to his dogs. There was a look in his eyes now when he raised
them again and tried to recover the drift of what he had been
saying that was like the look of a sportsman who saw the birds
rising in a semicircle over the wide green bog. But they were out
of shot. He could not remember where he had got to. ". . . We
talk things over," he said, "round a table." His eyes became mild
and vacant as if the engine were cut off, and his mind glided on
silently.

"The English talk too," said North perfunctorily. Patrick
nodded, and looked vaguely at a group of young people. But he
was not interested in what other people were saying. His mind
could no longer stretch beyond its beat. His body was still
beautifully proportioned; it was his mind that was old. He
would say the same thing all over again, and when he had said
it, he would pick his teeth and sit gazing in front of him. There
he sat now, holding a flower between his finger and thumb,
loosely, without looking at it, as if his mind were gliding on. . . .
But Delia interrupted.

"North must go and talk to his friends," she said. Like so
many wives, she saw when her husband was becoming a bore,
North thought, as he got up.

"Don't wait to be introduced," said Delia, waving her hand.
"Do just what you like—just what you like," her husband
echoed her, beating on the table with his flower.

———

NORTH WAS glad to go; but where was he to go now? He was
an outsider, he felt again, as he glanced round the room. All
these people knew each other. They called each other—he
stood on the outskirts of a little group of young men and
women—by their Christian names, by their nicknames. Each
was already part of a little group, he felt as he listened, keeping
on the outskirts. He wanted to hear what they were saying; but
not to be drawn in himself. He listened. They were arguing.
Politics and money, he said to himself; money and politics. That
phrase came in handy. But he could not understand the argument, which was already heated. Never have I felt so lonely, he
thought. The old platitude about solitude in a crowd was true;
for hills and trees accept one; human beings reject one. He
turned his back and pretended to read the particulars of a desirable property at Bexhill which Patrick had called for some
reason "a manifesto." "Running water in all the bedrooms," he
read. He overheard scraps of talk. That's Oxford, that's Harrow, he continued, recognising the tricks of speech that were
caught at school and college. It seemed to him that they were
still cutting little private jokes about Jones minor winning the
long jump; and old Foxy, or whatever the headmaster's name
was. It was like hearing small boys at a private school, hearing
these young men talk politics. "I'm right . . . you're wrong." At
their age, he thought, he had been in the trenches; he had seen
men killed. But was that a good education? He shifted from
one foot to another. At their age, he thought, he had been
alone on a farm sixty miles from a white man, in control of a
herd of sheep. But was that a good education? Anyhow it
seemed to him, half hearing their argument, looking at their
gestures, catching their slang, that they were all the same sort.
Public school and university, he sized them up as he looked over
his shoulder. But where are the Sweeps and the Sewer-men, the

Seamstresses and the Stevedores? he thought, making a list of trades that began with the letter S. For all Delia's pride in her promiscuity, he thought, glancing at the people, there were only Dons and Duchesses, and what other words begin with D? he asked himself, as he scrutinised the placard again—Drabs and Drones?

He turned. A nice fresh-faced boy with a freckled nose in ordinary day clothes was looking at him. If he didn't take care he would be drawn in too. Nothing would be easier than to join a society, to sign what Patrick called "a manifesto." But he did not believe in joining societies, in signing manifestoes. He turned back to the desirable residence with its three-quarters of an acre of garden and running water in all the bedrooms. People met, he thought, pretending to read, in hired halls. And one of them stood on a platform. There was the pump-handle gesture; the wringing-wet-clothes gesture; and then the voice, oddly detached from the little figure and tremendously magnified by the loudspeaker, went booming and bawling round the hall: Justice! Liberty! For a moment, of course, sitting among knees, wedged in tight, a ripple, a nice emotional quiver, went over the skin; but next morning, he said to himself as he glanced again at the house-agents' placard, there's not an idea, not a phrase that would feed a sparrow. What do they mean by Justice and Liberty? he asked, all these nice young men with two or three hundred a year. Something's wrong, he thought; there's a gap, a dislocation, between the word and the reality. If they want to reform the world, he thought, why not begin there, at the centre, with themselves? He turned on his heel and ran straight into an old man in a white waistcoat.

"Hullo!" he said, holding out his hand.

IT WAS his Uncle Edward. He had the look of an insect whose body has been eaten out, leaving only the wings, the shell.

"Very glad to see you back, North," said Edward, and shook him warmly by the hand.

"Very glad," he repeated. He was shy. He was spare and thin. He looked as if his face had been carved and graved by a multitude of fine instruments; as if it had been left out on a frosty night and frozen over. He threw his head back like a horse champing a bit; but he was an old horse, a blue-eyed horse whose bit no longer irked him. His movements were from habit, not from feeling. What had he been doing all these years? North wondered, as they stood there surveying each other. Editing Sophocles? What would happen if Sophocles one of these days were edited? What would they do then, these eaten-out, hollow-shelled old men?

"You've filled out," said Edward, looking him up and down. "You've filled out," he repeated.

There was a subtle deference in his manner. Edward, the scholar, paid tribute to North, the soldier. Yes, but they found it difficult to talk. He had the air of being stamped, North thought; he had kept something, after all, out of the hubbub.

"Shan't we sit down?" said Edward, as if he wished to talk to him seriously about interesting things. They looked about for a quiet place. He had not frittered his time away talking to old red setters and raising his gun, North thought, glancing about him, to see if by chance there was a quiet place in the room where they could sit down and talk. But there were only two office stools empty beside Eleanor over there in the corner.

She saw them and called out, "Oh, there's Edward! I know there was something I wanted to ask . . ." she began.

It was a relief that the interview with the headmaster should be broken up by this impulsive, foolish old woman. She was holding out her pocket-handkerchief.

"I made a knot," she was saying. Yes, there it was, a knot in her pocket-handkerchief.

"Now what did I make a knot for?" she said, looking up.

"It is an admirable habit to make a knot," said Edward in his courteous, clipped way, lowering himself a little stiffly onto the chair beside her. "But at the same time it is advisable . . ." He stopped. That's what I like about him, North thought, taking the other chair: he left half his sentence unfinished.

"It was to remind me—" said Eleanor, putting her hand to her thick crop of white hair. Then she stopped. What is it that makes him look so calm, so carved, North thought, stealing a look at Edward, who waited with admirable serenity for his sister to remember why she had made a knot in her handkerchief. There was something final about him; he left half his sentences unfinished. He hadn't worried himself about politics and money, he thought. There was something sealed up, stated, about him. Poetry and the past, was it? But as he fixed his eyes upon him, Edward smiled at his sister.

"Well, Nell?" he said.

It was a quiet smile, a tolerant smile.

North broke in, for Eleanor was still ruminating over her knot. "I met a man at the Cape who was a tremendous admirer of yours, Uncle Edward," he said. The name came back to him—"Arbuthnot," he said.

"R. K.?" said Edward. And he raised his hand to his head and smiled. It pleased him, that compliment. He was vain; he was touchy; he was—North stole a glance to add another impression—established. Glazed over with the smooth glossy varnish that those in authority wear. For he was now—what? North could not remember. A professor? A master? Somebody who had an attitude fixed on him, from which he could not relax any longer. Still, Arbuthnot, R. K., had said, with emotion, that he owed more to Edward than to any man.

"He said he owed more to you than to any man," he said aloud.

Edward brushed aside the compliment; but it pleased him. He had a way of putting his hand to his head that North remembered. And Eleanor called him "Nigs." She laughed at him; she preferred failures, like Morris. There she sat holding her pocket-handkerchief in her hand, smiling, ironically, covertly, *smiling* at some memory.

"And what are your plans?" said Edward. "You deserve a holiday."

There was something flattering in his manner, North thought, like a schoolmaster welcoming back to school an old boy who had won distinction. But he meant it; he doesn't say what he doesn't mean, North thought, and that was alarming too. They were silent.

"Delia's got a wonderful lot of people here tonight, hasn't she?" said Edward, turning to Eleanor. They sat looking at the different groups. His clear blue eyes surveyed the scene amiably but sardonically. But what's he thinking, North asked himself. He's got something behind that mask, he thought. Something that's kept him clear of this muddle. The past? Poetry? he thought, looking at Edward's distinct profile. It was finer than he remembered.

"I'd like to brush up my classics," he said suddenly. "Not that I ever had much to brush," he added, foolishly, afraid of the schoolmaster.

Edward did not seem to be listening. He was raising his eyeglass and letting it fall, as he looked at the queer jumble. There his head rested with the chin thrown up, on the back of his chair. The crowd, the noise, the clatter of knives and forks, made it unnecessary to talk. North stole another glance at him. The past and poetry, he said to himself, that's what I want to talk about, he thought. He wanted to say it aloud. But Edward was too formed and idiosyncratic; too black and white and linear, with his head tilted up on the back of his chair, to ask him questions easily.

Now he was talking about Africa, and North wanted to talk about the past and poetry. There it was, he thought, locked up in that fine head, the head that was like a Greek boy's head grown white; the past and poetry. Then why not prise it open? Why not share it? What's wrong with him, he thought, as he answered the usual intelligent Englishman's questions about Africa and the state of the country. Why can't he flow? Why can't he pull the string of the shower bath? Why's it all locked up, refrigerated? Because he's a priest, a mystery monger, he thought, feeling his coldness; this guardian of beautiful words.

But Edward was speaking to him.

"We must arrange a date," he was saying, "next autumn." He meant it too.

"Yes," North said aloud, "I'd love to. . . . In the autumn. . . ." And he saw before him a house with creeper-shaded rooms, butlers creeping, decanters, and someone handing a box of good cigars.

UNKNOWN young men coming round with trays pressed different eatables upon them.

"How very kind of you!" said Eleanor, taking a glass. He himself took a glass of some yellow liquid. It was some kind of claret cup, he supposed. The little bubbles kept rising to the top and exploding. He watched them rise and explode.

"Who's that pretty girl," said Edward, inclining his head, "over there, standing in the corner, talking to the youth?"

He was benignant and urbane.

"Aren't they lovely?" said Eleanor. "Just what I was thinking. . . . Everyone looks so young. That's Maggie's daughter. . . . But who's that talking to Kitty?"

"That's Middleton," said Edward. "What, don't you remember him? You must have met him in the old days."

They chatted, basking there at their ease. Spinners and sitters in the sun, North thought, taking their ease when the day's work is over; Eleanor and Edward each in his own niche, with his hands on the fruit, tolerant, assured.

He watched the bubbles rising in the yellow liquid. For them it's all right, he thought; they've had their day: but not for him, not for his generation. For him a life modelled on the jet (he was watching the bubbles rise), on the spring, of the hard leaping fountain; another life; a different life. Not halls and reverberating megaphones; not marching in step after leaders, in herds, groups, societies caparisoned. No; to begin inwardly, and let the devil take the outer form, he thought, looking up at a young man with a fine forehead and a weak chin. Not black shirts, green shirts, red shirts—always posing in the public eye; that's all poppy-cock. Why not down barriers and simplify? But a world, he thought, that was all one jelly, one mass, would be a rice pudding world, a white counterpane world. To keep the emblems and tokens of North Pargiter—the man Maggie laughs at; the Frenchman holding his hat; but at the same time spread out, make a new ripple in human consciousness, be the bubble and the stream, the stream and the bubble—myself and the world together—he raised his glass. Anonymously, he said, looking at the clear yellow liquid. But what do I mean, he wondered—I, to whom ceremonies are suspect, and religion's dead; who don't fit, as the man said, don't fit in anywhere? He paused. There was the glass in his hand; in his mind a sentence. And he wanted to make other sentences. But how can I, he thought—he looked at Eleanor, who sat with a silk handkerchief in her hands—unless I know what's solid, what's true; in my life, in other people's lives?

"RUNCORN'S BOY," Eleanor suddenly ejaculated. "The son of the porter at my flat," she explained. She had untied the knot in her handkerchief.

"The son of the porter at your flat," Edward repeated. His eyes were like a field on which the sun rests in winter, North thought, looking up—the winter's sun, that has no heat left in it but some pale beauty.

"Commissionaire they call him, I think," she said.

"How I hate that word!" said Edward with a little shudder. "Porter's good English, isn't it?"

"That's what I say," said Eleanor. "The son of the *porter* at my flat. . . . Well, he wants, they want him to go to college. So I said if I saw you, I'd ask you—"

"Of course, of course," said Edward kindly.

And that's all right, North said to himself. That's the human voice at its natural speaking level. Of course, of course, he repeated.

"He wants to go to college, does he?" Edward went on. "What examinations has he passed, eh?"

What examinations has he passed, eh? North repeated. He repeated that too, but critically, as if he were actor and critic; he listened but he commented. He surveyed the thin yellow liquid in which the bubbles rose more slowly, one by one. Eleanor did not know what examinations he had passed. And what was I thinking? North asked himself. He felt that he had been in the middle of a jungle; in the heart of darkness; cutting his way towards the light; but provided only with broken sentences, single words, with which to break through the briar-bush of human bodies, human wills and voices, that bent over him, binding him, blinding him. . . . He listened.

"Well then, tell him to come and see me," said Edward, briskly.

"But that's asking too much of you, Edward?" Eleanor protested.

"That's what I'm for," said Edward.

That's the right tone of voice too, North thought. Not cara-paced—the words "caparison" and "carapace" collided in his mind, and made a new word that was no word. What I mean is, he added, taking a drink of his claret cup, underneath there's the fountain; the sweet nut. The fruit, the fountain that's in all of us; in Edward; in Eleanor; so why caparison ourselves on top? He looked up.

A big man had stopped in front of them. He bent over and very politely gave Eleanor his hand. He had to bend, for his white waistcoat enclosed so magnificent a sphere. "Alas," he was saying in a voice that was oddly mellifluous for one of his bulk, "I'd love nothing more; but I have a meeting at ten tomorrow morning." They were inviting him to sit down and talk. He was tit-tupping up and down on his little feet in front of them.

"Throw it over!" said Eleanor, smiling up at him, just as she used to smile when she was a girl with her brother's friends, thought North. Then why hadn't she married one of them, he wondered. Why do we hide all the things that matter? he asked himself.

"And leave my directors cooling their heels? As much as my place is worth!" the old friend was saying, and swung round on his heel with the agility of a trained elephant.

"Seems a long time since he acted in the Greek play, doesn't it?" said Edward. ". . . in a toga," he added with a grin, follow-ing the well-rounded person of the great railway magnate as he went with a certain celerity, for he was a perfect man of the world, through the crowd to the door.

"That's Chipperfield, the great railway man," he explained to North. "A very remarkable fellow," he went on. "Son of a rail-way porter." He made little pauses between each sentence. "Done it all off his own bat. . . . A delightful house . . . Perfectly restored. . . . Two or three hundred acres, I suppose. . . . Has his shooting. . . . Asks me to direct his reading. . . . And buys old masters."

"And buys old masters," North repeated. The deft little sentences seemed to build up a pagoda; sparely but accurately; and through it all ran some queer breath of mockery tinged with affection.

"Shams, I should think?" Eleanor laughed.

"Well, we needn't go into that," Edward chuckled. Then they were silent. The pagoda floated off. Chipperfield had vanished through the door.

"HOW NICE this drink is," Eleanor said above his head. North could see her glass held at the level of his head on her knee. A thin green leaf floated on top of it. "I hope it's not intoxicating?" she said, raising it.

North took up his glass again. What was I thinking last time I looked at it? he asked himself. A block had formed in his forehead as if two thoughts had collided and had stopped the passage of the rest. His mind was a blank. He swayed the liquid from side to side. He was in the middle of a dark forest.

"So North . . ." His own name roused him with a start. It was Edward speaking. He jerked forward. ". . . you want to brush up your classics, do you?" Edward went on. "I'm glad to hear you say that. There's a lot in those old fellows. But the younger generation," he paused, ". . . don't seem to want 'em."

"How foolish!" said Eleanor. "I was reading one of them the other day . . . the one you translated. Now which was it?" She paused. She never could remember names. "The one about the girl who . . ."

"*The Antigone?*" Edward suggested.

"Yes! *The Antigone!*" she exclaimed. "And I thought to myself, just what you say, Edward—how true—how beautiful. . . ."

She broke off, as if afraid to continue.

Edward nodded. He paused. Then suddenly he jerked his head back and said some words in Greek: "*οὗτοι συνέχθειν, ἀλλὰ συμφιλεῖν ἔφυν.*"

North looked up.

"Translate it," he said.

Edward shook his head. "It's the language," he said.

Then he shut up. It's no go, North thought. He can't say what he wants to say; he's afraid. They're all afraid; afraid of being laughed at; afraid of giving themselves away. He's afraid too, he thought, looking at the young man with a fine forehead and a weak chin who was gesticulating, too emphatically. We're all afraid of each other, he thought; afraid of what? Of criticism; of laughter; of people who think differently. . . . He's afraid of me because I'm a farmer (and he saw again his round face; high cheek bones and small brown eyes). And I'm afraid of him because he's clever. He looked at the big forehead, from which the hair was already receding. That's what separates us; fear, he thought.

He shifted his position. He wanted to get up and talk to him. Delia had said, "Don't wait to be introduced." But it was difficult to speak to a man whom he did not know, and say: "What's this knot in the middle of my forehead? Untie it." For he had had enough of thinking alone. Thinking alone tied knots in the middle of the forehead; thinking alone bred pictures, foolish pictures. The man was moving off. He must make the effort. Yet he hesitated. He felt repelled and attracted, attracted and repelled. He began to rise; but before he had got on his feet, somebody thumped on a table with a fork.

A LARGE MAN sitting at a table in the corner was thumping on the table with his fork. He was leaning forward as if he wanted to attract attention, as if he were about to make a speech. It was the man Peggy called Brown; the others called Nicholas; whose real name he did not know. Perhaps he was a little drunk.

"Ladies and gentlemen!" he said. "Ladies and gentlemen!" he repeated rather more loudly.

"What, a speech?" said Edward quizzically. He half turned his chair; he raised his eyeglass, which hung on a black silk ribbon as if it were a foreign order.

People were buzzing about with plates and glasses. They were stumbling over cushions on the floor. A girl pitched head foremost.

"Hurt yourself?" said a young man, stretching out his hand.

No, she had not hurt herself. But the interruption had distracted attention from the speech. A buzz of talk had risen like the buzz of flies over sugar. Nicholas sat down again. He was lost apparently in contemplation of the red stone in his ring; or of the strewn flowers; the white, waxy flowers, the pale, semi-transparent flowers, the crimson flowers that were so full-blown that the gold heart showed, and the petals had fallen and lay among the hired knives and forks, the cheap tumblers on the table. Then he roused himself.

"Ladies and gentlemen!" he began. Again he thumped the table with his fork. There was a momentary lull. Rose marched across the room.

"Going to make a speech, are you?" she demanded. "Go on, I like hearing speeches." She stood beside him, with her hand hollowed round her ear like a military man. Again the buzz of talk had broken out.

"Silence!" she exclaimed. She took a knife and rapped on the table.

"Silence! Silence!" She rapped again.

Martin crossed the room.

"What's Rose making such a noise about?" he asked.

"I'm asking for silence!" she said, flourishing her knife in his face. "This gentleman wants to make a speech!"

But he had sat down and was regarding his ring with equanimity.

"Isn't she the very spit and image," said Martin, laying his hand on Rose's shoulder and turning to Eleanor as if to confirm his words, "of old Uncle Pargiter of Pargiter's Horse?"

"Well, I'm proud of it!" said Rose, brandishing her knife in his face. "I'm proud of my family; proud of my country; proud of . . ."

"Your sex?" he interrupted her.

"I am," she asseverated. "And what about you?" she went on, tapping him on the shoulder. "Proud of yourself are you?"

"Don't quarrel, children, don't quarrel!" cried Eleanor, giving her chair a little edge nearer. "They always would quarrel," she said, "always . . . always. . . ."

"She was a horrid little spitfire," said Martin, squatting down on the floor, and looking up at Rose, "with her hair scraped off her forehead . . ."

". . . wearing a pink frock," Rose added. She sat down abruptly, holding her knife erect in her hand. "A pink frock; a pink frock," she repeated, as if the words recalled something.

"But go on with your speech, Nicholas," said Eleanor, turning to him. He shook his head.

"Let us talk about pink frocks," he smiled.

". . . in the drawing-room at Abercorn Terrace, when we were children," said Rose. "D'you remember?" She looked at Martin. He nodded his head.

"In the drawing-room at Abercorn Terrace . . ." said Delia. She was going from table to table with a great jug of claret cup. She stopped in front of them. "Abercorn Terrace!" she exclaimed, filling a glass. She flung her head back and looked for a moment astonishingly young, handsome, and defiant.

"It was Hell!" she exclaimed. "It was Hell!" she repeated.

"Oh, come, Delia . . ." Martin protested, holding out his glass to be filled.

"It was Hell," she said, dropping her Irish manner, and speaking quite simply, as she poured out the drink.

"D'you know," she said, looking at Eleanor, "when I go to Paddington, I always say to the man, 'Drive the other way round!'"

"That's enough . . ." Martin stopped her; his glass was full. "I hated it too . . ." he began.

But here Kitty Lasswade advanced upon them. She held her glass in front of her as though it were a bauble.

"What's Martin hating now?" she said, facing him.

A polite gentleman pushed forward a little gilt chair upon which she sat down.

"He always was a hater," she said, holding her glass out to be filled.

"What was it you hated that night, Martin, when you dined with us?" she asked him. "I remember how angry you made me. . . ."

She smiled at him. He had grown cherubic; pink and plump; with his hair brushed back like a waiter's.

"Hated? I never hated anybody," he protested.

"My heart's full of love; my heart's full of kindness," he laughed, waving his glass at her.

"Nonsense," said Kitty. "When you were young you hated . . . everything!" she flung her hand out. "My house . . . my friends. . . ." She broke off with a quick little sigh. She saw them again—the men filing in; the women pinching some dress between their thumbs and fingers. She lived alone now, in the north.

". . . and I daresay I'm better off as I am," she added, half to herself, "with just a boy to chop up wood."

There was a pause.

"Now let him get on with his speech," said Eleanor.

"Yes. Get on with your speech!" said Rose. Again she rapped her knife on the table; again he half rose.

"Going to make a speech, is he?" said Kitty, turning to Edward who had drawn his chair up beside her.

"The only place where oratory is now practised as an art . . ." Edward began. Then he paused, drew his chair a little closer, and adjusted his glasses, ". . . is the church," he added.

That's why I didn't marry you, Kitty said to herself. How the voice, the supercilious voice, brought it back! the tree half fallen; rain falling; undergraduates calling; bells tolling; she and her mother . . .

But Nicholas had risen. He took a deep breath which expanded his shirt front. With one hand he fumbled with his fob; the other he flung out with an oratorical gesture.

"Ladies and gentlemen!" he began again. "In the name of all who have enjoyed themselves tonight. . . ."

"Speak up! Speak up!" the young men cried who were standing in the window.

("Is he a foreigner?" Kitty whispered to Eleanor.)

". . . in the name of all who have enjoyed themselves tonight," he repeated more loudly, "I wish to thank our host and hostess. . . ."

"Oh, don't thank me!" said Delia, brushing past them with her empty jug.

Again the speech was brought to the ground. He must be a foreigner, Kitty thought to herself, because he has no self-consciousness. There he stood holding his wine-glass and smiling.

"Go on, go on," she urged him. "Don't mind them." She was in the mood for a speech. A speech was a good thing at parties. It gave them a fillip. It gave them a finish. She rapped her glass on the table.

"It's very nice of you," said Delia, trying to push past him, but he had laid his hand on her arm, "but don't thank me."

"But, Delia," he expostulated, still holding her, "it's not what *you* want; it's what *we* want. And it is fitting," he continued, waving his hand out, "when our hearts are full of gratitude . . ."

Now he's getting into his stride, Kitty thought. I daresay he's a bit of an orator. Most foreigners are.

". . . when our hearts are full of gratitude," he repeated, touching one finger.

"What for?" said a voice abruptly.

Nicholas stopped again.

("Who is that dark man?" Kitty whispered to Eleanor. "I've been wondering all the evening."

"Renny," Eleanor whispered. "Renny," she repeated.)

"What for?" said Nicholas. "That is what I am about to tell you. . . ." He paused, and drew a deep breath which again expanded his waistcoat. His eyes beamed; he seemed full of spontaneous subterraneous benevolence. But here a head popped up over the edge of the table; a hand swept up a fistful of flower petals; and a voice cried:

"Red Rose, thorny Rose, brave Rose, tawny Rose!" The petals were thrown, fan-shape, over the stout old woman who was sitting on the edge of her chair. She looked up in surprise. Petals had fallen on her. She brushed them where they had lodged upon the prominences of her person. "Thank you! Thank you!" she exclaimed. Then she took up a flower and beat it energetically upon the edge of the table. "But I want my speech!" she said, looking at Nicholas.

"No, no," he said. "This is not a time for making speeches," and sat down again.

"Let's drink then," said Martin. He raised his glass. "Pargiter of Pargiter's Horse!" he said. "I drink to her!" He put his glass down with a thump on the table.

"Oh, if you're all drinking healths," said Kitty, "I'll drink too. Rose, your health. Rose is a fine fellow," she said, raising her glass. "But Rose was wrong," she added. "Force is always wrong,— don't you agree with me, Edward?" She tapped him on the knee. I'd forgotten the War, she muttered half to herself. "Still," she said aloud, "Rose had the courage of her convictions. Rose went to prison. And I drink to her!" She drank.

"The same to you, Kitty," said Rose, bowing to her.

"She smashed his window," Martin jeered at her, "and then she helped him to smash other people's windows. Where's your decoration, Rose?"

"In a cardboard box on the mantelpiece," said Rose. "You can't get a rise out of me at this time of day, my good fellow."

"But I wish you had let Nicholas finish his speech," said Eleanor.

DOWN THROUGH the ceiling, muted and far away, came the preliminary notes of another dance. The young people, hastily swallowing what remained in their glasses, rose and began to move off upstairs. Soon there was the sound of feet thudding, rhythmically, heavily on the floor above.

"Another dance?" said Eleanor. It was a waltz. "When we were young," she said, looking at Kitty, "we used to dance. . . ." The tune seemed to take her words and to repeat them—when I was young I used to dance—I used to dance. . . .

"And how I hated it!" said Kitty, looking at her fingers, which were short and pricked. "How nice it is," she said, "not to be young! How nice not to mind what people think! Now one can live as one likes," she added, ". . . now that one's seventy."

She paused. She raised her eyebrows as if she remembered something. "Pity one can't live again," she said. But she broke off.

"Aren't we going to have our speech after all, Mr. ——?" she said, looking at Nicholas, whose name she did not know. He sat gazing benevolently in front of him, paddling his hands among the flower petals.

"What's the good?" he said. "Nobody wants to listen." They listened to the feet thudding upstairs, and to the music repeating, it seemed to Eleanor, when I was young I used to dance, all men loved me when I was young. . . .

"But I want a speech!" said Kitty in her authoritative manner. It was true; she wanted something—something that gave a fillip, a finish—what she scarcely knew. But not the past—not memories. The present; the future—that was what she wanted.

"There's Peggy!" said Eleanor, looking round. She was sitting on the edge of a table, eating a ham sandwich.

"Come, Peggy!" she called out. "Come and talk to us!"

"Speak for the younger generation, Peggy!" said Lady Lasswade, shaking hands.

"But I'm not the younger generation," said Peggy. "And I've made my speech already," she said. "I made a fool of myself upstairs," she said, sinking down on the floor at Eleanor's feet.

"Then, North . . ." said Eleanor, looking down on the parting of North's hair as he sat on the floor beside her.

"Yes, North," said Peggy, looking at him across her aunt's knee. "North says we talk of nothing but money and politics," she added. "Tell us what we ought to do." He started. He had been dozing off, dazed by the music and voices. What we ought to do? he said to himself, waking up. What ought we to do?

He jerked up into a sitting posture. He saw Peggy's face looking at him. Now she was smiling; her face was gay; it reminded him of his grandmother's face in the picture. But he saw it as he had seen it upstairs—scarlet, puckered—as if she were about to burst into tears. It was her face that was true; not her words. But only her words returned to him—to live differently—differently. He paused. This is what needs courage, he said to himself; to speak the truth. She was listening. The old people were already gossiping about their own affairs.

". . . It's a nice little house," Kitty was saying. "An old mad woman used to live there. . . . You'll have to come and stay with me, Nell. In the spring. . . ."

Peggy was watching him over the rim of her ham sandwich.

"What you said was true," he blurted out, ". . . quite true." It was what she meant that was true, he corrected himself; her feeling, not her words. He felt her feeling now; it was not about him; it was about other people; about another world, a new world. . . .

The old aunts and uncles were gossiping above him.

"What was the name of the man I used to like so much at Oxford?" Lady Lasswade was saying. He could see her silver body bending towards Edward.

"The man you liked at Oxford?" Edward was repeating. "I thought you never liked anyone at Oxford. . . ." And they laughed.

But Peggy was waiting, she was watching him. He saw again the glass with the bubbles rising; he felt again the constriction of a knot in his forehead. He wished there were someone, infinitely wise and good, to think for him, to answer for him. But the young man with the receding forehead had vanished.

". . . To live differently . . . differently," he repeated. Those were her words; they did not altogether fit his meaning; but he had to use them. Now I've made a fool of myself too, he thought, as a ripple of some disagreeable sensation went across his back as if a knife had sliced it, and he leant against the wall.

"Yes, it was Robson!" Lady Lasswade exclaimed. Her trumpet voice rang out over his head.

"How one forgets things!" she went on. "Of course—Robson. That was his name. And the girl I used to like—Nelly? The girl who was going to be a doctor?"

"Died, I think," said Edward.

"Died, did she — died —" said Lady Lasswade. She paused for a moment. "Well, I wish you'd make your speech," she said, turning and looking down at North.

He drew himself back. No more speech-making for me, he thought. He had his glass in his hand still. It was still half full of pale yellow liquid. The bubbles had ceased to rise. The wine was clear and still. Stillness and solitude, he thought to himself; silence and solitude . . . that's the only element in which the mind is free now.

Silence and solitude, he repeated; silence and solitude. His eyes half closed themselves. He was tired; he was dazed; people talked; people talked. He would detach himself, generalise himself, imagine that he was lying in a great space on a blue plain with hills on the rim of the horizon. He stretched out his feet. There were the sheep cropping; slowly tearing the grass; advancing first one stiff leg and then another. And babbling — babbling. He made no sense of what they were saying. Through his half-open eyes he saw hands holding flowers — thin hands, fine hands; but hands that belonged to no one. And were they flowers the hands held? Or mountains? Blue mountains with violet shadows? Then petals fell. Pink, yellow, white, with violet shadows, the petals fell. They fall and fall and cover all, he murmured. And there was the stem of a wine-glass; the rim of a plate; and a bowl of water. The hands went on picking up flower after flower; that was a white rose; that was a yellow rose; that was a rose with violet valleys in its petals. There they hung, many folded, many coloured, drooping over the rim of the bowl. And petals fell. There they lay, violet and yellow, little shallops, boats on a river. And he was floating, and drifting, in a shallop, in a petal, down a river into silence, into solitude . . . which is the worst torture, the words came back to him as if a voice had spoken them, that human beings can inflict. . . .

"Wake up, North . . . we want your speech!" a voice interrupted him. Kitty's red handsome face was hanging over him.

"Maggie!" he exclaimed, pulling himself up. It was she who was sitting there, putting flowers into water. "Yes, it's Maggie's turn to speak," said Nicholas, putting his hand on her knee.

"Speak, speak!" Renny urged her.

But she shook her head. Laughter took her and shook her. She laughed, throwing her head back as if she were possessed by some genial spirit outside herself that made her bend and rise, as a tree, North thought, is tossed and bent by the wind. No idols, no idols, no idols, her laughter seemed to chime as if the tree were hung with innumerable bells, and he laughed too.

THEIR LAUGHTER CEASED. Feet thudded, dancing on the floor above. A siren hooted on the river. A van crashed down the street in the distance. There was a rush and quiver of sound; something seemed to be released; it was as if the life of the day were about to begin, and this were the chorus, the cry, the chirp, the stir, which salutes the London dawn.

Kitty turned to Nicholas.

"And what was your speech going to have been about, Mr. . . . I'm afraid I don't know your name?" she said. ". . . the one that was interrupted?"

"My speech?" he laughed. "It was to have been a miracle!" he said. "A masterpiece! But how can one speak when one is always interrupted? I begin: I say, Let us give thanks. Then Delia says, Don't thank me. I begin again: I say, Let us give thanks to someone, to somebody . . . And Renny says, What for? I begin again, and look—Eleanor is sound asleep." (He pointed at her.) "So what's the good?"

"Oh, but there is some good—" Kitty began.

She still wanted something—some finish, some fillip—what, she did not know. And it was getting late. She must go.

"Tell me, privately, what you were going to have said, Mr. ——?" she asked him.

"What I was going to have said? I was going to have said—" He paused and stretched his hand out; he touched each finger separately.

"First I was going to have thanked our host and hostess. Then I was going to have thanked this house—" he waved his hand round the room hung with the placards of the house agent, "—which has sheltered the lovers, the creators, the men and women of goodwill. And finally—" he took his glass in his hand, "I was going to drink to the human race. The human race," he continued, raising his glass to his lips, "which is now in its infancy, may it grow to maturity! Ladies and gentlemen!" he exclaimed, half rising and expanding his waistcoat, "I drink to that!"

He brought his glass down with a thump on the table. It broke.

"THAT'S THE thirteenth glass broken tonight!" said Delia, coming up and stopping in front of them. "But don't mind— don't mind. They're very cheap—glasses."

"What's very cheap?" Eleanor murmured. She half opened her eyes. But where was she? In what room? In which of the innumerable rooms? Always there were rooms; always there were people. Always from the beginning of time. . . . She shut her hands on the coins she was holding, and again she was suffused with a feeling of happiness. Was it because this had survived—this keen sensation (she was waking up) and the other thing, the solid object—she saw an ink-corroded walrus—had vanished? She opened her eyes wide. Here she was; alive; in this room, with living people. She saw all the heads in a circle. At first they were without identity. Then she recognised them.

That was Rose; that was Martin; that was Morris. He had hardly any hair on the top of his head. There was a curious pallor on his face.

There was a curious pallor on all their faces as she looked round. The brightness had gone out of the electric lights; the table-cloths looked whiter. North's head—he was sitting on the floor at her feet—was rimmed with whiteness. His shirt-front was a little crumpled.

He was sitting on the floor at Edward's feet with his hands bound round his knees, and he gave little jerks and looked up at him as if he appealed to him about something.

"Uncle Edward," she heard him say, "tell me this . . ."

He was like a child asking to be told a story.

"Tell me this," he repeated, giving another little jerk. "You're a scholar. About the classics now. Aeschylus. Sophocles. Pindar."

Edward bent towards him.

"And the chorus," North jerked on again. She leant towards them. "The chorus—" North repeated.

"My dear boy," she heard Edward say as he smiled benignly down at him, "don't ask me. I was never a great hand at that. No, if I'd had my way"—he paused and passed his hand over his forehead—"I should have been . . ." A burst of laughter drowned his words. She could not catch the end of the sentence. What had he said—what had he wished to be? She had lost his words.

There must be another life, she thought, sinking back into her chair, exasperated. Not in dreams; but here and now, in this room, with living people. She felt as if she were standing on the edge of a precipice with her hair blown back; she was about to grasp something that just evaded her. There must be another life, here and now, she repeated. This is too short, too broken. We know nothing, even about ourselves. We're only just beginning, she thought, to understand, here and there. She hollowed her hands in her lap, just as Rose had hollowed hers round her ears. She held her hands hollowed; she felt that she wanted to enclose the present moment; to make it stay; to fill it fuller and fuller, with the past, the present and the future, until it shone, whole, bright, deep with understanding.

"Edward," she began, trying to attract his attention. But he was not listening to her; he was telling North some old college story. It's useless, she thought, opening her hands. It must drop. It must fall. And then? she thought. For her too there would be the endless night; the endless dark. She looked ahead of her as though she saw opening in front of her a very long dark tunnel. But, thinking of the dark, something baffled her; in fact it was growing light. The blinds were white.

THERE WAS a stir in the room.

Edward turned to her.

"Who are *they*?" he asked her, pointing to the door.

She looked. Two children stood in the door. Delia had her hands on their shoulders as if to encourage them. She was leading them over to the table in order to give them something to eat. They looked awkward and clumsy.

Eleanor glanced at their hands, at their clothes, at the shape of their ears. "The children of the caretaker, I should think," she said. Yes, Delia was cutting slices of cake for them, and they were larger slices of cake than she would have cut had they been the children of her own friends. The children took the slices and stared at them with a curious fixed stare as if they were fierce. But perhaps they were frightened, because she had brought them up from the basement into the drawing-room.

"Eat it!" said Delia, giving them a little pat.

They began to munch slowly, gazing solemnly round them.

"Hullo, children!" cried Martin, beckoning to them. They stared at him solemnly.

"Haven't you got a name?" he said. They went on eating in silence. He began to fumble in his pocket.

"Speak!" he said. "Speak!"

"The younger generation," said Peggy, "don't mean to speak."

They turned their eyes on her now; but they went on munching. "No school tomorrow?" she said. They shook their heads from side to side.

"Hurrah!" said Martin. He held the coins in his hand; pressed between his thumb and finger. "Now—sing a song for sixpence!" he said.

"Yes. Weren't you taught something at school?" Peggy asked.

They stared at her but remained silent. They had stopped eating. They were a centre of a little group. They swept their eyes over the grown-up people for a moment, then, each giving the other a little nudge, they burst into song:

> Etho passo tanno hai,
> Fai donk to tu do,
> Mai to, kai to, lai to see
> Toh dom to tuh do—

That was what it sounded like. Not a word was recognisable. The distorted sounds rose and sank as if they followed a tune. They stopped.

They stood with their hands behind their backs. Then with one impulse they attacked the next verse:

> Fanno to par, etto to mar,
> Timin tudo, tido,
> Foll to gar in, mitno to par,
> Eido, tedo, meido—

They sang the second verse more fiercely than the first. The rhythm seemed to rock and the unintelligible words ran themselves together almost into a shriek. The grown-up people did not know whether to laugh or to cry. Their voices were so harsh; the accent was so hideous.

They burst out again:

> Chree to gay ei,
> Geeray didax . . .

Then they stopped. It seemed to be in the middle of a verse. They stood there grinning, silent, looking at the floor. Nobody knew what to say. There was something horrible in the noise they made. It was so shrill, so discordant, and so meaningless. Then old Patrick ambled up.

"Ah, that's very nice, that's very nice. Thank you, my dears," he said in his genial way, fiddling with his toothpick. The children grinned at him. Then they began to make off. As they sidled past Martin, he slipped coins into their hands. Then they made a dash for the door.

"But what the devil were they singing?" said Hugh Gibbs. "I couldn't understand a word of it, I must confess." He held his hands to the sides of his large white waistcoat.

"Cockney accent, I suppose," said Patrick. "What they teach 'em at school, you know."

"But it was . . ." Eleanor began. She stopped. What was it? As they stood there they had looked so dignified; yet they had made this hideous noise. The contrast between their faces and their voices was astonishing; it was impossible to find one word for the whole. "Beautiful?" she said, with a note of interrogation, turning to Maggie.

"Extraordinarily," said Maggie.

But Eleanor was not sure that they were thinking of the same thing.

SHE GATHERED together her gloves, her bag and two or three coppers, and got up. The room was full of a queer pale light. Objects seemed to be rising out of their sleep, out of their disguise, and to be assuming the sobriety of daily life. The room was making ready for its use as an estate agent's office. The tables were becoming office tables; their legs were the legs of office tables, and yet they were still strewn with plates and glasses, with roses, lilies and carnations.

"It's time to go," she said, crossing the room. Delia had gone to the window. Now she jerked the curtains open.

"The dawn!" she exclaimed rather melodramatically.

The shapes of houses appeared across the square. Their blinds were all drawn; they seemed fast asleep still in the morning pallor.

"The dawn!" said Nicholas, getting up and stretching himself. He too walked across to the window. Renny followed him.

"Now for the peroration," he said, standing with him in the window. "The dawn—the new day—"

He pointed at the trees, at the roofs, at the sky.

"No," said Nicholas, holding back the curtain. "There you are mistaken. There is going to be no peroration—no peroration!" he exclaimed, throwing his arm out, "because there was no speech."

"But the dawn has risen," said Renny, pointing at the sky.

IT WAS A FACT. The sun had risen. The sky between the chimneys looked extraordinarily blue.

"And I am going to bed," said Nicholas after a pause. He turned away.

"Where is Sara?" he said, looking round him. There she was curled up in a corner with her head against a table asleep apparently.

"Wake your sister, Magdalena," he said, turning to Maggie. Maggie looked at her. Then she took a flower from the table and tossed it at her. She half-opened her eyes. "It's time," said Maggie, touching her on the shoulder. "Time, is it?" she sighed. She yawned and stretched herself. She fixed her eyes on Nicholas as if she were bringing him back to the field of vision. Then she laughed.

"Nicholas!" she exclaimed.

"Sara!" he replied. They smiled at each other. Then he helped her up and she balanced herself uncertainly against her sister, and rubbed her eyes.

"How strange," she murmured, looking round her, ". . . how strange. . . ."

There were the smeared plates, and the empty wine-glasses; the petals and the bread crumbs. In the mixture of lights they looked prosaic but unreal; cadaverous but brilliant. And there against the window, gathered in a group, were the old brothers and sisters.

"Look, Maggie," she whispered, turning to her sister, "Look!"

THE GROUP in the window, the men in their black-and-white evening dress, the women in their crimsons, golds and silvers, wore a statuesque look for a moment, as if they were carved in stone. Their dresses fell in stiff sculptured folds. Then they moved; they changed their attitudes; they began to talk.

"Can't I give you a lift back, Nell?" Kitty Lasswade was saying. "I've a car waiting."

Eleanor did not answer. She was looking at the curtained houses across the square. The windows were spotted with gold.

Everything looked clean swept, fresh and virginal. The pigeons were shuffling on the tree tops.

"I've a car . . ." Kitty repeated.

"Listen . . ." said Eleanor, raising her hand. Upstairs they were playing "God save the King" on the gramophone; but it was the pigeons she meant; they were crooning.

"That's wood pigeons, isn't it?" said Kitty. She put her head on one side to listen. Take two coos, Taffy, take two coos . . . tak . . . they were crooning.

"Wood pigeons?" said Edward, putting his hand to his ear.

"There on the tree tops," said Kitty. The green-blue birds were shuffling about on the branches, pecking and crooning to themselves.

Morris brushed the crumbs off his waistcoat.

"What an hour for us old fogies to be out of bed!" he said. "I haven't seen the sun rise since . . . since . . ."

"Ah, but when we were young," said old Patrick, slapping him on the shoulder, "we thought nothing of making a night of it! I remember going to Covent Garden and buying roses for a certain lady . . ."

Delia smiled as if some romance, her own or another's, had been recalled to her.

"And I . . ." Eleanor began. She stopped. She saw an empty milk jug and leaves falling. Then it had been autumn. Now it was summer. The sky was a faint blue; the roofs were tinged purple against the blue; the chimneys were a pure brick red. An air of ethereal calm and simplicity lay over everything.

"And all the tubes have stopped, and all the omnibuses," she said, turning round. "How are we going to get home?"

"We can walk," said Rose. "Walking won't do us any harm."

"Not on a fine summer morning," said Martin.

A breeze went through the square. In the stillness they

could hear the branches rustle as they rose slightly, and fell, and shook a wave of green light through the air.

Then the door burst open. Couple after couple came flocking in, dishevelled, gay, to look for their cloaks and their hats, to say good-night.

"It's been so good of you to come!" Delia exclaimed, turning towards them with her hands outstretched.

"Thank you—thank you for coming!" she cried.

"And look at Maggie's bunch!" she said, taking a bunch of many-coloured flowers that Maggie held out to her.

"How beautifully you've arranged them!" she said. "Look, Eleanor!" She turned to her sister.

But Eleanor was standing with her back to them. She was watching a taxi that was gliding slowly round the square. It stopped in front of a house two doors down.

"Aren't they lovely?" said Delia, holding out the flowers.

Eleanor started.

"The roses? Yes . . ." she said. But she was watching the cab. A young man had got out; he paid the driver. Then a girl in a tweed travelling suit followed him. He fitted his latch-key to the door. "There," Eleanor murmured, as he opened the door and they stood for a moment on the threshold. "There!" she repeated as the door shut with a little thud behind them.

Then she turned round into the room. "And now?" she said, looking at Morris, who was drinking the last drops of a glass of wine. "And now?" she asked, holding out her hands to him.

THE SUN had risen, and the sky above the houses wore an air of extraordinary beauty, simplicity and peace.

Notes to *The Years*

I wish to acknowledge and thank the editors of the following editions of *The Years* for their illuminating introductions and, in the Penguin and Oxford editions, for their extremely helpful notes. While I have not slavishly copied any of their sources, I am indebted to both Jeri Johnson and Sue Asbee for guiding me toward some specific sources: *The Years*, introduction by Susan Hill and Steven Connor (London: Vintage, 2004); *The Years*, edited with an introduction and notes by Jeri Johnson (London: Penguin, 1998); and *The Years*, edited with an introduction by Hermione Lee and notes by Sue Asbee (Oxford: Oxford University Press, 1992). Details of other works referred to will be found in the list of works cited in the introduction, in the suggestions for further reading, or within specific notes below. The following reference works are cited by author's name only: Jeremy Black and Donald M. MacRaild, *Nineteenth-Century Britain* (London: Palgrave, 2003); K. Theodore Hoppen, *The Mid-Victorian Generation 1846–1886* (Oxford: Clarendon Press, 1998); William Kent, editor, *An Encyclopedia of London* (London: Dent, 1937); A. D. Mills, *Oxford Dictionary of Place Names* (Oxford: Oxford University Press, 2001); G. R. Searle, *A New England? Peace and War 1886–1918* (Oxford: Clarendon Press, 2004). References to *Three Guineas* (*TG*) cite the edition annotated and with an introduction by Jane Marcus (Orlando: Harcourt, 2005). *OED* refers to the *Oxford English Dictionary*.

Whiteley's [3]   One of the large London department stores, opened by William Whiteley in 1863 in Westbourne Grove, with over two thousand employees by 1870 (Hoppen 352).

Army and Navy Stores [3]   The first store opened in 1872 on Victoria Street and catered largely to middle- or aspiring middle-class customers. The 1870s saw the burgeoning of retail chains that began to compete with and often replace smaller trade and corner shops like Lamley's (Hoppen 352).

West end . . . East [3]   The two principal parts of London, the West end comprising Westminster, the area from Leicester Square's theater district through Kensington, and the East referring to the City of London, the square-mile area of the financial and commercial heart of London. The West end here represents royal and fashionable London; the East, professional working London.

landaus, victorias and hansom cabs [3]   Popular forms of transportation for the wealthier classes, landaus and victorias were larger carriages often owned or rented by families, hansom cabs smaller one-horse vehicles seating one or two passengers. See introduction, pages lxii–lxiv.

the season [3]   In the nineteenth century, the period between January and midsummer when the bulk of the debutante balls, dinner parties, and other social events occurred and when those who had residences both in the country and in the city came to the city. Kitty Lasswade, living in the north of England, also has a house in London but is about to give it up, as she tells Eleanor in the excised episode of "1921" (see introduction, page liii).

Hyde Park [3]   The entrance to the fashionable West end in Westminster, the park was used by Henry VIII as a royal hunting ground from 1536 and subsequently opened to the public in the seventeenth century (Mills).

St. James's [3]   St. James's Park, the oldest of the royal parks, dating from about 1531, when Henry VIII built St. James's Palace on the site of a hospital dedicated to St. James (Mills).

Marble Arch [3]   John Nash's monumental arch constructed in 1827 to commemorate Admiral Nelson's naval victories. Originally opening onto Buckingham Palace, it was moved in 1851 to Hyde Park Corner.

Apsley House [3]   Built opposite Marble Arch for Lord Chancellor Apsley in 1771–1778, it became the Duke of Wellington's residence in 1816 after the British victory at the Battle of Waterloo in 1815 (Mills). Woolf situates the London aristocracy and royalty between these two symbols of British military heroism.

Princess [4]   Alexandra (1844–1925), daughter of King Kristian IX of Denmark and wife of Edward, Prince of Wales, who ascended the throne as Edward VII after the death of his mother, Queen Victoria, in 1901.

Bermondsey and Hoxton [4]   Both London areas mentioned in the Domesday Book of 1086. In the nineteenth century they were less fashionable than Westminster or Kensington, Bermondsey on the south side of the Thames in Southwark and Hoxton in northeast London's Hackney, a popular site for music halls (Mills).

Round Pond and the Serpentine [4]   Man-made lakes in Kensington Gardens and Hyde Park, near Woolf's childhood Hyde Park Gate home.

the Bridge [4]   Possibly either Westminster or Waterloo Bridge, from which one can scan the city line with St. Paul's Cathedral to the east and the buildings of Parliament to the west.

the moon rose and its polished coin [4]   In *Three Guineas,* Woolf connects the opening of the professions to women in 1919 with the symbol of a woman holding a coin and looking at the moon, which suddenly seems "a white sixpence, a chaste sixpence . . . the sacred sixpence that she had earned with her own hands herself" (*TG* 20). The symbol of the sixpence will return in the "Present Day" section, when Martin offers the caretaker's children sixpence to sing a song (407).

Colonel Abel Pargiter [4]   See introduction, page lii, for speculations by Mitchell Leaska and Jane Marcus as to the origin of the name and its original definition in Joseph Wright's dialect dictionary.

club [4]   Possibly the Naval and Military Club at No. 94 Piccadilly, formerly the residence of Lord Henry John Temple, Viscount Palmerston (Mills).

India, Africa, Egypt [4]   Three sites of British imperialism and territorial expansion in the nineteenth century under the administrations of Lord Palmerston, and, particularly after midcentury, those of Benjamin Disraeli and William Gladstone.

omnibuses [5]   Horse-drawn vehicles first used in London in 1829, and later one of the most popular methods of public transportation. The authors of *A History of London Transport* define an omnibus simply as "a box on wheels with two forms placed lengthways inside, windows through which passengers could peer to discover where they were, and a door at the back providing easy entry and egress" (T. C. Barker and Michael Robbins, *A History of London Transport*, vol. 1, 14–15 [London: George Allen & Unwin, Ltd., 1963]). The omnibus could carry twelve to fifteen passengers and became especially popular after the Great Exhibition of 1851 brought crowds of visitors to London.

broughams [5]   Four-wheeled horse-drawn enclosed carriages with two doors, named after Lord Chancellor Henry Brougham. The carriage usually held two passengers inside and had room outside for a driver and footman.

Cologne Cathedral [5]   In the autumn (October 15 and 16) of 1880, the *Times* carried two long articles about the inauguration of

Cologne Cathedral in Germany, finally completed after 632 years. Colonel Pargiter, however, reads an article about the Cathedral in the spring of 1880, before the inauguration took place.

Green Park [6]   At one time part of St. James's Park, it was so named on a map of 1746 (Mills).

Westminster [6]   First recorded under a slightly different spelling in 975, then again in 1066, this section of London originally meant "the west monastery" because of its location west of the City of London.

the Abbey [6]   Westminster Abbey, the current building of which was begun by Edward the Confessor in the eleventh century, and where most of England's monarchs have been crowned since William I in 1066.

muffin man [6]   Deliverer of fresh muffins to households, a common feature of Victorian England. The prevalence of muffin men gave rise to the nursery rhyme, one line of which asks, "Do you know the muffin man who lives in Drury Lane?" Drury Lane was in the not-so-respectable theater district of London. Woolf may suggest here the same slightly disreputable area in which Mira lives.

Bogy [7]   According to the *Oxford English Dictionary,* bogy or bogey refers to an evil one, goblin, or devil. Curiously, it can also mean a detective in criminals' slang.

barrel-organ [8]   An organlike keyed instrument with a revolving barrel studded with metal pins (*OED*), this was a popular form of street entertainment from the eighteenth to the early twentieth centuries.

sixpence . . . sovereigns [8]   A silver coin worth six pennies, and a gold coin equivalent to a pound, first issued by Henry VII in 1489.

Sovereigns were continuously issued between 1817 and 1917, after which they were largely replaced by banknotes.

public house [9]   Since the seventeenth century in England, a pub or tavern (*OED*).

front drawing-room [9]   A room for the reception of company, often a formal living room. The drawing room was also the place to which women withdrew after dinner, leaving the men at table.

Nurse [10]   In Victorian middle- and upper-class households, a servant who acted as nursemaid to the children of the family. She usually lived in the house and occupied a room in the upper story near the children's nursery.

pinafore [10]   A sleeveless garment that fastened in back, worn to protect children's clothes from dirt (*OED*).

he *is—wearing his white flower* [12]   The first indication of Delia's fascination with Charles Stewart Parnell (1846–1891), an Irish Protestant landowner and from 1880 leader of Ireland's Home Rule Party. Supported by William Gladstone and the Liberal Party and opposed by the Ulster Protestant Unionists, Parnell advocated separation from England. His notorious affair with a married woman, Kitty O'Shea, and her husband's divorce suit against him in 1889 forced Gladstone to withdraw his support for Parnell (Hoppen).

Whiteley's [12]   See note to page 3.

florins [12]   English silver coins first minted in 1849 and worth two shillings (or about ten pence) (*OED*).

Mutiny [13]   An uprising (May 10, 1857) by Indian soldiers at Meerut in the North-Western Provinces against British officers. The Indian Mutiny, in part a response to the British seizure of land in Oudh, spread to Delhi and south toward Calcutta and lasted until July 1858. Hoppen notes the similarities between British imperialistic tactics in Ireland and India, and Woolf suggests a particular affinity between Delia and Colonel Pargiter.

Grove day [13]   Eleanor's social work among the poorer classes in London suggests that of both Woolf's half sister Stella (1869–1897) and Woolf's eldest cousin, Katherine Stephen (1856–1924), who was active in the foundation of the Lily Club for working girls and the Southwark Settlement. Though Katherine rose to become principal of Newnham College, Cambridge, there are sufficient parallels between Eleanor's and Katherine's lives, as well as hints of the other Stephen cousins, Rosamond, Dorothea, Herbert, Harry, and Jem, to indicate that Woolf may, in part, have based Abel Pargiter's family on the James Fitzjames Stephen family. In the holograph manuscript, *The Pargiters,* Grove is Lisson Grove in Marylebone, Westminster.

prep. [13]   Homework.

Greek . . . Latin [17]   Knowing classical languages was required for entrance to Oxford and Cambridge throughout the nineteenth century, and Edward, who becomes an Oxford don, later publishes his own translation of *Antigone.*

houses opposite [17]   A reference to the terraced houses, many of which were built along straight streets in the early to mid-nineteenth century as improvements in lighting, gas, and drainage made these more practical and sanitary than the older, back-to-back houses (Black and MacRaild 92).

perambulator [18]   A four-wheeled baby carriage, now commonly called a pram in England.

privets [18]   Evergreen shrubs often planted as hedges for privacy.

man in the frock coat with the flower in his button-hole [21]   See note to page 12 about Charles Parnell ("*he* is—wearing his white flower").

Mr. Parnell was by her side [22]   See note to page 12 ("*he* is . . .").

Liberty . . . Justice [22]   These words from Parnell's speech will be parodied in the "1914" section when Martin and Sara listen to the extemporaneous speeches at Hyde Park Speakers' Corner. (See note to page 227.)

night nursery [25]   A room usually in the upper story of a house where young children slept.

schoolroom door [25]   In Victorian households, female children and young male children were often educated by governesses and private tutors (and occasionally their parents) at home. This was the case with Virginia Stephen and her sister Vanessa, although their two brothers went to boarding school and then to Cambridge University. An Education Act of 1870 required children to attend school between the ages of five and thirteen, but this was not strictly enforced (Black and MacRaild 153).

British flag was still flying on the central tower [26]   Possibly another allusion to the Indian Mutiny of 1857, where the British flag flew over the besieged city of Lucknow in northwest India (Hoppen). In *The Pargiters,* Woolf states of Rose, "Her head was full of her father's old stories of the Indian Mutiny" (42).

pillar-box [26]   A public mailbox, first established in England in the 1850s (*OED*).

unbuttoning his clothes [28]   In the essay that originally followed this episode in the manuscript, Woolf notes the stringent Victorian convention that "forbids, whether rightly or wrongly, any plain description of the sight that Rose, in common with many other little girls, saw under the lamp post by the pillar box in the dusk of that March evening" (*The Pargiters* 51).

Shoreditch [29] A neighborhood in the London borough of Hackney, northeast of the City of London, where in the nineteenth century a large immigrant working-class population lived.

Jews [29] An example of both ethnic and class distinctions that underlie *The Years*. In 1880 London Jews were still associated with two traditional stereotypes: love of money and splendor and the vocation of tailor. Woolf's husband, Leonard, a graduate of Cambridge University, was by the early twentieth century no longer bound by the University Test Act, which barred non-Anglicans from graduating from Oxford or Cambridge.

devilling for Sanders Curry [31] Morris, a new barrister, is serving an apprenticeship before obtaining his own court briefs.

Common Law and the other kind of law [32] Eleanor's confusion is understandable in light of the recent Judicature Acts of 1873–1875, which had merged courts of common law with other courts (equity, probate, etc.) and formed a Supreme Court of Judicature. These acts also formally divided solicitors from barristers, the latter devoted to court cases (Searle). In the holograph draft of *The Pargiters,* Eleanor has forgotten the difference between Common Law and Chancery, a difference no longer relevant after 1875.

Lord Chancellor [32] The most highly paid cabinet minister, who acted as leader of the House of Lords and as head of the judiciary.

Lord Chief Justice [32] The second-highest judicial official (after Lord Chancellor) and head of the Queen's Bench Division.

dressing-bell [33]   In wealthier Victorian households, a gong was rung to summon people to dress formally for dinner.

day nursery [37]   A room in Victorian households used by the children during the day.

hear St. Paul's [39]   A reference to the bells of St. Paul's Cathedral in the City of London, at the top of Ludgate Hill.

sulphur in the dog's bowl [41]   Often used during warm weather to help keep dogs cooler and to ease itchy skin.

second post [42]   The second delivery of mail during the day.

red smoking-cap [43]   A soft fezlike cap, often with a tassel, worn indoors by men during the nineteenth century, especially after 1850.

a dozen of fine old port "by way of a stirrup-cup" [47]   Probably a reference to a dozen bottles of port sent by Colonel Pargiter as an encouragement before Edward's examinations. The stirrup cup was traditionally given by Scottish Highlanders to departing guests who were already mounted on their horses (*OED*).

Antigone [48]   A Greek tragedy by Sophocles (ca. 496–406 B.C.). Edward is studying for his examinations in classics, the results of which will determine his eligibility for a fellowship.

asphodel [49]   A flower found in southern Europe, especially, as in this case, in Greece, and said by the poets to be immortal. Edward imagines Kitty here as a Greek goddess.

Morris wall-papers [49]   Popular floral designs by William Morris (1834–1896), artist and poet associated with the Pre-Raphaelite Brotherhood and later the Arts and Crafts movement in England.

cubbing in September [49]   Hunting young foxes. The *OED* indicates the first use of the term in 1882, not 1880.

handy hack [49]   A horse for ordinary, as opposed to specialized, riding (*OED*).

keeper [50]   A gamekeeper or employee/servant who takes care of game on an estate to prevent poaching. Gibbs's comments indicate that he and his friends are fond of hunting on others' estates and possibly out of season.

pigging it [52]   Living slovenly (from the late 1800s) (*American Heritage Dictionary*).

masters of Katharine's [55]   A fictitious Oxford college, though a St. Catherine's Delegacy of noncollegiate, and therefore nonpaying, student society was founded in 1868.

Bodleian [56]   The principal library at Oxford University, founded in 1602 by Sir Thomas Bodley.

Blessed is he who has found his work [58]   From Thomas Carlyle (1795–1881), *Past and Present* (1843). The entire quotation reads: "Blessed is he who has found his work; let him ask no other blessedness."

Balliol [59]   The oldest college in Oxford, founded in 1263 by John Balliol, a lord of Henry III. During the late Victorian period, it was under the liberal reformist leadership of Benjamin Jowett from 1870 to 1893.

mugging up [59]   From the mid-1880s, to cram for examinations (*OED*).

bell came out with a jerk [60]   Victorian doorbells often consisted of two pieces—a brass ringer and either a lever or a turning knob.

Scarborough moors [61]   Rolling hills to the west of the tenth-century coastal city in North Yorkshire.

overall [64]   A smocklike outer garment worn to keep clothes underneath clean (*OED*).

Eton jacket [65]   A short dark jacket worn with a round white collar, a uniform made popular by junior students at Eton College, a boys' public school founded in 1440.

He was not Eton or Harrow, or Rugby or Winchester; or reading or rowing [67]   An allusion to the four most famous and prestigious of the British public schools. Woolf's father and uncle attended Eton. Pursued avidly by Woolf's father, Leslie Stephen, rowing was one of the principal sports of the aristocratic youth at Oxford and Cambridge.

stunner [67]   Colloquialism for an exceptionally attractive young woman (*OED*).

Gainsborough that was not quite certainly a Gainsborough [68]   Thomas Gainsborough was an English landscape and portrait painter (1727–1788) whose works were immensely popular throughout the eighteenth and nineteenth centuries. Here the Malones' painting is probably a copy, though the Lasswades' Gainsborough in the "1914" section may well be an original. Woolf subtly indicates class status by such allusions, with the Malones as middle and the Lasswades as upper class.

Take two coos, Taffy. Take two coos. Tak . . . [70]   Jeri Johnson identifies this refrain as a remnant of a children's rhyme about a Welshman who was a thief. She credits Andrew McNeillie with further linking the pigeon call to H. V. Morton's *In Search of Wales,* where Morton attributes the song to a border cry of wood pigeons (Johnson 328–29). Morton relates an archaeologist's version of the wood pigeon's cry along the Welsh border marshes: "Next time you hear wood-pigeons cooing, listen and you will be able to fit these words to the sound. . . . And you will notice that, like a determined raider, the pigeon, if disturbed and silenced, will resume his cry where he left off. For instance, if he stops at 'Take' he will begin next time with 'two cows, Taffy' . . ." (*In Search of Wales,* 166–67 [New York: Dodd, Mead & Co., 1932]). Woolf must have read this book when it was first published, and transformed "cows" to "coos" to create a refrain that runs throughout *The Years.*

pressing gentians on to a rough sheet of blotting paper [71]   Botany was a popular pastime in the nineteenth century. Dr. Malone is probably preparing the flower, found in the Alps, among other places, to be mounted in an herbarium.

Chingachgook! [71]   The Mohican Indian chief and companion of Natty Bumppo in several of American novelist James Fenimore Cooper's *Leatherstocking Tales,* especially in *The Last of the Mohicans* (1826).

dining in Hall [72]   Only male members of the colleges and their guests were permitted to dine in the university dining halls. Woolf's *A Room of One's Own* details the gastronomic differences between the impoverished meal of a women's college in the 1920s and a meal at one of the men's colleges.

took up The Times [73]   Johnson notes that this edition is from April 16, 1880, where all the articles mentioned are found (Johnson 329). Woolf refers throughout the novel to phrases from both the *Times* and the evening newspaper. The allusions serve to anchor the novel in the material world of fact that Woolf at first claimed would dominate the pull to vision.

leading article [73]   Presumably referring to the lead editorial in the newspaper.

from a tomb at Ravenna [74]   Probably from one of the Byzantine mosaics in Ravenna.

Pope, Tennyson [74]   Alexander Pope (1688–1744) was an eighteenth-century satirical poet about whom Woolf's father, Leslie Stephen, wrote a book for the English Men of Letters Series. Alfred, Lord Tennyson (1809–1892), was an acquaintance of Leslie Stephen and a poet he was fond of quoting to his children. In *To the Lighthouse,* Mr. Ramsay frequently quotes Tennyson's "Charge of the Light Brigade."

General Election [74]   Gladstone's Liberal government (1880–1886) won back control of Parliament from Disraeli's Tory government. Jeri Johnson establishes the date of this and the previous newspaper articles that Kitty and her mother are reading as April 16, 1880 (320).

experiment with electric light . . . the Rock [75]   According to the *Gibraltar Magazine,* "the humble quartz watch is a well-known example of the ability of quartz to structure energy, dating back to 1880 when it was discovered that electricity applied to quartz causes it to vibrate in a regular, consistent and harmonious pattern. So harmonious, in fact, that you can tell the time by it." In addition, the *Times* carried a spate of articles on electricity throughout 1880, particularly with reference to electricity in mines.

Whiteley's [79]   See note to page 3.

nothing but black all the summer [79]   Reference to the color of mourning clothes popularized in Victorian England by Queen Victoria after her husband, Prince Albert, died in 1861.

Mr. Parnell [80]   See notes to pages 12 and 21.

I am the resurrection and the life. . . . And fade away suddenly like the grass [80]   From the Anglican *Book of Common Prayer,* "For the Burial of the Dead." The service begins with the quotation from John 11:25–56. It continues later with verses particularly applicable to *The Years:* "For a thousand years in thy sight are but as yesterday: seeing that is past as a watch in the night. / As soon as thou scatterest them, they are even as a sleep: and fade away suddenly like the grass" (Psalms 90:4–5).

Man that is born of a woman [82]   From the *Anglican Book of Common Prayer,* "For the Burial of the Dead," just before the body is laid in the grave: "Man that is born of woman hath but a short time to live, and is full of misery."

Margate, Eastbourne and Brighton [84]   Popular seaside resorts in southeast England.

St. Martin's [84]   An allusion to St. Martin-in-the-Fields church in Trafalgar Square, the name designating the original position of the church in the fields adjacent to the royal mews (Mills).

Parliament Square [84]   The green area near the Palace of Westminster and Westminster Abbey containing statues of well-known British statesmen, including Victorian prime minister Benjamin Disraeli.

little boy in a pink frock [85]   Until early in the twentieth century, it was common to dress both male and female children in smock-like dresses.

drew on her blotting paper; a dot with strokes raying out round it [86]   In the holograph notebooks now in the Berg Collection of the New York Public Library, Woolf frequently uses a similar mark to indicate breaks in the sections of the manuscript.

barrel-organ [86]   See note to page 8.

Sur le pont d'Avignon [86]   From a French nursery rhyme, the chorus of which is:

> *Sur le pont d'Avignon*
> *L'on y danse, l'on y danse*

Sur le pont d'Avignon
L'on y danse tous en rond

(On the bridge of Avignon
We all dance there, we all dance there
On the bridge of Avignon
We all dance there in a ring)

visiting-cards [88]   Among the social elite of British society, it was a common practice to leave cards with one's name at residences called on when occupants were absent.

one bulky form; mercifully, it was yellow [88]   The London omnibus, the most popular form of public transportation in the late nineteenth and early twentieth centuries. Horse-driven until World War I, this type was replaced by motor-driven omnibuses after 1917. Eleanor especially frequently takes this middle-class form of transportation as opposed to the more expensive hansom cabs or, later, private motorcars. They were color-coded according to route.

leather apron [89]   A leather cover over the seats on an omnibus or other horse-drawn vehicle to protect passengers' legs: "When you have only a short journey to make, and the day is fine, it is not a bad thing to sit in the banquette . . . a seat immediately behind the driver, roofed in, but open to the front, a stout leather apron covering your legs . . ." (*London Society,* edited by James Hogg and Florence Marryat, 1865).

Bayswater Road [89]   Bordering Hyde Park and Kensington Gardens to the north, the long road was on a major east–west omnibus route.

Princess of Wales [90]   See note to page 4, "Princess." The detailed description of the portrait in the committee meeting room serves here as a reminder to Eleanor of the disparate attitudes of the working and lower middle classes toward the monarchy.

Varsity [91]   Slang for university.

a hansom [100]   A one-horse cab, replacing the hackney coach in the nineteenth century, accommodating one to two passengers and a driver.

Marble Arch [101]   See note to page 3.

Chancery Lane [102]   A street giving onto The Strand where the Courts of Law are located.

barristers [102]   Wig and gown–clad lawyers in the United Kingdom who represent clients in court, as opposed to solicitors, who give oral and written legal advice outside of court.

Lion and the Unicorn [103]   A coat of arms, with the lion representing England and the unicorn representing Scotland, signifying the union of the two countries since 1707.

the Strand [105]   A long street, close to the river before the building of the Embankment, that connects the City of London to Westminster.

Dead . . . Parnell [106]   Parnell's Irish Parliamentary Party had split in 1890, the majority opposing Parnell and his affair with Kitty O'Shea (whom he married in June 1891 after her divorce). Parnell died on October 6, 1891. His obituary, which Colonel Pargiter and Eugenie seem to be reading, appeared in the *Times* on October 8. Eugenie's comment, presumably about Parnell's wife, may be in response to the statement "Mrs. Parnell is completely overcome by this sudden and heavy blow, and yesterday absolutely refused to see any one." (See also note to page 12.)

divorce case [110]   See note to page 12.

Kitty O'Shea [113]   See notes to pages 12 and 106.

Lido [116]   A popular eleven-mile stretch of sandy beach in Venice, Italy.

this African business [119]   Colonel Pargiter's comment could be an allusion to a number of British-held areas in Africa. The *Times* contained over two hundred articles in 1891 about European concerns in Africa, the bulk of which concerned German and Portuguese interests in addition to English. On September 28, 1891, the *Times* carried a lengthy article on a "Serious Situation in British East Africa" about a threatened Imperial British East Africa Company withdrawal from Uganda. The correspondent warns that such action would result in "an immediate massacre of the native converts and European missionaries in that country."

Hammersmith to Shoreditch [121]   A western suburb of London, its eastern point in Hackney.

Wapping in the romantic Inn [122]   The Prospect of Whitby tavern on the Thames, dating from the thirteenth century.

green beetles' wings [122]   These were popular in jewelry, pins, and hairpieces from the Victorian period onward, perhaps also indicative of a fascination in the Edwardian period with Oriental decorations.

put the Government in a fix [123]   Probably referring to Liberal Welsh MP David Lloyd George (1863–1945), in 1905 president of the Board of Trade and subsequently chancellor of the Exchequer and prime minister. Lloyd George was partly responsible for helping to abolish the Lords' veto power in 1911. This remark likely refers to a *Times* article on June 21 (midsummer) on his speech to a dinner gathering of the City Liberal Club about the need to combat the Conservative government on issues of free trade and disproportionate Conservative membership in the House of Lords.

the world is nothing but... thought [124]   Sara may be reading the British philosopher George Berkeley (1685–1753), who argues that the mind relies on ideas that conflate perception and thought. Sara, the "visionary" character in the novel, may be said to represent the idealistic as opposed to realistic, empirical, or materialistic vein in British philosophy.

music had stopped [125]   See Woolf's sketch in her early diary from 1903, "A Dance in Queens Gate," for a close parallel to this scene (*Passionate Apprentice* 164–67). As Quentin Bell notes, at this time Vanessa had already "come out" (like Maggie Pargiter) into society and Virginia was about to be introduced to parties by her half brother George (*Virginia Woolf: A Biography,* 68 [New York: Harcourt Brace Jovanovich, 1972]). Autobiographical parallels between Virginia and Sara Pargiter surface throughout *The Years.*

Antigone of Sophocles [126]   Virginia Woolf comments to her brother Thoby in 1901 that she is reading *Antigone* (by Sophocles, 442 B.C.) with her Greek tutor, Janet Case. In the manuscript version, Sara (Elvira) makes Edward's gift of *Antigone* more explicit: "Because she was a humpback, she reflected, he gave her a book, taking it from his shelf in his room, that day when they went to Oxford..." ([*The Years*] The Pargiters, vol. 3).

unburied body of a murdered man [127]   Sara reacts to Antigone's burial of her slain brother, Polyneices.

Creon [128]   The king of Thebes who orders Antigone to be buried alive because she has defied his orders and buried her brother. Falling asleep in her tomblike bed, Sara mentally assumes the position of Antigone. In *Three Guineas,* Woolf describes Creon's hunger for power and absolute rule and links it to the rise of the tyrants of Fascism. She praises Antigone for resisting Creon's law (*TG* 98).

nothing but thought [131]   See note to page 124.

Rembrandt in the National Gallery . . . ruby in a Bond Street window [138]
This refers to a Rembrandt painting in the National Gallery in
Trafalgar Square, and a precious stone in the expensive shop-
ping district of Bond Street in Westminster.

Isle of Dogs [138]   A section of London in Tower Hamlets southeast
of Stepney, in previously marshy land near the Thames River.

dust cart [138]   Forerunner of a garbage truck.

Army and Navy Stores [138]   See note to page 3.

Pimlico [139]   A district in Westminster south of Victoria, first
recorded in 1626 (Mills).

King of Spain's daughter [140]   A sixteenth-century nursery rhyme Martin hums as he leaves his uncle and aunt's now empty house and
again later in the "1914" section (213). The first two verses are:

> I had a little nut tree,
> Nothing would it bear
> But a silver nutmeg,
> And a golden pear.
>
> The King of Spain's daughter
> Came to visit me,
> And all for the sake
> Of my little nut tree.

In her chapter on *The Years* in *Virginia Woolf and London,* Susan
Squier offers a feminist interpretation of the significance of
Martin's singing this rhyme as opposed to Eleanor's humming
the French nursery rhyme (see note to page 86). In spite of his
attraction to a number of women throughout the novel and his

dandyism, Martin remains single and oddly sterile, traits perhaps symbolized by this nursery rhyme.

Renan [141]   Ernest Renan, French historian and Hebrew scholar (1823–1892), whose work, probably *The Life of Jesus* (1863), along with the New Testament, Woolf tells Ethel Smyth in a letter of January 1935 she is reading (*Letters* 5: 362). In her diary entry for January 1, 1935, she notes that she is reading St. Paul and the Acts of the Apostles as well as Renan: "At last I am illuminating that dark spot in my reading. What happened in Rome?" (*Diary* 4: 271).

tea caddy [143]   A receptacle for tea, often with a middle compartment for sugar.

Tube [143]   First mention of London underground transport, which began limited operation in 1869. By 1906 most of the main Tube lines (District, Metropolitan, Northern, Central, and Bakerloo) were open, originally for a cost of two pence (Kent). In a 1907 diary entry, Woolf speaks of having made an "expedition" on "The Twopenny Tube" to Golder's Green on the Northern Line, which had just been extended in 1905 (*Passionate Apprentice* 365).

a spill [144]   A twist of paper with which to light a fire.

God is love, The kingdom of Heaven is within us [146]   See note to page 141. Also possibly an allusion to the writings of the Quaker Samuel Tuke (1784–1857), who, in addition to founding the York Asylum for humane treatment of the insane, advocated this principle. Woolf also would likely have been familiar with the stress on the inward kingdom of heaven from her Quaker aunt, Caroline Stephen. The biblical sources are 1 John 4:8 and Luke 17:20–21: "The Kingdom of God cometh not with observation . . . for, behold, the kingdom of God is within you."

holding meetings in the North [148]   Probably an allusion to the
Women's Social and Political Union (WSPU), founded in 1903
by Emmeline and Christabel Pankhurst, a more militant suffragette organization than the National Union of Women's
Suffrage Societies (NUWSS), whose members were termed suffragists and led by Millicent Fawcett. According to Searle, the
first incident of stone throwing by the suffragettes occurred in
June 1908 (458). See, too, Ray Strachey, *The Cause: A Short History of the Women's Movement in Great Britain,* 1928; reprint, Port
Washington, NY: Kennikat Press, 1969.

Queen Alexandra [152]   Wife of King Edward VII. Edward died on
May 6, 1910. See note to page 4, "Princess."

bald scrubbed space by the Marble Arch [152]   Speakers' Corner, where
since 1872 anyone could speak on any topic.

vans, cars, omnibuses [152]   Woolf alludes here to the shift from
horse-drawn conveyances to motorized vehicles. Frank E.
Huggett remarks of this transition: "By Edwardian times there
was an extraordinary variety of vehicles on the roads, including
electric cars and trams, horse-drawn omnibuses, steam-driven
lorries, petrol-driven motor cars, bicycles and all the old horse-
drawn vehicles from barouches to baker's vans" (*Carriages at
Eight* 131).

Whiteley's [153]   See note to page 3.

Damned humbugs! [154]   Having just glanced at the Houses of Parliament from either Westminster or, more probably, Waterloo
Bridge, Rose may be thinking of the Liberal ministers who were
divided over their support of female suffrage and unable to
come to any agreement. H. H. Asquith, the Liberal prime minister, was opposed to female suffrage. Woolf "officially" joined
the suffrage movement in January 1910. She wrote to Janet Case
on January 1 to see if she could help to address envelopes for the

"Adult Suffragists" (*Letters* 1: 421). On November 14, she confesses to Violet Dickinson, "My time has been wasted a good deal upon Suffrage. We went to two meetings, at which about a dozen people spoke, like the tollings of a bell" (*Letters* 1: 438).

Hyams Place [154]   In his discussion of Woolf's allusions to Jews and Jewish images in *The Years,* David Bradshaw suggests that Hyams Place and Rose's question "Who was Hyam?" are traceable to the Hebrew word *hayyim,* meaning "life." Bradshaw comments that "Woolf's choice of street name expresses both her sense of the 'life' of the capital in general and, more specifically, the contribution of Jews to that life" ("Hyams Place" 187).

Oh, blasted eyes of my deceased wife's sister [159]   An unidentified quotation, but suggestive of the recent act passed in 1907 that permitted a widower to marry his wife's sister.

They cooked their own food [161]   Rose observes that Maggie and Sara are too poor to hire a cook or a servant.

Campagna [162]   The countryside surrounding Rome. In the nineteenth century it was considered dangerous at night, both because of robbers and because it was a low-lying, swampy area connected in tourists' minds with fears of malaria.

drawing a spoke from the hole in the middle [167]   See note to page 86 ("draw on her blotting paper . . .").

Kew [167]   A southwestern suburb of London, in Richmond. Kew Gardens, the Royal Botanical Gardens, date from the eighteenth century. Woolf sets her short story "Kew Gardens" here.

Ealing [167]   A western London suburb, now a borough. Eleanor's snobbishness is apparent here, as she is surprised to learn that Mr. Pickford lives closer to the city center in the more fashionable Westminster.

What a magnificent car! [170]   Kitty's husband's car marks her here as upper class. After 1908, the motorcar became a sort of status symbol heartily endorsed by King Edward VII (Searle 437).

Force is always wrong [170]   Kitty's remark to Eleanor probably alludes to the split in the women's suffrage organizations between militant and constitutional suffragettes, exacerbated by an acid-throwing incident by a member of the Women's Freedom League (WFL) in October 1909 (Searle 459).

Covent Garden . . . Opera House [171–72]   The aristocratic Kitty Lasswade contrasts the public fruit and vegetable market of Covent Garden in Westminster with the Opera House, which borders the market.

Siegfried [172]   Richard Wagner's third opera in his *Ring of the Niebelungen,* performed at Covent Garden the night before King Edward's death on May 6, 1910. Kitty's musings lead her to connect Siegfried's rustic appearance and his hammering with Jo Robson from her youth at Oxford.

doctors have given him up [173]   A reference to the grave condition of King Edward the day before his death.

The Wanderer [175]   In act I of *Siegfried,* the god Woton appears in disguise as the Wanderer and exacts answers to three riddles from the dwarf Mime before Siegfried enters and begins mending the broken sword Mime was to fix for him.

May my bones turn to coral [177]   Possibly a loose allusion to Shakespeare's *The Tempest* (I.ii.399–400): "Full fathom five thy father lies; / Of his bones are coral made" (see Asbee 472). The literary allusions to *Antigone, Siegfried,* and *The Tempest* all hint at families disrupted by betrayal, incest, and craving for power. Set alongside the more mundane history of the Pargiter family, they seem to contrast the tragic with the bathetic. However, viewed in the buildup to World War I, they lend an ominous note to what will follow in 1914.

antre [179]   A cavern or cave.

Bring up your children on a desert island [180]   Another allusion to *The Tempest,* where Prospero raises his daughter Miranda far from corrupt civilization.

The King's dead! [181]   See note to page 172, "Queen Alexandra."

though the King, borne under a white and blue Union Jack, lay in the caverns at Frogmore [182]   This refers to the burial place of Edward VII, as well as of Queen Victoria, at Windsor near Windsor Castle. Curiously, here the red of the Union Jack is missing; the white and blue flag is Scotland's St. Andrew's Cross. David Bradshaw suggests that Woolf purposely associates the Zionist flag of blue and white (officially adopted in 1933 at the eighteenth Zionist Congress) with King Edward VII's pro-Jewish sympathies ("Hyams Place" 186–87).

portmanteaus [183]   Large traveling bags with two compartments; a term, no longer in use, for a suitcase.

old victoria [183]   See note to page 3.

chemist's [184]   British for drugstore or pharmacy.

Guadalquivir [184]   A large river in Spain that crosses Andalusia and empties into the Atlantic Ocean.

Jubilee [184]   An allusion to 1887, Queen Victoria's fiftieth anniversary as queen of England.

coconut shies [187]   A country village game in which players try to hit coconuts with wooden balls.

nankeen trousers [187]   Trousers made of buff-colored durable fabric originally from China.

Acropolis . . . Naples . . . Granada . . . Toledo [188]   All places in southern Europe—Greece, Italy, and Spain—that both Eleanor and Virginia Woolf visited. By this time Eleanor, unfettered by family obligations, has become the principal traveler in the novel.

Maidenhead [189]   A town on the Thames in Berkshire, about twenty-five miles from central London.

silver-plated salver [189]   A flat tray used for serving dishes or drinks.

up with him [190]   At Oxford University.

at the top of his tree [190]   At the peak of his profession.

an Embassy and a Legation? [190]   A legation is a diplomatic office or headquarters in a foreign country that ranks below an embassy.

situation in the Balkans [190]   In July and August 1911, the *Times* carried reports of unrest in Turkey, especially after the July 10 assassination of reactionary Turkish journalist Zeki Bey. The allusion here is to the increasing Balkan opposition to Turkey from disaffected populations both within and without. In 1912 the Balkan League (Greece, Serbia, Montenegro, and Bulgaria) declared war on Turkey but failed to capture Constantinople. The war ended with the Treaty of London in 1913 but exacerbated Austro-Hungarian and Russian hostility, which eventually led to World War I. The London Treaty saw the creation of Albania and the reduction of European Turkey and Bulgaria.

found myself in an old pair of riding-breeches standing under a peacock umbrella [191]   Sir William, formerly a British officer in India, represents a returned class of British civilians and soldiers who found themselves by 1911 largely redundant and unrecognized in British society.

She threw a brick [194]   The first brick-throwing incidents occurred in June 1908. The imprisonments resulted in hunger strikes and force-feeding by the government. Rose evidently aligns herself with Christabel Pankhurst's more militant faction, the WSPU, as opposed to Millicent Fawcett's alliance with the NUWSS (see note to page 148, "holding meetings in the North").

ear trumpet [198]   A funnel-like ear horn used as a primitive hearing aid. Woolf's father, Leslie Stephen, used one in his later years.

whist [198]   A card game popular in the eighteenth and nineteenth centuries, now largely replaced by bridge.

rubber after rubber [199]   Two out of three games won by the same person or team.

The Diary of a Nobody, Ruff's Tour in Northumberland *and an odd volume of Dante* [200]   *Diary of a Nobody* (1892), by George and Weedon Grossmith, was first serialized in *Punch Magazine*. *Ruff's Tour* was a nineteenth-century guidebook. Reading Dante's *Purgatorio* in 1917, Woolf found it "stiff, the meaning more than the language" (*Diary* 1: 84); but by 1935 she is again reading it (this time in Italian) while she revises *The Years* (*Diary* 4: 264), and tries to find bridges between revising the novel and reading Dante.

For by so many more [201]   Dante's *Purgatorio,* canto 15, lines 56–57. In this section of the canto Dante is torn between a focus on material vs. spiritual good until Virgil explains that all can share in spiritual good without envy of each other. Throughout the novel Eleanor seems to be searching for participation in a higher, more transcendent sphere, although she admittedly enjoys such small material goods as a nice bath and electric lights.

Wandsworth [204]   A London suburb (now borough of London) on the south bank, formerly inhabited by Huguenot immigrants (Kent 550). With the advent of rail travel in the late nineteenth century, Wandsworth expanded to entice commuters to the city. Woolf relegates a number of her middle- and lower-class characters in *The Years* to the outlying London suburbs.

four-wheeler [204]   Probably a horse-drawn carriage here instead of an early four-wheeled automobile.

Richmond [205]   The southern London suburb in which Kew Gardens and Richmond Park are located. The Woolfs lived in Richmond from 1914 to 1923 and founded the Hogarth Press there, so named because the house in which they lived had previously been named Hogarth House. At the time of her removal to Richmond, Crosby considers it a far inferior place to Abercorn Terrace in Kensington.

old Queen's funeral [207]   A reference to the death of Queen Victoria on January 22, 1901, and her burial at Windsor on February 4.

Brand's Essence [208]   A natural tonic, formerly Brand's Essence of Chicken.

Ebury Street [208]   In Westminster, near Sloane Square, a street dating from 1820 and previously marking the boundary between fashionable Belgravia and less fashionable Pimlico (Kent 501–2). That Martin lives on this boundary seems to fit with his dandyish lifestyle.

war in the Balkans was over [209]   See note to page 190. An allusion to the Treaty of London engineered by Foreign Secretary Sir Edward Grey.

King of Spain's daughter [213]   See note to page 140.

Apsley House [214]   See note to page 3.

statue of Queen Anne [214]   A copy of the original statue of Queen
    Anne (1665–1714) erected in 1712 by Francis Bird and replaced
    in 1886. It faces away from St. Paul's Cathedral and looks down
    Ludgate Hill. Four female figures at the base represent England,
    France, Ireland, and North America (Kent 470).

City chop house [216]   Traditional nineteenth-century London eat-
    ing establishments originally for workingmen, chophouses served
    simple English food with an emphasis on beef.

The father incomprehensible; the son incomprehensible [217]   From the
    Anglican *Book of Common Prayer,* the Athanasian Creed, rarely re-
    cited today: "The father incomprehensible, the Son incompre-
    hensible, and the Holy Spirit incomprehensible" (line 9).

tart . . . Brussels sprouts [218]   Woolf seems to have mixed up the
    luncheon courses here, with the waiter serving the tart before
    Martin helps Sara to the Brussels sprouts.

Round Pond [219]   In Kensington Gardens (just west of and adjoin-
    ing Hyde Park), opened to the public from the early nineteenth
    century.

see my sister in prison [219]   A reference to Rose's second brick-
    throwing incident, which landed her in jail. See note to page 194.

Sitting on a three-legged stool having meat crammed down her throat! [220]
    An allusion to the force-feeding first authorized by Home Sec-
    retary Herbert Gladstone in 1909 in response to hunger strikes
    by suffragettes in prison. This was suspended by the Cat and
    Mouse Act under Herbert Asquith's Liberal government in
    1913, so named because it allowed for the suffragettes to be

recaptured after they were freed from prison. Sara may not realize here that force-feeding has already ended.

Roll up the map of Europe [220]   A statement by William Pitt, prime minister 1783–1801 and 1804–1806, in response to the victory of France over Russia at the Battle of Austerlitz. The statement ends with "It will not be wanted these ten years," and appears here to predict the territorial scramble of World War I. Sara's following quotation, "I don't believe in force," links military maneuvering to the force-feeding of the suffragettes, a far less muted condemnation of militarism and patriarchal power than in Woolf's *Three Guineas.*

Fleet Street [221]   A busy former newspaper street leading to Ludgate Hill and St. Paul's Cathedral. Sara and Martin are walking west from the City toward Westminster.

figures lodged so uncomfortably against the pediment of Temple Bar [222] Temple Bar marks the western edge of the City of London. The statues of Queen Victoria and King Edward herald the entrance to Westminster from the City. Traditionally the monarch was not allowed to pass through the old Temple Bar gate to the City without knocking, representing the division between the citizens of London and the monarchy of Westminster. The bar or gate was removed in 1879. Temple Bar also carries violent associations, as executed criminals' and political prisoners' heads were displayed there on spikes through the first part of the eighteenth century. In his *Walks of London,* which Woolf reviewed, Augustus Hare notes the "contemptible pillar surmounted by a dragon" erected in 1880, upon which Queen Victoria and Prince Edward stand (55).

Charing Cross [223]   A train station in Westminster near Trafalgar Square, opened in 1864 on the site of the old Hungerford Market. Charing Cross was named from an Old English word meaning bend and from the last of twelve "Eleanor crosses" set up by Edward I to mark the spots where his wife's coffin paused on its journey from Nottinghamshire to Westminster Abbey (Mills).

news from Ireland [223]   This probably refers to the third Irish Home Rule Bill, which was suspended during World War I and never formally instituted. Home Rule would have established a two-chambered Parliament in charge of domestic policies.

St. George's Hospital [224]   Opposite Hyde Park Corner at the entrance to Belgravia.

the Row [224]   In Hyde Park, traditionally called Rotten Row because of the soft soil on which carriages and horses promenaded. It runs from Apsley Gate near Hyde Park Corner to Kensington Gardens. In earlier centuries, especially the eighteenth, it was a popular place to be seen in London society.

bald rubbed space where the speakers congregate [227]   Hyde Park Speakers' Corner. See note to page 152.

Bermondsey . . . Isle of— [227]   Areas in southeast and east London along the Thames. In the nineteenth century Bermondsey was a lower-class immigrant neighborhood known for its leather factories. "Isle of" refers to the Isle of Dogs, destroyed in World War II and now part of the Docklands.

Round Pond [229]   See note to page 219.

Palace and the phantom church [230]   Kensington Palace, erected in 1691 by Christopher Wren and residence of monarchs until the building of Buckingham Palace during the eighteenth-century reign of George III.

white figure of Queen Victoria [231]   An 1893 white marble statue of
  Queen Victoria erected by her daughter, Princess Louise, representing the queen at her accession to the throne in 1837.

boarding house at Putney [233]   Located in Wandsworth (see note to
  page 204), and in 1647 the headquarters of Cromwell's parliamentary army.

Canaletto [235]   Giovanni Antonio Canal, known as Canaletto, was
  a fashionable Venetian painter (1697–1768) who was wildly
  popular in England, and especially with the Grand Tourists of
  the eighteenth century. He was famous for his topographical
  style and as one of the earliest landscape painters to paint out-
  doors. Throughout this section, the Lasswades' possessions
  place them within the English aristocracy.

Racing; the Russian ballet; and . . . Ireland [237]   Martin refers to three
  conversational topics popular among Britons in 1914—horse
  racing, the Russian Ballet that was housed for a season at London's Palace Theatre, and the Irish question of Home Rule.

Who's taken my life of Wren? [238]   A reference to Sir Christopher
  Wren (1632–1723), architect of many of London's principal
  churches, including St. Paul's Cathedral, after the fire of London
  in 1666. Martin, who would have liked to have been an architect, has that day moved between two Wren edifices—St. Paul's
  and Kensington Palace.

Victoria [238]   A reference to Victoria Station, opened in Westminster in 1860.

game of spillikins [238]   A game popular in Victorian (and later) England, also known as pickup sticks (jackstraws in the United
  States), in which players try to pick up scattered sticks without
  touching other sticks. The sticks were originally made of bone,
  ivory, or wood but are now mostly plastic.

Gainsborough [239]   One of England's most famous eighteenth-century portrait painters, another emblem of the Lasswades' taste and class. See note to page 68 and to page 235, "Canaletto."

When I was in Ireland . . . in 1880 [240]   A possible allusion to the dispute between the advocates of Irish Home Rule with Parnell, the leader of the Land League of Ireland, against the Ulster Unionists, who were opposed to Home Rule. See note to page 12 ("*he* is . . .").

Have you seen the Russian dancers? [240]   Ann is referring to famous Russian ballet dancer Vaslav Nijinsky (1890–1950) and his company, who danced for a season at the Palace Theatre. Hermione Lee suggests (476) that Woolf has mixed up dates here, as Nijinsky danced for the final time in London in mid-March, but the day after Kitty's party the narrator notes, "It was a perfect May morning" (262).

Mortimer House [244]   Near Regent Street on Mortimer Street, frequently used for academic lectures.

Malta [244]   An island south of Sicily, acquired by the British in 1814 and of strategic significance during World War I.

Eton [244]   See note to page 67.

battledore and shuttlecock [245]   An ancient game popular in sixteenth-century England and revived in the Victorian period as badminton; the game was particularly popular among the British in India in the 1880s and '90s.

talking about a by-election [245]   The Conservatives gained a number of seats between 1910 and 1914, partly because of splits between the new Labour Party and the Liberal Party.

turned her upside down and slapped her . . . I'm so delighted he got in in spite of them . . . [245]   Lady Margaret is probably referring to the suffragettes, the Pankhurst-led members of the Women's Social and Political Union (see notes to pages 148 and 194). According to a number of historians, the militant suffragettes temporarily helped turn the political tide in the by-elections toward the Conservative Party (see, for example, T. O. Lloyd, *Empire, Welfare State, Europe: English History 1906–1992*, 44–45 [Oxford: Oxford University Press, 1993]).

Harrow [246]   See note to page 67.

That's the wise thrush that sings each song twice over [247]   See Robert Browning's "Home Thoughts from Abroad" (1845). It is reminiscent of Edward's nostalgic love for Kitty: "That's the wise thrush; he sings each song twice over, / Lest you should think he never could recapture / The first fine careless rapture!" (lines 14–16). Kitty has mistaken Edward's quotation as a reference to the actual bird, a symbolic instance of their incompatibility.

Mallarmé [248]   Stéphane Mallarmé was a French symbolist poet (1842–1898) known for his Tuesday evening salons (les Mardistes) and his elevation of complex sound over pure denotative content. Tony Ashton, like Mallarmé, represents an intellectual elitism that Kitty both admires and disdains. Mallarmé's poetry would be in direct contrast to that of the later World War I poets Wilfred Owen and Siegfried Sassoon, who voiced the agony of soldiers' experiences in the trenches.

Grosvenor Square [252]   The second-largest square in London, located in wealthy Mayfair and home to a number of past prime ministers, members of the nobility, and wealthy Americans.

unlocked the door of her carriage [255]   Kitty would have traveled in a first-class train compartment with a locking entrance and exit door.

bonnet [260]   English word for the hood of a car.

She was happy, completely. Time had ceased [263]   An ironic close to the "1914" section, as England would enter World War I that following summer on August 4, in response to Germany's invasion of Belgium.

lamps were shrouded in blue [264]   A precaution taken against sighting by German zeppelins, which began bombarding London in May 1915.

we are talking about Napoleon [265]   Renny (a Frenchman) and Nicholas (of Polish or Russian descent) are discussing the Napoleonic Wars (in which France and Russia were on opposing sides) a century earlier, the final ending of which was Napoléon's defeat at the Battle of Waterloo in 1815. Their conversation appears as a thinly disguised allusion to the World War I events of 1917, when the alliances shifted, with France, England, and Russia now on the same side.

turbaned and fantastic Turk [269]   Another of Sara's allusions to Shakespeare, this time to Othello just before he kills himself in act 5, but possibly suggesting a further political allusion to the declining power of Turkey, which led indirectly to the start of World War I in the Balkan state of Serbia.

Royal Regiment of Rat-catchers [270]   Sara's criticism of North's decision to join the military before conscription was mandated. *Three Guineas* is far more explicitly critical of war, but most of the criticism in *The Years* is relegated to Sara's statements.

God save the King, Happy and Glorious [270]   Sara's sarcastic rendition of the English national anthem and more evidence of her (and Woolf's) connection of militarism, patriotism, and patriarchy.

Poppycock [271]   Nonsense, rubbish, humbug (America, 1852). Renny mistakes Nicholas for an American since he uses this word.

But then he gave his bridle reins a shake and said, 'Adieu for evermore...'
[272]   Sara is quoting from Sir Walter Scott (1771–1832), "The Rover's Adieu":

> —He turned his charger as he spake
> Upon the river shore,
> He gave the bridle-reins a shake,
> Said 'Adieu for evermore,
> My Love!
> And adieu for evermore.' (lines 15–20)

Another raid [273]   See note to page 264. A reference to the German air bombing of London.

as if a light had gone out [273]   Sir Edward Grey (1862–1933), British foreign secretary, stated on the eve of World War I, "The lamps are going out all over Europe; we shall not see them lit again in our lifetime." Eleanor appears to echo this statement.

Hampstead... The Embankment [275]   Respectively, a suburb in northwest London and, closer to Maggie and Renny's Westminster home, the Embankment, which borders the Thames on the north side of the river.

They're only killing other people [277]   Renny is probably thinking of his fellow Frenchmen, in whose country the war was being fought.

bugles [279]   The "all clear" given by Boy Scouts with bugles as a signal to return to normalcy.

Nicholas... who ought to be in prison [281]   A reference to Nicholas's homosexuality, a crime under English law until the Sexual Offences Act in 1967 repealed the Labouchere Amendment of 1885 that had mandated up to a two-year prison term for homosexual activity, labeled "gross indecency."

war was over [289]   World War I ended at 11:00 A.M. on November 11, 1918. Woolf typically submerges momentous historical and political events within a character's consciousness, thereby giving priority to the everyday life of common people like Crosby, for whom the war can be summed up as "Them guns again" (288). Significantly, *The Years* will jump here from the end of the war to a summer evening in the early 1930s, ignoring events of the 1920s — the labor strikes, economic depression, the British Empire Exhibition of 1924.

sha'n't [291]   Shall not.

but she must be well over seventy [291]   In the chronology for "The Pargiters," Woolf places Eleanor's birth in 1856, making her one year younger than Morris and fourteen years older than Rose. Thus it is possible to set the "Present Day" section in the early 1930s, probably between 1932 (when Woolf started writing the novel) and 1935. It was first published in 1937. In the original manuscript, however, as Grace Radin notes, "Present Day" is 1927. That she omitted the date in her revision indicates that Woolf did not want to tie the last, long chapter to a specific date.

Milton Street [293]   Until 1830, Grubb Street was in the City, near Barbican. Significantly, in the seventeenth century the street was associated with journalists and literary hacks (Mills). Sara is a part-time writer, though she disdains commercial writing. See, too, David Bradshaw's interpretation of Milton Street as a link between John Milton's possible negotiation of the reentry of Jews into England in 1655 ("Hyams Place" 188).

near the Prison Tower [293]   Sara lives in the less fashionable part of East London, near the Tower of London. The name carries a sense of irony here, as Sara has prided herself on her own freedom from social conventions.

a circle on the wall with a jagged line in it [294]   A reference, according
to Bradshaw, to the British Union of Fascists' anti-Semitic activities in the mid-1930s ("Hyams Place" 183). Founded by Os-
wald Mosley in 1932, the organization was in part funded by
Mussolini. Its members and supporters wore black shirts and re-
taliated against attacks by Jewish youths and Communists. The
organization was outlawed in 1940, but just prior to the publication of *The Years,* Woolf would have read accounts of the
Battle of Cable Street on October 4, 1936, when 1,900 BUF
members marched in the East End of London (*Oxford Companion to British History,* edited by John Cannon, 128–29 [New York:
Oxford University Press, 2002]). Woolf alludes to Mosley's activities in her diary on December 5, 1934 (*Diary* 4: 337).

regular lodging-house skivvy [298]   From 1902, a female servant, maid
of all work.

barrel-organ [301]   See note to page 8.

A shadow like an angel with bright hair. . . [301]   From Shakespeare's
Richard III. Clarence, elder brother of Richard, dreams he has
entered Hell and describes to the Keeper in the Tower the following vision (I.iv.52–56):

> . . . Then came wandering by
> A shadow like an angel, with bright hair
> Dabbled in blood, and he shrieked out aloud
> Clarence is come — false, fleeting, perjured Clarence
> That stabbed me in the field by Tewksbury.

Woolf was reading Dante's *Inferno* while she wrote parts of *The
Years,* though this passage also echoes the water themes of *The
Tempest,* a play to which Sara also intermittently alludes. That
Sara compares in the next passage North's metaphorical descent
to England as dropping from the clouds "in an aeroplane"

seems both to foreshadow the impending war and to explain North's disoriented feeling returning to London after the remoteness of his farm in Africa.

Strand [304]   The street running from Trafalgar Square in Westminster to Temple Bar—the entrance to the City of London.

Coward; hypocrite . . . [305]   Sara's letter to North echoes images of T. S. Eliot's poem *The Waste Land* (1922), published after World War I. The first section of the poem, "The Burial of the Dead," concludes with this line: "—You! Hypocrite lecteur!—Mon semblable, —mon frère!," which quotes from Baudelaire's preface to *Fleurs du Mal.* North and Sara have been alluding to North's participation in the war and the armistice on November 11, 1918—"a still autumn night; the lights lit; and people padding along the pavement with wreaths in their hands."

Ten and six . . . half a crown [307]   Ten shillings (£1 = twenty shillings) and sixpence. Half a crown was two shillings and sixpence, currency common in England until decimalization in 1971.

air ball [307]   Balloon.

Westminster Cathedral [311]   The largest Roman Catholic church in England and mother church of the Roman Catholic community in England and Wales, situated in Victoria, Westminster.

You know they'd flown the Channel not so very long before [312]   Eleanor is referring to the first flight from France to Dover, England, on July 25, 1909, by Frenchman Louis Blériot.

wireless [313]   Forerunner of present-day radio, the wireless was invented by the Italian Guglielmo Marconi, who successfully transmitted the first signal across the English Channel in 1899. Eleanor is recapitulating the numerous technological inventions she's seen in her lifetime, including electricity and hot water taps.

a fat man gesticulating [313]   Possibly Mussolini, who from 1927 increasingly tightened his Fascist hold on Italy. The *Times* carried front-page articles on his activities throughout the late 1920s and early 1930s, though here Eleanor appears to be reading another evening newspaper.

pillar-box [315]   A mailbox, but the reference also recalls Rose's encounter with a man standing by the pillar-box on page 26.

figure of a woman in nurse's uniform holding out her hand [319]   A monument to nurse Edith Cavell (1865–1915) in St. Martin's Place near Trafalgar Square. Cavell was head of a clinic in Belgium that assisted Allied soldiers to escape. She was imprisoned and executed by the Germans. The statue was unveiled by Queen Alexandra in 1920, with the base inscribed with the words "Devotion," "Fortitude," and "For King and Country." In 1924, Cavell's statement "Patriotism is not enough" was added (Kent).

Society is all but rude— / To this delicious solitude [322]   End of the second verse of "The Garden" by Andrew Marvell (1621–1678). The verse momentarily unites North and Sara in their preference for solitude over society:

> Fair Quiet, have I found thee here,
> And innocence, thy sister dear!
> Mistaken long, I sought you then
> In busy companies of men;
> Your sacred plants, if here below,
> Only among the plants will grow.
> Society is all but rude,
> To this delicious solitude.

Polluted city, unbelieving city, city of dead fish and worn-out frying-pans [323]   Sara paraphrases "The Burial of the Dead," the first section of T. S. Eliot's *The Waste Land* (see note to page 305), and possibly also Baudelaire's *Fleurs du Mal,* the former of which compares London to Dante's *Inferno:*

Unreal City,
Under the brown fog of a winter dawn,
A crowd flowed over London Bridge, so many,
I had not thought death had undone so many (lines 60–63)

your conspiracy [323]   See Woolf's discussion of a Society of Outsiders in *Three Guineas,* where she proposes an alternative to joining the society proposed by the writer of the third letter, requesting a guinea to help prevent war (*TG* chap. 3).

sponge-bag trousers [324]   Trousers made of checked cotton fabric.

Burnt as brown as a nigger! [326]   Probably lacking the offensive connotation of today, in the early twentieth century "nigger" could refer to a dark-skinned person of any origin. It's likely here that Eleanor is referring to her recent trip to India.

drawing a line with a tube of some sort round her lips [326]   Lipstick, invented in the 1880s, became popular after World War I in the 1920s. To Eleanor it is clearly a mark of the new generation of young women.

Don't spoil a good ship for a ha'porth of tar [327]   An English proverb used in the nineteenth century (but originally referring to sheep instead of ships) to denote the pointlessness of saving "in a small matter of detail, referring to the use of tar to protect sores or wounds on sheep from flies" (William George Smith, *Oxford Dictionary of English Proverbs* [Oxford: Clarendon Press, 1935]).

coppers [327]   Slang for copper money, usually a penny or a halfpenny (*OED*).

He's killed the king [328]   According to Alice Fox, this is an allusion to Macbeth, evincing Shakespeare to follow tragic events with comic relief (*Virginia Woolf and the Literature of the English Renaissance,* 103 [Oxford: Clarendon Press, 1990]).

a rocky island in the middle of the sea [328]   Suggests Shakespeare's play *The Tempest.*

There was the cause . . . Ireland, you know. Parnell [338–39]   See note to page 12 ("*he* is . . ."). In response to Peggy's question about whether Delia was in love, Martin instead remembers Delia's devotion to Parnell and Home Rule in Ireland and avoids answering the real question.

your red ribbon [341]   Rose has presumably been decorated for her service during World War I, in which suffragettes moved to support the country.

For what do I care about his "I, I, I" [343]   This echoes Woolf's point in both *To the Lighthouse* and *A Room of One's Own* about men's self-absorption. In *To the Lighthouse,* Lily Briscoe knows the dining-table etiquette of flattering men by questioning them about themselves, and in *A Room,* Woolf's narrator notes Professor Von X's absorption in his own work in the British Library.

phantom wheel-barrow [343]   Probably a reference to the Big Dipper constellation, called the Plough in England, part of Ursa Major.

Candles—that sort of thing [357]   Hugh is referring to the High Church affiliation of the Anglican "parson," though he mixes his terms here since parson typically suggests Low Church (more Protestant) and priest, High Church (closer to Roman Catholicism in its emphasis on sacraments and ritual over preaching).

For cubbing in September [361]   See note to page 49.

La médiocrité de l'univers m'étonne et me révolte [364]   From Guy de Maupassant's (1850–1893) *Sur l'eau* (1888), a journal of his travels along the Mediterranean coast in which he notes in his preface that the journal contains nothing interesting. Translation: "The mediocrity of the universe astonishes me and revolts me." Strongly influenced by Gustave Flaubert, Maupassant was best known for his short stories. In a reading notebook dated October 16, 1934, Woolf notes of Maupassant's journal in a reference to biography, "That what starts us wanting to know about Maupassant is the conflict of 2 things in him — the emotion & the hardness" (Brenda Silver, *Virginia Woolf's Reading Notebooks,* 213 [Princeton, NJ: Princeton University Press, 1983]). The conflict accurately describes Peggy's character.

what do dreams mean? [365]   Eleanor supposes that because Peggy is a doctor, she understands dreams. Freud's *Interpretation of Dreams* had been published in 1900, but Peggy cynically dismisses doctors' knowledge of the mind. Woolf's younger brother Adrian was a psychoanalyst, though by her own account, Woolf began reading Freud only in the late 1930s.

Tosh [367]   Rubbish, nonsense, a word first coined in 1892, according to *OED.* That Eleanor does not know some of the new slang signifies her age. She has moved from Victorian to modern in her use of inventions such as electricity and running taps, but she has not caught up with the latest psychological theories or the most recent slang words.

of people toiling, grinding, in the heart of darkness [368]   An allusion to Joseph Conrad's novella *Heart of Darkness* (1902), a book largely concerned with imperialism and the question of civilization. Woolf admired Conrad and wrote several critical essays about his work.

picture palace [369]   Early movie theaters became popular in the decades after World War I, with sound introduced in 1927.

Highgate [369]   A northwest London suburb adjacent to Hampstead Heath.

On top there was a woman's head like Queen Alexandra [370]   Another allusion to the wife of Edward VII, but here as an imperialistic figure representing the various countries partly colonized by England, India as a tiger and Africa as an elephant. North's quotation of Christopher Marlowe's *Doctor Faustus,* "The face that launched a thousand ships" (V.i.97)—referring to Helen of Troy—is ironic in this context, indicating possibly either World War I or the impending threat of another war.

Viceroy of India [373]   North cannot remember whether Kitty's husband, Lord Lasswade, was governor of a province in India or the principal governor-general (viceroy) of British India.

Government House [373]   Both a residence and place of business and receptions of British governor-generals, governors, and lieutenant governors in British Empire and Commonwealth countries.

Nijinsky [373]   See note to page 240.

nox est perpetua una dormienda [374]   From the Latin poet Catullus (ca. 84–ca. 54 B.C.), *Poems* 5, line 6, the last line of the couplet: "For us, when the short light has once set, remains to be slept the sleep of one unbroken night" (*Catullus, Tibullus and Pervigilium Veneris,* edited by C. P. Goold [Cambridge, MA: Harvard University Press, 1913]). The poem is addressed to Lesbia and is a *carpe diem* plea to enjoy love now and ignore the talk of old men (Patrick) and the "evil eye" of any "malicious person" (for a time here, Peggy). Both North's random reading and Peggy's do indeed indicate their separate states of mind at the party.

Spoons for the widow of the Governor-General! [377]   See note to page 373, "Viceroy of India."

Twopence [378]   Two pennies.

Covent Garden [379]   Kitty may be referring either to the ballet or opera, both held at Covent Garden's Royal Opera House.

He won't be happy till he's got Dublin Castle back again [379]   The Irish Free State was formed in 1922, with Ireland becoming a republic (Eire) in 1937. With the establishment of the Free State, Ireland achieved the same Commonwealth status as Canada, Australia, New Zealand, and South Africa (*The Oxford Companion to Irish History*, edited by S. J. Connolly [Oxford: Oxford University Press, 2002]). Patrick, ironically given Delia's fierce early support of Parnell, has remained loyal to England and pessimistic about Ireland's future.

Force [381]   Kitty remembers the meeting she had attended before the opera in 1910 at which she met Rose, Sara, and Eleanor. See note to page 170. Delia appears unwittingly to have chosen the same building in which to rent rooms for her party.

Now these ladies have got the vote [381]   The first franchise bill in England granted suffrage to women over thirty in 1918 and was followed in 1929 by a bill granting the vote to all women over twenty-one. Patrick's conservative view conflates the Irish Free State with women's new rights and indicates his pro-monarchy, patriarchal stance.

glad enough to join the Empire again [381]   Patrick here laments the separation of the Irish Free State (southern Ireland) from the Union, believing that the Irish Free State's inhabitants have not benefited economically or socially from the split.

English settlers [381]   Patrick traces his family roots in Ireland three centuries back, to the English Protestant settlements in the seventeenth century under James I and Cromwell.

Harrow [383]   See note to page 67.

Stevedores [384]   Workmen who load and unload cargoes of merchant vessels (*OED*). North is cataloging typical nineteenth-century working-class occupations and noting the absence of this class at Delia's party in spite of her earlier revolutionary leanings.

Spinners and sitters in the sun [388–89]   See Shakespeare's *Twelfth Night,* where Lord Orsino asks the Clown to sing a song from the previous night:

> Mark it, Cesario; it is old and plain.
> The spinsters and the knitters in the sun,
> And the free maids that weave their thread with bones,
> Do use to chant it: it is silly sooth,
> And dallies with the innocence of love,
> Like the old age. (II.iv.43–48)

black shirts, green shirts, red shirts [389]   See note to page 294. The first reference is to the black-shirted uniform worn by the British Union of Fascists in the 1930s. A French peasant right-wing organization wore green shirts in 1930s France, and an anti-Fascist group at Oxford University wore red shirts. Red shirts were traditional symbols of freedom and rebellion worn by Italian leader Giuseppe Garibaldi's army in the fight for Italian unification in the 1850s. North is here dissociating himself from any faction, right or left.

Commissionaire [390]   An indication of the elevation of working-class occupations such as porter to a loftier-sounding title. The Corps of Commissionaires was founded in London in 1859 and was largely composed of pensioned soldiers.

heart of darkness [390]   See note to page 368. Although North uses this as a metaphor, he has just returned from Africa and finds himself unable to connect with those around him at the party.

"caparison" and "carapace" [391]   In both cases, types of coverings; "caparison" is defensive armor, ornament, or cloth over a saddle; "carapace" is the hard upper body of a tortoise or a hard case protecting the body of other animals, and metaphorically of humans.

Shams, I should think [392]   Eleanor and Edward betray their upper-middle-class ancestry here by mocking the nouveau-riche Chipperfield, "son of a railway porter" and eager to collect art as a mark of his new social class. See notes to pages 235, "Canaletto," and 239, "Gainsborough," for references to copies of Old Masters as indicators of the social class of the Malones and Lasswades.

He was in the middle of a dark forest [392]   See the beginning of Dante's *Inferno,* where Dante finds himself alone in the dark wood: "In the midway of this our mortal life, / I found me in a gloomy wood, astray / Gone from the path direct . . . (*The Vision: or Hell, Purgatory, and Paradise* of Dante Alighieri, translated by Henry Francis Cary, 3: lines 1–3 [London: Frederick Warne, 1844]). North's allusions to Conrad and Dante indicate the isolation he feels upon his return to London in the 1930s after both his service in World War I and his years in Africa.

Antigone [392]   See note to page 48. Edward has made a career of teaching classics and translating Greek.

said some words in Greek [393]   From *Antigone:* " 'Tis not my nature to join in hating, but in loving," in response to Creon's remark about her dead brother, whom she wishes to bury, "A foe is never a friend—not even in death" (*The Tragedies of Sophocles,* trans. Sir Richard C. Jebb, line 254 [Cambridge: Cambridge University Press, 1904]). See, too, Woolf's note 40 to chapter two in *Three Guineas* (*TG* 202), where she quotes this line and gives Jebb's translation, and wherein she states, "Consider Antigone's distinction between the laws and the Law. That is a far more profound statement of the duties of the individual to society than any our sociologists can offer us" (*TG* 98). Through a series of literary allusions in this final section, Woolf cleverly pits Edward, the classical scholar, and North, the modern man of action, against each other, though she suggests North's yearning for this other side of life he feels he has missed.

Paddington [396]   An area in Westminster and location of Paddington Station, opened in 1847. The station is presumably near the Pargiters' old home in Abercorn Terrace.

"She smashed his window," Martin jeered at her, "and then she helped him to smash other people's windows..." [399]   Possibly an allusion to David Lloyd George, chancellor of the Exchequer (1908–1915) and influential in securing Allied resistance to Germany in World War I. Martin is mocking the suffragists' prewar opposition to the government and their collusion with the government during the war. See notes to pages 148, 194, and 245. In 1913 suffragettes had bombed Lloyd George's home in London.

Aeschylus. Sophocles. Pindar [405]   Greek dramatists and lyric poet of the fifth century B.C.

here and now [405]   One of the working titles for *The Years* was "Here and Now."

Now — sing a song for sixpence! [407]   See Shakespeare's *Twelfth Night* (II.iii), where Sir Toby Belch says to the Clown, "Come on; there is sixpence for you: let's have a song." This comes in the scene immediately preceding the allusion to the play on pages 388–89. See note to pages 388–89, "Spinners and sitters in the sun."

Etho passo tanno hai [407]   Various critics have puzzled over this unintelligible song, as do the characters at the party. Jane Marcus notes its class-leveling tendency: "Our ears cringe at the accent, Latin words and Cockney English mixed with echoes of Greek. . . . No false note of nostalgia intrudes; no utopian pretense of class comradeship mars the clarity of vision" ("*The Years* as Greek Drama, Domestic Novel, and Götterdämmerung" 294–95).

God save the King [411]   The English national anthem, but here ironically undercut by Eleanor's reference to the cooing pigeons (a recurrent sound throughout the novel) and not to the patriotic song (see note to page 270). By the end of the party nature, symbolized by the cooing pigeons and the rising sun, has drowned out the modern technology of the blaring gramophone.

A Note on the Text

The text of this edition follows the first U.S. edition of the novel, with the following variations: the obvious typographical error "Eleaner" that appears in the first edition has been corrected here on page 97; the error "the Colonel doubting" has been corrected to "the Colonel doubted" on page 114; and a necessary question mark has been added after "red and gold" on page 217.

Suggestions for Further Reading:
Virginia Woolf

Editions

The Complete Shorter Fiction. Edited by Susan Dick. 2nd ed. San Diego: Harcourt, 1989.

The Diary of Virginia Woolf. Edited by Anne Olivier Bell. 5 vols. New York: Harcourt, 1977–84.

The Essays of Virginia Woolf. Edited by Andrew McNeillie. 6 vols. [in progress]. San Diego: Harcourt Brace Jovanovich, 1986–.

The Letters of Virginia Woolf. Edited by Nigel Nicolson and Joanne Trautmann. 6 vols. New York: Harcourt Brace Jovanovich, 1975–80.

Moments of Being. Edited by Jeanne Schulkind. San Diego: Harcourt, 1985.

A Passionate Apprentice: The Early Journals, 1897–1909. Edited by Mitchell A. Leaska. San Diego: Harcourt, 1990.

Biographies and Reference Works

Briggs, Julia. *Virginia Woolf: An Inner Life.* San Diego: Harcourt, 2005.

Hussey, Mark. *Virginia Woolf A to Z: A Comprehensive Reference for Students, Teachers, and Common Readers to Her Life, Works, and Critical Reception.* New York: Facts on File, 1995.

Kirkpatrick, B. J., and Stuart N. Clarke. *A Bibliography of Virginia Woolf.* 4th ed. Oxford: Clarendon, 1997.

Lee, Hermione. *Virginia Woolf.* New York: Knopf, 1996.

Marder, Herbert. *The Measure of Life: Virginia Woolf's Last Years.* Ithaca, NY: Cornell University Press, 2000.

Poole, Roger. *The Unknown Virginia Woolf.* 4th ed. Cambridge: Cambridge University Press, 1995.

Reid, Panthea. *Art and Affection: A Life of Virginia Woolf.* New York: Oxford University Press, 1996.

General Criticism

Abel, Elizabeth. *Virginia Woolf and the Fictions of Psychoanalysis.* Chicago: University of Chicago Press, 1989.

Bazin, Nancy Topping. *Virginia Woolf and the Androgynous Vision.* New Brunswick, NJ: Rutgers University Press, 1973.

Beer, Gillian. *Virginia Woolf: The Common Ground.* Ann Arbor: University of Michigan Press, 1996.

Cuddy-Keane, Melba. *Virginia Woolf, the Intellectual, and the Public Sphere.* Cambridge: Cambridge University Press, 2003.

DiBattista, Maria. *Virginia Woolf's Major Novels: The Fables of Anon.* New Haven, CT: Yale University Press, 1980.

Fleishman, Avrom. *Virginia Woolf: A Critical Reading.* Baltimore: Johns Hopkins University Press, 1975.

Froula, Christine. *Virginia Woolf and the Bloomsbury Avant-Garde: War, Civilization, Modernity.* New York: Columbia University Press, 2005.

Guiguet, Jean. *Virginia Woolf and Her Works.* 1965. Reprint, New York: Harcourt Brace Jovanovich, 1976.

Harper, Howard. *Between Language and Silence: The Novels of Virginia Woolf.* Baton Rouge: Louisiana State University Press, 1982.

Hussey, Mark. *The Singing of the Real World: The Philosophy of Virginia Woolf's Fiction.* Columbus: Ohio State University Press, 1986.

———, ed. *Virginia Woolf and War: Fiction, Reality and Myth.* Syracuse, NY: Syracuse University Press, 1991.

Majumdar, Robin, and Allen McLaurin, eds. *Virginia Woolf: The Critical Heritage*. Boston: Routledge, 1975.

Marcus, Jane. *Art and Anger: Reading Like a Woman*. Columbus: Ohio State University Press, 1988.

———, ed. *New Feminist Essays on Virginia Woolf*. Lincoln: University of Nebraska Press, 1981.

———, ed. *Virginia Woolf: A Feminist Slant*. Lincoln: University of Nebraska Press, 1983.

———, ed. *Virginia Woolf and Bloomsbury: A Centenary Celebration*. Bloomington: Indiana University Press, 1987.

———. *Virginia Woolf and the Languages of Patriarchy*. Bloomington: Indiana University Press, 1987.

McLaurin, Allen. *Virginia Woolf: The Echoes Enslaved*. Cambridge: Cambridge University Press, 1973.

McNees, Eleanor, ed. *Virginia Woolf: Critical Assessments*. 4 vols. New York: Routledge, 1994.

Minow-Pinkney, Makiko. *Virginia Woolf and the Problem of the Subject: Feminine Writing in the Major Novels*. New Brunswick, NJ: Rutgers University Press, 1987.

Phillips, Kathy J. *Virginia Woolf Against Empire*. Knoxville: University of Tennessee Press, 1994.

Roe, Sue, and Susan Sellers, eds. *The Cambridge Companion to Virginia Woolf*. Cambridge: Cambridge University Press, 2000.

Ruotolo, Lucio. *The Interrupted Moment: A View of Virginia Woolf's Novels*. Stanford, CA: Stanford University Press, 1986.

Silver, Brenda R. *Virginia Woolf Icon*. Chicago: University of Chicago Press, 1999.

Zwerdling, Alex. *Virginia Woolf and the Real World*. Berkeley: University of California Press, 1986.

SUGGESTIONS FOR FURTHER READING:
The Years

(in addition to the works cited in the introduction)

Bradshaw, David. "Hyams Place: *The Years,* the Jews and the British Union of Fascists." In *Women Writers of the 1930s: Gender, Politics and History.* Edited by Maroula Joannou, 179–91. Edinburgh: Edinburgh University Press, 1999.

Cramer, Patricia. "'Pearls and the Porpoise': *The Years* as a Lesbian Memoir." In *Virginia Woolf: Lesbian Readings.* Edited by Eileen Barrett and Patricia Cramer, 220–40. New York: New York University Press, 1997.

———. "Trauma and Lesbian Returns in Virginia Woolf's *The Voyage Out* and *The Years.*" In *Virginia Woolf and Trauma: Embodied Texts.* Edited by Suzette Henke and David Eberly, 19–50. New York: Pace University Press, 2007.

Dalgarno, Emily. "A British War and Peace? Virginia Woolf Reads Tolstoy." *Modern Fiction Studies* 50 (2004): 129–50.

Gottlieb, Laura Moss. "*The Years:* A Feminist Novel." In *Virginia Woolf: Centennial Essays.* Edited by Elaine K. Ginsberg and Laura Moss Gottlieb, 215–29. Troy, NY: Whitson, 1983.

Hanson, Clare. "Virginia Woolf in the House of Love: Compulsory Heterosexuality in *The Years.*" *Journal of Gender Studies* 6 (1997): 55–62.

Hargreaves, Tracy. "'I Should Explain He Shares My Bath': Art and Politics in *The Years.*" *English: The Journal of the English Association* 50 (2001): 183–98.

Hoberman, Ruth. "Aesthetic Taste, Kitsch, and *The Years.*" *Woolf Studies Annual* 11 (2005): 77–98.

Levenback, Karen L. *Virginia Woolf and the Great War.* Syracuse, NY: Syracuse University Press, 1999.

Linett, Maren. "The Jew in the Bath: Imperiled Imagination in Woolf's *The Years.*" *Modern Fiction Studies* 48 (2002): 341–61.

Lipking, Joanna. "Looking at the Monuments: Woolf's Satiric Eye." *Bulletin of the New York Public Library* 80 (1977): 141–45.

Moore, Madeline. "Virginia Woolf's *The Years* and Years of Adverse Male Reviewers." *Women's Studies* 4 (1977): 247–63.

Phillips, Kathy J. "Woolf's Criticism of the British Empire in *The Years.*" In *Virginia Woolf Miscellanies: Proceedings of the First Annual Conference on Virginia Woolf.* Edited by Mark Hussey and Vara Neverow-Turk, 30–31. New York: Pace University Press, 1992.

Proudfit, Sharon L. "Virginia Woolf: Reluctant Feminist in *The Years.*" *Criticism* 17 (1975): 59–73.

Saariluoma, Liisa. "Virginia Woolf's *The Years:* Identity and Time in an Anti-Family Novel." *Orbis Litterarum* 54 (1999): 275–300.

Schlack, Beverly Ann. "Virginia Woolf's Strategy of Scorn in *The Years* and *Three Guineas.*" *Bulletin of the New York Public Library* 80 (1977): 146–50.

Swanson, Diana L. "An Antigone Complex? The Political Psychology of *The Years* and *Three Guineas.*" *Woolf Studies Annual* 3 (1997): 28–44.

Zimring, Rishona. "Suggestions of Other Worlds: The Art of Sound in *The Years.*" *Woolf Studies Annual* 8 (2002): 127–56.

ILLUSTRATION CREDITS

PAGE

ii–iii: E. V. Lucas, *London Revisited,* 3rd ed. (London: Methuen & Co. Ltd., 1917)

xiv, xlii, xliv, xlv, xlvii, lv: The Society of Authors as the Literary Representative of the Estate of Virginia Woolf

lxiii, lxiv: © TfL/London Transport Museum

lxvi: © TfL/London Transport Museum

lxviii: *The Blue Guides: Short Guide to London,* 3rd ed., edited by Findlay Muirhead, 1933

lxx: *The Blue Guides: Short Guide to London,* 3rd ed., edited by Findlay Muirhead, 1933

Virginia Woolf Annotated Editions

Top Woolf scholars provide valuable introductions, notes, suggestions for further reading, and critical analysis in this paperback series. Students reading these books will have the resources at hand to help them understand the text as well as the reasons and methods behind Woolf's writing.

Between the Acts
Annotated and with an introduction by Melba Cuddy-Keane
978-0-15-603473-9 • 0-15-603473-5

Jacob's Room
Annotated and with an introduction by Vara Neverow
978-0-15-603479-1 • 0-15-603479-4

Mrs. Dalloway
Annotated and with an introduction by Bonnie Kime Scott
978-0-15-603035-9 • 0-15-603035-7

Orlando: A Biography
Annotated and with an introduction by Maria DiBattista
978-0-15-603151-6 • 0-15-603151-5

A Room of One's Own
Annotated and with an introduction by Susan Gubar
978-0-15-603041-0 • 0-15-603041-1

Three Guineas
Annotated and with an introduction by Jane Marcus
978-0-15-603163-9 • 0-15-603163-9

To the Lighthouse
Annotated and with an introduction by Mark Hussey
978-0-15-603047-2 • 0-15-603047-0

The Waves
Annotated and with an introduction by Molly Hite
978-0-15-603157-8 • 0-15-603157-4

The Years
Annotated and with an introduction by Eleanor McNees
978-0-15-603485-2 • 0-15-603485-9

Each volume includes a preface by Mark Hussey, professor of English and women's and gender studies at Pace University, and editor of *Woolf Studies Annual*.

Harcourt | HARVEST BOOKS

www.HarcourtBooks.com